BOOK ONE

RISE
OF THE
SIX

MATT RYAN

THE **PRESTON SIX** SERIES

For information on new releases
or if you want to chat with me, you can find me at:
www.facebook.com/authormattryan
or www.authormattryan.com

Cover: Regina Wamba
www.maeidesign.com
Editor: Victoria Schmitz | Crimson Tide Editorial
Formatting: Inkstain Interior Book Designing
www.inkstainformatting.com

RISE
OF THE
SIX

PRELUDE

"ARE THEY SAFE?" HARRIS ASKED.

"The kids? Yeah." Tears absently fell from Minter's puffy red eyes. The orange glow from the massive fire skittered across his face.

"I'm so sorry, Minter."

"Karen's alive." He spoke as if reading from a dictionary. "I sent her and our baby to the storm shelter."

Blankly staring at the town bar, Minter's thoughts shifted to his friends; their dead bodies strategically placed in the raging inferno.

Harris sighed. "I don't think he'll come for the babies. All of our intel says Isaac acted alone. Marcus never knew." He was obviously grasping for a positive.

"What in the hell do we do now?"

"You live. Find a way to move past this. You have a special

kid to raise." Harris put a hand on Minter's shoulder. "I don't think you'll see me again, but know I'll be watching."

"He has his mother's eyes."

"Hmm?"

"Joey. Joey has Karen's eyes. It's what we named him."

"That's a good, solid name."

"Promise me, Harris. Promise me they won't come back and try to take him."

"I can't."

CHAPTER 1

JOEY FLIPPED THROUGH THE PAPER and searched for his parent's names.

"Look at this." Samantha handed him a faded article.

He took it and scanned the headline, 'Six Local Teens Pregnant.' He'd read it before, they all had, but he skimmed through the sentences again—looking for any clue they might have missed. Peering over the top of the paper, he stole a glance at Samantha while she was preoccupied. She eventually felt his attention and he quickly shifted his gaze back to the yellowing paper before she looked up.

"I've read this a hundred times," Joey said. "But I just feel like we're missing something."

Samantha sighed and leaned back in the chair. "We're never going to figure out what really happened."

MATT RYAN

Joey set the paper down on the table, watching Samantha rub her eyes. He sympathized with her exhaustion; they had been searching through the town's papers for a few hours.

The librarian walked by for what seemed like the umpteenth time. She slowed down, lingering on the numerous papers spread across the table. "Make sure you put all of those back in chronological order," she said with a sneer.

"Of course we will," Samantha politely responded. Last time they hadn't, and now they were red-flagged as unsystematic troublemakers.

He waited for her to leave the area. "Let's see the birthday article."

Samantha's eyes lit up and she rushed to the filing cabinet. Retrieving the newspaper, she sat next to Joey and placed the paper on the table before them. *The Preston Six Are Born* read in bold across the top of the article.

"Look at your mom and dad." She smiled and pointed to the picture on the front page. "They are so young."

He lifted the paper's edge and tilted it to get a better look in the light. All six sets of parents held their newborn babies. Their eyes looked innocent and happy. He loved that picture. It was a different time.

"Your parents looked happy." Joey pointed to her parents. Her mom held a baby Samantha in her arms.

Samantha sniffed. "I wonder what my dad would look like today?"

Joey didn't answer. He kept quiet when the talk of dead parents came up. He was the only one of the six who still had both parents.

"Sometimes I think I can find clues in these pictures, like

something is hidden in the background," Joey said.

She gave him a questioning look and leaned closer to study the picture. *It worked.* Her hair brushed over his face as her shoulder pressed against his. He took in her scent, knowing she wasn't going to find any clues; if there were something in it, he would have found it years ago. She shook her head and leaned back.

"I don't see anything unusual."

"Well, you never know. Sometimes we find things where we least expect it." Joey felt the velvet box in his jacket pocket and fought the urge to give it to her right then.

"You okay?"

He let go of the box. It wasn't the right time. He had a plan for the party, later that night. "Yeah, why?"

"You're just acting kind of strange today."

"I don't know, I guess I just get nervous around the big day."

"You think he'll show?"

"Yeah, Trip's always at the birthday parties."

"You think he'll talk more about you know what?"

He looked at Trip's picture, eighteen years younger, in the paper. He had become their best chance of finding out what really happened that night. He leaned across the table, pulled another newspaper toward him and turned it right-side up. Samantha slid her chair back and turned away. It wasn't easy for Joey to look at it, but he had to find out what happened and he always felt this was the critical article.

"Tragedy" was the only headline, followed by a picture of a burning bar. A single stream of water landed on the roof. Fire bellowed from the front windows, reaching the Molly's sign above. He forced his eyes to stay on the picture. If there was anything hidden, this would be the picture. After a minute, his mind only thought of the people in the bar, behind the flames.

He turned the paper over and pushed it away.

Samantha returned to his side, happy to find the newspaper gone. She looked at him with a smirk. "Joey Foust, have I said 'happy birthday' yet?"

"Well, no you haven't, Samantha Roslin."

"Happy birthday."

He bowed his head slightly. "And happy birthday to you as well." Joey glanced at the clock—two hours until the party. He felt the box again and thought of the words he'd prepared to say to Samantha.

"You have a plan for getting Trip to talk tonight?" she asked.

"He hasn't needed much encouragement in the past."

Trip never came to the other events like Easter or Thanksgiving, but he had always come to the birthday parties; and after a few drinks, he liked to talk about the past.

She smiled. "We should make it a goal tonight to get the whole truth."

"Done." Joey dealt himself in, but he had another goal in mind. He rolled the box in his hand and couldn't stop the smile spreading over his face. She was going to freak out when she saw what he found.

CHAPTER 2

JOEY PUSHED THE WRAPPED BOX deeper into his pocket and knelt next to his bed. He searched under the blanket and pulled out a folder. It was a collection of documents from the library and internet; all forming the unbelievable picture of what their parents were telling them.

He flipped it open, turning the old pages and stopping on his handwritten notes from his previous birthdays, making it a third of the way down the page.

16th birthday: Trip talked about telling us the truth before the other parents shut him up.

- What truth? The bar fire?
- How did they all get pregnant at the same time?
- How did they all give birth the same day? Was it just a coincidence?

to catch up with Samantha to have that 'talk.'

"What?" Lucas followed him inside.

The sounds of the party grew louder as he walked down the stairs. Music played from his dad's old stereo, mixed with several conversations going on at the same time. He found all of the parents huddled in small groups around the family and dining rooms.

Lucas brushed against his arm. "Hey, sorry if I messed with you guys up there." Lucas raised an eyebrow with a wide grin. "Was there something going on?"

Joey shrugged and shook his head, as if nothing were amiss. *Was there nothing?* He needed to find Samantha. He scanned the room and met eyes with a few parents at the dining room table, but they quickly looked away and whispered to each other.

"The whole reason I came to find you is because Hank's dad is drunk and startin' to talk about stuff," Lucas said, grinning and rubbing his hands together.

Joey jerked toward Lucas. "Already?" He may have blown one goal with Samantha, but the other still had a chance of success. More than a chance.

"Oh yeah, he's been pounding 'em back." Lucas chugged from a pretend glass in his hand.

Joey stared at Trip across the family room, holding a small glass. His mom, Karen, stood next to him. She met Joey's gaze before looking away quickly, returning her attention to Trip. He owed it to Samantha—to the rest of the six—to find out what happened.

"Let's go find out what he's saying," Joey said.

CHAPTER 3

JOEY HAD TAKEN THE STORIES their parents told at face value, until their sixteenth birthday. Trip had been drunk and made a few comments about the past that hadn't quite added up to the stories told in the newspapers. Ever since then, the parents kept him under constant supervision.

Trip's arms moved around as he conversed with Karen, but Joey was too far away to hear the words. She cuddled a glass of water next to her face and sucked on the straw, glancing at the moms talking around the dining room table. With a nervous smile, she listened to whatever Trip was rambling on about, giving him intermittent nods and encouraging smiles.

"Told you." Lucas couldn't contain his smug look, as he rubbed his hands together in excitement.

He wanted Samantha at his side when Trip inevitably spilled the information, but she was nowhere to be seen. Not wasting the chance, he got close to the action.

Keeping out of sight, he snuck up behind Trip's large back. Like a hawk, his mom poked around and spotted his approach. She gulped down the water in her mouth and blurted out, "Yes, Trip. We *do* need to be careful. The dirt roads are awful right now."

"What?" he asked, confused.

"Hey, Trip," Joey said to his back.

The big man turned around, glazed eyes widening. "Happy Birthday, Joey." An enormous arm enveloped him as he spoke. The hard liquor smell burned Joey's nose and stung his eyes.

"Thanks," Joey wheezed.

Trip's hand clasped Joey's shoulder and shook him around. The shaking slowed for a bit, only to start up again.

"Ha, it's crazy to think I was just a little older than you when Hank was born." Trip lowered his head, his smile turning to a blank stare at the brown carpet. "Well, you're turning into a fine young man, Joey."

"Thank you." Joey attempted to regain some personal space, but Trip held him in place. Looking around for help, he found Lucas, but he just stood back, smiling at the encounter. Exasperated, he returned to Trip's unblinking stare.

Joey felt a large hand on the back of his neck. He turned and saw Hank's arm extended to him. Hank sighed and shook his head.

"Dad, I need to talk to Joey for a minute," Hank said. "Let's grab a drink in the kitchen."

Trip released him and lifted his glass as Hank pulled him away. Joey staggered toward the kitchen, looking back at Trip.

The noise of the party diminished as they entered the

kitchen. The smell of meatballs hung in the air. A birthday cake lay on the counter with each of their names written on it.

Happy Birthday, Hank, Poly, Julie, Samantha, Joey, and Lucas.

His mom always wrote the names on the cake; she probably didn't want to explain it to the grocery store people. Last year's party had not even made it to the cake before Trip's mouth ran the parents out of the house.

Joey sat on the kitchen island, his legs dangling. Hank grabbed two water bottles from the refrigerator, tossed one to him, and leaned on the kitchen island. He was never one to say very much, so Joey was interested in what the big man had to say.

"How'd the present go?" Hank asked.

He choked on the water, forgetting he told Hank about the present. He looked around the kitchen to make sure no one else heard.

"Fine. Well . . . I don't know." Joey set his water bottle on the counter. When thinking about it, it sounded stupid and embarrassing. "I tried to kiss her, but she turned her head at the last second," he whispered.

Hank raised his eyebrows. "Wow. What'd she do after that?"

"I don't know. She said she didn't think I was going to do *that*. Then Lucas interrupted us and she ran off."

"Hmm . . . pretty bold, going for a kiss."

Bold was one word for it . . . stupid was probably more accurate. Joey sighed and slid off the island.

Lucas entered the kitchen, rushed to their side, wedging his way into the fray. With a wide grin, he bounced his attention back and forth between the two. He raised his hands dramatically

Marcus? Who the heck is that? Joey's heart raced and he felt dizzy.

"I've been training my boy to defend himself and I suggest you all do the same." Trip turned and walked past Julie and Samantha, leaving behind a birthday gift of silence and nervous glances from the remaining parents.

Samantha's hand covered her open mouth.

"I'll make sure he gets home safe," Minter offered, grabbing his coat from the coat rack and the keys hanging next to the door.

The front door slammed and Joey stared at the closed door to his answers.

Nobody talked or moved. Parents began exchanging worried looks.

Samantha stared at him, but Joey couldn't talk to her. He felt as if he was going to pass out. The smell of beer, booze, bean dip, and tension overloaded his senses. He rushed to the back door.

"Who the hell is Marcus?" Lucas asked the room.

Joey opened the back door and stumbled onto the porch.

The cold air entered his lungs and slapped his face. Laying his hands on the worn, painted rail, he tried to pull Trip's thread, but it kept knotting up. Another name, but no answers.

The back door opened and the planks creaked as Hank and Lucas stepped across them.

He braced himself for one of Lucas's wild recaps.

"What do you think he meant about your dad being the lucky one?" Lucas asked. "He seemed to be accusing your dad of something."

"I don't know," Joey said. And he didn't. His parents had

parents. "You all know it. He's got all the time in the world and will never stop."

Another thread tossed out, but Joey couldn't find a way to grab it.

"We didn't fail, Trip." Opal tiptoed closer to Hank. "All you need to do is look at your son and you can see our success." She pointed at Hank.

Trip considered his boy, blinking as if trying to solve the puzzle Opal had laid out for him. He shook his head and shoved his glass on the coffee table. It fell over and rolled, landing on the carpet.

He fidgeted with his jean jacket, smoothing it out with his hands, watching as Karen cleaned up his mess.

"Come on, Trip. Let's get you home." Minter pulled on his arm.

He seemed puzzled by the offer, pulled his arm free, and continued to stare at Karen. "Minter, you're the luckiest of us all. You—you got to keep yours," gesturing to Karen. "While my Mary was taken from me, taken from our son. Why do *you* get to be lucky?"

"I think you've said enough." Minter took one large step, closing the distance between them. Trip met his gaze, stepped a few inches closer, and then stomped past him toward the front door.

The front door opened and Samantha and Julie stepped into the house, talking. Julie's gaze swept over the room and she placed her hand on Samantha's to stop her from talking.

Trip turned to face the room. "Marcus will never stop looking for these kids. You all know it."

Karen gasped when she heard the name Marcus.

Marcus? Who the heck is that? Joey's heart raced and he felt dizzy.

"I've been training my boy to defend himself and I suggest you all do the same." Trip turned and walked past Julie and Samantha, leaving behind a birthday gift of silence and nervous glances from the remaining parents.

Samantha's hand covered her open mouth.

"I'll make sure he gets home safe," Minter offered, grabbing his coat from the coat rack and the keys hanging next to the door.

The front door slammed and Joey stared at the closed door to his answers.

Nobody talked or moved. Parents began exchanging worried looks.

Samantha stared at him, but Joey couldn't talk to her. He felt as if he was going to pass out. The smell of beer, booze, bean dip, and tension overloaded his senses. He rushed to the back door.

"Who the hell is Marcus?" Lucas asked the room.

Joey opened the back door and stumbled onto the porch.

The cold air entered his lungs and slapped his face. Laying his hands on the worn, painted rail, he tried to pull Trip's thread, but it kept knotting up. Another name, but no answers.

The back door opened and the planks creaked as Hank and Lucas stepped across them.

He braced himself for one of Lucas's wild recaps.

"What do you think he meant about your dad being the lucky one?" Lucas asked. "He seemed to be accusing your dad of something."

"I don't know," Joey said. And he didn't. His parents had

told him they'd decided at the last minute not to go to the bar. When he'd pushed them for answers, they got angry with him and shut the conversation down.

"What danger are we in?" Hank said.

"I don't know." Joey rubbed his temples in frustration.

The door creaked. He peered back over his shoulder and saw Samantha standing in the doorway. He spun around to face her, waiting for her to speak.

"Looks like I missed it this year," Samantha said. "Party seems to be over. Hey, Joey. Can we talk?"

He nodded, unable to move his mouth.

Samantha walked onto the porch and glanced at Hank and Lucas.

They took the cue and said their goodbyes, heading back into the house.

"Later, guys," Joey said, heading back to the railing. He was unable to keep his eyes on Samantha, expecting her to give him the 'friend' rejection.

"Joey?"

He turned to face her. His oversized jacket draped over her shoulders.

Taking a step closer, she removed the space between them. Then Samantha rose up on her tiptoes and kissed him. He got lost in her warm lips and moved his hands up to her hair. He felt a chill run down his neck and the moment seemed frozen in time. The sounds dulled until a loud car horn honked.

She pulled away and smiled.

"My mom's waiting for me out front." She kissed him quickly one more time. "I expect full details about what Trip said tomorrow."

"Yeah." He licked his lip, tasting Samantha's lip-gloss.

Taking off the jacket, she flung it over him. "See you tomorrow, Joey."

He watched her leave the porch and then turned back to the rail. Putting his hands in his jacket pockets, he felt the velvet box. Looking back at the door, Samantha was gone. Joey took the black box out, opened it, and watched the earrings jostle as he moved. Snapping the lid shut, he rolled the velvet box in his hands and stared into the darkness.

See you tomorrow, Joey . . . The way his name rolled off her tongue, gave him chills.

He spent a while longer on the porch, not wanting to lose the feeling, or the taste. Smiling like an idiot, he kept thinking about Samantha. *She liked him.*

The music shut off inside the house. The party was over. Another birthday without making it to the cake.

Joey stuffed the box back into his jacket and went to his room. Sitting on the side of his bed, he pulled the folder from under his blankets and jotted down the few snippets revealed tonight, before stuffing the folder back under his bed. He wanted to write that Samantha kissed him in the book, but thought against it in the end.

Laying on his blankets, he heard a light tap on his door.

"May I come in?" Minter peeked in, holding a wooden box.

"Sure." Joey stared at the box as he sat up and moved to the edge of his bed.

Minter sat next to him and put the mysterious item on Joey's lap. "A birthday gift."

Joey gripped the side of the box, feeling its high-polished

finish.

His dad never got him gifts. That was his mom's job. At best, his dad signed a card or helped him build whatever it was he got. It wasn't that he was a bad dad; just, shopping wasn't his thing.

"What's this?" Joey held the box to his face. It had weight to it and felt expensive.

"Open it."

Feeling the edges, he found the lid and cracked it open. Smells of metal and oil rose from it. He couldn't believe what he was staring at . . . two handguns, neatly nestled in the box. He absentmindedly slid his fingers across the metal barrels.

Did these have something to do with Trip's warning? His dad had taught him how to shoot and said Joey was a natural, but never hinted he should own a gun.

"I think you should have these for protection," his dad said. "This can be a—a dangerous world." He looked past Joey and toward the bedroom window. "There are no bullets in them, but tomorrow after school, we'll go shooting."

"Thanks," Joey said, struggling to find the questions he wanted to ask. "Dad, are we in danger?"

"No, but better safe than sorry." He glanced out his window again.

"Trip mentioned Watchers Woods . . . that you had been tricked. Is there something in there?"

Minter ran his hand through his hair and looked out Joey's window. "I know you kids are searching for the answers, the librarian told me about your excursions there." He paused and struggled to get the words out. "When we were young, Karen and I went to the woods with your friends' parents."

Joey's mouth hung open. He couldn't believe his dad was talking about the past.

Minter sighed. "I wish I could just explain things to you, but even if I tried, you'd think it was a lie."

"Please?"

He breathed out a quick laugh. "I have as many questions as you do about that night."

"Yeah, but—"

"The fact is, a lot of my dear friends ended up dead." He took a deep breath. "Listen son, I see the look in your eyes. You have to promise me you will never go into those woods. You're a special kid—"

"Dad, I'm eighteen now."

"You are turning into a man, I know, but you'll always be my kid. What I'm trying to say is you and your friends shouldn't go there."

"Okay," Joey said, thinking of the path that led to the woods from their house.

"Good night, Joey." He placed a hand on Joey's shoulder, got up, and left the room.

JOEY LAY IN HIS BED for an hour, spinning the empty cylinders and feeling the rosewood grips and cold metal. He got out of his bed and went to his window. Under the moonlight, he saw the treetops of the Watchers Woods. Every morning he took his dog, Bull, for a walk. Maybe tomorrow would be the day he entered the forest.

CHAPTER 4

AN ALARM CLOCK WENT OFF and Joey slammed the snooze button quickly. He rolled over and watched as the sun peeked over the distant trees of the forest, illuminating the golden grass in the field below. Sitting up, he thought about his father's warning.

Watchers Woods had always been a forbidden place. Through the years, the stories about why it was dangerous changed. When he was young, it was simple boogey man stuff, progressing over the years to kidnappers, murderers, and pedophiles.

Getting up, he jumped in the shower and got dressed for school. Before leaving, he turned to his nightstand, and glanced at his new gift. After staring at the box for a while, he took a deep breath and opened it. Two 586 Smith & Wesson .357 magnum revolvers sat in the box.

He pulled the guns out, one in each hand. He pushed the

cylinder over then flicked his wrist, locking it back in. He held them tight in his hand and thought about what kind of recoil they might have.

Then, he noticed a black bag at the bottom of the box and pulled it out. Inside the bag were several black straps with Velcro weaved in and around two holsters.

He stood, put his arms through the straps, and clipped the front straps together over his chest. The holsters fit high on his sides, just below his ribs. He grabbed the guns, slid them into the holsters, and looked at his closet door mirror.

He frowned at the reflection, pushed the mirrored slider across, and pulled his jacket out from the closet. Putting the jacket on, he closed the closet and looked at his reflection again. He moved from side to side, happy to see the jacket almost completely hid the bumps his guns created.

Tiptoeing down the stairs, he listened for his parents—silence. He looked at their bedroom door. It was early, but he and his parents were early risers. When he was younger, he always thought his dad battled the sun to see who could get up first. Maybe last night got the better of him. Joey skipped down the rest of the stairs.

He passed through the living room, still reeking of the beer and dips from the party, and left out the front door.

The smell of oil and soil hit his nose as he stepped onto the dirt driveway. Patches of weeds collected around his dad's two project vehicles. The grass field beyond the broken down vehicles swayed in the morning wind, kicking up bits of dust and seeds that floated into the Watchers Woods beyond.

Eyeing the gloomy trees, he strained to make out the details. It looked like any other forest he and his friends had been in . .

. but it wasn't. This was the forbidden forest. The Preston Six had played games around the woods; running in and out of the forest's edge before hearing a cricket or bird chirp, spooking them away. He stared at the distant, dark tree line, summoning courage from within.

He slipped his right hand into his jacket and felt a polished grip. He was only missing one thing, Bull.

"Well, speak of the devil," Joey said, as his chocolate Lab came running from under the front porch. He smiled and got down on one knee to greet him. Bull's body shook in excitement as he tried to pet his head.

"It's the first day of school." He glanced back at the edge of the dark forest. "Think we have time for a walk?"

Bull barked.

"Shh," he said and glanced up at the second-story window.

He followed the trodden path leading to the edge of the forest, squinting into the sunrays shooting over the top of the trees. A cool breeze swept over the field and he watched the grass sway. Holding out his hands, he let the overgrown grass graze his palms. When they reached the edge of the clearance, he stopped and stared at the forest, building up nerve.

Joey kicked the ground and ran his hand through his hair. Bull sat down and gazed up at him, cocking his head.

"You think I'm crazy, don't ya?"

Bull had seen him do this every time they got to the clearing, only to turn back. He looked at his house, thinking of sizzling bacon with eggs and an English muffin. No, he had to see what was in Watchers Woods.

"Let's do this," he said.

Bull wagged his tail.

As he breached the woodlands, he crunched his head and shoulders together, tensing his body. Keeping a steady pace for over a minute, he finally stopped and relaxed. The thick canopy cast a deep shadow over the forest floor, while the dense trees and foliage made it difficult to see beyond thirty feet. He stepped forward and a fallen branch cracked under his foot. He noticed the lack of other sounds—no birds chirping, no squirrels rustling about, no leaves swishing.

Bull nudged him with his nose.

"Okay, let's keep going. Just keep an eye out."

He followed his dog deeper into the forest, trying not to blink, afraid to miss a clue. There was nothing but oak trees and bushes.

Hairs rose on Bull's back. Joey knelt down, placed a hand on his stiff body and focused on the direction the dog faced.

"What's the—"

His dog barked and bolted ahead. Joey startled and chased after him.

"Slow down," Joey yelled, jumping over a fallen tree, struggling to keep him in sight. After a few minutes, he caught up to him sniffing around a small clearing.

"What's gotten into you?"

He watched Bull slow his methodical path around the fallen trees, sniffing a place and then moving on. Joey studied the fallen trees. They lined up, as if someone had set them in place. Bull dug on a spot and he moved toward him, trying to pull him back. This was when Bull pulled something free from the soil. He pulled the garbage from his mouth—a cracked, red plastic plate with dirt stuck to the bottom. He shook the dirt loose and tossed it to the ground. Continuing the search, he looked around and saw a row of bushes, almost like a hedge, nearby.

Bull sniffed the thick hedge line, stopped, and stuck his head into it. Then, he barked and pushed through, disappearing from sight.

"Not again," he muttered and chased after him. The branches scraped his arms as he pushed through the bushes and came into a clearing. "What the hell, Bull?"

The hair on Bull's back stood up, and he growled at a stone in the center of the circular clearing.

"What is it?" Joey held out a hand and stepped closer. Bull turned toward him, but looked past him, growling. Joey spun around thinking someone would be there.

"Stop it. There's no one there." He spoke harsher than he wanted and Bull's ears lowered.

Joey knelt next to him, patted the back of his neck and looked around the open space.

The trees formed a dome over the circle, but the precision of it looked unnatural. Pacing under the curved canopy, he stopped next to the stone in the center.

The stone jutted from the ground, reaching to the height of his knees. It seemed out of place, as if put there purposely, in the center of the clearing.

He bent over and studied the top of the beige stone. Fingertip-size divots pitted the surface. He rubbed his hand over the rough surface and the stone hummed. Yanking his arm back, he frowned. There was no explanation for the sound, so he stepped back from the stone.

Bull growled at it.

The humming sound grew louder, like a slow rumble growing in speed. A few leafs stacked at the base of the stone shook and tumbled away. He backed up until he hit the shrub line. He turned and pushed through, keeping the shrubs separated long enough for Bull to make it through. After a few seconds, he found a thin spot to see through. Everything in him told him to run, get away from the stone, listen to your dad but he had to know what this was.

Bull whimpered.

He kept his gaze on the stone.

Joey blinked and a man dressed in all black was suddenly standing in the circle. Stumbling backward, Joey barely kept himself from falling. The man turned in his direction and he froze, hoping the man didn't see him. Bull matched his stillness.

Behind the man, a small silver animal stepped away from the stone. The creature sniffed the air, a dagger hanging from its belt. It bared its pointy teeth. Joey swallowed hard and felt his hands shaking. He breathed hard through his mouth and felt his whole body starting to shake from the fear.

The creature took a step toward him and sniffed the air, looking around and blinking his large yellow eyes. It placed a slender hand on its dagger.

Joey's body was screaming for him to run, but he felt as if he was stuck to the ground. He didn't even want to move his arm. Everything told him not to let this man and his silver companion know he was there, but they were moving closer. It wouldn't be long before something broke free, either Bull or they would finally see his silhouette among the foliage.

"You got something?" the man asked.

"Yes," the thing hissed out. "They're here."

"You sure?" the man sighed and lifted a tablet to his face. "You've been wrong before."

"One is close," the creature slurred. It inhaled again, walking toward Joey. Its yellow eyes passed over the hedge.

He had to use all his will to move his leg back a half step, then the next. *Slow and easy*, he told himself.

The silver creature sniffed and moved closer. Its slender fingers grasped the dagger at its side and pulled it out of its sheath. The dirt stirred under its bare feet as it took a few steps, tasting the air with each inhale.

A crow cawed in the sky and the silver thing turned to the bird.

Joey looked at Bull and his brown eyes stared back at him. He wanted to project a single thought into his dog's brain. *Run!*

He turned, dug his foot into the dead leaves, and took off toward home. Bull bolted ahead in a second. The creature behind him hissed and he heard a rustling of leaves.

Don't look back.

He ran as fast as he could, jumping over rocks and fallen trees. Water splashed as he stomped through the shallow creek.

After a few minutes, the muscles in his legs balked at the assault. A few minutes more and he spotted the light shining over the clearance. He kept pace and ran out of the forest. Half way through the field, he slowed and looked back.

Nothing.

He walked sideways, expecting the silver creature to leap from the shadows of the forest. After a few sidesteps, he jogged the rest of the way his house. Reaching the front porch, he stopped and paced, staring at the forest in the distance.

Bull sat at the bottom of the stairs and with his head cocked to the side, watched his master walk back and forth.

"You saw that, right?"

The dog stood and wagged his tale. Joey kept glancing at the forest. It had to be real . . . but how could it? People don't appear out of nowhere and small silver creatures definitely do not exist. It had to be a trick of his mind.

He glanced up at the second window and smelled the air for his mom's morning cooking but only came up with the smell of dirt and pollen kicked up from the wind. They had to be sleeping. He knew well enough not to disturb his dad from sleep, let alone to tell him he just gone and done the very thing he told him not to do.

Joey jogged into the house. In a few minutes, he came back out without the guns. He had to tell his friends what happened. He needed someone to laugh at him and tell him he was crazy.

"Bull, get under the house porch, okay?" He glanced back at the forest and sighed. "Dad will protect you from anything, but you better not go to that forest again." He pointed to the forest. "No."

His dog eyes gleamed with intelligence but not enough to show him he had any clue what he was talking about.

"Go on," Joey pointed to the house and Bull trotted under the front porch.

Looking at the clock on his phone, he knew he was going to be late for school if he didn't move. He jumped on his old bike and pedaled hard down the driveway.

CHAPTER 5

THE BACK TIRE KICKED UP puffs of dust from the driveway as he picked up speed. Relaxing his grip on the handlebars, he slowed his pace, sat on the seat and turned onto the dirt road. It was a four-mile ride to school. He wanted to push it, but after the run back to his house, he had to pace himself.

Under most circumstances, he enjoyed the ride to school. Even as every other kid his age, or younger, seemed to have a car to drive to school, he didn't mind the time traveling down the unkempt dirt road. However, this morning he dared glances at the forest to his right, expecting things to appear among the yellow trees. Nothing did. He stopped looking once he got to Main Street and the dirt road changed to asphalt.

The school was a block away and the street was crowded with cars, yellow buses, and kids bustling around the drop-off zones. The first day of school was always more chaotic than usual, as parents jostled for positions at the Kiss-n-Go.

After crossing the street, he dodged a couple of kids, and then slid his front tire into the bike rack. The younger kids stared at him. Being eighteen and riding a bike to school was bad, but doing so on a bike that looked like he had pulled it from a dumpster made it embarrassing. He slapped the cable around his front tire, fastening it to the rack.

The school held grades from kindergarten to twelfth; at full capacity, it housed no more than two hundred students. He watched the nervous faces of kids as their parents sent them on their way. They must be thinking about being beat up, picked on, trashed-canned, or many other first-day fears. As a senior, he didn't have any of these first-day anxieties.

Joey scanned the nearby faces, looking for the Six. He needed to tell someone what he saw. Most of the kids were piling into the front doors. *Had the warning bell rung already?*

"Joey," Hank yelled from across the front yard, his large size making him easy to spot. They made their way toward each other. "Been waiting for you. Thought you were going to be late," he said.

"Well, I have a story for you." Joey pulled out his cellphone to check the time. "We've got a minute to get to class."

Mrs. Nires didn't care if he'd seen silver creatures in the forest. She would give him detention if they were one minute late. His after-school plans were forming in his mind and he didn't want to spend his first day in detention.

The school was a single-story building, and the wood siding's paint peeled off in large sections, revealing the aging cedar planks. Red flakes clung to the brown shake roof in patches. The cracked concrete steps leading to the front door tilted to the left and the handrail shook loosely as he grasped it.

The double doors stood open to the main hallway of the school. Lockers lined each side of the hall, broken up by the classroom doors. Students bustled in every direction, making last minute decisions in their lockers or speaking a quick word to a friend.

Joey always liked the first day of school—something about the open-ended feeling—as if anything could happen. He nodded to some, and said "hi" to others as he hurried to class.

"Hey, Joey," the younger classman said. She positioned herself in front of her friend and clasped her folder over her chest as she gazed at him from under her lashes.

Joey smiled to her and searched for her name. "Hello." He could see his classroom door behind her, but stayed, not wanting to be rude.

"Ok, well see ya." The two girls giggled and ran away.

"Day one and you've got a harem brewing." Hank came up beside him, shaking his head.

"They're just saying hi."

"Didn't say hi to me."

A pretty girl made eye contact with Joey as she strode by. "Hey, Joey."

"Hey." He watched her walk away.

Hank gave him an I-told-you-so expression. "You're just *too* sexy, Joey Foust." He batted his eyes at him and Joey jokingly pushed him into the lockers.

Rushing into the class as the bell rung, he spotted his friends sitting in a cluster near the windows. Lucas waved at him and told the kid attempting to sit next to him to move on.

Joey didn't look at the teacher and quickly took his seat;

detention would ruin his plans. Poly sat in front of him and turned to give him smile. Samantha sat next to Poly in her own desk. He took a quick breath and wanted to blurt out everything he'd seen to them right then. He opened his mouth and saw Mrs. Nires rise from her desk.

"Miss, put away that cellphone." She pointed at Julie.

"Busted," Lucas whispered to Julie.

She sneered at him and put her phone on her lap.

Joey closed his mouth. Mrs. Nires wouldn't have allowed the outburst building in him. He swallowed it down and glared at the clock—a few hours until lunch.

The teacher wrote *Mrs. Nires* in large cursive letters across the dry erase board. She gave the morning orientation and discussed how it was going to be a great year. For the next two hours, she laid out the curriculum for the year. Once finished, she had them get out their U.S. history books and read about what had led up to the civil war.

He wasn't much of a student—nothing like Julie—but he usually had a deep curiosity of the past.

Staring at the words on the page, he pretended to read, but all he thought of was yellow eyes. It had to be real. Would his friends even believe such a wild story?

He watched the second hand move around the clock. Closing the history book and rubbing his eyes, his stomach growled—two minutes until lunchtime. He wanted to get to the cafeteria first and claim their table. Each year, some under classmen would mistakenly sit at their table. He needed that table if he was going to have any privacy with his friends.

The bell rang for lunch and he hurried to the cafeteria, not waiting for anyone. First in line for the taco/pizza cart, he bought two slices of pizza and a soda, taking his food to their usual table. It was the ideal corner spot with a view of both the outside and the cafeteria. *Preston Six* was carved into a spot on the table. Each of them took a turn carving in a letter or two.

With the first slice down, his stomach felt better. His friends found their way in and sat down with their trays of food or home-packed lunches. He watched Samantha stride across and take a seat near him. They locked eyes and he smiled.

She grinned and covered her mouth with her hand. She glanced at their friends. He didn't think she told anyone about the kiss.

Lucas talked with Hank as they sat down next to him. Julie and Poly sat next to Samantha as they filled their table. Joey decided to wait and pick his moment.

"Did you guys know the school went digital this year?" Julie asked. She smiled and held her cellphone. Not that you would ever catch her without it. It was her spirit animal, and she'd probably die if it was detached from her.

"Yeah, thanks for the update there, Julie. They added a new urinal in the men's bathroom, but I was saving that groundbreaker for a dull moment." Lucas leaned back.

"Check this out." Julie held her phone out for them to see. She leaned and whispered, "I hacked their system last week. I have total control over the bells, intercoms—"

"Can you change my grades?" Hank interrupted. Day one and the poor guy was already worried about his grades.

Joey would make sure Hank got the grades to graduate, even if he and the rest of the six had to write every report for him.

"I'd think they'd notice something like that, but we can

have a bit of fun with it. Watch this." Julie held her phone to her mouth and whispered into it. Joey couldn't hear the words, but her mischievous look as she pressed the button gave him all sorts of ideas of what she had just done.

The intercom crackled to life and the speaker blurted out in a deep, modulated voice, "Attention. Can a Lucas Pratt please come to the front office? I repeat, Lucas Pratt, to the front office. Your mom is here with a pair of underwear and your anti-diarrhea medication."

The cafeteria broke out in laughter, many pointing at Lucas.

He stood up and waved his hands toward himself as if saying, "Bring it on." The laughter slowed to a few chuckles and he sat down.

"Oh, no you didn't." Lucas said, leaping across the table for Julie's phone.

She dodged his grab.

"Come on. You have to show me how to use that." He shook his head and his eyes twitched. "There are a billion awesome things I could do. You're just going to waste it."

"You'd abuse it, and you know it. If you can come up with a written request, I may entertain the idea." Julie held the phone against her chest and gave Lucas a smug look.

"A written request?" Lucas plopped back in his chair and crossed his arms.

"No, really, can you change my grades?" Hank asked again.

"No, Hank, I can't."

"Are you Julie?" A different voice drew Joey's attention away from their circle. A young man he didn't recognize—maybe a junior—swept his gaze over the table, and then locked his attention on Julie. "I heard you're the resident computer queen?"

"Well, I guess my reputation has preceded me."

He stuffed his hands in his pocket and cocked his head. "I was wondering if maybe you could help me with an app I've been working on."

"She's busy, pal." Lucas slid his taco plate to the middle of the table and leaned back in his chair.

The new guy didn't back down. "I think she can talk for herself, and the name's Brent."

Lucas rolled his eyes and mouthed the word "Brent" under his breath. Joey reveled in the banter and leaned back in his chair to see what would unfold. Samantha and Poly raised eyebrows at each other.

"I think I can as well." Julie scowled at Lucas. "I'd be happy to help you out," she answered the new guy.

"Thanks, Julie. I'll hit you up after school and we can trade numbers." Brent paused and glanced over them, his arrogant gaze passing over Joey and stopping on Lucas. "Next time, just let Julie speak for herself, pal." He turned and walked away.

Lucas stared at Brent's back. "Who was that? Some new kid?"

"Must be, I think I would've remembered him." Julie fanned her face with her hand.

"Yeah, well, if you're into looks and stuff." Lucas folded his arms.

"Too full of himself. The balls on him to come up to a group like us, and hit on Julie." Poly appeared annoyed. Julie smiled and looked like she just realized she was hit on.

"Yeah, the nerve." Lucas looked vindicated as Poly took his side.

"You want me to rough him up for you, Lucas?" Hank asked sarcastically.

"Actually, I would."

Hank laughed. "It'll be okay, buddy." Then his attention jerked to Joey. "Oh yeah, Joey has a story for us."

Joey's eyes went wide. He took a deep breath and looked at his friends. The more he ran it through his head, the more difficult it was to say aloud without sounding insane. "Something happened this morning when I took Bull for a walk," he started, and then continued to tell them everything that happened.

When he finished, Lucas's mouth hung open. "You're messing with us right? Freaking Gollum is in Watchers Woods. For real?" he asked with skepticism

"There must be an explanation," Julie said, examining the tater tot in her fingers. "The bean dip looked pretty sketchy last night; did you have a bunch of that?"

"It wasn't the bean dip. I think that thing was after me— after us. It said, '*They're* here, one is close.'"

"This is strangely familiar to when you told us about going through Watchers Woods and seeing witches," Lucas said.

Joey had forgotten about that story. "No, I was like eight when I told you guys that. This time it's for real."

"What about when you told us you thought your dad was an alien?" Lucas asked.

Joey sighed. "Can you bring up a story where my age is in the double digits?"

Lucas put his hands behind his head and smiled.

"I've been through Watchers Woods several times and I've never seen anything," Hank said. "I've heard of vagrants going through the woods though."

"Maybe it was some homeless guy and his pigment-challenged pigmy friend," Lucas hypothesized.

Joey breathed in deep breath and blew it out through his nose. "It wasn't some homeless guy."

"I believe you," Poly said.

"Thanks, Poly, but it's not just the two guys in the forest. Don't you think our parents are acting weirder?"

They shared uncomfortable glances with each other.

"My dad's acting stranger than normal," Hank agreed. "He's been showing me how to defend myself, like hardcore martial arts stuff."

"Not sure how that fits in, Hank," Julie answered.

"Just seemed weird is all," he said and forked his chicken salad.

Poly leaned forward and motioned with her hand for everyone to do the same. Joey slid his plate aside and leaned forward on the table so he could hear. She brought her backpack onto the table and unzipped the front pouch. Looking around, she slowly pulled out a long knife and set it on the table. There was a collective gasp. Joey could not believe she had a weapon, and at school no less. She would be expelled, if anyone saw.

"What the hell, Poly?" Samantha blurted out.

"Why do you have a knife?" Joey whispered.

"My mom's been acting strange this summer as well. I hear her talking on the phone with Trip and I think he convinced her to teach me self-defense." She spun the knife in her hand and slid it back into the backpack.

"With knives at school?" Julie's mouth hung open and she raised her eyebrows.

"Mom's amazing with blades," Poly bragged with a glowing smile. "Who knew?"

Joey stared at Poly's backpack. "There's something else." He hadn't planned on telling them. "My dad, last night, gave me a birthday present. Two hand guns." He put his hand on the side of his face, rubbing his temple.

"What's going on?" Samantha asked.

"You think this has something to do with what you saw in the woods?" Julie asked.

"I don't know," Joey said.

"I got it!" Lucas exclaimed. "Last night, Trip said *he* would never stop looking for us. I bet it's this guy you saw in Watchers Woods."

Julie frowned at Lucas. "When did you start to make sense?"

"Hey, I have my moments."

"Well, what are we going to do about this?" Poly asked, leaning forward on the table.

Joey sighed and looked at Samantha. She'd been quiet since she heard him tell his story. "What do you think, Samantha?"

"I don't like this. I think there is something bad going on. Maybe we should tell our parents about what Joey saw."

"What?" Lucas said. "No. All they'd do is freak out and stuff us away in the storm shelters."

"Lucas is right," Julie added. "Remember when we were twelve and they got freaked out about some 'tornado'? We spent the entire day stuffed underground. I checked the weather reports, there wasn't a chance of a tornado happening on that day."

Joey remembered it well. His mom wouldn't stop shaking

as she held him. There was not a cloud in the sky, so it hadn't made sense.

"If we aren't telling our parents, then what are we going to do?" Samantha asked.

"If this person knows anything about what happened to my dad, I want to find him," Poly said. "I say we go to this stone tonight. We get our weapons and meet at Fletchers path."

Fletchers path ran along the edge of Watchers Woods. It would be a good central meeting place. The woods were spooky enough during the day; Joey didn't like the idea of being there in the dark. If he had his guns loaded, maybe he could protect his friends from that thing. It could be running around the woods right now or waiting for him in his house.

His friends didn't completely believe him, he saw it in their faces. Except for maybe Poly. If this forest man and his dagger-carrying companion were part of what happened to their parents, then they had to pursue it. He was sick of looking at old newspapers and articles; he wanted to find out what really happened.

"We can tell all our parents we're staying at Hank's," Joey said.

"Fine, but I'm bringing some of the fun to the party tonight," Lucas said. "You know, just in case this silver thing doesn't show."

"I think it'll show," Julie said.

"Why's that?" Lucas asked.

"Joey said it was attracted to scent and your particular odor, carries a *long* way."

"Oh, ha-ha," Lucas rolled his eyes. "I'm going out there to have fun tonight. If we can summon something from the depths of Watchers Woods, great. I'll bring something to take it down."

Joey frowned at Lucas. He didn't know what he meant about bringing something to take it down, but he didn't think it would be fun if those yellow eyes appeared in the dark.

"Is it cool if I invite Brent?" Julie asked with a poorly contained smile.

"Oh, that's it." Lucas flung a tater tot at Julie.

"Ugh, how dare you throw food at me?" Julie played shocked and appalled, but the hint of a smile gave her away.

The bell rung.

"I think we should go right after school." Joey said in a hurry. Truth was he did not like the idea of being in or near Watchers Woods in the dark.

"Fine, let's just grab our stuff at our houses and head out." Lucas said.

"I'll bring a blanket," Poly said, smiling at Joey.

"Okay, I'll just bring my guns because there's a silver thing with a huge dagger trying to get to us," Joey said.

Lucas laughed.

Joey shook his head. He was starting to want Lucas to see this creature. Maybe he'd take him right to the circle and have him touch the stone.

The cafeteria filled with the clatter of trays and slapping trashcan lids. Joey stood and tossed his food away. Leaving the cafeteria, a hand touched his arm and he turned to face Samantha.

"I got another present last night," she said.

"Don't tell me your mom got you nunchucks or something?"

She laughed. "No, I wish. Nunchucks would be awesome. She got me a car."

"What? No way. That's unbelievable."

"I was thinking, if we have some time tonight, maybe we can skip out on the rest and take a drive to the lake."

His eyes widened. A trip to the lake, at night, in a car, alone with Samantha . . . that sounded much better than waiting for his friends to decide if he was crazy or not.

"Okay, yeah," he tried to sound only mildly interested, but failed.

She smiled, reached out and touched his hand. "Well, I'll see you tonight then."

CHAPTER 6

JOEY GLANCED BACK AT HIS house. He was far enough away. Pulling each gun from his bag, he holstered them one at a time. The weight of them pulled on the rig over his shoulders.

He almost wished his parents had questioned him about going to Hanks. He hated lying to his parents, and didn't want to add another layer of sediment to their history of lies. Pulling the bag over his shoulder, he picked up his pace to Fletcher's Path. It was only a couple miles away from his house.

Approaching the meeting spot, he saw what looked like smoke. It covered a large section of the dirt parking lot and the forest next to it. Joey jogged toward it and heard the roaring motor of a car. The car emerged from the cloud and then turned hard right, sliding sideways.

A person screamed in excitement from inside the car. He squinted and leaned forward, looking at the person driving.

Poly had one hand on the wheel and the other sticking out of the window.

The car's front tires spun and flung gravel and dust into the air, expanding the cloud filling the area. Lucas sat in the passenger seat with a huge grin.

Skidding to a stop, the dust cloud washed over Joey. He coughed and attempted to wave the dust away from his face, as he walked up to the car.

Poly shot out of the car. "That. Was. *Awesome.*"

Lucas climbed out, reached back and moved the front seat forward. Julie and Samantha stumbled out of the back of the two door Civic. Samantha scowled at Poly as she backed away from the car.

"My turn," Lucas said.

"Hell, no," Samantha said. "Poly nearly gave me a heart attack doing that. I can't imagine what you'd try to do."

"Hey, guys," Joey said.

"Hey, Joey, you see my driving?" Poly asked as she skipped over to him.

"Yeah, pretty impressive donuts."

"I wanted to do some e-brake slides, but Samantha got all motherly on us."

Samantha crossed her arms. "When you get your own car, Poly, I want to be the first to drive it."

Poly rolled her eyes so only Joey could see. "You see anything in those woods again?"

"Nah, nothing. But I'm telling you, I think it's dangerous in there." He looked at the woods.

"What can stop the six of us?" Poly tapped her fingers on her thigh strap holding a row of thin knives.

Hank walked through the settling dust, carrying a small bag over his shoulder. "Awesome car, Samantha," Hank called out.

"Thanks," Samantha replied with a smile.

"Great, we're all here now." Lucas pointed to Hank as he approached. "Let's go check out this circle thingy," he said. "Oh wait." Flinging the car door open, he pulled out a bow and quiver. "You're not the only one with something to shoot. I've been practicing all summer with my dad."

"That's a cute bow you got there, Lucas," Poly said.

"Cute?" Lucas studied his bow. "What'd you bring, a bunch of kitchen knives?"

Poly sneered. "These are stainless steel throwing knives and if something gets close. . . ." She unsheathed a dagger from her hip.

"You wouldn't get within a hundred feet of me with that stuff," Lucas taunted.

"Well, when one of these silver things comes at us, I'll leave it up to you to take it out."

"If it's real." Julie looked doubtful. "And how do we even know if they are dangerous? We could be the first people on Earth to respond to an alien visitor. What if we attack and create a war?"

Joey gritted his teeth.

"Let me show you what I'll do if one of those things comes at me." Poly slid a knife out from her thigh and threw it. It stuck into a nearby tree.

"Nice, Poly," Lucas said. He cocked an arrow and pulled back his bowstring, releasing it. The arrow flew into a distant tree. Lucas smiled with a smug face.

"What tree were you aiming for?" Julie asked.

Lucas glanced at Julie and shrugged. "The one next to it, but a tree's a tree." He leaned forward and stared at the arrow in the tree.

Joey pulled out his left gun and held it out. Everyone but Lucas watched him. He lined the sights and fired. The sound cracked through the forest and knocked some bark off a tree. Lucas jumped at the sound.

"Holy Christ!" Lucas said, holding his chest. "Don't just shoot that thing without a warning."

"You okay?" Poly asked.

"No, I think I need to go back home and change my underwear now."

"Good thing your mom brought you an extra pair this afternoon." Joey laughed. "Sorry man. I thought you were looking." He holstered his gun.

"Freaking ear is ringing now," Lucas whined, covering his ear.

After the dust settled, they walked into Watchers Woods. Joey kept his right hand near his gun. His friends laughed and joked around as they walked deeper into the woods, but he kept silent, his attention on the edges of visibility.

He led the way toward the stone. On the ground, he spotted a path ahead. It seemed familiar. Was this the path he'd taken this morning?

"I think we should be quiet," Joey urged.

Samantha nudged up against him. He wished they could have just taken the car ride to the lake and forgotten about the things in Watchers Woods, but he had to find out who the man in black was, and the silver creature with him.

She looked at him. "You think we're close?"

He looked at those brown eyes. Did he really just bring them all to see what he saw? Panic built as he studied Samantha's face. He turned back to his friends. Julie typed into her phone, Lucas inspected the string on his bow, Poly raised an eyebrow and tapped her fingers on her knives, and Hank's head pivoted around as he searched the forest.

"Yes," Joey said.

He turned back and faced the path ahead. The stone was close and a deep fear had begun to creep in. He thought about taking the path to the right, it led to his house.

"I don't think we should have come," Joey spoke out.

"I agree. We don't get any cell coverage out here." Julie frowned.

"Oh no," Lucas protested. "I need to see this circle."

Joey stared at the path ahead. It would only be a few minutes to get to the circle. "Fine, but let's be quiet for the rest of the way. That thing could still be around here." He sighed and walked down the path leading to the stone. He spotted Bull's paw print over an anthill.

"Hello?" a man's voice called out.

Joey stopped and looked at the man standing in the middle of the path ahead. He wore a black jacket and jeans. He smiled and waved a hand. Joey adjusted his jacket so the man couldn't see his guns.

Samantha and Poly stood next to him and Lucas sneered at the man.

"This the guy from the circle?" Lucas whispered.

"No." Joey didn't recognize him.

The man approached and stopped within talking distance. "What are you kids doing out here?" His gaze swept over them with a weak smile, plastered on his face.

"We're hunting rabbits," Lucas said.

"You look familiar, what's your name?" The man stared at Joey.

"Joey."

The man winced and looked at the ground. He brushed back his hair, pulled out a tablet from the inside of his jacket, and started typing. Joey spotted it for a split second—a gun, holstered to his side.

With wide eyes, Joey tried to send a warning to his friends. He mouthed the words to Samantha, but she shook her head in question.

"Joey Foust?" the man confirmed.

"Yes. How do you know my last name?"

The man took them in again, passing over each of them. "I don't suppose your parents told you who I am?"

Joey raised an eyebrow and glanced behind him. This man knew them. This man had a gun. He'd brought his friends to danger. He leaned close to Samantha's ear and whispered, "Go tell our parents about this. This guy has a gun. Run."

Samantha looked shocked. She glanced at the man and then to Joey.

He urged her with his eyes to run. "Run," he said between his teeth.

Samantha turned and ran.

"Wait," the man called out. "Whoa, Joey, you don't need to point that at me."

Joey kept his shaking hand on the gun. The heavy steps of Samantha running faded away. She'd reach the car in a few minutes and get to his parents' house in a few more. Within ten minutes, his parents should be here. He just needed to keep his gun trained on the man until they did.

The man raised both hands. "I wish I could explain everything to you kids right now, but we don't have time. They're moving around us as we speak. We need to get out of here."

Joey mouth twitched with words. "Who are you?"

"My name is Harris."

CHAPTER 7

"I KNOW YOUR PARENTS, JOEY. Your dad, Minter." Harris looked at Poly. "Opal is your mom, isn't she? You look just like her." He smiled and this time it reached his eyes. "And from that bow you're holding," he said to Lucas, "I'm guessing Rick is your dad."

Poly stood next to Joey. He spotted the blade gripped in her hand. "We've heard your name mentioned. Are you the one that killed my dad?"

"No." Harris sighed. "I know I'm asking for a major leap of faith, but in a minute we are going to have company. It's too late to run now and I hope you know how to use those guns, Joey."

Joey glanced back at the path Samantha took while keeping his gun on Harris. He wanted to trust Harris, but everything told him to run away. His parents would be there in a little bit if he could stall for a little longer. "If you really were with our parents, then how did they die?"

"We put their bodies in a bar as a cover story. I'm so sorry for your losses, but we really need to get ready." Harris glanced at the tablet in his hand. "One's here already." He lowered his hand and started walking forward. "You're going to have to make a decision right now, Joey, if you're going to kill me." He kept his pace toward them.

Joey tapped the trigger with his shaking finger and lowered the gun. He couldn't kill the man. He glanced at Poly, who looked at his lowered gun. He shook his head and she lowered her knife.

An arrow hit Harris in the shoulder. He winced in pain and yanked out the arrow.

Lucas scrambled to get another arrow from his quiver.

"Lucas, no," Joey yelled.

Blood soaked into the jacket around Harris's wound. "Don't do that again," he warned.

"Sorry man, I just thought you were about to do something to us."

Harris grimaced and took out his gun. He pointed it in Lucas's direction.

"Hey, man—"

He fired and Lucas winced. A small silver creature skid on the dirt next to their feet. A dagger fell from its limp hand. Lucas looked at it and jumped back. "Those things are real?"

Joey pointed his gun at its dead body. "What the hell are they?"

"Arracks." Harris fired another shot into its head. He sighed and scanned the area around them. Stepping forward, he fired into a bush. An Arrack fell forward with its dagger in hand, black blood running down its chest. It scrambled on the forest floor, clawing over dead leaves and branches while black blood slid down the hole in its chest. Harris shot it in the head.

"No, no, this can't be happening." Julie clutched her phone in her hands and stared at the dead Arrack body.

"I wish it wasn't," Harris said, glancing at his tablet. "They're concentrating the attack at our rear and they are going to do everything in their power to get to you kids."

"Samantha went that way," Joey said.

"I think she made it. But if we don't get moving to the stone, they'll have us cornered." Harris jogged down the path toward the stone.

Joey looked at the path leading to his house before taking the other path behind Harris. His friends kept pace as they jogged. Stopping at their destination, Joey recognized the placed logs and saw the thick hedge blocking the circle from view. He turned, pointing his gun into the dense forest. Bushes rustled and fallen branches cracked in all directions, too many for him to concentrate on.

Silver streaked past a tree and then to another one. Joey fired, sending chunks of bark flying. Another silver streak, then another, they were forming a circle around them, pushing his back to the circle.

"I won't let you take them," Harris called out.

A man stepped out from behind a tree, dressed in a similar black uniform the other man had on this morning, but with R7 written on his chest on one side and MM on the other.

"Well done, Harris. Thanks for rounding them up," the man in black said. He smirked and rubbed his hands together.

His face contorted with joy and his eyes twitched as he gazed at each of them. "There should be six. No matter, five will do."

Joey clinched his jaws and trained his gun on Harris.

Harris faced the end of his gun and gave him a subtle shake of his head. "Simon, you know I won't let you take them," he called out.

Simon laughed and placed a hand on the gun at his hip.

Joey moved his gun from Harris to Simon. His sweaty hand slipped and he adjusted his grip. The gun fired and the bullet went directly for Simon, but hit the air a foot away from him and shimmered. A spark flew off the spot it hit. He didn't even flinch. *Was that a force field?*

Simon laughed. "Got a reckless one here." He locked eyes with Joey. "I'll have fun watching him suck the life from you." He raised his gun at Joey.

Harris stepped in front of him, as a human shield.

"I'm not going to shoot the kids, but I have no problem ending you, Harris."

"You shoot me and that bullet will go right through me and into him."

Joey looked at Harris's back and took a step back.

"Don't move if you want to live," Harris whispered.

Simon shook his head in amusement. "I'll tell you what. You leave the kids with me, and I'll tell Marcus I killed you. You can go about your life in complete ambiguity."

"I won't let you take them."

Gunshots sounded from deep within the forest. Simon frowned and looked in the direction of the noise. More gunfire and Joey thought he heard yelling. He took out his second gun and kept one pointed at Simon and the other at the noise moving toward them.

A silver creature flew into view, landing on the dead leaves of the forest floor. Then, Trip jumped and landed on the Arrack's head. Sweat poured down his face as he rose to look at them. His eyes went wide.

"They're at the stone!" Trip yelled.

Another Arrack launched at him with its dagger extended. Trip grabbed a branch off the tree next to him and swung it at the beast.

A gunshot sounded and the Arrack fell to the forest floor. Minter walked toward it with his gun drawn, smoke coming from the barrel. Samantha was with him.

"Joey," she shouted.

"Enough!" Simon screamed. He took out a whistle from his pocket and blew into it.

The forest around them rustled with sounds of shaking bushes and crunching leaves. Arracks emerged from all directions.

Joey spun around, looking at the hundred or so Arracks standing shoulder to shoulder. Some had necklaces and yellow stripes on their shoulders. Some sniffed the air. All of them had yellow eyes trained on them.

"As you can see, it's hopeless. I could start a blood bath here, but I don't want to risk damaging the merchandise." Simon pointed at them.

"Mom," Poly called, as Opal ran up next to Minter.

Opal whispered in Minter's ear, as Rick ran up behind, carrying a bow.

"All that matters is the kids, Harris," Minter said. "We don't matter. You take care of them."

Harris nodded and Joey stood, mouth open, looking at his

dad. An unspoken plan developed. His dad stared at him, an apology formed over his face, as if to tell me he was sorry for getting me into this mess, or maybe he was disappointed I came to the forest. Minter took out his second gun and nodded to Harris then to the parents. Opal clutched a deck of knives in her hands and Rick pulled out an arrow.

Simon sighed. "Guess we're going to damage the merchandise." He raised his gun and shot Harris.

Joey checked his body, finding no wounds.

Harris fell to his rear and raised both guns. He fired at Simon. The bullets dinged off his face. Sparks flew around, but nothing struck him.

Joey fumbled with his gun and managed to get it pointed at Simon. He fired several shots and they too bounced off the shield.

Simon backed up, blinded by the barrage of bullets striking his face; he fired wildly into the forest, striking a few Arracks. Harris kept firing into his face.

"Get to the stone," Harris said to Joey. "Now!" he yelled.

Joey looked back at his dad and his dad nodded to him.

Simon blew two sharp whistles and Arracks ran at them.

Joey turned and felt a chill run down his neck as he saw the Arracks charging. The sounds dulled and the Arracks froze. Joey took a step and stopped. Poly stood next to him. Her arm extended, a knife suspended in air a few inches from her hand. Lucas held an arrow back in the bowstring. Joey spun in a quick circle; everything had frozen. No, not quite frozen. He watched Poly's knife inching away from her.

The sounds and action crushed back to him and her knife flew toward its intended target. Joey didn't have a second to think about what happened. He pulled his gun on the Arracks and fired into them.

"Get them to the stone," Trip yelled. He jumped on Simon with Minter. Opal stood next to the dog pile and threw knives at the Arracks as they got close.

Harris staggered to his feet and grabbed onto Joey's shoulder. "We need to get you kids out of here."

Joey shot two more bullets and then his gun clicked—empty. He reached into his jacket for speedloaders, jamming them in and raising his gun. The Arracks moved behind trees and scattered around. A few still ran at them though. He timed his shots and fired on them.

"Joey!" Harris grabbed his shoulder. "We've got to get out of here."

"I'm not leaving my dad."

Harris raised his gun and shot two Arracks as they ran toward them. One of their daggers skipped across the ground and stopped at Joey's feet.

"Get to the circle and we have a chance of saving them."

Opal howled.

"Mom." Poly ran toward her.

Opal gripped her arm in pain. She spotted her daughter moving toward her. "No, Poly." She held out her hand and Poly stopped. "Harris, get them to the circle."

Trip, Minter, and Rick pinned down Simon on the ground. Simon laughed and pushed Trip off him. Then he stood and punched Minter. Rick grabbed Simon's neck and pulled him to the ground. Trip, Opal and Minter piled on him.

"Just kill him!" Poly yelled.

"They can't, he's shielded," Harris said. "If we can get to

the circle, we can save everyone." He fired at the advancing Arracks, pushing his way through the hedge.

Joey glanced at Poly. "If this can save them."

She nodded and followed him through the hedge. Julie, Hank, and Lucas ran through as well.

Harris grabbed his stomach and fell the ground. Blood covered his hands.

Joey ran to his side. "What do we do? How do I save them?"

"Pull me to the stone," Harris instructed, before raising his gun and shooting an Arrack trying to jump into the circle.

"Hank, pull Harris to the stone over there." Joey turned as Hank grabbed Harris. The hedges rustled with Arracks pushing through. He fired into each set of yellow eyes.

"Samantha," Joey yelled. He searched for her through the hedge.

Harris's hand touched the stone and it started to hum.

"Samantha!"

An explosion from Simon blasted past Joey. The shock wave knocked him back, sending leaves flying into his face. Through the hedge, he saw Samantha tumbling over the forest floor.

Joey ran for Samantha.

Simon ran at the hedge screaming, "No!"

CHAPTER 8

BLACKNESS.

Joey's face hit something hard and fell to the ground. He couldn't see anything. Holding out his hands, he felt the steel wall he ran into. He slapped the wall, wanting to get to Samantha. *Have I gone blind?* Then he heard shuffling footsteps and turned from the wall.

"I can't see anything," Lucas said.

"Everyone okay?" Hank called out in the darkness.

"I'm here," Poly said.

"What happened?" Julie asked.

"Joey?" Hank called out.

"I'm here, man," Joey said, but his thoughts raced with his last image of Samantha. He wanted to run and find her, but everything was black. Holding his hands out like a mummy, he searched for the trees and bushes in front of him. The forest floor no longer crunched with leaves under his feet. There was only soft dirt under his shoes. The sweet forest air was gone—replaced with the smell of musty, dry dirt.

Where are we?

A moan came from someone on the ground. Joey turned to the sound to find a glow emanating from Harris's hand. He held a tablet out in front of him. It lit up the room in a soft white light.

Joey stumbled away from the metal dome surrounding them. The enclosure looked small. He avoided taking deep breaths of the stale air. *How much air could be in here?* He bounded to the spot he last saw Samantha, clenched his fist and hit the steel curved wall.

"Samantha!" Joey yelled. She had to be right there, just past the metal enclosure.

"Joey, what's going on?" Poly asked as she walked in a circle, taking in the metal dome.

"I have no idea—"

"We've got to get out of here. Did you feel that blast? They need our help," Hank said.

Joey was about to ask the same question and stared at the one man in the dome who might have a clue of what was actually going on.

"We can't help them," Harris said, struggling to get to his feet. "We're not even on Earth anymore. We can't get back."

"You're kidding, right? This is just some protective dome. Dad, we're in here!" Lucas yelled the last bit with his face as close to the metal as he could get.

Harris touched the wet spot on his jacket with his free hand and inspected a few pockets on the inside. He pulled out a small white jar, bit the lid with his mouth, and untwisted the cap. He spit the lid away and lifted his shirt.

"They can't hear us. We are gone. I'm sure they think they know where you are." Harris looked at the ceiling. "Even if I don't." He dipped his fingers into the white goo and spread it over the hole in his stomach. Wincing, he closed his eyes. Grabbing another blob, he reached into his shirt and rubbed it on his shoulder.

"This is impossible." Julie moved close to the curved steel wall and felt it.

Joey rapidly breathed in and out. "No! We need to get back."

"Your parents should be fine—"

"We left Samantha back there!" Joey pointed in the direction he saw her last.

Harris grimaced. "I'm sorry. This is a one-way stone." He held his side tight and shined his light around the room. "Opal and the rest of your parents are tough kids. Well, not so much kids now, but they are tough people."

"I don't know who you are or where you've taken us, but we need to get back to them, now," Joey demanded.

"Yeah, some freaking psycho was all over them back there." Poly pointed to the wall.

"I wish Samantha had come with us, but we can't change what happened," Harris said.

Joey paced around the stone. It had a few marks on it and looked similar to the one in Preston. He needed to learn how to use this stone and get back to Samantha.

"Your mom's Opal, right?" Harris asked.

"Yes, I'm Poly."

"And the rest of you?"

"That's Joey, Minter's son. Hank, Trip's son. Lucas, Rick's son, and Julie, Beth's daughter," Poly said, then looked around the room.

Joey knew she was looking for Samantha. It didn't feel right not to have her here. Everything in his body was screaming to get back to her. He had to find a way.

"If we're not on 'Earth'. . . ." Lucas used air quotes and rolled his eyes. "Then where are we?"

Harris tapped the screen on his device, shook it and then shined the light on the stone. He let out a heavy sigh. "I'm not sure. I got bumped when putting in the code and we missed the intended destination."

"Great, so you don't even know where we are." Lucas put his hands on his head.

"My Panavice isn't getting a signal," Harris tapped his fingers on his tablet and lowered it down in frustration.

Joey shook his head. "It's a real bummer your Panavice isn't getting a signal, but we need to get out of here."

Julie stared at Harris's Panavice lighting the room and let out a huff. She pulled out her cellphone and pushed a button. Light emanated from her phone and she raised an eyebrow. She studied the ceiling and walls with her own light as she made her way around the room. Lucas stood near her with his mouth open, looking at the ceiling.

Harris got to his feet and took a step. He clutched his side, wincing.

"You okay?" Poly asked.

"Yeah, this old body can take a lot."

Joey didn't think he was much older than his thirties, which is old, but not old enough to say "this old body."

"We're underground, I think." Julie tapped the walls and they thudded. "It sounds solid behind this steel." She took small steps around the dome, tapping the wall until her tap resonated through the room. She felt the wall in front of her. "There's a door over here."

Hank moved over to the steel door with an iron hand crank. He grabbed the crank and unlocked the door. The steel moaned as he struggled to open it. Joey rushed to the door, still hoping to see the woods on the other side. Dust stirred in the opening. As everything settled, a stone staircase, came into view—no forest.

Damn it.

Hank and Julie stepped through the doorway.

"There are stairs here," Julie said, lighting upward with her cellphone.

"Okay, let's get out of this hole," Harris said. He walked toward the door and stumbled a bit. Poly grabbed his arm to help steady him.

In the dim light, Joey glanced back at the stone in the middle of the room. He couldn't go back. Joey sighed and strode up the staircase.

Everyone crowded the stairs.

"Joey, take a look at this." Hank pointed at a stone wall. Julie moved aside and gave him as much room as she could in the confined space. He studied the wall and grasped a metal handle protruding from it.

"It's a door." Hank pushed against it and it slid back an inch. "Help me with this?" He leaned his shoulder against the stone door.

Joey pushed with Hank and it slid back farther. A ray of light shone through the top and they pushed again until the opening was large enough to get through. He wanted out of the cave-coffin, but he waited for each of his friends to pass through. "Right behind you, Harris," he said, motioning his hand forward.

Harris nodded and squeezed through.

Joey tried not to push Harris out as he followed behind him. Stepping from the cool confines of the cave, he raised his hand to block the rays of the unforgiving sun. He squinted, waiting for his eyes to adjust, and counted his friends as they stood on rocks surrounded by sand.

He reeled from the shock of being somewhere entirely different. There wasn't a tree in sight, not even a bush; nothing but desert everywhere he looked.

They stood about halfway up a hill made of sand and rocks. Rock pillars jutted out of the sand, and when he looked back, the door appeared camouflaged against the landscape. He scanned the desert surrounding them. *Where are we?*

"Great," Lucas said, holding out his hands. "You brought us to a freaking desert."

Harris brought out his Panavice, held it up and tapped on the screen, then put it back in his pocket.

"Do you know where we are?" Julie held her cell phone up, as if trying to find a signal. "You getting a signal?"

"My Panavice isn't working properly, so I'm not positive where we are. We need to get up there." Harris pointed up the hill. "For a better vantage point."

"You need help?" Poly asked.

"No, I'm feeling better now." Harris threw her a fake smile.

Joey looked up the sandy, rocky hill and then to the sun. It would be a difficult climb, but if it got him closer to Samantha, he would endure much more.

Near the top of the hill, he reached back and took Poly's hand to help her over the last few rocks. She used her arm to wipe the sweat off her red face. He hunched over, breathing hard, but was glad to be at the top.

Harris strode past them, looking composed and dry. The holes in his jacket were the only reminder of his encounter with Simon.

A small plateau on top of the hill gave them a vantage point to take in the vast desert. The rest of them looked around, but all he could do was look down the hill and control the urge to go back into the cave to find a way back home.

"We're going to die." Lucas paced in a circle. "There is nothing here."

"Shut up, Lucas," Poly beseeched.

It was hard to argue with Lucas. Joey wiped the sweat from his forehead and longed for the thick canopy of the forest.

"Look around and see if you can find anything," Harris asked.

"Sure," Joey said.

This side of the hill looked just like the other side, with a desert spanning all the way to the horizon. Cactuses and bushes scattered the landscape. A dried, sandy riverbed snaked its way through the desert. At the end of the dry river and over a hill, he spotted something. A glimmer of a reflection. He stepped forward, squinting, making out the straight lines of a building.

"There's something over there," Joey said and pointed to the horizon.

"Is there?" Harris replied, his eyes following to where Joey was pointing. "So there is. Nice spot."

"Do you know this place?" Joey asked.

"I hope I don't," Harris said.

Joey didn't understand what that meant but didn't push for an answer. The sun pulsated and sweat rolled down the side of his face. Oddly enough, Harris didn't seem affected by the heat. No sweat formed on his brow, even with all the layers of clothes he wore.

"Who are you?" Joey asked.

Harris stopped looking at the horizon and faced Joey. "I tried to help your parents and now I will try to help you and your friends."

"Half our parents died."

"I hope to do better this time."

"What happened? How did they really die?" Poly jumped in.

"Do you all want to get back home—back to Samantha and your parents?" Harris said.

They nodded.

"Then we need to go in that direction." He pointed to the place Joey found. "We don't have time to waste on old stories." Harris glanced back down the hill. "We can make it by morning if we keep a steady pace."

"Wait. How is going over there," Julie pointed, "going to help us get home if we're not even on Earth?" she asked with her arms crossed.

Harris gave a hint of a smile and took his Panavice from his jacket. "There's a master Alius stone in the same direction. We can use it to get out of here. On the way, we can stop at that building for supplies." Harris pointed to the horizon.

Joey wanted to start moving. Moving meant he was getting closer to home. His thumb rubbed the small velvet box in his pocket as he took the first step down the hill.

They reached the bottom with ease, and Joey looked back at their footprints trailing down the hill.

Over the next hour, the horizon swallowed the last bits of sun light, the air cooling. Darkness enveloped the desert and the night bugs chirped. They trudged over the sandy riverbed; it was their own personal yellow brick road.

Joey walked next to Hank and Lucas at the rear, and Julie and Poly took the middle. Harris kept quiet, but Joey kept watching him. That mind held the answers to their riddles.

The desert valley wasn't as barren as it appeared from above. There were plenty of cacti, bushes, and spikey plants with flowers on top, and the occasional bird would fly from one bush to the next as they passed.

"Can we use our lights, Harris?" Julie asked.

"Better not, might draw attention to us."

"Like, from wild animals?" Poly asked, looking into the darkness.

"Maybe, but I would be more concerned with the human kind."

Julie raised her hand to the sky. "I'm no astronomer, but I'm pretty sure that is the moon, as in *our* moon, and there's the big dipper. And look at these plants, cactus and stuff, same as we have." She jumped up and down twice. "And gravity, it feels exactly the same. What are the chances of all this?"

Harris stopped and turned around. "You're smart and I won't try to placate you, however, when I said we aren't on

Earth, I meant it. This is a similar version in another dimension."

"Like a parallel?" Julie abandoned her jumping and looked Harris in the eye.

"Yes."

"There could be another group of us here?" Julie shot a glance at Lucas.

"Not likely, I just hope this isn't the planet I think it is. We could be in danger." Harris turned and started walking.

Julie lowered her arms and huffed, annoyed by Harris ending the conversation. She took out her cellphone and held it in the air as she walked.

Great, more dangers . . . as if Arracks and strange men in black weren't enough.

Joey noticed Poly frantically scanning the darkness around her. He jogged to get closer to her. "How are you two doing?" he asked, coming up between the girls.

Julie nodded as she played with her cellphone. Poly smiled at him and hid the knife back in her jacket, moving close enough to rub shoulders.

"You think Samantha's okay?" she asked.

"I hope so," Joey said.

"Oh, I bet she got out of there just fine. I *did* just give her a pretty kickass driving lesson."

"Yeah, she is probably whipping donuts as we speak."

Poly laughed and he smiled. He always liked how she could find a way to brighten any situation. He felt relaxed around Poly, as if he could tell her anything.

She leaned in to whisper, "You think we can trust this guy?" She nodded at Harris.

"Doesn't seem like we have a choice," he replied. *Whom*

else did they have?

"I have your back if anything goes bad." Poly flashed a blade. He saw it for an instant and then it was gone.

"Same here," he whispered, and then looked over to Julie with a questioning nod.

"She keeps texting Samantha, even though there's no cellphone coverage."

"I'm right here," Julie said.

He wished it were simple as calling Samantha. He lowered his head and dragged his feet in the sand.

Poly sighed. "We're finally seniors. It was supposed to be our year. *Now* look at us." She extended her arms and looked back at Hank and Lucas. "I think Lucas is right. This whole situation is crazy."

He didn't know how to respond. He had the urge to comfort her, but he knew she was too smart for such things. They were on a crazy path and no comforting would change that. He smiled at her instead. "Want to take bets on what our parents will say to the school about our absence?"

"Ooh! Yes. I'll put twenty down for Alien abduction, of course," Poly said.

"The town's going to be suspicious. Our families have a history," Julie reminded.

Lucas chuckled. "The town will probably think there's a Preston *Three* on the way."

Joey glanced back at Lucas and laughed aloud, "I'll put my money on that!" He could feel Poly staring at him, smiling. He smirked at her and bumped her arm, as he took in her brightness. She bit her lip and faced forward. He looked at her a moment longer—the softness of her smile, mixed with the determination in her eyes. She had her mother's eyes.

"I better get back. Lucas gets scared if I leave him for too long in the dark," Joey whispered in her ear. He slowed down so Hank and Lucas could catch up and Poly rejoined Julie.

WALKING WAS EASY, BUT WALKING with the weight of the unknown and in the thick sand of the riverbed, dragged Joey to near mental exhaustion. After a few hours, without many words spoken, he filled the silence with his own insane thoughts and theories. He refused to believe they were somewhere different from earth. Everything around them seemed familiar. They just needed to get to the building in the distance, back to civilization and a phone. A quick call could end the thick lump in his chest, if anything, a car to get back home.

"Can we get something to drink?" Julie asked.

Harris stopped and looked around. He walked close to a bank, carved back by flowing water at some point. Harris got on his hands and knees and felt around in the sand below it. He must have found what he was looking for because he started scooping handfuls of sand, digging a hole.

Julie moved in, closer to Harris.

"Hold this." He handed her his Panavice, and continued to dig in the sand.

"What the heck is this?" Her face shone from the light of the Panavice. Her wide eyes didn't blink. "Can I make calls with this?"

"It's a Panavice." Harris pulled out handfuls of sand from the deepening hole. "You can make calls, sort of like that phone of yours . . . but not here. We're off the net."

Her fingers slid across the screen. "What OS is this using?" she said to herself.

Harris pulled out a wet clump of sand. "Hank, could you help me out and dig this hole deeper?"

"Yeah, sure." Hank knelt down and reached into the hole, pulling out handfuls of sand. "There's water down here," he said with a big smile.

"Sand is a great filter, but this bag will filter it even more." Harris pulled out a clear plastic bag. "Hank, see if you can fill this bag up."

Taking the bag, he lowered it into the hole and pulled it out, full of water. It looked dirty at first, but in a matter of seconds, it turned clear.

Joey patiently waited his turn for the water bag as Julie passed it to him. He took two mouthfuls of water before passing it to Lucas. Hank took the empty bag and filled it again. They continued until everyone was satisfied.

Harris took a couple of small sips, but was too busy spreading white cream on his wound to take any more. A streak of blood ran down his stomach.

"You going to be okay?" Poly asked.

"Yeah," Harris replied, but it didn't sound convincing.

"Do you know what happened to my mom, eighteen years ago?" Hank asked.

The group froze, as if a cobra dropped in the middle of them. Everyone stared at Harris in the moonlight.

He let out a long breath and pushed his shirt back down. "They told you nothing?"

"Yeah, that they died in a fire." Lucas said, rolling his eyes.

"I don't think it's right of me to tell you what they didn't, but I'll admit we put their bodies there." Harris's voice cracked and he cleared his throat. "I'm so sorry."

"Yeah, but why?"

Harris placed a hand over his gunshot wound. "We needed to protect you. That man back in the forest has been searching for you for a long time. They want what's *in* you."

Joey looked at his body. "What are you talking about?"

"So this Simon guy is after us because of something inside us?" The Panavice's light shone on Julie's raised eyebrow.

"He works for another man, Marcus. Marcus wants you. And, it's not an object he is after, it's your DNA." Harris pushed against his wound and cringed. "If we're on the planet I think we're on, I can show you a little more. Basically, you are the end-line of a chain of experiments."

Harris turned and walked down the riverbed. Joey took another swig from the pouch.

Over the next few hours, they quietly talked to each other as they walked. Occasionally, they would stop to drink and rest. Harris would not let them stop long, and would speed up the pace for a mile after water breaks to make up time.

The moon crossed the night sky. Joey felt some fatigue building in his legs, but with each step, he was getting closer to Samantha. On the horizon, the inky sky faded and morphed to a dark blue. The sun was on the urge of showing itself.

"Let's stop for a water break," Harris suggested.

Joey plodded over and took a seat on a sandbar, facing the rising sun. Poly passed him the water bag.

"Look at this," Julie said. She reached down and pulled a bottle out of the sand. "It says Pemberton Cola."

Harris grimaced as he viewed the bottle.

"Never heard of it." Lucas looked confused when Julie handed the bottle over and he rolled it around in his hands.

"Look." Poly pointed to the horizon, over the hill behind them. "They don't have sunrises like that in Preston," she said. The yellow sun crested over the distant desert mountains. Streaks of red stretched across the sky.

"There's something I need to warn you guys about," Harris said. "The town's over this hill. I think it's empty, but if it's not . . . Don't wander off, don't lose one another, don't talk to anyone, and don't touch anything. We don't want to disturb *anything*. Everyone understand?"

He hadn't left any room for a disagreement, but they all nodded. The way he'd said "disturb" concerned Joey.

What are we walking into?

CHAPTER 9

JOEY FOLLOWED HARRIS UP THE small hill. At the top, he spotted the building he'd seen yesterday wasn't a building after all, but a large, metal water tank on a hill. It sat above a small town of similar looking houses, all lined up down a single street.

An asphalt road split the town down the middle with houses on each side. The road ended at a store parking lot on the far side of town. Sand took over parts of the black road, covering it in large patches. Something about the town just didn't feel right.

"Let's try that store first," Harris suggested.

Joey nodded, letting the rest walk by as he assessed the town below. Nothing moved, no sounds, no cars or people, no cell phones ringing—just the houses and the store. He counted sixteen homes on each side of the street. But where were the people?

Harris led them down the sandy hill toward the store. As he got closer, the bright green grass stood in sharp contrast to the dead bushes and trees, many that had blown against the dirty houses. The sand reached the bottom row of the small white picket fences surrounding the backyards.

Joey brought up the rear as they walked along the backyards of the houses toward the store. Nothing moved behind the cloudy house windows. The only sign of life was the green grass. Joey stepped over the small plastic fence and onto the green lawn, and then reached down to touch it. Plastic blades flicked at his hand as he brushed the grass.

"Stick close, everyone," Harris said.

Joey jumped off the fake grass and caught up to the group.

"I don't think we should be here," Poly said.

He saw the knife in her hand, and reached for the grip of his gun. He felt the same vibe. The town felt abandoned, dead. Even more than that, he felt as if someone, or something, was watching them.

"Keep an eye out for anything," Harris said.

Joey rubbed his brow and looked at the sweat on the back of his hand. He gazed up to the sky and the merciless sun had barely cleared the horizon.

Grateful they'd passed the last house, Joey stepped onto the asphalt parking lot of the store. *ShopMart* displayed on a faded sign over the windows. Joey thought it was all pretty generic as they crossed the empty parking lot. It looked like any gas station he'd ever visited.

Advertisements clung to the dusty store windows with unfamiliar brands. Pemberton Cola, Twickster candy bars, Energy Volcano, and various others. The glass front door listed the hours of operation. Reaching the glass wall of the mart, Joey peered into the store, looking for any movement. Empty shelves lined the store but nothing moved.

Harris crouched low along the storefront and stopped at the door. He held his fist up as if he was hand signaling for a right turn. "Get low and stay behind me."

They followed his instructions, watched as he opened the door, and followed him into the store. Joey crouched next to an empty barrel of Shocker Cola. Harris pointed to the other aisles. Joey shuffled his feet to the white metal shelves. He imagined them filled with every sort of candy and snacks, but nothing except a thin layer of dust remained. He passed each aisle with the same disappointment.

Harris, hunched over, moved down the last aisle Joey inspected. Getting on his knee, he held a finger to his mouth. Joey pinched his lips together and knelt close to him.

"Don't look at it, but there's a camera above the register. It buzzed when I was over there. Get close and see if you hear it," Harris said and walked away.

Joey strode to the register and resisted every urge to peek at the camera. Standing next to the register, he heard a faint electrical whirring. He turned his back to the camera and folded his arms. Was the camera on some automatic mode or was someone watching them?

"Oh my god!" Julie yelled standing just inside the store.

Joey stumbled against the counter at the sound.

"What?" Lucas ran to her.

Joey darted over to join them. She held up the printed newspaper and he examined it.

"What's the date?" Hank asked.

"July 2022," Julie said.

"Where the hell are we, Harris?" Lucas demanded.

"A parallel," Julie said. "There's a theory that in the quantum world, even the tiniest of things move between all realities and every decision is played out. In some other reality, Russia got to the moon first, or all our parents lived."

"What the heck does that mean?" Lucas asked.

"We're on a different Earth." Julie's eyes narrowed and she faced Harris. "But what is it about this planet, Harris? You know this place. I've seen it on your face since we found that soda can."

"I knew we were on a similar planet from the plants, but there were no planes, no distant smog, no drones, or highways. So I wasn't sure."

"Great, so we're interstellar, inter-dimensional time travelers now?" Lucas threw up his hands and turned his back.

"My goal was to get you to safety at any cost. If I hadn't been bumped by Simon's blast wave, we'd be at my compound."

"So where is here?" Joey asked. He looked to the ceiling and walls, then out to the parking lot and beyond. The thought of it being true made him dizzy. How could they be on another version of Earth? He turned back to Harris, waiting for the answer.

"Ryjack. A planet ruined by Isaac and MM's failed experiment. I was afraid we might be here. That article will probably explain it." Harris pointed to the printed article.

Julie read it aloud.

Panic crushes the world as the CDC struggles to find a cure for the ZN1 virus. ZN1 knows no borders; it has passed

through checkpoints and jumped oceans. The virus's inception point appears to be near the L.A. area, but every major city in the world is now infected. The whole world holds its collective breath as we bunker down and attempt survival.

Details continue to emerge from ERs and morgues. Symptoms of infection start with a simple cough, followed by a mild fever. As the fever sets in, the virus attaches itself to white cells, shutting down the body's functions one by one. The time from first exposure, to time of death, is about 2 weeks. The mortality rate is one hundred percent. The President, in his Address to the Nation, called for everyone to stay home and seal their houses. The military will be stopping by each city to distribute supplies.

Making a bad situation worse, there are reports of murders in L.A. and San Diego areas, involving possible cannibalism. We have some shocking footage, at INT.OUR-TIME.MAG, showing a graphic video of multiple murders, committed by what looked to be infected people. Some are saying the fever has driven people to schizophrenia; others are claiming it is the dead rising. Please use caution when watching these videos; they are traumatic for most viewing audiences.

Julie stopped reading the yellowed paper. "How long ago do you think this was written?" She looked out the store windows.

"Nineteen years ago," Harris said. "When I said you were the end line of experiments, this planet is where it started. Marcus Malliden wants to live forever. He and Isaac conducted longevity experiments here, changing the DNA of their victims. It didn't work. He lost control of one of his labs and the infected escaped."

"Infected people?" Julie echoed.

"Are we going to get infected?" Poly pulled her jacket tight around herself and looked at the air surrounding them.

"Only if you come in contact with the infected," Harris said.

Joey looked out the store window to the empty parking lot. Still nothing moved—no signs of any life or infected. He touched the hilt of his gun. He would make sure nothing came close to his friends.

"I don't think we have to worry about viruses because we'll die in days without any food," Lucas sagely pointed out.

"Yes, we do need food." Harris nodded. "Let's drink some water."

Joey's stomach rumbled, as he happily took the water from Harris. Infected or not, he needed to take some weight off his legs, if only for a bit. He sat down with his back against the wall. Hank sat next to him, the smell of sweat wafting past Joey. Poly slid in on the other side of him with her bag of water sloshing around. Lucas and Julie sat in front of them.

After a night of trudging in sand, his legs hurt. He tried to rub the pain from his legs, but when he saw Poly eyeing him with her weary face, he stopped and took another drink of water. All of his friends slumped against whatever they could find. A night without sleep came at a cost, unless you were Harris. He didn't look beat at all, even with gunshot and arrow wounds.

"Gas station's empty. What do you guys think we should do for food?" Harris asked.

Joey choked on the water. He assumed Harris had a plan.

He stared out the windows to the houses lining the street, searching for a simple answer that wouldn't make him seem stupid. "Uh, well, we can go to the houses in town and search for supplies. Maybe they left stuff behind?"

"Sounds good to me," Harris said.

Lucas sighed and fell against Julie. She shoved him off with a disgusted look. "You're all sweaty and gross." She brushed the spot his face touched.

"Can't we rest for a while?" Lucas asked.

"It's only going to get hotter," Harris said.

Joey climbed to his feet and the rest followed. He snuck a glance at the camera while leaving the store.

Outside, the heat radiated from the black asphalt as they crossed the parking lot. The bottoms of his feet felt the heat and he picked the few remaining white painted lines to walk on.

They stopped at the sidewalk in front of the first house on the street. The front porch battled against the desert, as sand covered most of the concrete. Dried weeds clung to the house in large stacks. Streaks of brown ran down the stucco walls.

"Let's go over how we'll search the houses," Harris said.

He formed two teams: one outside, which consisted of Hank and Julie, and one inside the house with Harris, Poly, Joey, and Lucas. He then gave instructions on how to enter a house, covering each other as they cleared each room of any danger.

Harris opened the front door with his gun drawn. Joey, Poly, and Lucas took up the rear. He motioned Joey past him and he stepped into the entryway. A faint smell of decay and mildew hit his nose. The family room couch lay on its side with clothes and broken glass scattered across the floor. He paused, examining the black smears on the wall.

"Old blood stains," Harris whispered. "Keep a look out for anything and be as quiet as you can."

Joey gave the bloodstains a wide berth and tried not to think about how they got there. He half expected a creepy kid on a big wheel to come by and say, "*Redrum.*"

Harris moved to a door behind the family room and they put their backs to the wall on each side of the door. He rotated the handle, opened the door, and went in first. Joey followed next. Poly and Lucas mimicked their movements, as they too entered the kitchen.

The room appeared untouched compared to the family room. The tablecloth draped on the table, anchored down with a bowl of vibrant fake fruit. The white kitchen cabinets showed some aging, a yellow tint creeping in around the edges. He ran his hand on the painted cabinet door and opened it to find a stack of plates. Poly yanked open a cabinet door next to him.

"Cups," she reported.

Harris opened the long cabinet door and pointed to the contents inside. Joey walked next to him to see the food pantry, still full of various foods. It reeked of mildew and decay, but one shelf held a few canned items. Harris pulled out a black bag from his jacket and placed the cans in it.

They went from house to house, taking turns. Most of the other houses had less in the way of can goods and nonperishables, but they still managed to find a dozen cans. There were a few more houses left on the street.

"Let's hit one more house and get some blankets for the cold nights ahead," Harris suggested.

Nights, as in plural? Joey sighed. Not knowing if Samantha was okay, if his parents were okay, caused fear to build. His shoulders slumped and he sighed as he stepped onto the porch of the next house. It was his turn to go in this house with Harris, Poly and Lucas. Poly and Lucas looked as tired as he felt. A cold night under a blanket sounded like a vacation.

Harris, as cautious in this house as he had been in the first, had them work in twos, clearing the house. This time, they went upstairs to retrieve blankets from the bedrooms. Dragging his feet, Joey climbed the stairs.

"Maybe we can just stay here today, ride out the heat," Joey suggested.

"Quiet," Harris whispered. "You don't want to stay in these houses. Trust me."

Joey sighed and lifted his tired legs up the remaining stairs. They hadn't seen a single person the entire day, but at every step, Harris seemed on edge.

Harris stopped in front of a bedroom door and Joey put his back on the wall next to the door. He held up three fingers, then lowered one and then another. When he swung the door open, Joey got a peek into the dark room—blankets covered the windows, and the bed lay on its side.

Once Harris took a step into the room, a high-pitched scream sounded and made Joey fumble his gun. A man with nothing but brown-stained underwear on lunged at Harris. Two booming shots rang from his gun and the man slid onto the gray carpet near the door.

Joey's heart pounded and his ears rang. He looked at the man lying in front of him. His skin was dark and saggy-looking, with a large portion of his arm missing. He saw more movement in the room. The woman, or at least what *looked* like a woman, opened her black mouth, growling, with dark eyes and gray skin. She clawed at the turned-over mattress, thrashing at the bed, trying to get to Harris. Scaling the mattress, she jumped at them. Two more booming shots cracked and the thing slid next to the man on the floor.

Frozen in place at the doorway, Joey gawked at the two bodies. He couldn't breathe. Harris walked up to the bodies, inspecting them. He pushed the man over with his foot, revealing the gaping hole in its head. Black blood seeped from its wound.

"You killed them," Joey said.

The sound of pounding footsteps came from down the stairs. Poly was there first, with her knives out. Lucas followed closely behind, holding his bow with an arrow cocked.

"They were dead a long time ago," Harris said. "This is what happens if you get bit by one of these creatures." He pointed at the bodies. "You'd become a mindless monster." He holstered his guns. "Only a shot to the head stops them."

"Everyone okay in there?" Hank called from the front door.

"Yeah, just killing zombie people up here!" Lucas yelled back in a sarcastic tone.

"What?" Hank ran up the stairs. "Holy cow," he said as he reached the top of the stairs.

Joey couldn't take his eyes away from the couple on the floor. Why were they in this room? Were they complete monsters, or did they still have some kind of humanity behind the rotting skin?

Covering his nose, he took a step back and leaned on the railing. Up to this moment, part of him wanted to believe he was still on Earth. But after looking at the things on the floor, it was confirmed. His only chance of getting back home now belonged in the hands of the man holding a gun in front of him.

"Guys!" Julie yelled from the front door. "I think you should get down here now! There are freaky looking people coming our way."

CHAPTER 10

JOEY RAN DOWN THE STAIRS as Julie closed the front door and backed away.

Harris got to the door first and pulled up a wooden slat on the blinds. He peered out the opening, and then slammed it back in place. "Get down." Harris laid on the floor and motioned with his hands for them to do the same.

Joey slid to the floor and found himself face to face with Poly. He looked past her to Julie. "What's out there?" he asked.

"I don't know. They look like humans, but all mangled and wrong." Julie's hands shook. "Are those the infected?" Something hit the front door and she let out a small squeak and crouched her body against the floor.

Harris held his finger over his mouth and motioned with his hand for Joey to come over to him. More bodies thumped against the house. Joey cringed at each noise made. If the things outside acted anything like the things upstairs, they were in deep trouble. Poly's face quivered in fear.

"Be right back," Joey whispered to Poly.

"Be careful," she warned, as another thumped into the wall. She held her dagger in her hand and stared at the wall.

Joey crawled under the window next to Harris.

"Joey, take a look through the blinds and let us know what you see," Harris said.

He leaned up on his elbows and squinted through a crack in the blinds. Out front, the street had dozens of zombies, similar to the ones on the second floor, coming toward the house. Most had chunks of their body torn off. Just then, one brushed up against the window and Joey fell to the floor, squeezing his eyes closed, hoping it didn't see him. The thumping sounds grew and the noise of feet stomping around on the porch filled the room.

"What did you see?" Harris asked.

"The street's full of them, and a bunch are on the porch already," he answered.

"Oh my god, they're going to kill us," Julie whimpered, "I won't die, not here." She pulled her knees to her chest and held herself. Lucas scurried over the floor to her and whispered in her ear. She nodded her head and seemed to relax some.

"They won't go crazy unless they see us," Harris said. "They are as violent as they are dumb."

"Maybe they haven't surrounded the house yet. The back could be clear." Joey leaned forward a bit so everyone could hear.

"Sounds good. Let's do it before it's too late." Harris crawled toward the kitchen.

They followed him on their hands and knees. The unobstructed windows gave them a view of the backyard—no zombies. They stood next to the back door and Harris placed his hand on the handle.

"Everyone needs to get ready for what we might face out there." His gaze passed over each of them. "There's a group out front, and if we're lucky, we can sneak away without them noticing. But, if it all goes wrong, make a run for the store."

Joey stretched his fingers and nodded, feeling for his guns. Lucas took his bow out and Poly flipped a knife in her hands. Hank carried the trash bag of supplies, while Julie stayed in the middle between Lucas and Poly. They formed a loose circle as they exited the rear door of the house.

Once outside, Joey heard the grunts and thuds as the zombies stumbled on the front porch. Not ten feet past the back door and he cringed at a hissing sound, like a huge cat. He turned toward the noise and saw one running at them. Its insane eyes locked on him, mouth open, showing its yellow teeth and black tongue.

"Lucas, shoot it," Harris whispered.

Lucas hesitated, struggling to get the arrow in the bow. He secured the arrow and pulled his bow back, letting it fly. The arrow missed, striking nothing but a few strands of silver hair. He cocked another arrow and shot it, hitting it in the head. It fell onto the fake grass in front of them. Joey had his finger on the trigger and kept it aimed at the back of the thing's head.

Lucas stared at it, the bow shaking in his unsteady hands. "I had to, it was going to kill me," he pleaded.

Julie covered her mouth, tears rolling down her cheek.

"Uh-oh." Hank pointed past the fallen zombie.

The first errant arrow had hit a zombie rounding the corner. It hissed and ran toward them. Lucas unleashed another arrow and hit the thing in the neck. It slowed, grabbed the arrow, and yelled in a guttural, gargling voice.

Moving faster, the creature closed the gap. Joey held his gun out, pointing directly at its disturbed face. Lucas fumbled with his arrow again and Joey put his finger on the trigger.

Come on, Lucas. Don't make me do it.

Poly leaned forward and threw her knife. It plunged into its head, falling face first on the fake grass. Joey took his shaky finger off the trigger, terrified by the fact he was going to shoot it.

"I can't do this. We need to get out of here." Julie shook her hands up and down, frantically looking for an escape.

The need to move hit Joey hard as he looked up to see a dozen zombie-things rounding the corner of the house. Each of their sunken faces changed when they spotted them. Their mouths widened and gaped abnormally. Many of the zombies hissed and growled as they ran at them.

"Run to the store," Harris ordered, as he pushed them in that direction.

Joey didn't need a push. He ran full speed, out in front. Glancing back, he saw the creepy group increasing in numbers and closing in.

Harris ran at the rear of the pack. He fired and the gunshot echoed through the houses. He fired again and with each shot, Joey winced. If there were any not aware of their presence, they were now.

Every hundred feet they had to jump over a small, white picket fence separating one fake lawn from the next. Joey ran with his gun in hand, bobbing up and down. He didn't think it was possible to make a shot on the run the way Harris did.

"Joey, ahead of us, to the right." Harris nodded.

The large zombie stumbled toward them with his withered, sagging face and open black mouth. Joey slowed down and grasped his gun with a shaky hand. He took aim and fired while walking, striking the thing in the shoulder. He shot again and hit the chest. Panic built as it trotted toward them. Black drool spilled from its mouth. It must have been salivating.

Gunshots blasted from behind. Joey stopped at a picket fence and held up his gun, looking down the sights. Frustrated, he felt the pressure of not letting his friends down. Lucas pulled back an arrow and fired into the ones coming down the side of the house. It struck one in the chest but it kept coming.

"We should get into a house," Julie screeched.

"No, they'd break down the windows and we'd be stuffed like chickens in there," Harris said. "We need to get to the store." He fired six more shots into the group behind them. Some fell onto the fence while the rest pushed it over and kept coming.

Joey saw the fear in Poly's eyes and the distress in Lucas as he fired another arrow. He had to do something or they were going to die.

Gritting his teeth, he let the anger flood through his body. A chill started in the back of his neck, sweeping over his whole body—not the normal kind of body chill, but a shudder that felt as if his bones were brittle. The chill wasn't the only thing different, the sounds of the world around him became muffled, and Poly stopped running at his side.

He stopped and turned around, facing his friends. They inched along, legs barely moving. He watched Harris's gun as it fired. The flame sparked out of the barrel followed by the bullet flying toward a zombie.

Can I actually see that bullet? He traced the bullet's path to where it would strike a zombie in the head. *Holy shit.* Joey looked ahead to the drooling zombie and leveled his sight on its head. He pulled the trigger. Before the bullet even left the gun, he knew it was a hit. He wasn't sure how he was doing it, but he didn't want to waste a second of it.

He turned his gun to the next zombie. It went down in a heap. Behind him, four more went down. He shot at everything around him, reloaded, and shot it again until it was empty.

Joey hopped the next fence and shot the large zombie ahead, as well as the many staggering between the houses. He stopped at the last house before the parking lot and looked back at his friends. They had barely moved in the last minute. Before he could get his mind around what was happening, the sounds rushed to him and his friends accelerated back to running and yelling at a normal level.

"Come on," Joey said and waved for them to follow him.

They ran, jumping over the last few lawns and reached Joey at the edge of the asphalt parking lot. Lucas still had the arrow cocked and was looking wildly around for a target.

"They're all dead. How the hell did you move so fast?" Lucas asked, out of breath.

Joey opened his mouth to try to explain, but Harris broke through the group, still running.

"Keep moving!" Harris yelled as he ran across the parking lot.

Nausea swept over Joey. He stumbled forward, but kept his feet moving. He ran at the back of the pack and watched his friends run into the store. Harris stood next to the open front door, motioning for him to get in. Joey holstered his guns and ran. He turned the corner and put his hands on the glass door. A man in tighty whities broke from the front of a new zombie crowd as it reached the edge of the parking lot.

Joey held the door as Harris ran through.

"Lock it!" Harris yelled.

They slammed the door shut, but fumbled with the lock as underwear zombie guy crashed into the door. Harris and Hank held the door closed, but the creature pushed back hard. Poly jumped in and pushed against the door. Harris reached up to the top and grabbed a metal bar that lowered across the door and locked it in place.

The zombie frantically punched and ran into the glass door, its black mouth open as he growled—spit droplets of black splattering on the glass.

The slower zombies made their way across the parking lot at varying speeds. Each zombie crashed against the glass like birds against a clean window.

Joey, unable to hold back the nausea, staggered over to the plastic Shocker Cola bucket display and threw up into it. Julie held onto Poly and sobbed. Poly, with one arm holding Julie and the other holding a knife, stared at the creatures slamming against the windows. Hank stood next to Harris near the front door, bent over and breathing hard. The bag of supplies sagging over his feet.

"Lucas, get the back door closed and locked," Harris ordered.

Lucas jerked at his voice and lowered his bow, dropping his arrow. He plucked the arrow off the floor and struggled to get it into the quiver.

"I'll go with you," Joey offered, standing up and wiping his mouth. He already felt better, but some of the nausea still clung to his stomach.

They went to the back door and secured it in the same manner as the front, with a steel bar across the door. In the hallway were two other doors, one a bathroom, and the other marked *Employees Only*.

Joey sighed at the sight and sound of the zombie's deranged bodies pressing against the glass. Some pounded with the hands and heads while others slapped and kneed.

The loudest pounded its face and hands against the glass door, turning them into mush, leaving black smears on the glass. Joey held his hand over his stomach and thought he might add to the cola bucket.

He didn't consider himself claustrophobic, until being trapped in the store and the urge to flee swelled. He looked over to Poly, who still held Julie with one arm. She glared at the wall as if daring them to break through. The glass bulged in and vibrated with each hit. How long could the glass take such a beating?

Poly met his gaze and nodded. He nodded back and reached for the grip of his gun, knowing full well, the glass would break. This was it. They were going to die right there. Her nod gave him the will to stand, to push the panic down. He pointed his gun at the window, waiting for it to happen; but the glass didn't break—not even a crack. The zombies pounded, yelling and heaving en masse, but the glass held.

"It's bullet-proof glass. Should keep them out for a while," Harris said. "I saw it when we first got here. This is some sort of a hold-out place."

Julie stopped crying and, with tears still wet on her cheeks, marched close to the glass. Rage filled her face as she edged next to the window. Her proximity created a frenzy as they clawed and battered the glass. She screamed, loud and hard, letting it go until she had no breath left. Hank stumbled back from the scream.

She lowered her head, wiping a tear from her cheek, and turned to Harris. "You knew!"

His steel expression never faltered as he and Julie stared at each other. "I knew it was possible, but this town seemed clean."

"Clean!" Julie pointed at the windows.

"Yeah, this is not cool. We could've died out there," Lucas said.

Harris's cool gaze focused on him. "I wouldn't let that happen."

"Did you make that same promise to our parents?" Julie asked.

His face showed signs of creases as he stared at the floor. He didn't respond and Joey thought it was clear he *had* made that promise. Julie trembled as she glared at Harris.

Joey walked over to her. "Can you check the back door, and see if they are trying to get in?"

She looked at him with her hazel eyes, and his heart hurt as he saw the raw emotion. He didn't really need her to watch the back door, but she needed something to do right then.

"I'll go with you, Julie," Poly said, taking her by the arm.

Joey turned his attention to Harris. "What are we going to do?"

"We can't stay here. This glass won't hold forever." Harris examined the glass.

"What about the camera?" Joey whispered and nodded to

the camera behind the front counter.

"Let's see if we can ask them," Harris said. He crossed to the front counter and jumped onto it, waving in front of the camera. The lens of the camera shifted as he continued to wave. After a minute, Harris jumped down.

"What the hell was that about?" Lucas said. "Is there someone watching us?" He moved in front of the camera and looked into it. "Hello? We're trapped in this store with freaking zombie things outside."

"I don't think there's sound." Harris shook his head. "No microphone that I can find."

Poly and Julie came from the back hallway to look at the camera. Julie glared at Harris, then inspected the area around the cash registers, as if not willing to rely on his ability to spot for a microphone.

"That camera doesn't mean there's a person behind it. It could be automated, as most security cameras have back-up power," Julie said.

Crack.

Joey winced at the sound from the front of the store. Julie squealed as each of them turned to view the long crack in the front door. More spider cracks formed around the main one.

"There was a door marked for employees next to the bathroom," Joey said.

They crowded the hallway in front of the door. He grabbed and twisted the handle—locked.

"Kick it in, Hank, right at the handle." Harris stood back.

They gave Hank room as he reared back and kicked the door. The jamb splintered and the door swung open, revealing a small office with a cluttered desk.

"Great, now we have an office to die in," Lucas said under his breath.

"We're not going to die," Poly answered.

"Poly's right," Harris said. "At least, not here and not now."

Lucas's face contorted with a mixture of fear and anger. "Listen, you freaking freak head." He pointed his finger at Harris's chest. "You've taken us to some other world and dragged us through miles of desert, only to arrive at some town filled with crazy dead people . . . and *now* you say we're not going to die? I don't think you have a clue what's going to happen. None of us do!" He picked up the printer on the desk and threw it to the floor.

The printer struck the orange carpet with a *dong* and bounced, breaking into two pieces. The odd sound resonated and the room went silent.

"Poly, cut out the carpet," Joey said.

"With pleasure." She took out a knife from her thigh and bent over to cut the old carpet from the floor. She made quick work of it, cutting a large circle. Hank grabbed the carpet and peeled it up.

"That's no floor," Julie said.

A metal, circular hatch lay on the floor.

"Where does it go?" Lucas asked.

Joey looked to Harris in desperation and hoped he knew what to do. There was no handle, no hinges, just a smooth steel door on the floor.

"I think it can only be opened from the other side," Julie said.

Harris shrugged his shoulders, bent over to the door, and knocked three times. "Hello in there. I know you can hear us.

You saw on your video camera that we're not infected." No answer. "If you don't answer, then I have to assume no one is down there and it will be safe to use my explosives to blast the door open," he continued.

After thirty seconds of silence, they heard from below the door, "Have any of you been bitten?"

"No," Harris responded.

The sound of steel creaking and a latch clanking filled the silent room as it opened. Joey leaned back from the opening, gripping his gun. An old man appeared, squinting as he gave everyone a quick look over. He stood on a ladder over a dark hole.

Crashing glass, a sound worse than the first, came from the front of the store. A windowpane had finally given to the pressure and shattered.

The sounds of crunching glass and zombie hisses filled the small office. Joey grabbed the desk at the same time Harris did. They pushed it against the broken door, and as soon as the desk was in place, a thud from the other side hit the office door. He pushed against the desk, but the door inched open and grimy fingers clawed their way into the sliver of space.

CHAPTER 11

JOEY FROZE, APPALLED BY THE fingers. Harris kicked the bottom of the door and wedged his boot there. The door stopped opening, but two more sets of slender fingers joined the first.

The old man on the ladder let out a cry and tried to slam the hatch-door closed, but Hank caught the door with his hand and shook his head at him. The old man pulled at the door in panic, but it didn't budge. He finally let go, giving Hank a defeated look.

"Quick, get in here before they break through that door," the old man squealed, climbing down the ladder.

"Everyone, move," Joey yelled as he pushed against the door, his muscles straining under the pressure. He watched as each of his friends climbed down the ladder into the darkness. He looked from Harris to the hole. The opening was only a couple feet away, but he felt the pressure against the desk and knew Harris would be in trouble the second he let go.

"Go, Joey. I can hold them back," Harris ordered.

He stared at Harris, not wanting to leave him. "You sure?"

"Just go."

Joey took his hands off the door and shot down the ladder. He looked up at Harris struggling with the door. "Come on."

"Get out of the way," Harris said. In one motion, he jumped into the stairwell, grabbed the steel door, and closed it. He spun while hanging on the wheel, locking the door. Feet pounded on the steel door and hands scratched on the steel. He let go and dropped to the floor.

Joey stared at him in amazement. "How'd you do that?"

"All those years training in Parkour."

Joey couldn't tell if he was joking or not. The zombies pounded at the hatch.

"Will that thing hold?" Poly asked.

"Yup." The old man nodded. Or maybe he wasn't nodding, as his head seemed to shake uncontrollably of its own accord. His tattered, dirty clothes clung to his frail body, but he smiled at his new visitors.

In the dim lights, Joey saw the steel walls and ceiling, a long desk with a wall-mount TV above it, and a couch on the opposite side, facing the TV. A closed door stood at the end of the room. It had a musty, subterranean smell. There wasn't enough room for everyone to exercise, but it was far better than the alternative. He looked to the ceiling, thinking of all the zombies overhead and shuddered.

"Wow." Lucas stared at the ceiling. "Good thing I found that hatch."

Harris moved toward the old man with his jacket pulled

back on one side. "Thanks for letting us come down here. You alone, sir?" Harris asked.

"Yep. You can call me Ferrell. Sorry for the mess in here, but I haven't had company in a long time." He laughed and whistled at the end of his laugh. "Don't worry, missy. Those things can't get through steel," he said, looking at Julie who stared at the ceiling. His chuckle sounded like a motor trying to start.

Joey slid his foot forward and took a big step toward Ferrell, keeping Julie behind him.

"How long have you been in here?" Julie asked.

"Oh, not too sure on that, maybe a few years." Ferrell grinned, keeping his eyes on Julie. "You sure are a beautiful thing there, young lady."

Lucas frowned and stepped toward Ferrell as well.

"Hey now, meant no harm in that. Just an observation," he said, looking at Poly and Julie, and then licking his cracked lips. "It's not like I get to look at young pretties every day, you know."

Hank put a hand on Lucas's shoulder, as Harris spoke.

"Let me introduce everyone, I'm Harris and this is Joey, Lucas, Poly, Hank, and Julie."

Ferrell smiled and laughed at each name. He mouthed the word 'Julie.' "It's nice to meet you all. Since you're down here, I might as well give the tour. Built this whole thing myself, ya know. Well, I had it built from my design. I didn't actually put it together myself." He laughed and turned with his hunched back and slow walk, waving for everyone to follow.

Ferrell told them about how he was part of the house community and one of the lead developers for the whole project, but he was most proud of his bunker. Each word describing it was like a doting parent referring to their child. He explained that it consisted of five, eight-by-forty-foot cargo bins welded together. Joey was amazed at the size of the place after the initial shock of the first room. He had two bedrooms, a bathroom with shower and toilet, a kitchen, and a living room. He had backup generators, a large storage of batteries, a solar power system on the roof, a well for water, and a septic system for all wastes.

He grumbled a few times because the place didn't fit seven people, but it would do fine for a little while. Joey didn't intend to stay for any longer than needed. The feeling of having earth over his head made him uneasy.

The tour ended at the same room they started in. Joey stared at the couch in the center of the room. It looked inviting even with its cotton showing at the corners. His muscles ached from trekking through the desert all night, taking goods from the houses, fleeing from the undead and finally touring an old man's bunker. The occasional scratch and thump on the ceiling above didn't discourage his need for sleep.

He yawned and stretched his arms. His friends' faces said the same thing. Harris, however, looked fresh and had a strange smile as he looked around the room. *Does this fascinate him?*

Ferrell brought some chairs from the kitchen into the family room so everyone had a seat.

Joey longed for the soft cushions of the couch, but decided to take one of the fold-up chairs from the kitchen. Hank and Lucas sat next to him. Poly and Julie plopped on the couch. Harris stood with his back to a wall and crossed his arms with one of his hands stuffed into his jacket.

Joey sank into the wooden seat. He blinked, but they wanted to stay shut. Ferrell hovered around, near the kitchen. Joey wasn't going to sleep with that man looking over him. Maybe Lucas could take the first shift; he seemed more awake. He opened his mouth to speak, but Lucas spoke first.

"What happened to this world?" he asked.

Ferrell gave a quizzical look. "Where have you been, boy, stuck on the space station?" he laughed. No one echoed his laughter and Ferrell cleared his throat. "How could you guys not know? It's everywhere, isn't it?" his voice went into a high pitch at the end, full of hope. "Is there any place where they aren't?"

"Our religion had us living in a cave for years. We've had no contact with the outside world for some time," Harris said.

Ferrell perked up at this. "Cave dwellers, eh? Well, as far as I know, the world still belongs to them." He pointed to the ceiling. "We built this place before those things entered this world. When it all went south, we hoped this town would be far away from it all, thinking that maybe it wouldn't get here.

"Then a group of those *things* came and washed over the town one night. If I hadn't been working the night shift. . . ." he appeared to drift off into old memories. Shaking his head, he said, "They all thought I was crazy, building this bunker. Now look at them."

Harris interrupted his rambling. "We've had a long night and day. Is there any way we can have some sleeping arrangements here?"

"Oh yes, yes," their host said, opening a cabinet next to the TV. "So many, so many, I don't have enough." He rummaged through the cabinets, tossing blankets behind him.

"We'll sleep in the family room if it's okay with you," Harris said.

Ferrell turned around and faced them, holding two blankets. "Sure, no problem. I have some blankets in here, not enough for everyone, but the nights are good, just like the days are good. Nothing ever changes down here." He whistle-laughed as he passed out blankets and pillows.

"Thank you much for this hospitality." Harris smiled.

"Nothing to it," Ferrell said. "I don't have much, but does anyone need something to eat?"

Joey perked up in his chair at the mention of food. Perhaps he could stay awake long enough for food.

"Very kind of you, but we brought our own supplies." Harris pointed to the large bag of food they took from the houses. He pulled out the cans of food and passed them around like Santa. Joey ate his potato soup.

Ferrell stood near Joey, watching everyone eat. His hands shook and he bobbed up and down. The corners of his mouth moved and Joey heard soft laughter from him. He may have been having a discussion with himself. Perhaps it was a funny joke.

"How long has it been since you've seen another person?" Joey asked.

"Oh, not long. People come and go."

"Really?" Lucas asked.

"Sure, just a few weeks ago my daughter visited."

Lucas raised an eyebrow, but didn't ask any more.

After everyone ate, Joey moved his chair back into the kitchen and found a spot under the TV to lie down.

"Well, I'll be right in there if you need me." Ferrell pointed to a door that wasn't part of the tour. Must have been his bedroom. His gaze hung on Julie for a moment. "Good night," Ferrell said and left the room.

Joey relaxed with that creeper out of the room. Harris gave him a nod, as if to say that it's okay to sleep. Julie stood from the couch holding an empty can. She looked around for a place to throw it away. She shrugged and walked toward the kitchen.

Lying down, Joey watched her cross the room and pass Ferrell's door. In a flash, his door flung open and his wrinkled arm grabbed Julie. She screeched as he yanked her into his room and slammed the door. For a split second, Joey thought he had seen it wrong, that he'd imagined it. Then her muffled screams came through the door, and the reality of it hit him hard.

Ferrell had just taken Julie.

Joey jumped to his feet but a second slower than Lucas. Lucas bolted to the door, grabbing the handle and throwing his shoulder into it.

"Open this door." Lucas twisted the handle and slammed his body against the door. "Open this goddamned door, *now!*"

Joey saw the panic taking over his friend. He nudged next to him and put pressure on the door, but it wouldn't move. It felt solid as a stone. Another scream from Julie sent Lucas into a fresh fit.

"Hank!" Lucas called. "Kick this door in." It came out in a high-pitched scream.

"Don't touch me," Julie called out.

Hank ran to the door and kicked at the handle. He kept kicking, but it held. Joey felt the panic overwhelming him as well, a completely helpless feeling. A stupid two-inch thick door stood between them and a friend.

Lucas and Hank pounded the door with their feet. "Let her out of there," Lucas howled.

Joey pulled out his gun with a shaky hand. He pointed it at the door but didn't know where Julie was on the other side. She could be leaning against the door for all he knew.

Lucas spotted his gun and stepped back. "Shoot the door," he demanded.

"Don't shoot it, it's steel," Harris said.

Joey slowly lowered the gun and breathed out. Lucas looked at his gun for a moment and Joey stuffed it into the holster. Lucas had lost all control of his emotions as he punched at the door and screamed into it. He continued to kick at the handle with Hank.

"Julie!" Lucas yelled, pulling at his hair.

She yelled out an intelligible sentence, but the tone in her voice told Joey they needed to hurry. His mind ran wild with what the old man could be doing to her in there. The panic swelled and he moved his hand to his gun again. He had to get through that door no matter what.

"Joey, grab the tool box in the next room over," Harris muttered to him.

He breathed hard and took his hand away from the gun. A toolbox . . . Joey knew where it was. He ran to the mechanical room and grabbed the metal toolbox. "Here." He handed it to Harris.

Harris grabbed a hammer and crow bar from the box. Lucas took half a step back but hovered over him. Harris shoved the crowbar between the jamb and door. He pushed against the crow bar and hit it with the hammer, wedging the crow bar deeper into the jamb. Harris pushed hard, letting out a groan as he strained.

Lucas pushed Harris out of the way and took a hold of the crow bar. He screamed as he pushed against it, his face turning red. Hank grabbed the crow bar with Lucas and for a moment Joey thought the bar itself would fold over before the door opened but then the door popped open.

Joey ran in the room behind Lucas. One lamp on the nightstand next to the bed gave enough light to see Julie and Ferrell on his bed.

Julie sat on the bed, sobbing. Ferrell sat behind her in his underwear, one arm holding her in place; the other ran over her hair as he brushed it. He didn't look up as Lucas lunged at him.

"You sick bastard." Lucas punched Ferrell.

The old guy fell off the bed and landed on the floor. Lucas pounced on him and kept beating him. He raged with incoherent words and flying punches. Julie hadn't moved and kept sobbing. Joey rushed to her side and took her hand.

She wiped a tear from her face and looked back at Lucas. "That's enough, Lucas."

Ferrell moaned. Lucas stood over him and kept kicking him.

"Stop it!" Julie yelled.

Lucas's cheeks flushed red and his matted hair stuck to his face. He regarded Julie for a moment and then Ferrell. He kicked him one last time before bounding to Julie, pushing aside Joey. "You okay? Did he touch you?"

"He didn't do anything but comb my hair. Kept calling me Janice."

"Janice," Ferrell cried out.

"Shut up," Lucas warned to the man over his shoulder,

before turning back to Julie. "You sure you're okay?"

"Yes, I just want to get out of here," her voice shook and sounded weak.

Lucas hugged her and helped her to her feet. Joey watched them leaving the room. Ferrell moaned on the floor, and Joey thought about going over there and finishing what Lucas started.

"What's wrong with your leg?" Lucas asked, noticing a limp.

"When he grabbed me, I fell and twisted my ankle," Julie explained as she lifted her leg.

Lucas turned with fresh rage and Joey wasn't about to stop him.

"Leave him." She grabbed his hand and stopped him.

He huffed and left the room with her.

Ferrell cried on the floor and rocked back and forth.

Harris walked over to him and propped him into a sitting position. "I'm going to tie you up so you don't cause any more problems. If you stay quiet, I'll let you loose in the morning."

Ferrell nodded his head. Blood trickled from his nose.

"Good." Harris tied him to the bedpost. Joey paced behind Harris, watching the knots, making sure the sick old man had no chance of getting free. Satisfied with the knots, they went into the family room.

Lucas paced in front of the girls, as Poly sat on the couch, holding Julie.

"We should just kill the guy," he said.

"We're not killing him," Julie interrupted him before he went too far. "He's just some sick old man." She left Poly's shoulder and crossed her arms. "I think he thought I was his sister or some other family member."

Lucas walked toward Ferrell's room.

"Stop it, Lucas."

He turned around and paced once again. "Well, I'm not staying here . . . with that guy sitting in the next room."

"He's not going to harm anyone," Harris assured. "I've tied him up and I'll stay up all night, watching over him."

Lucas grumbled more, but Julie was able to calm him down from murderous rage. They took their positions back on the floor. Joey made his bed under the TV and stared at Ferrell's open bedroom door. He thought he heard Ferrell sobbing. He rolled over and faced Harris.

"All night?"

"All night."

Joey closed his eyes, but it would be a long time before the adrenaline left his system. After more time passed, he got used to the sounds of a whimpering Ferrell and eventually exhaustion overtook him.

JOEY WOKE TO SEE HARRIS rubbing medical goo on his gut wound. He didn't notice Joey's stare and winced in pain. Harris closed his eyes and pulled down his shirt. Joey sat up, making sure not to wake anyone.

"Is it morning?" Joey whispered.

Harris looked at his Panavice. "It will be soon."

He took a seat next to Harris on one of the folding chairs. Soft thumps above reminded him of the danger overhead.

"That bastard try anything last night?" Joey nodded toward Ferrell's door.

"Nah, I heard him crying for a while, but he's been silent for a long time. Lucas did a number on him I think."

Joey took in a deep breath; Lucas's rage was still fresh in his mind and thinking of it made his pulse race.

"We can't stay here," Harris stated the obvious.

"Who would want to?" Joey didn't want to be in this hole for any longer than necessary. Chills ran down his arms as he thought about where he was.

"What happened yesterday? You moved faster than I could see," Harris said.

Joey leaned forward on the steel chair, placing his elbows on his knees. How could he explain something he didn't understand himself?

"Has it happened before?" Harris prompted.

"I don't know, maybe back in Watchers Woods?"

Harris nodded his head, looking into his Panavice. "What's it like?"

Joey thought of the chills that swept over his body. "It's like the whole world is in slow motion. I don't feel like I'm moving any faster. Everything else is slower."

"Fascinating," Harris said.

"What's going on? Did Isaac do this to me?"

Harris put his Panavice in his jacket and looked at him. "They did something to you, to all of you, but I think it hit you more than the others."

Joey shook his head. "What do you mean?"

"I'm not sure yet." Harris took a deep breath. "You know Isaac and Marcus started their experiments on the few natural people left on Vanar—the ones who lived were sent to Mutant Isle. But the experiments all came to a halt when they found

Ryjack." He looked to the ceiling. "They had a whole world to mess with and not a person or thing to stop them. That is until Isaac messed something up and created these zombies. They rule this planet now."

"What's a natural person?"

"On my planet, everybody is a product of genetic modification. Early on, they put blockers in our DNA. You can't adjust it. But naturals, such as you, can be played with."

Joey buried his face in his hands, rubbing his forehead. "You're joking, right?"

Harris laughed. "This planet is a product of Isaac's testing. You tell me." He stared at Joey with his piercing eyes, full of wisdom and pain. "I don't believe in fate, but I think it's too large of a coincidence that out of the endless possibilities, we ended up on this planet."

"Bad luck seems to run through our families."

"Now you get to see the failed versions of what eventually became of you. It's important to know who we are up against and how far they are willing to go to get what they want," Harris said.

"I just want to get home and back to my old life. I want to make sure Samantha is okay and my parents . . . their parents."

"We will."

They didn't speak for a while and the thoughts of the zombies above being some kind of precursor to what he was sent shivers down his body. He didn't feel comfortable in his own skin, thinking of what was running through his blood.

How could his parents have kept so much stuff from them? He remembered his dad saying the truth would probably sound like a lie and maybe he was right. How could you explain jumping to different planets, or that a person from another planet changed their DNA? He wouldn't have believed it even if his dad told it with a straight face.

A thump on the steel door resonated through the family room.

"What's the plan?" Joey asked.

"Let find another way out of here. I don't think we got the full tour." Harris said.

After some searching, they found another way out—a ladder hidden behind boxes of dried food. Joey climbed the ladder and opened the hatch. The hatch thumped against the concrete floor of the garage. He pushed himself out through the hole and stood, gawking at the vehicle filling most of the space in the garage.

"Get the others. We're getting out of here."

CHAPTER 12

JOEY STARED WITH WONDER AT the vehicle in front of him for a while before taking in the rest of the garage. Cabinets lined both side walls, and a large steel roll up door filled the back. Light poured in from windows at the top of the door.

Lucas climbed from the hatch and into the garage. "Yes," he called out as he jumped next to the car. "There is no way in hell I was walking past the things out there."

The others emerged from the hole in the floor and filled the space around the vehicle. Joey slid his fingers across the paint and the emblem H1. Large steel bumpers lined the front of the massive SUV, perfect for plowing through those zombie things outside.

"It's like a Hummer," Joey said. He'd seen one a few years ago in Preston. *A monstrosity on wheels* his mom had said.

"Think it'll run?" Hank asked.

"I don't know. I bet Ferrell planned on it running. Look, it's some kind of diesel hybrid." Joey shuffled through the empty boxes of fuel stabilizers sitting on a workbench. "Here's a fuel drum and there's a pump on top." He had used a pump like this once to fill a tractor his dad rented. He pulled the handle over to the gas cap and stuck it into the tank. "Pump it—on top of the tank."

"Wow, a combustion engine," Harris said. A wide grin spread across his face as he touched the back of the Hummer. "I have a collection of combustion vehicles, but nothing like this one."

"Who's going to drive?" Julie asked as she held onto Poly.

"Let's have Poly drive. She probably has more experience than the rest of us," Joey suggested.

Poly's face lit up. Harris eyed at him, but didn't say anything.

Gas spilled out of the cap. "It's full," Joey said. "Hank, once we're all in, open the garage door."

"Let's get the hell out of here," Lucas said as he opened the car door and helped Julie get in. Harris climbed into the third row back seat.

"Amen to that. I never want to see this place again," Julie said. "What about Ferrell?"

"Let him rot down there," Lucas seethed.

"I untied one of his hands and gave him a case knife to cut the rest of the rope. It will probably take him a half hour to get loose," Harris said.

Lucas huffed and crossed his arms.

Poly clapped her hands and climbed into the driver seat. Joey ran to the front passenger side and slid onto the tan leather seat, elated to have an option other than walking to death in the desert. The keys dangled from the ignition.

Poly stared at Joey and placed her hand on the ignition. "Okay, here we go." The SUV growled as the motor cranked, and for a second, Joey's heart stopped, thinking it wasn't going to start. Then the motor roared to life and smoke puffed out the back.

They cheered.

Joey leaned out the window and looked back at Hank standing next to the garage door. "Okay, Hank, let's get out of this hell hole."

Hank slid the sliding garage door up and ran to jump in the car, slamming the door behind him. The sun barreled into the garage. Joey squinted at it and felt the heat blazing on his face.

"Turn on the AC," Lucas said, wiping the sweat from his face.

Joey turned the dial and felt the warm air blowing on him. After a few minutes, the air started to cool. He let the cool air blow into his jacket sleeves. He pulled his jacket off and tossed it to the floor. He turned his arms over, looking at all the dirt and filth on them. His shirt stuck to his chest and the straps holding his holsters left sweaty marks on his body. If alone, he might have torn down to his underwear and let the cool air blow over his whole body. It wasn't as good as a shower, but he somehow felt cleaner.

"There are water bottles back here," Hank mentioned from the back of the car, holding a case of Aquis water.

Spotting a camera pointed at them through the windshield, Joey leaned forward far enough for the camera to see his middle finger.

"This must be that creeper's bug-out vehicle," Julie said.

Poly reversed the Hummer and a pair of zombies hit the back window.

"Floor it!" Joey ordered.

The Hummer accelerated and the two zombie rolled under the tires, bouncing everyone inside. Poly glanced at him as she turned the wheel. She backed up, swinging the front of the car around, hitting another zombie and knocking it to the ground.

Joey watched Poly; her expression was one of cold determination as she shifted into drive and ran over a few more bodies. He kept his eyes on her as she drove around the side of the store, steering around a small group running at them. She shot him another glance and smiled as she saw him watching her.

"Wooo!" Poly cried out as the Hummer bounced over a dirt mound.

"Drive through the parking lot and get on the main road," Harris instructed. "And don't slow down for them."

Poly followed the advice and drove through a pack of zombies at the edge of the parking lot. The vehicle jumped the curb and landed on the main road through the center of town. Passing by the houses, they saw some zombies still standing on the porch of their last house visit.

Joey looked out the back window, watching the zombies stumbling after them. His attention turned to Julie's strained face. She rubbed the bottom of her leg. Lucas sat next to her, his hands hesitantly close to her leg. Hank and Harris sat in the back row. Hank looked out the window, and Harris moved his fingers over his Panavice.

"Where we headed?" Poly asked, looking in the rearview

mirror.

"New Vegas. Just keep on this road." Harris spoke without looking up.

Poly nodded and kept both hands on the steering wheel.

"New Vegas." Lucas rolled his eyes. "*New* Vegas? Really?"

"What?" Poly asked.

"I don't know. It's like, why don't we just call the Prime Minister of America, who lives at the beige house in Washington A.C. We can meet with him in the square room and share some Alligatorade, eat some Kwinkies and drink some Dan Jackneils."

Harris laughed. Joey looked back over his shoulder to see it in person and memorize this new expression. Julie smiled too, but quickly went back to tending her leg.

"Julie, how you doing?" Joey asked.

"My ankle's sore," she replied. The hummer hit a bump in the road and she winced.

Lucas glanced back and muttered something under his breath. Joey caught the name Ferrell. Another bump and Julie winced taking Lucas's attention away from the rearview. He moved closer to Julie and unbuckled her seatbelt. "Lie down, Julie, and put your leg on me."

Once she laid down, he held her foot gingerly on his lap.

"You doing okay, Poly?" Joey asked.

She smiled. "You think I can do donuts in this thing?"

"The rear wheel drive should make it exceedingly easy," Julie said before wincing from another bump.

"Let me know if you need to pull over and switch drivers," Harris said in a higher tone than he normally used.

"I think I can handle driving on these roads." Poly's head

bobbed from side to side. The corners of her mouth pulled back as her lips pursed. When she turned to face Joey, a big smile spread over her face. It was infectious. He found himself smiling and trying to forget Ferrell's small town and the horrors it held.

A burnt car sat in the middle of the road. Poly slowed down and passed by it using the dirt shoulder. The Hummer bounced as she navigated the large sandbars stretching across the road next to the car. Joey had driven his dad's truck down the dirt road a few times, but his dad became so nervous he had him pull over.

"I'm okay back here, if anyone's interested," Hank said.

"Good to hear, Hank," Joey replied. "That really takes a load off."

"How far to New Vegas?" Julie asked after a few minutes.

Harris answered, "About a hundred miles."

"Is the Alius stone in Vegas?"

"Yeah."

JOEY STRETCHED HIS LEGS OUT and took a deep breath. He kept his gaze on the landscape as it passed by. With his eyes open, the world seemed normal. Cactuses and bushes . . . nothing in the desert showed what happened to this world. Did the animals know? Did the jackrabbits still run, snakes slither, and vultures scour?

"I guess I'll be the one who asks the question." Lucas broke the silence. "Joey, what's going on with you? How did you move so fast? You were in one place, one second, and in another, the next."

He kept his forehead against the glass, looking at the desert.

He had expected this question from his friends at some point, but he didn't understand what happened himself, and felt like some freak. "A chill goes over my body and the world slows down. I'm at a normal speed. Everything else is just going slow." Hearing himself explain it aloud sounded ridiculous. Joey turned his head to look at Poly, but she kept her face toward the road.

"Holy crap, are you serious?" Lucas asked.

"Yeah."

"You must be moving near the speed of light," Julie said. "The closer to the speed of light you get, the slower time goes, sort of."

"Harris, what do you think?" Poly asked.

"Isaac manipulated your genetics. I've seen many mutations, but nothing like this," Harris said.

Joey looked at his hands, studying his fingers. He wondered what was under his skin, deep in his cells, all the way to his DNA. He wasn't normal. Putting his forehead against the window again, he made note of how the hot glass made an interesting contrast to the cold interior.

"I'm still the same Joey," he said.

"We can call you Flash if you want," Lucas offered. "Give you some kind of superhero name."

Joey groaned. He hated this.

"Speedster," Hank said.

Julie chuckled and added, "Joey Lightyear."

"Come on, guys," Poly reprimanded, looking in the mirror. Joey sighed in relief at the end of the names. "Speedy Gonejoey is the obvious choice, anyway." She reached over and squeezed his hand, giving him a wink.

He laughed at the ridiculous name and saw Poly eyeing him, smiling. She kept her hand wrapped over his and eyed him again, with a softer smile and the look in her eyes gave him a warm feeling in his gut. She pulled her hand back to steer, but he kept his hand in place, looking at it and back to Poly. He watched her glowing face with new eyes.

"Harris, if that small town had all those zombies, wouldn't a city like Vegas be a terrible place to go?" Hank asked.

"Yes."

"Are there any . . . regular people left on the planet?" Poly asked.

"There are pockets of people, here and there. They're usually fortified underground, like Ferrell, or in enclosed compounds."

Joey adjusted himself in the seat. Hearing Ferrell's name made him uncomfortable. He glanced back at Julie and she brushed her hair back with a disgusted look. If there were more people like that on Ryjack, he would make sure to avoid them.

Julie, with her feet resting on Lucas, pulled out her cellphone. She sighed and stuffed it back in her pocket. "Hey, Harris, can I have a look at that smart phone of yours?"

"My Panavice? Sure." Harris took it out of his jacket pocket and handed it over. Her eyes lit up under the soft glow of the screen. "It's a bit tricky to use the first time, if—"

"Oh my god, you can scan everything electronic around you." Julie interrupted Harris as her fingers flew across the screen. "I can see the Hummer's computer, and even my cellphone." She slid her fingers around the screen. "Ha, I can access my phone and get the data out of it. Lucas, I can get into your cell phone as well."

"Yeah, well, if you happen to see anything weird in my search history, it's probably that time my phone was taken. . . ."

"When was your phone taken?" Hank asked.

"Dude, remember that time, like the end of last year?"

"Don't worry. I'm not going *near* your demented places. I do have some hacking morals, you know."

Lucas visibly relaxed and Joey thought the whole thing hysterical.

Julie's face scrunched as she tapped at the screen. "It locked up on me."

"It's biometrically attached to me. I can only put a two minute-timer on it for guest users."

"Oh, whatever." Julie huffed and handed it back to Harris.

Lucas smiled at the exchange. His browser history was safe.

"I didn't see one thing about our parents in there."

Joey looked back at Julie and then to Harris.

"Were you there when it happened?" Lucas asked.

Poly hands fidgeted on the wheel and she stared into the rear view mirror more than what Joey would consider safe. But then, he had the luxury of turning around in the front seat.

"I was."

"Can you tell us what happened?" Julie pushed the issue.

Harris sighed and pulled at the edges of his jacket. "When Isaac came to get you from your parents, he wasn't counting on them fighting back. It was our best advantage. What we had not counted on was the group of Arracks he brought with him. We had a plan, but it went terribly wrong and some of your parents died in attempt to save your lives."

"Why the bar?" Joey asked.

"Your parents didn't think they could explain what happened,"

Harris's voice cracked.

"Yeah, but how did they all get pregnant at the same time, and go into labor on the same day and stuff?" Lucas kept the conversation going.

"That, I'm not sure of. Your parents didn't talk too much about it."

"Was this Simon guy involved?" Poly gripped the steering wheel and looked in the rear view mirror.

"No one knew what Isaac was doing. But he must have left something behind because not long after we dealt with Isaac, Simon began his search for you."

"He's been searching for us for eighteen years?" Julie asked.

"Yes, and now that he has your scent, I suspect others will be helping him. Simon isn't the only dangerous person working for Marcus; in fact, he isn't even the most lethal. You may have all of MM searching for you now."

Joey turned and faced the front of the car. He slid into his seat and adjusted the seatbelt, exhaling as he stared at the windshield. He wanted it all to end . . . and wished he had never taken the path into Watchers Woods. Anger built and his hand balled up into a fist.

Poly touched his hand and he loosened his tight grip. She glanced at him. "We're not going to let them get any of us. If we get caught, our parents died for nothing."

Joey nodded and looked out the window.

A LARGE GREEN SIGN APPEARED on the horizon. *New Vegas: 12 miles.*

"We'll see the city after this hill," Harris said.

Joey saw the large city below. The setting sun reflected its yellow light off the glass of the towering buildings. The thought of going into the sprawling city gave him the chills. Millions would have probably lived there.

"Stop the car," Harris said. "We better not go there at night. We can camp here and head out in the morning."

Poly pulled off the road and parked the Hummer behind a dirt bank. Joey gritted his teeth at the idea of wasting more time, but going into the city at night seemed like a bad idea.

Poly cut the engine off, and in the stillness, he realized how jarring the ride had been. His arms and legs tingled as he opened the door to stretch. It did not take long in the hot, dry air to find comfort back in the front seat.

Looking through the dirty windshield, they watched the sunset over the distant mountains. He was getting sick of sunsets. With each passing one, it felt as if he were disappointing Samantha. He was in a different world, a new reality. If he thought about it too much, his brain hurt. He turned to Poly, hoping for a warm smile. She turned and gave him what he wanted.

They made themselves comfortable in the Hummer for the night. Poly and Joey up front, with Julie on the middle bench, and Lucas on the floor underneath. Hank and Harris shared the back seat. The car shifted as Hank struggled to find a comfortable spot. Joey reclined his seat back until Lucas complained.

"What's your world like, Harris?" Julie asked.

"Vanar? It has some amazing places. The Three Falls of Benri is the most astounding sight I've ever seen on any planet."

"You married?" She was on a roll.

"I was," he said, putting his hands behind his head in an

effort to lean back in the rigid third-row seat.

"What happened?" Julie asked.

"In a way, MM killed her. In a way, it was my fault," Harris said.

Joey was glad she did not press the questions any further. The awkward silence was better than hearing about a man's dead wife. If Harris thought he had any responsibility for his wife's death, how did he live with himself? If Joey got any of them killed he wouldn't be able to . . . well, just thinking of it tightened his chest.

He stretched his legs and pressed on the floor mat. The city of Vegas filled his view. Somewhere down there was the next step to getting off this planet. He slid his hand into his jacket pocket and felt the velvet box. He thought about going to Vegas at some point in his life, but not like this. He watched TV shows about Las Vegas, how the city illuminated at night with huge screens and millions of lights. New Vegas sat in complete darkness, disappearing into the black abyss.

"We'll get back to them," Poly said, touching the top of his arm.

He smiled at her and placed his hand over hers. Some of the tightness in his chest unwound. Poly was an amazing woman, a knife-wielding, hummer-driving, zombie-killing woman. She gave him hope.

CHAPTER 13

"TIME TO GET UP," HARRIS SAID.

Joey opened his eyes to the dark surroundings, jolted forward in his seat and grabbed his gun on the dash. He scanned the surrounding area but nothing moved. He relaxed and holstered his gun.

Poly stretched and yawned as she woke up. The rest of them rustled from their slumber.

After drinking some of the bottled water, they left their spot next to the mountain and drove back to the main road.

"Drive slower as we get closer to the city," Harris instructed.

The sun rose behind the distant mountain range, giving off a faint glow, enough light for him to see the sprawling city and the roads leading to it. As they got closer, the cars lining the road grew denser. Arriving at the bottom of the hill, the road clogged with rusted, aged cars. Poly drove on the dirt shoulder when she had to, which made for a bumpy ride.

He recognized the large pyramid casino, even with its dust-covered glass façade, its white peak shined like a diamond. The morning sunlight spilled over the city, lighting up the massive glass structures, putting life into it. If he narrowed his vision to the reflecting towers, the city seemed normal, as if he could pull into a casino with his friends and turn over the keys to a valet.

Poly stopped the car and Joey jerked his attention away from the towers. Ahead, rows of cars blocked the shoulders and median with no easy way around. It stretched this way for the remaining mile into the city.

"Where do we go now?" she asked, lifting up in her seat and trying to see past the car pile.

"We're in a Hummer. We off-road," Lucas said.

"I've never off-roaded." Poly tightened her hands on the wheel and gazed at the open field next to them.

The car roared and the rear tires spun in the dirt. Joey grasped the grab bar over the glove box and gave Poly a sideways look. A small dirt berm on the side of the road became a speed bump as she launched it into the barren desert that surrounded Vegas.

"Yeah!" Poly cheered.

The car bumped wildly as she navigated around the bushes and rocks. The smaller obstacles she disregarded. Joey braced his body for each impact. He searched the dash in front of him until he saw the airbag symbol.

"Take it easy," Julie warned.

Poly hit a large dip. The Hummer jumped out of it, locking his seatbelt tight against his body as he bounced around in his seat.

"Yeah! Go, Poly!" Lucas yelled from the back seat. Julie punched him.

Poly, with a wide grin, didn't respond but did slow down. Joey glanced back and saw Harris smiling.

"Poly, you see that house with the pink-painted stucco?" Harris asked, looking at his Panavice.

"Yeah."

"Take us over there please, and get on Olive Street."

She saluted. "Yes, sir!"

Joey spotted the house as well. It was hard to miss a pink house in a sea of beige. As they got closer, he saw the windows were broken out and sand had piled up against the house. He adjusted his guns at his sides. Nothing moved around the houses, but nothing did in Ferrell's town at first, either.

Getting closer to the house, Poly slowed to a crawl. He felt the pressure in his chest come back, the danger sensors in his head making their statements. Poly hopped the curb and drove onto Olive Street.

Houses lined both sides of the street. Some had broken windows and graffiti while others appeared untouched beyond the dirt and weeds that grew over them. The desert sand covered a lot of the street, but he made out the yellow line in the middle here and there.

"They spread everywhere," Harris explained. "Most people weren't even aware of it until it was too late."

There was spray paint on some of the houses, an X or an O. Others had slash lines on the front door. He stared at a turned-over Big Wheel in the middle of the driveway. He owned one just like it, but his was red.

"Sometimes they stay in houses, kind of like what you saw

in that one house; a lot of them went into hibernation when the food supply ran out. While others never quite rest and roam at all hours. You have to always be vigilant while on Ryjack."

"How much farther?" Julie asked. She wrung her hands as her head swiveled to each window.

"A few miles, make a left on Tulip Street, coming up."

The sign below the dead stoplights listed Tulip Street. Poly turned left.

The corner gas station's windows were all broken, but one displayed *No Power, No Food, No Gas* in faded paint on the glass. Parked cars filled the gas station's parking lot, hoses still sticking out of cars.

A skeleton lay on the hood of a blue sedan. It was the first body he'd seen in the city. He gripped his gun. With only a few bullets left, he would make them count.

"Look," Poly said.

Joey took his fixation off the skeleton to look ahead. A clear lane in the middle of the road opened in front of them, all vehicles pushed to the side. At the end of the street, the backs of the huge casinos lined up along a strip.

"Keep on this road until we get to the strip and then make a right," Harris said. "And make sure you're quiet, one loud noise and . . . well, let's just not find out. I can drive if—"

"I got this." Poly slowed down and put her hands at the ten and two position. She leaned closer to the wheel and moved her head from side to side. The path appeared narrow for a regular car but for a behemoth Hummer, it seemed impossible.

Joey leaned forward as she approached the first choke point. If she scraped anything, the screech might awaken the terrible things he knew lurked about. Joey held his breath as Poly closed in on it. He winced as the front bumper came within inches of hitting an overturned car. She avoided the crushed, upside-down cars jutting into the cleared path. A tractor must have come through and pushed through the cars like a snowplow.

With each car Poly passed with ease, Joey relaxed more. He gazed at her and shook his head. She surprised him at every turn. They made the next few miles without a scratch. The cars lessened as they got closer to the strip and Poly gained some speed.

Harris spoke up, "Take a right on the strip."

Sand covered much of the strip's wide asphalt road. Weeds dominated the medians, with a few palm trees hanging on for their lives.

"Where to now?" Poly asked after a few blocks.

"Just up here, on the right—Venice Hotel. The Alius stone is inside."

To the right, another hotel lay in a heap of ash, with parts of its steel structure sticking out of the remains. Hotel Venice, though, remained intact. Its dusty glass could not stop the beauty forcing its way out. The marble pillars lined the entry to the driveway. Statues of angels and pipers spread with vigor. A gold valet sign welcomed them as Poly pulled into the covered entry.

"Same rules apply in here as they did in the town. Stay close. Don't make a sound," Harris said.

"You okay to walk, Julie?" Lucas asked.

"I think I can put some weight on it." Julie tested it out by pushing her foot on the floor.

Joey opened the door and pulled out one of his guns. Even in the shade of the hotel, the heat hit him and he instantly felt the sweat glistening on his face. He ignored the heat and stared at the broken glass from the front doors lying in front of them. At any second, a wave of zombies could crash through those doors and block them in.

"Lead the way, Joey," Harris said.

Joey winced at the words, but nodded and gripped his gun. He wanted to be first. If a zombie attacked, he would have the best chance to stop it.

Joey stepped through the broken front door. The grand entry hallway looked like something he had only seen on shows about Italy—scenes of people picking grapes or gathering water, all displayed on large tapestries. Stained-glass windows let in an array of colors that shone off the marble floors. The dust and weeds had not infiltrated the foyer yet. A reception desk across the hallway sat unattended.

"It's beautiful," Poly admired. "I've dreamed about coming to Vegas."

"Incredible," Lucas echoed her sentiments and ran down the marble walkway, sliding on his feet to the reception desk. "Excuse me, Garçon. I would like to request your best suite for me and my friends," he said in his mock-British accent. "Oh, a comped room? Why, thank you."

"Lucas, cut it out," Joey yelled in a forced whisper.

"Dude, we've got the place to ourselves," Lucas said. "Look, a mall." Lucas pointed up. At the end of the entrance hall, there was a large marble staircase with escalators and a sign at the top read *Venice Shops*.

Joey didn't think about shopping, but Lucas, Poly, and Julie laughed as they stepped on the bottom marble stair. Lucas bounded to the top and jumped in a circle with his arms raised in his best Rocky impersonation. Poly shook her head and kept an arm around Julie to help her.

"I don't like this." Hank walked sideways to the stairs, eyeing the dark casino.

Joey smiled. He didn't like it either, but he couldn't stop his friends from having a little fun. They needed a distraction, even if for a few minutes. Joey ran up the stairs to help Poly with Julie. He took Julie's right arm and walked with her the rest of the way up.

At the top, he released her arm, amazed at the mall in front of him. It looked untouched with windows still displaying clothes and jewelry. *Crombie & Mitch, Gianni's, Coco's & Louis Malletier*, and many more stores filled the sides. A canal carved into the middle of the mall drew his eye. With the water gone, the canal had a brown, dirty substance on the sides and bottom.

"Oh my god, look at that dress!" Poly said, running into the *Gianni's* store. A black, sleek dress was on display on the storefront mannequin.

Joey wanted to tell Poly not to go into the store, but the door had already swung behind her. He grimaced at the noise his friends made. He scanned the mall, searching for any movement.

"She likes dresses." Julie shrugged. "Ooh, look at that." Her shaking finger pointed at the cellphone store displaying a human-sized cellphone in the window. Julie hobbled toward the store.

"What are the chances they have a gun store?" Joey asked.

"About zero, I'd imagine," Harris answered.

"Dude, look at that store." Lucas ran to its window display.

The store's sign said, *Hooper's Top Hats*. Behind the storefront glass stood a mannequin holding a cane, dressed in a black tuxedo with, of course, a top hat.

"I'm so getting that." Lucas disappeared into the store.

Julie, holding a white box, hobbled up to him. "Guys, this phone has a charge!" she said and dropped the white box. She held the phone so they saw the display lit, then took it back and slid her thumbs across the screen. "Boo. No coverage." She frowned.

Joey watched her fumble with the new phone. He thought of the time he spent playing with the menus and features preloaded into his own phone. It was the first time he had seen Julie happy since leaving Earth. Her eyes lit up under its dim light. Her fingers flew around the screen.

"Whoa, this has totally different games preloaded."

Joey caught movement from his side and spun, drawing his gun. He lowered his aim and exhaled as he saw it was just Poly exiting Gianni's. The mannequin stood naked in the window. Poly twirled when she saw him watching. The black, sleek dress with embroidered designs at the fringe, formed tightly around her body. He gawked at her for an inappropriate amount of time, jerked his head away, and looked at the empty canal that once carried romantic couples in fake Venetian boats. He snuck another glance at her as she sauntered to him.

"What do you think? Isn't it amazing?" Poly said with her hands on her hips. "And look." She lifted her dress up, revealing her bare thigh and the knives strapped to her leg. "You can barely see my knives through the dress, right?" She caught his lingering eyes and smiled as smoothed her dress out.

Joey cleared his throat. With heat in his face, he said, "Yeah, barely notice them."

"Top o' the morning, chaps," Lucas announced as he promenaded from *Hooper's Top Hats*, decked out in a black tuxedo and a white shirt with no tie. A black top hat, kicked to one side, sat on his head and he clasped a black cane with a crystal ball on top with his right hand. The only thing throwing the outfit off was the bow and quiver strung across his back.

Poly laughed and ran over to Lucas.

"Well 'ello, m'lady." He tipped his hat and held out an arm. She looped her arm through his and they skipped in a circle around Joey, Harris and Hank.

Joey chuckled as Lucas paraded around with Poly in tow. The smug expression he imitated made the whole thing hysterical. Harris cracked a smile as well. Lucas slapped his cane on the marble floor and began to tap dance around it. Poly danced around Lucas, laughing.

The sound of a chair falling behind them made everyone stop their antics and turn to face the dark casino.

CHAPTER 14

BEYOND THE MARBLE STAIRS AND the first row of empty chairs and blackjack tables, darkness filled the casino. Joey stepped to the edge of the stairs and squinted into the blackness. *Please, let the sound be a bird, a dog, or anything but the black-mouthed dead.*

A chair scratched against the floor, past the edge of their vision. Another chair moved and made the scratching sound mixed with a slap, like some patron slapping a bar top for another drink. A chair next to the roulette table shifted. Something on the ground moved the chair.

He gripped his gun.

"Harris, where's the stone?" Julie asked.

"Down in the service basement, well below the casino." Harris pointed to the casino floor.

"What is it?" Lucas used his cane to point into the casino.

"I don't know, but it's coming our way," Joey replied, as another chair shifted and fell over, only a few rows back from the edge of the casino floor.

Lucas pulled an arrow from his quiver and adjusted his top hat. He cocked the arrow and held it there. Poly held a throwing knife in each hand.

A chair in the last row fell over and a hand reached out beyond the chair. It slapped the marble floor and pulled its body into the sun-lit entry. Then it repeated the movement and pulled out further, showing its legs dragging behind. A paraplegic zombie out to kill them—great.

Joey watched the thing, hoping it didn't spot them.

Using the one arm to lift its body, it made eye contact with Joey. The disfigured remnants of a human let out a loud hiss and began flailing and screaming, making its way to the bottom of the stairs. The sounds echoed off the marble floors and bounced around into the recesses of the casino.

"Lucas." Joey nodded his head toward the slapping zombie.

Lucas nodded, never blinking as he drew back an arrow. He fired into the creature's head and its hand fell for the last time on the bottom step.

"That's disgusting." Julie turned her back from the scene.

They heard another sound from deep into the dark casino, more chairs moving—a lot more—and it grew in volume.

Joey's eyes went wide and he took a few steps back. "Oh crap."

Hisses, hundreds of them from the sound of it, spilled out of the casino at them.

"Come on!" Lucas fired an arrow into the darkness. "Let's put down a few of these things."

"No we need to run, now," Joey searched the mall for an escape path.

"There are stairs at the far end of the mall," Hank pointed out.

"Okay . . . let's go."

They ran sideways away from the casino. Chairs fell and pushed across the floor. The blackjack table came into the light and crashed down, knocking over a row chairs. Zombies pushed their way through the chairs and into the light coming through the massive windows. Some stumbled over the fallen chairs, but most filled the spaces in between the last row of blackjack chairs and into the light.

Julie limped, trying to keep up, but fell to the ground. Joey slid on the marble floor as he stopped and ran back, but Lucas got to her first.

"Grab my shoulder," Lucas said, leaning over her.

She wrapped her arm around his shoulders and he helped her to her feet.

"Don't leave me behind," Julie begged as she glanced back at the zombies running to the top of the stairs.

"Never," Lucas said.

Joey grabbed Julie's other arm and they picked her up and ran down the mall.

She slipped on his shoulder and Joey slowed down to adjust her, but Lucas had not, and they fell in a tumble. Glancing back, he spotted a couple rotting bodies nearing. He looked ahead and saw Harris standing at the doorway of the stairs.

"Go, Lucas. Get Julie to the stairs," Joey said. He had to give them a chance to make it.

Lucas helped Julie to her feet and they moved as quickly as

Julie's ankle would allow. Joey spun to his feet with his gun in his hand and stumbled backward as a zombie reached for him. Jogging backward, he shot the thing in the head. It fell to the ground and another stomped over its body and staggered toward him. He glanced ahead to see Lucas and Julie reach the stairwell. He stowed the gun and made a run for the door.

Harris held the door for him and Joey ran in, knocking into Hank. The door slammed shut behind him, the sound vibrating through the stairwell. He stopped to give his eyes time to adjust, and something began thumping on the door behind him. A crack of light escaped through the top of the door with each blow.

The stairwell lit up as Harris held up his glowing Panavice.

"Now what? The stairs only go up," Julie said, sitting on the bottom stair and rubbing her ankle.

"We go up," Harris said.

"How do we know more of those things aren't up there? They could be everywhere." She glanced around as if expecting them to come through the walls.

"We don't, but I'll stay in front as added security."

Julie seemed half convinced and took a small hop toward the stairs on her good ankle. "Anything is better than being right here."

"Julie, I'll help you." Lucas took off his hat, bowed and held out his hand. "Oh here, you can use my cane." He pulled a cane out of his quiver.

She took the cane and stood. Leaning on it, she found she was able to climb the first few stairs. "Thanks," she replied with a small smile.

The zombies continued their assault on the door. With each thump Joey jerked back, as if the door would come crashing in. "I'll take lead," he said, bounding up the stairs until he reached the first door labeled *Floor 4.*

"If we can get to the top floor, there's a service elevator that can take us to the basement," Harris said, looking at his Panavice.

Joey nodded and walked up more stairs until he stood in front of the *Floor 8* sign. Past the door, in the middle of the stairs, a steel plate stood like a monolith, blocking the path. He breathed hard, waiting for the others to see the block. Poly arrived next to Harris.

"Great . . . is there another way?" Poly asked.

"No, but I think I can get through this." Harris moved next to the plate with his Panavice. He held it up and a red light shot from the end of the Panavice, striking the steel, sending sparks to the ground.

"Oh, come on. That thing can cut through steel?" Julie gawked at Harris's device.

"Mine can."

Julie crossed her arms. "Someone put that there. What if they were keeping something in?"

"Maybe they were." Harris continued cutting the steel. He made a hole large enough for them to crawl through.

Joey climbed through first. A jagged edge jabbed him in the rib and he winced. He slowed down and made sure the edges of steel didn't scratch him. The smell of urine was the first thing that assaulted his senses. He jerked his arm against his nose and tried to breathe through his jacket sleeve. Searching around the dark stairwell, he noticed boxes and chairs pushed on each side of a walk path.

He turned back to the steel opening and helped the rest. Harris picked up the steel he cut, put it back in the hole and spot-welded in a few places.

"Dear God, what a horrible smell," Lucas said.

Poly covered her mouth and nose while holding a knife in her other hand. Julie seemed to ignore the smell, but Joey saw her eyes watering.

Joey jogged up the next flight, trying to escape the smell. Light from a partially open door on floor nine spilled into the stairwell. He pushed the door, and it opened a few more inches. He shoved it until a mattress moved and knocked over a dresser. He climbed over, then stepped off the dresser and landed on the carpeted floor of the hallway. The hall smelled of old, musty laundry and burnt carpet but anything was better than the smell of the staircase. A window at the end of the hallway glowed with sunlight.

Hotel mattresses and chairs filled the hallway, leaning on the walls. Trash and furniture piled up on each side, creating a path of sorts.

The others climbed through and piled into the hallway.

"You think someone's still here?" Poly asked.

"Well, someone did this." Julie stepped off the dresser onto the carpet and avoided a nearby mattress.

"I doubt they're still here," Joey said. The hall felt stagnant, stuffy. The furniture hosted a thick layer of dust. He thought it would take years to collect dust like that in here.

The defined path led to a closed door marked *932*. Poly moved passed him and he nodded as she took a stance on the opposite side of the door. They did this type of entry several times in Ferrell's town. He put his back on the wall next to the door. Joey held his fingers up. *Three, two, one.* He pushed the door open, gun drawn.

Two decomposed bodies laid on the floor near a bed. The largest, wore jeans and a button-up shirt, while the smaller figure, had a dress on, bones sticking out from the clothes. The one with a dress on would have been the size of a young girl. Joey kept his guns on the two long dead corpses, unsure if they were going to rise from their stupor.

"Oh my god," Poly said, pointing to a pile of bones.

Human skulls and assorted bones lay in a mound in the corner of the room. Next to the bones, a large skillet with a black smoke stain streaking up the wall.

"You don't think they. . .?" Poly looked sick.

"I think when things get bad, they can get *real* bad," Joey said.

Poly backed out of the room, holding her mouth. He stared at the bone pile and the two bodies. He wished he had stayed in the foul-smelling stairway. He could forget a smell. Lucas and the others peeked into the room, but left quickly. Joey's stomach felt sick and he pulled his eyes away from the horrors in the room.

"I hate this planet." Poly had her back turned to them.

"You can't blame them." Julie pointed to room 932. "This world, this reality, was delivered to them from Isaac, Marcus, and MM. They did *that* to these people."

Harris rubbed his chin and nodded. "Julie's right, but we have a saying on Vanar. 'You are truly judged when the world stops looking.' This man thought the world had stopped looking. He felt free to break the rules that kept this world civilized. Beware of men like this."

"'The ultimate measure of a man is not where he stands in moments of comfort and convenience, but where he stands at times of challenge and controversy.' – Martin Luther King," she replied.

"Smart man," Harris said.

"I have a saying." Lucas used his British accent and adjusted his top hat. "He who loiters on a floor of dead cannibals, shall be named stupid."

Joey chuckled. "Agreed."

He climbed to the next floor. The door was open and the hallway beyond looked similar with beds and chairs filling the halls, but Joey didn't want to enter any more rooms.

Floor after floor the same thing, burning, rotting, and mildew smells mixed with human waste. Joey swallowed, trying not to think about it. They hadn't seen any sign of zombies though.

After what seemed like a million stairs later, his legs screamed at him to stop. Hank breathed hard, helping Julie walk up the stairs. Joey stopped at the floor thirty-one landing, glad for the closed door.

"This hotel blows," Lucas said. His shoulders sunk and sweat dripped down his face.

"How many more floors are there?" Julie asked.

"I think we're near the top," Harris said.

"Let's just keep pushing then," Joey suggested and started up again. He stopped, gazing at the end of the stairs and a door marked *Floor 32*. This door looked different from the rest, wood inlayed into the steel door, a digital keypad next to the door handle. Hammer marks pocked the door around it.

It had a ten-key pad, with a small digital screen above. With the buttons worn, none of the markings remained. The once square buttons were worn smooth, rounded on the edges. He imagined the people here trying for months if not years to get past this door. So much so, they had warn each button to a nub trying to guess the combo. Had that little girl's fingers touched these keys, hoping for some kind of chocolate factory behind it? He pressed a few buttons, but nothing responded.

"Let me see if I can get it open. My Panavice can possibly charge it," Harris said.

Julie suddenly looked pain-free as she again tried to study the device in his hand. "That thing can power other stuff?"

"If you can get within range." He held the Panavice close to the lock and slid his fingers across the screen. The keypad next to the door beeped and a green light blinked. Then they heard a satisfying *click*. Harris motioned for Joey to open it. He felt wrong opening it. As if it wasn't his right to access it with such ease, but the feeling fleeted and he grasped the handle.

CHAPTER 15

NO FLOWING RIVERS OF CHOCOLATE but a large room with intricate furniture, hanging lights, stone floors, TVs on the walls, and windows around the whole floor.

Lucas pushed him into the room.

"Whoa, it's freaking MTV cribs in here," Lucas said and jumped onto the couch.

Poly rushed to the windows.

The room appeared untouched. The granite counters were clean and the windows unbroken. Joey looked at the door holding back the foul smells and took deep breaths of the clean, stale air. His stomach rumbled at the sight of the kitchen.

"Guys, look at this," Poly said. She opened the sliding glass door and stepped onto the balcony.

He followed her outside. The hot breeze hit his face, but the pure air felt amazing. Poly stood at the edge of the glass railing. Standing next to her, he looked out at the city of sin. Thirty-two stories up, they could see the whole city. It almost seemed normal from some angles.

Down the strip, about half the hotels had burned to the ground and he saw the piles of cars lining the streets. Cars clogged the freeway. Residential districts lay in ruin, partially burnt.

"You see it?" Poly said, pointing down the strip.

He shook his head.

"On top of the . . . the one with all the fountains," Poly said.

Joey had seen enough shows about Vegas on TV to know what she meant. "The Bellagio?"

"I see it. How's it possible?" Julie said.

Then he saw it as well. The roof of the Bellagio had green plants all across it. There must have been acres of them. He squinted and thought he saw broken-out windows with green growing out of them. Then he saw the sign, painted black in contrast to the white hotel. *Sanctuary* spelled out in huge letters on the side of the building.

"There are people in there?" he asked.

"Yes, that's one of those hold-outs I was talking about," Harris said.

"Think they could help us?" Julie inquired.

"Them? No, I don't think they could."

"You know them?"

"I spent some time there," Harris said. "It's best if we stay far away from them."

The sign made Joey smile. It was a small victory over MM. He wondered if anyone on the planet knew the truth about what happened. Would they come to the stone with them and help them fight against MM? Would anyone believe the truth? He laughed at his thoughts and walked back into the hotel room. If someone told him a few weeks ago, there were other Earths, Arracks, and zombies; he would have thought they were crazy.

"So where's this service elevator?" Julie asked, as the rest came back into the room.

"It's on this floor, in this suite, somewhere," Harris said.

They spread out and searched the sprawling suite. Joey walked to the other rooms—an office, a bedroom, a bathroom. Then, he opened a door that led to a short hallway with an elevator door. "Found it," he yelled.

They came to him and he walked to the elevator door.

"Should be able to pry it open," Julie said.

"Here, let me." Poly stepped forward, pulling a knife from her leg sheath. She wedged it between the two elevator doors, opening them an inch.

Joey stuffed his fingers in and pulled the door open.

"Holy moly." Lucas peered down the shaft.

Joey glanced down and reactively stepped back. It went down farther than he could see, and then the hole disappeared into darkness. Steel cables ran down the middle of the shaft.

"See these cables? Maybe we can rig something to them to get us down," Julie said.

Harris looked down the elevator shaft, then up, and took a step back. He placed his hand on his chin and took his Panavice out. He didn't seem happy with it and stuffed it back in his pocket.

"We're over thirty floors up. There's no way we're going

down that shaft," Lucas said.

"I can't control the elevator from here, but if I go down, I can get it going and send it up to you guys," Harris said.

"You're okay going down those cables?" Poly asked.

"I think I can handle it." Harris took something that looked like a wallet from his inside jacket pocket and jumped into the elevator shaft, grabbing onto the cable. "When the power is back on, press the call button." Then he slid down the cable, disappearing into the darkness below.

Lucas shook his head. "Wow."

"What a frickin' lunatic," Julie said in awe.

"I think the guy is pretty incredible," Hank added.

"You think he's pretty?" Lucas teased.

Hank pushed him.

Joey looked at the black hole. The cables jostled with Harris attached somewhere below. What if the elevator wouldn't run after sitting for so many years? Could Harris get back up those cables? "I guess we have to wait."

"What if he doesn't come back?" Julie asked. "What if he dies down there? We'll be stuck in this hell. I mean, do we even know who this guy is, really?"

Joey paced near the elevator door, listening to her concerns. They quickened his steps, as well as his breath. They didn't really know much about Harris . . . but he *had* saved their lives, probably several times now. Plus, his dad seemed to trust him taking them away. "He'll be back," he said and looked back at his friends.

Julie crossed her arms and leaned against the wall. She slid down to her rear and Poly took a seat next to her. "You okay?" she asked Julie.

"No. This whole time we've been hunting down the secrets of our past, I've wanted to believe what my mom told me. But look at this . . ." She flung both hands up. "She freaking lied."

Joey grimaced and rubbed his chin. He'd felt the same way since the first zombie skidded across the bedroom floor. He always knew there was more to the story, but this was too much. They weren't just hiding a lie, they were hiding a whole different world.

Lucas sat against the opposite wall from Julie, laid his bow at his feet and adjusted his top hat. "They all lied to us, true. But what was the alternative? I'm sure they all thought this was behind them. Plus, would we really have believed them?"

Hank shook his head. "My dad would tell me stuff so outlandish I never believed him. Even when I heard the truth, I thought he was lying. In fact, I wish he had lied to me." He took a deep breath blew it out. "It's not fun living alone in a house when you think your dad is going crazy." He laughed halfheartedly. "But he wasn't . . . this is real."

Joey thought of his house and his parent's refusal to say anything. Living in a house of secrets felt like the walls were moving in on you. For over a year now, they had eaten in near silence. He would slide his fork against the plate because he knew it annoyed his dad. It wasn't that he didn't like his parents; it was more about the pink elephant in the room crowding out the spaces of comfort. He almost felt he owed his parents an apology.

"Well, I can't wait to get home and have a talk with my mom," Julie said.

"I forgive my mom," Poly chimed in. "I'm with Hank. I think it would have been worse if they told us the truth."

"If I have kids, I'm telling them everything," Joey said, but he felt as if he was trying to convince himself as much as anyone.

"Same here," Lucas agreed. "The stuff we've seen will make for the awesomest stories ever. We've freaking world-jumped, fought off zombies, and now we are in some super suite in what has got to be the fanciest abandoned hotel in the world. And did you see the headshot I made on that slappy zombie down below?"

"Not to mention your sweet outfit." Hank smirked.

"Thank you, Hank. You're right. This hat is the topper of my head and of my future stories." He slapped the top of the hat.

Joey glanced over to Poly and her new dress. Her position on the floor revealed her high upper thighs. He turned and looked at the open elevator doors.

The distinctive sound of electricity and motors came to life and the doors slid shut. Joey ran over to the call button and pressed it. It lit up and the number above the door changed, counting up until it stopped at floor thirty-two. The bell dinged. He brought his gun out, ready for anything.

The doors slid open, revealing an empty elevator. He relaxed and lowered his gun.

Lucas sauntered in first. He turned to face them with his tuxedo and top hat and bowed before them, spreading his arms out, inviting them into the elevator. Joey didn't think Lucas would be changing out of his ridiculous outfit anytime soon.

"Bottom floor I guess." Julie pushed the button marked *B3* and the elevator began its descent. It creaked and moaned the entire trip down.

"This thing seems to be in excellent working order," Lucas

said sarcastically.

Joey watched the numbers fall and concentrated on that, instead of the creeping fear of entrapment in a tiny elevator. He felt a hand on his and looked over to see Poly smiling at him. He tightly laced his fingers through hers and watched the numbers until they displayed B3 and came to a hard stop.

Julie let out a cry of pain. "Well, that sucked." She hopped on one leg.

The doors slid open, and the cab lights filled the immediate space in front of the elevator, but beyond ten feet—darkness enveloped. Joey gripped his gun, scanning for anything in the darkness. Something cloaked in the shadows moved. He took a step closer and pulled the hammer back on his gun.

CHAPTER 16

AT THE END OF JOEY'S sights, Harris stepped into the light.

"Took longer than I thought," Harris whispered. "Come on. It isn't far from here."

Joey let everyone out of the elevator first. The elevator clicked as the lights went out. He stepped out quickly, catching up to Harris's Panavice light.

"We really need to be quiet this time and watch your step. I'm keeping the light at a minimum," Harris said quietly.

A musty smell of dirt and waste filled the basement. Harris led and Joey stayed in the far back, behind Poly. Pipes ran in every direction and large, metal boxes lined the walk paths. He relied on his ears as much as the faint light from Harris. He listened for the soft steps in front of him and the soft breathing of Poly next to him.

He bumped into Poly. "Sorry."

Harris stopped ahead and shared close words with Lucas. He waved his hand for them to come up to the front. The soft glow from his Panavice lit Lucas's worried face as he huddled close with them.

Harris whispered, "Look ahead."

Joey followed the light as Harris pointed his Panavice and saw why they had stopped. Ahead on their path, a zombie leaned face-first against a wall with its back to them. Harris pulled the light back.

"Hibernating," Harris said.

Joey cringed and shook his head. If one found its way down there, a hundred could have. He reached for his gun and glanced down the hall, into the darkness.

"Can we sneak by?" Joey whispered.

"Too risky," Harris said.

Joey nodded towards it. "Lucas, shoot it in the head."

"No problem," he said with a smile and nocked an arrow.

Harris illuminated the thing again. Lucas pulled back his bowstring and let go. The arrow flew into its head. It slumped to the concrete floor without a sound.

Lucas fist-pumped his bow. "You see that shot?"

"Can we just keep moving?" Julie asked through gritted teeth. "And shut up, you idiot."

Lucas stopped congratulating himself and joined the group as they walked by. They centered around Julie and Harris's lights and stayed near the middle of the walkway. Harris lifted his light every few feet, just enough to check ahead of them, but not enough to give them away.

Joey whipped his head around, thinking he heard something in the darkness. Maybe it was a scratch on metal, or a heavy footstep or a creak of the building. It was as if every sound in the basement was a zombie. His foot caught on a crack in the concrete and he stumbled forward. His foot skidded on the concrete as he stopped himself from crashing into Poly. She spun around with a knife in her hand. Looking at him, she shook her head and lowered the knife.

"It should be right here," Harris whispered, shining his light around the hallway. There was a concrete wall on one side and rows of metal containers on the other. Harris paced around the small space, searching every crack.

"There might be a door somewhere."

Joey looked around, but it looked exactly like the rest of the hallways.

Harris stepped on the gap that had made Joey trip. He dropped to his knees and passed the light over it. "Here. It's below us." He pointed at the crack. Jumping to his feet, he looked around the room. "Hank, grab that steel bar."

Hank took the metal bar leaning against the concrete wall and brought it to him.

"We're going to have to punch a hole through this."

"That's going to be ridiculously loud." Julie shook her head. "All of the freaking zombies in a fifty mile radius will be running here."

"Can't you use that laser thing and cut through it?" Lucas asked.

"No, not through concrete." Harris sighed. "It is going to be loud. They will be coming."

Hank stared at the crack in the concrete and shook his head.

Harris placed a hand on his shoulder and looked at him. "Hank, you're going to have to quickly break a hole big enough for us to get through. There's already a hole started, you just need to hit the edges and build on it. You can do this."

Hank nodded and gripped the steel bar with both hands.

"Joey, you take the west hallway with Poly. Julie, you light the way for them to see what's coming. Lucas, you and I will take the east hall. Make sure each shot counts." Harris paired with Lucas and stood on the other side of the room, shining his light down the hall.

Joey spent a moment looking at Poly. She gazed up at him with a hint of fear in her eyes. He felt the same way. He wanted to hug her, but she turned to face the dark hall.

Julie walked in between them, her cellphone light guiding the way. Joey sighed, took out his gun and followed Julie. He glanced back at Hank and had the horrible feeling they were about to do something incredibly stupid. The bar shook over his head as he glared at the floor.

Joey held his breath.

"Go," Harris ordered.

Hank slammed the bar on the concrete. Joey flinched. It echoed around the metal boxes and bounced off the concrete walls and floor. Hank slammed it again and got into a steady rhythm.

Joey stared down the hall, trying to make out the deepest regions the lights reach. He felt his pocket, feeling the two speed loaders. He sighed and gripped the gun.

The sound pounded into his head. He strained to see the ends of the hall—searching for the first signs of movement. Something moved. He took a small step forward.

"You get the far, I'll get the near," Poly said. She held a stack of throwing blades in her left hand and one in her right.

Joey gave a slight nod and didn't lose sight of the dark figure. It moved toward them and its wrinkled skin took form in the light. Julie gasped and the light wobbled as the cellphone shook in her hand. The thing opened its mouth and hissed at them.

"I got this one," Joey called. He trained his sights on the things head. He waited until it shuffled close enough for a sure head shot. The gunshot boomed through the small space. It fell to the floor.

"Another one," Julie said.

The light shook, bobbing the zombies head in and out of the darkness. A second one moved faster. It squealed at the sight of them and shuffled its bare feet quicker toward them. Joey timed his shot and killed it at the same spot as the first. He waited for another slower zombie and shot it in the head.

"See? No problem." Joey gave a nervous smile.

Poly glanced at him but turned her attention back on the hall. "Four more," she said.

He turned back to the hallway. The zombies stumbled toward them. He took out his second gun. "I got 'em." He shot the first three in the head but the fourth, hit in the neck. Black blood dripped from the hole, and it kept moving. With one gun empty, he switched the loaded gun to his right hand, dropping it on the floor. When he darted to pick it up, he stood up to see the creature falling, a knife sticking from its head.

"Thanks."

"I told you, I got the near."

He slipped a speed loader into the empty gun and locked the cylinder in place. A zombie staggered over the pile of bodies. He shot it in the head and it fell backward on top of the heap. Between the loud clanking from Hank and his rod, Harris fired his gun.

"I'm getting low on arrows," Lucas said loudly.

"Joey!" Poly said.

He squinted into the darkness. A group of zombies filled the hallway. A few opened their black mouths and hissed as they entered the light. He fired into the front line. They fell, only to be replaced with a fresh group. Joey looked at Poly. She stood with her stained throwing knives in hand. He fired into the next row.

There were just too many. "How's that hole coming, Hank?" he asked.

"It's not big enough," Hank said between heavy breaths. "Maybe Poly could fit."

"Poly, get in the hole."

"I'm not leaving you."

Harris's gun blasted several shots.

Joey emptied his gun into the advancing horde. He reloaded by feel as he watched them struggle to get past the dead. The hallway filled with zombies, pushing against the slowing front line.

"Get in the hole and if we're not there in a few minutes, just type in any code, anywhere is better than here."

She shook her head with her mouth open, looking hurt. "We're in this together." She reared back and threw a knife.

He emptied his gun again. They fell on top of the others and for a second he thought their bodies might form a barrier, but they stepped and stumbled over the bodies. Holstering one gun, he held the other. The last bullets he had were in it.

Hank's thumps were sounding less powerful and less frequent.

"Hank, they're coming," Joey shouted.

The steel bar resumed its heavy hits and the sound of

Harris's gunshots blasted through the basement. Zombies slowed next to the pile of dead and Joey shot a few more. One crawled over the pile and staggered toward them.

"He's yours, Poly."

Joey saved his last few shots for the pile. The horde pushed against the bodies. He fired his last shots and plugged a few holes with the falling bodies. The front zombies struggled to get over or through the dead pile.

Poly threw a knife at the approaching zombie and it struck it in the head.

"That's not going to hold them back." Julie's voice shook with fear.

He stuffed his guns back in the holsters and turned to Hank, who was grunting with each hit.

"Can you fit in that hole?" Joey asked.

"I don't know," he said between hits. "You guys get down there first."

Joey glanced back at the pile. It was holding them back but the middle was pushing out and soon the dam would break. He pointed at Poly. "Either you get in the hole or I'm throwing you in."

Poly shook her head, looked at the pile, and brandished her dagger. "You first, I can kill them still."

"Poly—"

"Get out of the way, you two." Lucas pushed Joey aside and climbed down into the hole. He hung from his fingertips before falling into the blackness below.

Julie sighed and got in the hole behind him.

Harris fired a few more shots and then ran back with his light. He shone the light on Joey's hall just as the pile collapsed and the zombies began to claw their way over the heap. "Time to go," he said.

Poly dropped into the hole.

Joey climbed down right behind her. The sharp edges of concrete felt like broken glass as he scraped through. His hands slipped off the concrete and he fell backward. He landed hard on his side and felt a sharp pain through his ribs. Groaning, he rolled onto his knees.

Julie's light lit up the dome and the stone in the middle of the room.

"Go, Hank," Harris said.

Hank dropped the steel pipe into the hole. He fell through and landed on the floor. He grabbed his leg in pain, but got to his feet.

Footsteps of the zombies sounded overhead. Harris fired many shots in rapid succession and then jumped down into the hole, landing on his feet. He rushed to the stone lit by Julie.

A zombie fell through behind Harris. Joey rushed to the zombie and kicked it. Another fell right next to him, then another. He stepped back as a steady flow of zombies flooded into the room.

Hank yelled and grabbed the steel pipe off the floor. He swung it and struck one in the head and it fell in a heap. He swung wildly around, hitting any zombie close to him.

Joey pulled out his gun and held the barrel, ready to use it as a club.

Hank rushed toward the group of zombies, yelling and swinging his pipe. They converged around his body as he struck them.

Joey moved toward Hank when the room hummed and exploded in gunfire from above.

CHAPTER 17

"GET TO THE GROUND," HARRIS yelled over the gunfire.

Joey reactively went to the ground, looking up at the ceiling and the guns mounted to it. They rotated and shot out with rapid fire. A bullet whizzed by his head. Each shot flashed, causing a strobe light effect. The stop-motion horror film played out as Joey, paralyzed with fear, covered his head and waited for the bullets to shred his body.

Then silence. He looked up. In the dark room, he saw the two barrels glowing red as they rotated. A zombie moaned and moved on the floor. A gun moved and fired a single shot into its head.

Joey breathed and searched in the darkness for his friends. "Lights, Harris," Joey said.

Two lights from Harris and Julie lit the room.

"What the freak was that?" Lucas pointed to the ceiling and

the still glowing guns. "Where did you bring us?"

"Somewhere that could take care of our unwanted guests. I don't think you'd want one of those loose on your planet," Harris said, pointing to the ceiling. "We found a way to install those outside of the transport dome. They are a defensive measure, in case we get unwanted visitors."

Lucas nudged a zombie with his foot.

Joey rushed past the bodies scattered around the room, searching for Hank. He had been right there, before the machine guns started.

"Anyone see Hank?" Joey asked, trying to catch his breathe.

"Over here," Hank said and pushed a zombie body off him.

"You okay?" he asked.

"Yeah, I think so," Hank said, getting to his feet. He pinched his shirt, keeping the soaking, bloody material away from his body.

Joey scanned for each of his friend's faces and each of them looked around the room at the dead bodies scattered around. Joey looked at the ceiling to make sure the hole was gone.

"Oh crap." Hank held up his arm, and in the dark, Joey saw the red streaks of blood running down his arm. "One of them scratched me."

"If you're scratched, you should be okay," Harris said, holding his Panavice in his direction.

"If he's bitten?" Poly asked. She held a throwing knife in each hand and glared at the zombies lying on the floor in front of her. She favored one leg as she stepped toward Hank.

"Well, let's hope he's not," Harris said.

In the dim light, he saw Hank's arm had several marks on it but he couldn't be sure if they were scratches or bites.

"How do you feel, Hank?" Joey asked.

"Okay." He shrugged, but he looked anything but okay. His hair was slick and matted with zombie goo, and his hand shook as he held his scratched arm.

"You okay, Poly?"

Poly limped over to Joey and wrapped her arms around him, burying her head against his chest. "Just tell me we're never going back there," her words wobbled.

"Can we get out of this freaking zombie coffin?" Lucas asked.

Harris stepped over bodies to get to the door. He turned on his heel to face them. "I have to warn you," he said. "Behind this door is help for the wounded, but also a world you won't be familiar with." He paused. "While there aren't many people here, they may be strange to you and I ask you keep an open mind. Everyone is here to help you and you should treat them as such."

"Can it get any stranger?" Lucas used both arms to point at the floor of bodies surrounding him.

"I guess not." Harris opened the steel door. Artificial light flooded the dome and illuminated the motionless zombies. Julie gasped and moved toward the door, holding her hand over her face.

Joey ushered Poly to the door. "One step closer," she said when they reached the door.

She looked up and made eye contact with him and he held it. She gave him a weak smile. He tried to turn up the sides of his mouth, but he couldn't find the joy. His stomach felt queasy. He needed to get out of the dome. Poly stepped through the door first.

He held his ribs and stepped past the steel door, pulling the door closed behind him. The lights muted the gray walls of the hallway. It was clear they were in another world, a clean one, free of the horrible smells and cannibals—hopefully one without zombies, as well.

At the end of the hallway were three women dressed in tight, shiny, white suits. Each donning a symbol of an oak tree on her chest, and had a thin, metal table levitating in front of them. One walked toward him and the floating gurney lowered next to him. She motioned for him to get on it. He stepped back from the floating table. There was no way it could hold his weight.

"No, take the others first. I can walk," he said.

"Aren't you the noble one?" she said with a smile.

Poly waved away the table as well, and then helped Julie on one. Lucas pushed Hank aside and jumped on the floating table, lying on his back. He waved at the woman next to his table. Hank sat on the edge of his table and the table bent up, forming a chair.

The women in white pushed them down the hallway. Lucas smiled at the women. They smiled back, but didn't say anything. A light flickered above and reflected off their high-gloss outfits.

"What is this place?" Joey asked.

"This is Haven 14," Harris said.

The vague answer annoyed Joey, but they stopped at a pair of doors. The double doors swung open and everyone walked into the room.

Joey smelled a hint of ozone. White, sterile-looking machines lined the white walls. Large lights dangled over some of the machines, giving off bright light. A woman in an all-white outfit, and an oak tree on her chest, stood in the center of the room holding a thin screen in her hands. Pens and thin metal objects stuck out of her pockets.

"Hello, I'm Doctor Almadon. I understand some of you have sustained injuries. Let's take a look at you, young man. What's your name?"

"Joey. But please, take care of the others. They're hurt worse."

Almadon raised an eyebrow. "Let's leave that for me to decide, young man." She motioned with one finger for him to come forward.

Joey looked to Hank, who shrugged. He took three steps. She peered over him while pulling a screen down next to his body. Almadon slid her fingers over the screen. He couldn't decide what felt more violating, the machine or Almadon's penetrating gaze. He leaned forward to peek at the screen.

"Stay still," she said. "You fractured three ribs, Joey. Nurse, can you please take him to the Makings?"

The nurse nodded and took Joey by the hand. He looked at her hand on his as she led him toward an adjacent room. He stopped at the metal door and looked back at his friends. Poly stood in front of the scanner as Almadon pointed at her leg.

The nurse let go of his hand and pushed open the door. "Please, step into the room." She motioned with her hands.

A stainless steel coffin sat in the middle of the room with light bars around it like a tanning booth. He looked to the nurse and she gave him a reassuring smile. What wasn't as reassuring was the size of the tiny room, which was not much bigger than the table itself.

"Please, lie down on the Makings," she said.

His ribs had hurt when he landed on the floor of the Alius

stone room—pain had shot through his body. He rubbed them, touching the tender parts and feeling the dull pain. His whole chest and back started to ache—each deep breath jolted pains along his ribs.

"This thing safe?" he asked.

"You'll be fine." She smiled and nudged him toward the table.

The climb into the Makings, as she called it, took a few grunts and a couple groans. But he made it and let the nurse position his body as she saw fit. He tensed up as she pulled the top side of the bed overhead. A crack of light peeked between the two.

"You may feel some tingling inside. It's the bones resetting and healing. Try not to move." The nurse left the room.

Joey wanted to jump off the Making machine and be out of the confined space in which she placed him. He moved his foot to get out, but the bars in the table lit with blue light. The tingling sensation started in his chest and spread through his whole torso. A warm, electric feeling, deep in his chest, radiated out. He struggled to stay still.

He closed his eyes, concentrating on a boat ride he had with Samantha over the summer. She had worn her red bikini; the mist from the boats wake sprayed into the air, misting her body before evaporating away. It was the day she lost her earrings.

"Ok, all done," the nurse said from a speaker in the room.

"What?"

The door lifted and she peeked her head in. "All done."

Confused, he stared at her while propping himself into a sitting position. He held his ribs and winced at the expected pain, but it wasn't there. He touched his side and pushed. They were fine.

"The body can be easy to heal. The mind is more difficult," the nurse said tapping on her temple.

He stumbled out of the room.

"You okay?" Poly asked, standing in line for the Making with the rest of his friends.

"Yeah . . . I feel good," he said, rubbing his ribs. He looked around the room. "Where's Harris?"

"He had other matters to attend to," Almadon spoke up.

"Where are we? Not this room, but where are we?" Julie said, standing in line, looking around the room.

"I think you better ask Compry. She'll be here as soon as you're all healed."

She tried to get Almadon to talk more, but she just smiled and gave polite responses.

Joey paced near the door as each of his friends came out of the Makings room, completely healed. Hank, the last one done, walked out of the room confidently walking on his right leg.

"It really worked," he said, dumbfounded. Even the scratches on his arm were thin red lines now.

"Told ya. Thing's freaking incredible," Lucas said.

The double doors swung open and a person came into the hospital room. Almadon rose from her chair and nodded to her. She wore black, sleek clothes, and commanded the room with an air of confidence. Lucas's attention swiftly stayed on the beautiful woman as her gaze swept over them. She didn't look much older than Almadon, maybe late twenties but they each held such wisdom in their eyes. He felt as if they were his senior by a much longer time.

"Hello, all. I'm Compry." She strutted across the room and

stopped in front of Almadon. "Harris wants them all vaccinated."

Almadon raised an eyebrow and paused for a second. "Of course," she said. "I'll get the vaccines ready right now. Oh, and make sure you tell him to get back down here so I can fix that hole in his gut."

"I will."

"He also got hit in the shoulder . . . with an arrow," Lucas said and adjusted his bow over his shoulder as he looked at the floor.

Compry smirked.

The doc opened a cabinet and pulled out a black box, setting it on a steel table. "Okay, everyone form a line here." She pointed to the ground next to her.

Joey walked over first, frowning at the black box on the table. Almadon pulled out a black gun with a black handle and glass barrel. His mind felt so frazzled, he didn't think to question anything. He would have normally said something about being stuck with a needle, but at that point, he obliged to whatever command given; shuffling around like a herded cow.

"Stay still, this goes in your neck." Almadon placed a vile in the barrel and brought it up against his neck.

He heard the shot, like air released from a tire, and felt the pinch. It didn't hurt as much as it felt weird—like something cold wiggling under his skin. Joey rubbed his neck and walked away.

"Next," Almadon said.

"What's this vaccinating against?" Julie asked.

"We have different diseases. This will protect you from those."

Julie narrowed her eyes but stepped forward. Joey felt dumb

for not asking what they stuck in his neck. He felt the injection site and the small lump it left.

The rest took their shots without argument.

"Come with me," Compry ordered and marched out the door.

Joey ran to keep up with her, as she turned left down the hallway. He glanced back to make sure each of his friends were with him. Lucas jogged up to him and nudged his elbow, nodding his head at Compry, and stared at her backside. Joey sighed and rolled his eyes. Lucas continued to ogle—the guy had no shame.

Compry stopped at a pair of doors. They slid open and she stepped into an elevator. Julie nudged up between Lucas and Compry as they entered the elevator.

"Where are we going?" Julie asked.

"To your quarters." Compry pushed the *B23* button on the elevator.

They moved downward and then stopped. Out of the elevator was another hallway with gray walls. Doors with nametags lined the passage.

"You've been assigned rooms. Hank and Lucas here. Julie and Poly here. Joey, you are here. There are fresh clothes and linens on the beds. Please get cleaned up. If there is something else you need, let us know." Compry turned on the last part of the sentence and started speed walking down the hallway.

"Um, yeah. I do need something else." Lucas held one hand in the air, as if he was in school.

She stopped her quick pace and turned to face Lucas. "Yes?"

He lowered his hand. "Is anyone going to tell us what's going on here, or where we even are?"

Compry took a few steps toward Lucas and then regarded all of them with a concerned expression. "I'll let Harris explain everything to you. Now, it looks like you kids have been through some bad stuff, and I think it's best if you get cleaned up. Everything's in your rooms." She regarded Hank and his zombie blood soaked clothes. "There is an incinerator in the room as well, right next to the hamper. Use it."

"When's Harris coming?" Julie asked.

"He'll be back soon. Now go on." She pointed to the rooms. "Get going." Compry turned and strode down the hallway and into the elevator.

Joey dragged his feet to his door, staring at his nametag. He felt the grime on his shirts and the oil in his hair. Was that blood? He smelled his shoulder and winced.

"Let's get cleaned up and meet in the hallway in thirty minutes," he recommended.

The others nodded and disappeared into their rooms.

Staring at his door, Joey searched for a handle of some sort. His fingertip touched the door and it slid open, revealing a small room with a bed and a tiny kitchen in the back. Another door led to a bathroom with a shower.

He stepped inside the room, and the door slid closed behind him. He took a deep breath, closed his eyes and felt the velvet box in his pocket. Was she okay? It had only been a few days since he'd given her the present. The memory of them on the balcony seemed a lifetime ago.

He let go of the box.

Fresh clothes draped off the edge of the bed with a note on

top.

Please place soiled clothes into laundry cabinet

He turned around to the cabinet on the wall marked *Laundry*. He emptied his pockets, placed the velvet box on the nightstand, and his guns and holsters on the bed. He peeled off the rest of his clothes and placed them in the plastic box in the laundry closet. A red button blinked on the face of the laundry closet door. He pressed it and it changed to a green light. It hummed from behind the door. He gathered the new clothes and headed to the shower.

After a few minutes of staring at the control panel in the shower, he figured out the digital screen and the small metal pipes coming out of the walls dispensing soap and shampoo.

HAPPY TO BE IN CLEAN clothes, he strapped his guns back on. The laundry drawer dinged and a green light blinked above. He opened the door to the laundry closet. Steam and the smell of soap puffed from the cabinet. Yanking the jacket out, he inspected it. It appeared clean . . . clean enough, anyway. He closed the door and put on his jacket to cover the guns. He grabbed the velvet box off the nightstand, stuffed it into his pocket and went into the hallway to meet his friends.

Poly stood in the hallway. She smiled when she saw him exit. He couldn't help but notice her black outfit. It was similar to his, but she wore it well—nothing like the black dress though.

"What did you think of the showers?" she said, feeling her hair. "The auto dry was amazing."

"Yeah, I couldn't really get it going," he admitted. He'd

given up trying to figure out the menu and dried off with a towel. "How you doing?" He pointed at her leg.

"All better now," she said and kicked the air.

"How's Julie?"

"She's fine. She found some kind of computer in there. So, she's basically in heaven."

"We should go check on Hank and Lucas." He knocked on their door.

Hank opened it and had on a similar outfit to his. "Joey." His face lit up. "How are the ribs?"

"Good, how about you guys?"

Lucas came to the door. "My leg feels good," he said. "But we should be talking about the real hero here," he thumped Hank hard on the back.

The big guy looked at the floor. "It was nothing."

"Breaking through that floor and taking on those zombies . . . that wasn't nothing," Joey pointed out.

"Yeah, thank goodness you have the massive amount of weight it took to break through concrete." Lucas swiped his forehead.

"Strength. It's called *strength*." Hank stretched out his arms and flexed.

"Or sheer mass. . . ." Lucas pushed his point.

"Yeah, well, we wouldn't be here if he didn't have mass or strength," Joey added.

"Speaking of *here*, where the heck are we?" Lucas asked.

Joey looked to the ceiling. "Must be some kind of bunker."

Julie, who must have heard the talking, came out of her room. She still wore the clothes she arrived in. "I've been reading about this place on their computer. This is an old complex, discovered and dug up partially, until some war happened. Harris is the one who found it and now he's rebuilding it as a base of operations."

"Yeah, but where is here?" Lucas asked.

"We're basically at their south pole. I believe there's miles of ice above us." Julie looked at the ceiling.

"South pole?" Joey swallowed and looked up again. He felt heavier, the miles of ice pushing down on his shoulders. He controlled the expression on his face, keeping a calm appearance. He didn't want the others seeing him freak out.

"Okay great, so we're at some secret south pole base with a group of rebels," Lucas said, throwing up is arms.

"I don't know if we're rebels. . . ." Harris interjected, coming up behind them. "You all should be getting something to eat and then catching some sleep. You're going to need it for tomorrow."

Tomorrow. Joey's eyes widened and his thoughts went wild with anger. He wanted to get home now. He didn't want to wait another day to see if Samantha was okay.

"We've been fighting the man who's hunting you for a long time. We've lost great people along the way." Harris shook his head and looked at the floor. "As long as he's around, you won't be safe. What you guys did back in the basement of that casino was pretty impressive for people your age, but you need training."

"Training, but what about going back home? We need to see if Samantha and our parents are okay," Julie said.

She had taken the words out of Joey's mouth. He didn't care about training.

Harris frowned. "That zombie-filled room will take days to clear out and days more to sanitize. If your planet was exposed to one drop of blood, we could have another Ryjack."

Joey felt a twitch in his eye as he struggled with a valid argument, but failed. "I want to know the second it's cleaned out."

"Of course," Harris said. "In the meantime, I encourage you to consider training with us. I think we have something that would interest each of you. You'll need more than your current skill set to defend yourselves against MM."

Poly held a dagger in her hand. "You just get me in stabbing distance." She had a fire in her eyes.

"Good, you'll need that determination to get past the defenses they've put up." He continued, "There are a few rules while you're here."

Lucas rolled his eyes and paced next to his door. "Great, what are the rules? No colors allowed?"

"No, but you will stay in your rooms or this hallway, no wandering."

"Why? Is there something you don't want us to see?" Julie asked.

"Yeah, what's up with this place?" Lucas added.

Harris sighed and then smiled, as if visiting a fond memory. "Your parents had trouble following the rules, as well."

"Wait, our parents were here? All of them?" Julie asked, stepping toward Harris.

"For a time, yes." Harris lowered his head. "We had hoped to keep them safe, but with six pregnant women, they wanted to get back home."

Poly studied the walls and floors, touching the grey paint. Joey knew the feeling; their parents had shared this same space at some point. Each looked around with wonder.

Joey thought about his mom and dad running down these halls around his age, breaking the rules. "They stayed right here, in these rooms?"

"Yes and a few on the other side as well," Harris took a deep breath and crossed his hands at his waste. It was the first time Joey had seen him look uncomfortable.

"You knew my mom?" Lucas asked.

"Tamara, yes. I knew all of your parents. Each one of them was an amazing person."

"You should have kept them here, locked them up or found a place to make them safe," Julie said with tears building in her eyes.

"Free will is necessary. Otherwise, they were just prisoners. Your parents chose to return and face Isaac. They did it for you. Every one of them was ready to sacrifice their life to ensure you kept yours. I don't intend on letting their sacrifice go in vain."

"Yeah, but look at what happened in the end," Julie said.

"Yes, look." He pointed at them. "They kept you alive. However, the dangers are much greater now. Marcus and MM know you exist and they have sent Simon to fetch you. They know I have you. They will do everything they can to find us. So please, stay in this area unless you're with me or one of the trainers."

"You going to hold our hands to cross the street and cut our food up for us while were here?" Lucas asked.

Harris laughed. "Now everyone back to your rooms and get some sleep. Tomorrow, you can decide on how you want to train."

CHAPTER 18

JOEY WANTED TO TALK TO his friends, but Harris stood in the hallway until they all were back in their rooms. Being alone in the room didn't feel right with so much to talk about. He was the only one by himself. Jealousy crept in, but he pushed it away and sat on the edge of his bed. He wouldn't allow for such petty emotions.

Had his parents sat on this very bed? He felt the soft comforter and looked at the lights above. Thinking of his parents here, in another world, in an underground bunker, made his head hurt. They had kept so much from them.

Joey couldn't begin to understand what his friends were feeling. They were sitting on what could have been their dead mom or dad's old bed. They might be walking on the same floors their dead parent had walked on so many years ago.

One thing was for sure, his parents were far more interesting than they were letting on.

He stared at the door and thought about checking on Poly. He wondered how she was doing in the next room, and if she was okay. It would've been nice to check on her before they went to sleep.

A bell rung and a green light lit on the wall near the bed. Below the light, a small door slid open, revealing a plate of food. Steam streamed from the plate. His urge to eat overtook his cautious mind and he bounded to the plate, taking it and sitting back on the bed.

He ate the mashed potatoes and meat. Half way through, he placed the plate on the nightstand. Even a small pleasure, like eating a hot meal made him feel guilty. The unknowns weighed on him.

Joey took the small jewelry box out of his pocket and rotated it in his hands. Rubbing the smooth velvet surface, he opened the box. The two earrings slid around as he moved it. These were supposed to bring him and Samantha closer, an icebreaker he had hoped would open the door for something more; and it had.

He spent most of the summer searching for the earrings, searching for an impossible find, until finally he had them. Now, Samantha felt as far away as the earrings had at the bottom of the lake.

He snapped the box closed and placed it on the nightstand. Swinging his legs over the bed, he stood. His mind raced with too many thoughts to stay still, so he strode to the door and touched it. *Forget the rules.* It slid open and he stepped into the hallway.

"Thought you might step out," Harris said.

"I'll go back to bed. . . ."

"Why don't we go for a walk?"

"What about my friends?" Joey asked.

"Come on, just you and me." Harris led the way down the hall and onto the elevator. He pressed a button on the panel and the doors slid closed.

"How's the zombie cleaning going?"

"Slow."

Silence filled the moving elevator and Joey put his hands in his pockets, staring at the side of Harris's head. "Where we going?" Not that Joey cared. Anything would be better than lying in bed, trying to capture sleep.

"I think you'll like this."

The elevator came to a stop. The doors slid open and the icy air swept in. He stepped from the elevator with his mouth open, gazing at the huge cavern, large enough to fit an entire mall in. Along the ceiling and flowing down one wall, was a huge ice sheet. There were a few people working in heavy coats, shooting a beam of light into the ice.

"Wow, what is this for?"

"This is the bottom of the ice sheet. We collect all our fresh water here."

A metal platform stood off the elevator and Joey walked to the edge and placed his hands on the cold steel railing. The ice glistened from the light beams. A stream of water ran down the ceiling like an upside-down river, collecting on the floor, and down to a drain.

"It's beautiful," Joey murmured, but he didn't think Harris wanted to talk about ice and water.

For a bit, Harris was silent.

"You see the water runners over there?" Harris pointed and Joey nodded. "The motors on the lights broke yesterday and to keep water flowing through the compound, we have to manually melt the ice. This old place is breaking down more every year."

"Why did you bring me down here?"

Harris turned to face him. "Marcus is ill, he's dying. He needs *you*, if he wants to keep living. Simon has had the terrible task of finding you amongst countless worlds. It's driven him over the edge of rational thinking; he's a dangerous man."

Joey frowned, watching the water runners melt the ice. Its shiny surface reflected some of the light back to him. "Why are you telling me this?"

"I need you, Joey. I see your wavering commitment. I don't think you guys realize what is after you. And if you do not at least train and learn some of the basics, you won't be able to protect yourself or your friends."

He shook his head and glared at the water runners. His parents had spent eighteen years running from this. And now, when the same offer was placed at his feet, he felt a wavering. "Do you think we can end it?" That's all he wanted. He wanted his safe home back.

Harris crossed his arms and his warm breath flowed out in a quick cloud. "If we can keep them from getting to you, then eventually, he'll die."

"Why don't you kill us?" Joey studied Harris's face for a reaction. They must have thought it. How could they not? They just kill the problem and Marcus would wither away.

Harris raised an eyebrow at him. "If he thinks you're dead, what do you think he'd do with the new, shiny planet they just discovered?"

New planet? Joey gasped. "You think he'd go after earth?"

"No question about it. Marcus would play with your world like a kid in a sandbox."

"Ryjack."

"Exactly."

Joey stood in silence for a while, watching the water melt. It fascinated him. He wanted to go down there and operate one of the lights, carve his name into the wall and watch it melt away.

"You think we can learn enough to stop them?"

"Together? Yes."

Joey took his hands off the ice-cold steel and rubbed them together. His whole body felt like it needed a thaw. He glanced back at the elevator.

Harris turned to face him. "There's one thing I want to ask you. Do you think you can control your accelerated movement?"

Joey turned from his gaze. He didn't want to talk about his mutation. It made him feel like a freak exhibit. "It seems to happen without my control, so I don't know how I'd control it."

"If they find out what you can do, they may try and use it."

His breaths floated out in front of his face. "They can have it. I don't want it."

"If they figured out how to replicate what it is you do, they'd be unstoppable. I know I'm dumping a lot on you all at once, but time is not in our favor. We don't have the time to waiver. Joey, I need you to back this."

The cold air numbed Joey's hands and the feeling crept up his arm. He rubbed his wrists and breathed into his hands. He'd had enough of the cold room. "I'll do what I think is best for my friends. If we are stuck here, it seems foolish not to learn from you."

Harris nodded his head. The cold didn't seem to bother him. "Let's go."

"Please." Joey rushed to the elevator. "You think you can train me to shoot like you?"

"If you can do what I think you can, you should make me look like a child with a dart gun."

Joey shook his head. The idea of being better than Harris seemed ludicrous. "I just want to shoot straight."

"It's not just about the weapon in your hands." Harris pointed to his head. "Up here is the real weapon. I hope you're ready."

CHAPTER 19

A LIGHT TAP ON THE door woke him up. Joey smoothed out the wrinkles in the jacket he slept in, and felt for his guns. Another light tap on the door, too dainty for Harris. He touched the door and it slid open. Compry stood on the other side.

"Time for breakfast," she said matter-of-factly and strode away.

He looked at the small door that delivered his dinner—no green light. Then he spotted his friends in the hallway. Was he the last one awake? He stepped into the hallway, glad to be out of his room and back with his friends. He smiled and felt better about the day. He wanted to put as much time between him and the zombie world as possible.

Compry led them to a pair of doors marked with a fork and knife. The cafeteria was large and circular, filled with rows of empty chairs and tables. At the edge of the circle, he saw more doors with numbers on them. He looked back at the door he came through and it was marked 2.

Harris sat at a table with his back to them. He put his Panavice on the table as they approached. The chair screeched across the white floor and Harris stood to face them.

"Everyone sleep okay?" he asked, lingering on Joey as they nodded. "Good, we have an interesting day planned." He turned his attention to Compry. "But let's eat and get some fuel for what's ahead."

Compry scowled at Harris as she pushed the metal tray cart and let it smack against the table. The plates clattered and slid about on the top of the cart. "Breakfast is served."

Joey sat at the far end of the white table, away from Compry and avoided her cold gaze as she surveyed them.

"Eggs, milk, and some ham." Compry picked up a glass of orange juice and placed it next to Harris. "Orange for you, Harris." He tapped his finger on the table as he stared at the orange beverage. He grasped it, swirled it in his glass, and slammed it down his gullet.

"Eggs and ham? Sounds good," Poly said.

Joey knew what she was doing, trying to put a brighter light on the situation. Compry eyed Poly with curiosity, before returning her attention to the cart. She slapped the first plate down on the table next to Lucas. "Pass the plate down . . . *please.*"

Lucas complied without a comment and passed the plate down.

After the plates were out, Joey looked at the slice of ham and scrambled eggs. How did they get stuff like this here? He forked a piece of ham and inspected it. It looked fine, so he popped it in his mouth. It was all right. He shoveled the remaining food down and picked up his empty plate, looking around for what to do with his dishes. "Where should I put this?"

"Compry will handle the dishes." Harris smirked.

She pursed her lips, but held her tongue. Joey avoided her eyes and held his plate in his hands. He'd rather throw it away than have Compry looking at him like that. Maybe he could take it to his room and wash it in that laundry-cleaning thing. He'd probably be able to fit everyone's plate.

Harris stared at him.

Joey gave up on his plate and set it back on the table. "You said last night you wanted us to consider training here, what kind of training do you have in mind?" he asked.

"That's up to you. We have people with varied skills here."

"I want one of those Panavice things. I want to learn everything about them," Julie spouted out.

"Almadon is the best tech person on the planet, in my opinion. She'd be happy to train you."

Julie almost fell out of her chair with excitement.

"You're telling me you have an archer in this place?" Lucas asked.

"Sure do. His name is Nathen. I'll let him know about you."

"I take it you can train me with guns?" Joey asked looking at Harris.

"I can." He nodded. "What about you, Poly?"

"My mom trained me. I don't need any other teacher, but her."

"What if it was the person who trained your mom?" Harris glanced at Compry.

Compry looked at Poly and raised an eyebrow.

"You serious? You taught my mom about blades?"

"I sure did. I'm glad to hear she passed it down to you."

"Do you have any gorilla handlers for Hank?" Lucas smirked. "Or anyone with a zookeeper background?"

"Oh, you're so funny, Lucas," Hank said. He stood from his chair and stepped toward him.

Lucas laughed and hid behind Julie. "Mommy, help. The rhino's getting too close to the car."

Hank smiled, but grabbed for Lucas. He darted under the table and exited out the end, moving to the opposite side of the table from Hank.

"Those toothpicks you shoot won't help when I come running for you."

"If you could run, I'd be worried."

Hank ran to one side of the table, but Lucas matched his moves and kept away from him.

"Can you two stop it?" Julie asked, exasperated.

Lucas stood straight and pulled at the end of his shirt. "Hank started it."

"Oh, you're dead, funny man," Hank warned.

"Enough," Compry slammed a plate against the table. It rattled and spun to a stop.

Harris filled the silence. "We should get to training. Lucas, I want you to take Hank and go see Nathen over on floor twenty-three. I sent him notification. He will be waiting for you."

Lucas rolled his eyes. "You better not try anything, Hank. I was just messin' around."

Harris continued, "Julie, you'll find Almadon waiting for

you in the medical wing. Joey, you'll come with me."

"That's just leaves me and you," Compry said to Poly.

THE IDEA OF TRAINING WAS exciting to Joey, but the realization of why they were training, brought about thoughts of his family. He'd learn as much as he could from Harris and take it with him back to Preston. If he could learn to control his slow-mo stuff, he'd be unstoppable.

Following Harris through a few elevator stops and two hallways, they made it to a white room.

Joey had been in gun ranges before, but this room didn't look like any gun range he'd ever seen. It was a long white room, with white walls, floor, and ceiling. It was completely stark white, except for the black line on the floor at the start of the room.

"Stay behind the black line," Harris said. "Get ready."

"For what?"

The whole room changed to look like a Wild West version of a town. Wood buildings were on each side of the street, with horses hitched to a post in front of the *Dusty Saloon*. A few dingy-looking people walked around, and one old man threw Joey a sneer. A man in a cowboy outfit hitched his horse and stepped into the saloon. Joey shook his head and squinted at the movement in the saloon windows. Was he missing something?

A gunshot cracked through the dirt-ball town and in the same instant, an electrical shock hit his shoulder. Joey grabbed at the pain in his shoulder and searched the town for the shooter. Then he saw an out of place movement; a man standing on the roof of the general store, with a rifle pointed at him. The end of the barrel flashed and another crack echoed through the town.

Joey stumbled backward at the second electrical shock, this time in the middle of his chest. He raised his gun to the man, took aim, and pulled the trigger—striking his target in the chest. The man froze like a still picture, then melted into a white goo, and disappeared. Everything in the town froze and dissolved into white.

"Whoa," Joey said. His heart pounded in his chest. It felt as if he were there, in the town. It was so real. He rubbed the shoulder the electrical shock hit, a reminder of how real it was. "That was crazy. What is this place?"

"It's a training room. We can create almost any scene we want within these walls."

Joey stared at said walls, questioning their reality. "How's this possible?"

"Better to ask Almadon, but let's get back to your training. What do you think happened there?"

"I don't know. Some guy just shot me from the roof?"

"The people in the open are not always the dangers, you have to look beyond the obvious and find the true danger," Harris said. "Let's try again."

"Did you train my dad here?" Joey turned to him and asked.

Harris's expression didn't change, but he paused. "Yes."

"How was he?"

"Good. He was your age. Young and enthusiastic," Harris stated. "We don't have much time, let's continue."

Joey readied himself, this time with gun in hand. A new scene popped up in front of him—a park. He scanned the grass fields, oak trees, a man selling balloons with a smile, a weird kid walking toward him, and a group of emo kids giving him looks from a picnic table they were carving into with a screwdriver. A man glided by on a set of roller blades. He couldn't find anything.

Glancing over at Harris, he shrugged. Then, Joey felt an electrical shock in his back and lurched forward. He spun around and saw the guy on rollerblades holding a knife.

"Near is important as well. The bad guys aren't always obvious. Sometimes he/she/it is right in front of you before you know it."

"I don't know, just seemed like regular people."

"The brain is an amazing thing. Your subconscious takes in way more information than can be processed consciously. Everyone's brain cleans out the clutter and presents only what we think is important. Think again about that guy."

Closing his eyes, all he could remember was the guy stabbing him with black eyes staring at him.

"Black eyes, his pupils were all crazy looking."

"Good, let's do some more."

The next scene appeared. An indoor two-story mall. He was on the bottom floor. Everything looked different from any malls he'd been in. The men wore suits and the women wore dresses, but the styles and colors were wild like a futuristic version of the fifties. The hats on the women were large and curved in all shapes, and many wore glasses with only one pane of glass in them. Most were holding a Panavice like Harris's in their hands as they walked.

He couldn't begin to think of a single strange thing in this scene. Everything was strange to him. Even the stores were strange, with interactive holograms projecting in front of them, selling to passersby. Then a man stuck out. He sat with a newspaper folded out in front of him, blocking his face. A big newspaper didn't seem likely in this world of digital. He narrowed his vision on the man and the woman walking next to him. The man lowered his newspaper, looking straight at him. Joey didn't hesitate and shot the man. He dropped the newspaper to reveal a gun pointed at him. The scene went white.

"Why him?"

"He was reading a paper in this digital world, and when the woman who walked by him, looked scared, I knew it was him. He confirmed it when he lowered his paper, and was looking directly at me."

"Good, let's do some more."

Harris had him run through more scenes and he began to spot the ones who didn't quite fit into the scene much quicker. In one scene, Joey shot a guy driving a car and Harris asked him why.

"There is a broken window on the passenger side and a dead body in the back. He was the killer; I saw blood on his hands."

"Wrong, the person in the back of the car was injured at a nearby construction site. His friend was driving him to the hospital."

Joey felt the heat in his face. He'd been shooting people like in a video game. "I don't think I can do this in the real world. How do you know when you have to shoot?"

Harris sighed. "I'm glad you asked that question. It's the right question and the answer is simple. When the time comes, you'll know. Trust me. When it's time to end another's life, it's because they intend on ending yours or those around you."

Joey sheathed his gun and looked at the blank room.

"Why don't we do some target drills for a while, work on that aim." Harris pushed the screen on the Panavice.

Joey wondered about the others training, but he didn't have much time to think as an open gun range appeared in front of him. Paper targets floated in the air.

Is that Simon's face on one?

POLY STARED AT COMPRY AS she explained to her about knife throwing. She patiently waited for her to finish and for her to turn on this machine she kept talking about. Her fingers tapped the hilts of her new throwing knives on the sides of her hips.

"Do you follow?" Compry asked.

Poly resisted the urge to roll her eyes. She gave a small nod, yanked two knives from their sheaths, and spun them in her hands. Compry watched on with that curious look again. She'd give her a show.

The white walls morphed into targets and Poly took a step back in confusion. The whole room changed in a nanosecond. It reminded her of a carnival game with wheels spinning, rectangles rocking back and forth, objects popping up from the floor, and each target had several colors on them.

"Yellow," Compry said.

Poly threw a knife through a hole in the wall and hit a yellow spinning target, then the yellow floating circle and finally the yellow rectangle metronome.

"Green," Compry said.

A green rectangle popped up from the ground and she hit it with her knife before it retreated below. Then she spotted a green dot on the far side of the room. She reached back and threw hard, not waiting to see if it hit, she drew another knife from her side and threw it at the floating green target. The target retreated into the floor and the room returned to white.

"Well, you've got some skill I see."

"My mom's a good teacher."

"Opal was a natural." Compry smiled warmly. It fit her face nicely.

Poly thought it was the first time she'd seen the woman express a positive emotion. Maybe it was the mention of her mom. Knowing her mom trained in the same place she was training, made her well up with pride. She'd grown even closer to her over the summer, as she learned how to handle all kinds of bladed weapons. "Yeah, she's amazing with blades," Poly said, relaxing as the room went white.

"Even when she was pregnant with you, she insisted on learning blades," Compry said.

"Who taught you?"

With eyebrows raised, Compry pulled out a dagger from the sheath at her side, a black blade with a dragon etched into it. "My father."

"Really? That's so cool. I love training with Mom. Is he part of your group with Harris?" A little bit of jealousy crept in when anyone spoke about their dad.

"No, he runs a city. He doesn't approve of what I'm doing." Compry sheathed her knife.

"I'm sorry." Poly had trouble imagining not having her dad's approval. If he were still alive, he'd be calling her his little princess and embarrassing her in front of all her friends. At least that's what she pictured in her mind.

"Don't be."

Poly fidgeted with her fingers, avoiding eye contact.

Compry smiled. "You're the real deal, aren't you?"

"What do you mean?" Poly forced her hands to stop touching and looked into Compry's friendly face.

"People here may look young, but we are old. Moreover, when you've lived for hundreds of years, you lose innocence. But you, you're like a beam of light . . . just like your mom." Her gaze passed over Poly. "I almost forgot what true youth was like."

"I'm not some china doll," Poly said, annoyed at her making her sound like some child.

Compry laughed. "I know. You're a kickass woman. Now let me show you how to be a little more badass." She pushed a button on her Panavice. A human dummy appeared. She showed the vital areas to slice or hit if you wanted a kill, and the places to target to incapacitate someone.

Poly spun her blades around the dummy, slicing it in the areas marked with red for kill.

"Only kill blows?"

"No one tried to incapacitate my dad," Poly said.

"Fair enough, but there will be situations where a kill isn't necessary."

If she could get closer to the people responsible for killing her dad, she wouldn't need to know how to incapacitate them. She gave Compry a smile and nodded her head, but they could skip the lesson on wounding a person.

"I think you're ready for some more intimate simulations."

The scene changed and there stood a man with a gun pointed at her. Poly, with knife in hand, sneered at the digital man. He shot her in the gut. Poly winced and grabbed at her stomach. It felt like the time she walked into her neighbor's stupid electrical fence. She flung her knife and hit the man in the eye. He dissolved into white and spread into nothing on the floor. The knife lay on the white floor where the man once stood.

"Guns win in a duel. However, most cannot shoot worth a damn. Give them a moving target next time, okay?"

The room changed to a man with a sword, moving toward her. Poly threw her knife, striking him in the head. The whole scene dissolved back to the white room.

"You're quick to kill."

"Better them than me." Didn't she get it? What was the use of learning how to wound a person when you could kill them?

"Yes it is. But when you grossly overmatch a person, mercy can be shown."

"Mercy . . . really?" Poly huffed air through her nose and spun the blades into the sheaths on her hips. "Can I expect mercy from them?"

"Yes. All humans can make the choice. When you stop making the choice is when you become less than human."

Compry seemed like she had a question, but didn't ask it until after practice. "Is everything okay with you and your friends?"

"Yeah, they're my best friends." Poly scrunched her brow in. What was she after?

"So I've heard." Compry pulled back her hair.

Was she really hundreds of years old? She looked to be in her late twenties. Poly would've asked if her mom hadn't always told her it was rude to ask a woman's age.

"But maybe one of them is more than a friend? I saw you checking out Joey more than once."

"I have no idea what you're talking about." Poly fiddled with her knives.

"He's super cute, so I can't blame you."

It was as bad as her mom trying to have the 'talk.'

"But if I may make a suggestion. . . ."

Oh God, when is she going to stop?

Compry bulldozed ahead. "It's okay to give a boy a push in the right direction."

"Thanks for the advice," Poly said between her teeth, a blush rising up her neck.

Compry laughed, as they left the room. "I see him sneaking looks at you as well."

Do we really have to talk about this? Maybe silence will get her to stop.

Poly glanced at the high fashion, beautiful woman walking next to her. She'd probably have any man she wanted with just a single look of her fierce eyes. She couldn't possibly understand watching a man from the sidelines—for years.

Compry smiled and looked over. "I'll say one more thing and then stop. If I've learned anything in my years, it's that time is a gift, but by the time you learn that lesson, it can be too late. You wait too long for something, and it may never happen. Sometimes, you need to act. Sometimes . . . fate needs a gentle nudge."

"YES!" LUCAS JUMPED IN THE air with his bow in his hand. "That was awesome."

He stopped his theatrics as Nathen, the trainer, gave him a stern look. But how could he not be excited? He just shot flaming balls coming at him while riding in a zeppelin.

Best. Video. Game. Ever.

"I noticed a few times where you stopped smiling and just made the shots," Nathen said. He paced next to Lucas and tapped the end of his chin with his finger.

"I call it the Zone. Like a poor man's version of what Joey does, the world around me just comes into focus. When I'm in the Zone, I'm the best shooter in the world."

"Let's strive for more of these in-the-zone moments, shall we?"

"Bring on the next game," Lucas said in the calmest voice he could manage.

The jungle formed in front of him with large trees pressing in on all sides. He couldn't stop smiling even after he saw the half-man, half-monkey things holding knives. They were jumping around in the trees and screaming at him.

A knife flew by his head and he spotted the man-monkey that threw it. Oh, *hell* no. No digital man-monkey was going to throw knives at his pretty face. He pulled back an arrow and let it fly, replaced it with another, and fired it into the trees at other mankeys. *Ha-ha! Mankey* . . . Just thinking of it made him smile. The mankeys fell from the trees with arrows in each one. Nathen patted Lucas on the back and the room dissolved into white

"Take *that*, mankeys," Lucas cheered.

Nathen chuckled. "Okay, good job. But let's say there's a situation where you have to keep your friends alive."

"Like when my parents fought MM?"

"Yes, like then."

Lucas lowered his bow and shuffled his feet. "Did you get to meet my mom?"

"Mm–hmm, while she was pregnant with you."

"What was she like?"

"I didn't have much interaction with her," Nathen said. "But your dad loved her very much. There wasn't a training session that went by where he didn't talk about her. His face lit up at the mere mention of your mom's name."

Lucas controlled his breathing and felt tears in his eyes. He wasn't going to cry in front of this guy, but no one ever spoke of his parents like that. He dreamed of being able to see them the way Nathen described. He and his dad had love, but it felt colder. There was a wall between them that kept him from getting close.

"I think you'll like this next scene." Nathen pushed on his Panavice.

The room changed to a ledge. Lucas stood on the ledge and looked down at the half-mile drop. A flying pig squealed with large fangs. It flew at him and he pulled back an arrow, letting it fly—sending it sailing past the pig.

The pig growled, showing its pointy white teeth. Lucas yanked another arrow in place and took a breath, lining up the shot. He fired and struck the monstrosity in the gut, sending it falling to the earth below.

"I found a bow in my dad's closet a few years ago. I bet it was the same one he used here."

"Maybe."

"Was he a good shot?"

"He wasn't too bad, but he had his mind on other things

while they were here." Nathen chuckled. "He must have spent a long time training you."

Lucas frowned. "No, he didn't. Even this summer, when he finally started showing me a few things, it was like pulling teeth." Lucas took a deep breath and looked way down to the bottom of the cliff where there should have been a splattered pig. "I think I was too good for him. I just got the feeling I was disappointing him by picking it up so much."

"Sometime parents don't want us stepping in their footsteps. Especially when they've stomped in the mud."

JULIE SAT IN FRONT OF her very own Panavice. She caressed the cold edges of it with her hands and tried to contain her excitement while sitting next to Doctor Almadon.

"While the barbarians play with tools, we'll be learning the true weapon of this world, technology. Everything is connected, in some way, digitally. Once you find your way around the digital walls, the world will be yours." Almadon pressed the screen on her Panavice. "I'm sending you the first training round."

Julie stared at her screen. *Level One* appeared.

"You're going to go against a level-one com."

Julie held the Panavice in her hands. It was thicker than her cellphone, but the screen was larger and clearer. When she tilted it, the tabs on the screen moved from the background, giving it a 3D look.

She pressed the tab with the cracked safe and it opened a new page. From there she saw every computer nearby. Each one had a label, *Medical Equipment, Elevator 4, Lighting, Panavice - Almadon.* Then she spotted it, a level-one label. She pressed it and a wall of code floated on the screen.

"There is software I installed on that Pana to help you break through many of the walls."

She saw the walls, but why use a sledgehammer when she could tip toe around it and sneak in? The codes on her screen scrolled with her finger swipes. Then she saw what she was looking for and typed into the keyboard. She pressed the last key and she was in.

The wall dissolved and a digital flower twirled on the screen.

"Nice, Julie. Now again, but this time try using the built-in software. It'll help you when you can't find a sneak. Level two."

Level two went down in under a minute. Julie set her Panavice on the table.

Almadon set hers down and furrowed her brow. "I suspected something on the first go, but now I am certain. Where did you learn these systems?"

Julie locked eyes with Almadon. She fidgeted with her hands in her lap and felt like a kid in the principal's office, confessing to prank gone wrong. "I used the computer in my room."

Almadon leaned back and touched her chin. "Find anything interesting?"

"I searched through MM's mainframe. . . ."

"What? That was incredibly foolish." Almadon jolted forward in her chair. "How? Those are meant for watching shows and browsing the net."

"I found a cloud that had unlimited storage and set up a basic operating system to penetrate walls," Julie said. "But I made sure I used a stack of proxies. They shouldn't be able to find me."

Almadon's mouth hung low. "Why, what were you looking for? Not to mention how dangerous that is. There are things on this net not to be trifled with."

"I know, and I found something strange. Deep in the code, it seemed like a hidden underground river, streaming through the background."

Almadon raised an eyebrow. "Probably just a data feed."

"I thought that as well, but then I wrote a program and found a back door into the stream."

Almadon's eyes twitched and she leaned closer. "And?"

Julie looked at the table. "Nothing at first, it just seemed to be a backup stream, but then I saw it deleting things, everywhere, like a virus."

"The Harris virus."

"Yes, but it did more. It pulled in vast amounts of info, yet had a very limited output, like it was being choked."

"Anytime someone writes anything about Harris on the net, this program finds it and deletes it. It's common knowledge."

"I know." This was the hard part for Julie. She almost didn't want to say anything to Almadon about it, but she needed to tell her. "It found me. It called herself Alice and appeared on my screen as a young woman. She asked me who I was, but it freaked me out so bad I turned off the computer."

"Alice actually talked to you?"

"Did I screw something up?"

Almadon stretched her fingers out in front of her and then proceeded to take great interest in smoothing out her shirt. "Alice is a whisper on the net. A myth to most. Some think the net itself birthed an A.I."

"I thought artificial intelligences were illegal."

"They are, but this one is different. MM has let her be, which makes me think she is part of MM. Possibly implemented by Marcus himself."

"Did I mess up? I'm so sorry; I just got all caught up in the level of computing power. I didn't think there was any limit to what I could do within your internet."

"It's probably nothing, but if you can get into systems like that, I think we should jump to level twenty."

She looked at the screen and *Level 20* popped up. There were more layers to this one, but she had already seen the flaw. She typed quickly and saw the swirling flower on her screen.

CHAPTER 20

THE NEXT MORNING AT BREAKFAST, Compry pushed the food cart, hitting the table again. Joey jerked back at the noise of plates clattering. Thoughts of creepy rollerblading people and old gunslingers floated around in his mind.

"Breakfast is served," Compry said as she handed plates out.

"Thank you." Poly got up from her chair and helped her pass out the plates.

Compry rolled her eyes.

"Easy on the plates, lady." Harris smirked.

She scowled. "This is the last day I'm the breakfast maker."

"Actually, the deal was for a few more days after this," Harris said and leaned back in his chair. He grinned and linked his fingers behind his head.

Compry's eyes widened. She pointed at Harris and her eyes narrowed. "Not another day."

Harris made a face and winked at her. After some silent communication between the two, he sat forward, and directed his attention to the group. "Would you guys like to meet the person behind everything? The man who wants to suck the life from your very veins?" He grabbed his Panavice and flipped it around towards the aisle. "Let me introduce you to Marcus Malliden."

Joey choked on his eggs and reached for the gun at his side, scanning the room for the man. Then he noticed the image projected from Harris's Panavice. He finished swallowing and sat down. The projection showed a man in a white robe, typing into a computer.

Marcus turned to face the camera. A good-looking young man with unkempt hair and an innocent smile. He turned back to his computer. Joey leaned forward in search of the horns he was sure would be coming out of Marcus's forehead. The plainness of Marcus made him think there had to be a mistake.

A voice-over started.

"There was a time in history when we had no path, no solutions to our problems. Our lives lasted mere decades. Birth defects were rampant."

The video showed a two-headed baby, and then another mutated baby that Joey couldn't watch.

"Then, we were rescued by the wonders of genetic breakthroughs. Marcus Malliden saved the world by creating the first, perfect baby. Free from defects, we no longer have to roll the dice between two people's DNA. Marcus took the guessing out of reproduction and brought a new age to the world, where people don't die of disease or aging. As long as you keep Orange in your life."

The screen switched to the voice-over guy, who took a drink of an orange liquid and smiled at the camera. A line of text scrolls across the bottom of the screen. *Orange, it makes you live.*

Harris turned the screen off.

"What the hell was that?" Lucas asked.

"That's a commercial for Orange, an old one, but a classic," Harris said and Compry let out a small laugh.

"You see, at the start of MM's new genetic design, the world was against it, but when the babies he designed lived far longer and healthier than any naturals did, the world became obsessed with having their babies modified. Unfortunately, MM didn't factor in the problem at hand. He played God and God fought back. It was as if your life span was a rubber band, pulled and stretched way out, but eventually, the band would break. People started to become ill and long-closed hospitals starting opening. Marcus, in a scramble, invented Orange."

Harris lifted his glass of orange liquid.

Compry said, "This drink is the torture and stranglehold that MM has on the world. Once he had the world on Orange, he knew every person who wanted to live was at his fingertips." She took a drink. "This drink keeps you alive, but also makes you the slave of MM." The disgust spread over her face. "Some chose death, but most simply fell in line and took the drink. MM Corp, with its massive power, gobbled up any competitors; they bought all the politicians and turned them into a one-world order."

"This is a video our group had made and are sometimes able to get into the state TV broadcasts," Harris added, and tapped his Panavice.

A similar voice-over started, but it sounded just different enough. *"Marcus Malliden, the man behind Orange. He brought you life and he brings you death."* A montage of towns getting bombed, and old people dying, flashes on the screen. *"Orange and MM allow you to live, for now."*

Harris turned it off. "If your town or province gets out of line, the shipments of Orange stop. Then people turn on each other and the town falls into chaos. This gives MM cause to step in and crush the towns."

"If your population is addicted to this Orange drink, how can you remove it? Won't you just all die?" Julie asked.

"Yes, we'd die without it. We are not looking to remove Orange, but the man who controls it. Marcus Malliden keeps the world under his thumb and he presses hard," Harris said. "You see, this man is the one who killed your parents to get what he wants."

"And what does he want?" Joey asked.

Harris made direct eye contact with him, "You, Joey." He paused and then continued, "Marcus would take any of you, but he wants what's *in* you. Isaac's experiments resulted in his greatest accomplishment with you. You're his best chance of staying alive and he wants to keep living very much."

Everyone at the table stared at him. Joey felt his heart beating hard as he shared looks with each of them. It felt like another weight thrown on his back.

"Is that why I have my . . . ability?" Joey struggled to get the words out, even if he already knew the answer.

"Yes. Isaac experimented heavily on the people of Ryjack and . . . well, you saw the result, but I think he perfected it with you kids."

"All this effort and death is for one man's wish to live forever?" Julie asked.

"It is a deeply personal mission for Marcus. He is the last naturally born person on the planet. Everyone else is a genetically modified MM baby."

"How's he still alive then?" Lucas asked.

"He used to have a man named John Smith. His body kept him alive for a while, at least until Harris ended that lifeline," Compry said. She placed a hand on his arm for a moment.

Harris lowered his eyebrows at Compry. "He finds unusual ways to stay alive. Not too long ago, we were able to take one of those things away from him, John Smith, a man we believe they made in Ryjack. He was sort of a cheap version of you guys."

"Where's this John Smith now?" Julie asked.

"Dead." Harris pushed his plate forward and stuffed his Panavice in his jacket pocket. "Let's get back to training." He stood from the table.

TRAINING WAS SIMILAR TO THE first day, with many scenes popping in and out. By the end of the day, Joey's eyes hurt and he stumbled into his room, burying his face in his blankets. He was glad to have the room to himself. He didn't want to see the looks they might give him for being different, or worse yet, pity. He heard a quiet knock on his door.

Poly stood at the door and smiled at Joey. She was wearing a yellow dress with a floral print. The flowers changed colors as she moved. "You like my dress? Compry gave it to me."

"It's very . . . nice," he said. He kept his eyes focused on her face. Otherwise, his eyes tended to wander and travel over her body.

"You're all by yourself in there. Aren't you getting lonely?"

"Not really, my thoughts keep me occupied," he lied.

"I thought you might need a break." Poly grabbed his hand. "Come with me. Julie found something I wanted to show you."

CHAPTER 21

"YOU HAVE TO WALK LOW," Poly said, crouching down.

"Why's that?" Joey asked.

"It's only sneaking around if you're crouching, duh." She playfully rolled her eyes.

He laughed and watched her sneak up to the elevator button and press it. He played along and crouched down, putting his back against the wall and looking left to right. "Where we going?" Joey asked in an exaggerated whisper.

"It's a surprise."

The elevator doors slid open. He followed Poly in, hugging the walls. She pressed the button and spun around, smiling. He couldn't help but feel happier around her. She was a bright light in a dark room.

Upon exiting, Joey crouched lower and followed Poly through a few hallways and into a room with white walls and ceiling. He raised a questioning eyebrow; half thinking she was going to run some training drills with him.

"Just wait for it." She slid her finger against a screen on the wall, it lit up, and she pushed a button. "It worked!" She pulled a Panavice off the wall next to the screen.

The room changed to a grassy meadow with a large oak tree at the top of a grass hill. Poly laughed and ran to the top of the grass hill.

The heat from the sun felt good. He took in the fabricated fresh air and looked at the blue sky; taking in the moment, as if it was real.

"I even have a blanket here so we don't get our clothes dirty." She laid the blanket on the grass next to the oak tree. Laying down on it with her face to the sky, she clasped her hands behind her head. Her dress pressed against her body.

He took in her form, for probably too long.

She raised her head and smirked when she caught his observing eyes. "Come on." She patted the space next to her.

Joey wiped his sweaty hands on his pants. Looking at the blanket, he reluctantly laid down on it, keeping a large gap between them. His heart raced lying next to Poly. The Preston Six travelled as a pack. He could count on one hand the times he and Poly were alone together. He kept his eyes on the leaves above his head, fidgeting with his hands. Why was he so nervous?

"Let's get a nighttime setting so we can see the stars." Poly pushed on the Panavice.

The sun fell off the horizon, and the darkness covered them with sparkly stars in the sky. The cold air crept in with the sun gone. They lay there in silence, looking at the stars.

He had a spot on his roof at home, where he would lay down and stare into the darkness above. So this was peaceful, familiar, and he relaxed a tad, moving his hands behind his head.

Poly rubbed her arms.

"You okay?" Joey asked.

"Just getting cold out here." She shifted her body next to him, her arm rubbing against his side.

He tensed up with her close to him.

"Don't worry. I won't stab you," she joked.

He laughed, felt her warmth, and relaxed a bit more as he looked at the stars. The crickets chirped and a flying bug buzzed by. It felt like home, as if he could be sitting under the oak in his back yard, and not stuck in this stagnant, recycled world of a bunker.

A glowing firefly buzzed above them. "Look," he said.

"Oh wow," she said.

The single firefly became two, then three, and then they popped into a mass of soft glowing bulbs above them. They landed in the oak tree and blinked randomly, forming a light show. Joey stared at the magical swarm doing their dance for them.

She laughed and pointed at them as they swarmed in different shapes. The maelstrom of lights above was mesmerizing—almost as much as Poly's glee at the sight of it all. He took his first easy breath since leaving Earth. It was the best thing he could think of doing right then. The dots of light flew high into the night sky and blinked out into stars.

"Poly?"

"Yes?"

"Thank you."

She turned on her side and draped an arm over his chest, squeezing him in a hug. "You're welcome."

They lay there, watching the night sky in silence, holding each other. For the first time in days, he felt some weight lift off his chest. He let his body relax, enjoying the moment. It was so natural lying with her; at some point Joey brought his hand down and was drawing circles on the arm she left draped across him. Her head nestled on his shoulder.

"Joey?"

"Yes?"

"Do you think MM is going to find us here?" She propped up on her free arm as she splayed her hand across his chest. "I keep having nightmares about him. He takes us and does horrible things," she said, looking somewhat panicked.

He wouldn't let them take her. He would protect her to his death, if that's what it took. He looked over at her, and laced his hand with hers. "Poly, I'll do anything . . . I'll make sure that never happens."

She nodded, their faces so close, he could feel her sweet breath on his cheek. She laid her head back on his shoulder and snuggled in closer, putting a leg between his.

He tilted his head to her hair and breathed in deeply. Then, it suddenly hit Joey, how close they were—what was happening. Her body pressed against his. They were holding each other, face's inches apart. He exhaled and his heart started racing. He could actually see his chest moving in rapid rhythm. She had to feel it.

"This is really nice," Poly said, looking up at him.

She continued to talk, saying something about trying to get him alone ever since their birthday party, but he just couldn't follow along. However, he was keenly aware of her lips moving and the connection of her body against his. The words didn't matter as much as he knew what she was telling him.

Poly's sentence trailed off when she noticed his focus on her lips. She moved her hand over his heart. Feeling the pounding in his chest, her face changed indecipherably. She tightened her leg on his, and parted her lips as she slightly moved her chin forward.

Everything happened so fast.

Joey stopped thinking and went in for what he wanted. Rolling her on her back, he lay on top of her, their lips meeting in a heated kiss. Grabbing both sides of his face, she tilted her head and opened her mouth to him. He groaned as their tongues entwined. Pushing his weight into her, he—

"What are you two doing?"

Joey and Poly froze, breathing hard. *Who was there?*

The scene turned off and the grassy ground turned to a white floor. The hill of white flooring lowered to the ground. Joey jumped off Poly, adjusting his clothes and putting his hands in his pockets. She quickly followed suit, keeping her eyes averted to the ground.

Harris was at the edge of the grass field. "This machine uses a massive amount of power, and if not properly channeled, it could be traced back to here," he said, frowning.

"Sorry," they both said in unison.

Still looking at the ground, Poly continued. "It's my fault, sir. I brought Joey here."

"Dang, you're as bad as your parents were, always sneaking around and getting into stuff. Your dad couldn't keep his eyes off your mother either."

Poly's face turned red at the conversation.

"Why don't you lovebirds get back to your rooms." Harris held the door open with a smirk.

They hustled through the door, without making eye contact, and didn't talk until reaching Poly's door. She turned around to face him. It was awkward, and then they both broke into soft laughter over Harris catching them.

Just when Joey didn't know how to say goodbye, Poly got on her tiptoes and leaned in, kissing him lightly on the mouth. She winked and darted into her room.

He turned and smiled to himself the entire way to his room. Throwing himself across his bed, Joey lay there, trying to figure out what had happened. He took off his shoes and set them next to the nightstand and that is when he saw the small velvet box. He picked it up and his thoughts drifted from Poly and him on the blanket, to the night on the balcony with Samantha. Guilt washed over him. He bit his lip, remembering Samantha's lip-gloss. What had he done?

THE NEXT MORNING WAS THE same. Joey kept thinking of that kiss during training, and he missed a man with a bow and arrow in the tree. The electric shock didn't seem to bother him. Harris called training early and told Joey to clean his weapons.

Dinner was meat and mashed potatoes again. Afterward, Joey saw everyone in the hallway, but told them he was going to go to bed early and avoided eye contact with Poly. He lay in his bed worrying about Samantha, but his mind kept floating back to Poly. He thought on his actions a long time, rolling the jewelry box in his hands.

Had Samantha made it to the stone and gone with them, would things be different? Would he have kissed Poly and enjoyed her body against his? When he got back to Samantha, what would he tell her? He thought he wanted to be with Samantha but each moment spent with Poly made him question it. Nevertheless, it didn't excuse the fact he'd made a move on both of them. He couldn't imagine hurting either of them, but he couldn't escape the sinking feeling he had done just that.

Joey slept roughly again.

THERE WAS ANOTHER SOFT KNOCK in the morning for breakfast. Followed by training. After training, Joey avoided the others again and headed to his room.

CHAPTER 22

HARRIS FELT THE GRIP OF his guns and let out a long breath. They were some of the few items he'd kept from his childhood; his father had given them to him so many years ago.

He sat at the desk across from Compry, Nathen, and Almadon. "How are they all doing?"

Compry answered first. "Poly is as lethal as anyone I've seen with a knife, but she's weaker in her emotions. It could be her age, or that she has a thing for Joey."

"Yes, I saw that as well. We should keep those two apart if we can," Harris said. "Ever since I caught them in the scene generator, Joey's been distant."

"Young love," Almadon said.

"I don't know. There's something else going on with Joey," Harris said. "How's Lucas doing?"

"Lucas is a natural with the bow. He could play at world

games, I think, with some of the stuff I've seen from him. But he needs some time to mature," Nathen reported.

Harris witnessed Lucas in action and wasn't surprised at Nathen's response. "And Hank?"

"He's something of a physical phenomenon. He took me to the ground in our first sparing session and has progressed quickly from there. I think he might give you a run for it, Harris."

He raised an eyebrow, but in all honesty, he hadn't expected much less. However, there was a person he was most interested in hearing about. "How's Julie?"

"Julie's learning fast." Almadon paused.

After many years with Almadon, he knew how to spot when she was holding back. "What is it?"

"She got into MM's network and found Alice, or I should say, Alice found her."

Harris leaned forward with shock. Alice was known to very few people in the world, and most of them sat in that room. "Alice came to her?"

"Yes, she asked Julie who she was—probably unable to recognize someone from another planet."

"Did she find us?"

"No, Julie did it right. She kept us hidden."

"Unbelievable." Harris knew the kids were quick to learn, but this seemed beyond anything he expected. "What do you think about this?"

"I don't know. She is progressing almost too fast. Beth was good, average really, but Julie is scary. I think she could hack our mainframe if she tried."

Harris leaned back in his chair. He thought the same thing

of all the kids. Joey was far better at shooting than he should be and he absorbed every instruction the first time shown.

"Yeah, I was thinking the same thing with Hank and Lucas. Their skills are far above where they should be," Nathen added.

He knew what they were getting at. "Did you run all the tests yet?"

"Yes, there are a few anomalies in each of them. It will take me some time to go through and make any sense of it," Almadon said.

Harris gazed at her. "But one of them stands out from the rest?"

"Yes. Joey's a bit different from the rest. Whatever Isaac did, it seemed to take hold of Joey the most."

"Yeah, his time manipulation is something I've never seen in any mutation."

"How is he doing?" Compry asked.

"He's okay. I've been working with him a lot on picking targets and making the right decisions."

"Has he done his slow-mo thing with you?" Almadon asked.

"No, it seems to trigger in extreme situations only." If he could get Joey to harness that skill, he'd be unstoppable.

She nodded. "If we can monitor him while it's happening, we might be able to figure it out—replicate it even."

"Let me see if I can even get him to do it again," he said. "Any news from MM?"

"The insider said he's still holed up in the bowels of their bunker," Almadon informed. "I've noticed a lot more negative traffic online about MM. There's even been rogue programmers that have a 'kill MM' program going at some of the scene centers, but they were murdered."

Harris took in the information. While it was encouraging to hear people posting negative things on their blogs and websites, it was a whole other thing for them to stand in arms against him. So, Marcus was still holed up in the bunker. With John Smith gone, he'd be suffering, probably clinging to life. The man deserved everything he got. Harris realized he was touching his ring finger. He hadn't worn his wedding ring in fifteen years, but he found himself feeling for it lately. He stopped, extending his fingers and placing them on the table.

"How long are we going to stay here, Harris? It won't take MM long to see where a massive power surge went to," Almadon pointed out.

"We better show Julie and Lucas a few stone locations, just in case," he replied. "I don't want any surprises this time around." He wouldn't let another group of kids die for his cause.

JOEY THRASHED AROUND IN HIS sleep as he dreamed of Simon grabbing Samantha by the neck and choking the life from her. Then he morphed into Simon. His own hands around her perfect neck, choking the life from her. She communicated with her eyes, asking why, why was he hurting her. He woke up sweating and breathing hard.

The soft knock at his door was the morning wake up call.

He went to breakfast for the eggs and meat again. At the end of the day, he walked to his door and saw his friends talking in the hallway. Hank shot him a hurt look as Joey stood in front of his door. He sighed and walked toward the group.

"Hey, look who's come down from his mountain top to

grace us with his presence." Lucas gestured with sweeping bow.

"Yeah, I haven't been feeling well," Joey said. He glanced at Poly, who looked at Julie.

"Well, good to have you talking again, man. We were starting to worry about you," Hank said.

"Hey, we're going to go sneak into the scene generator and go somewhere that isn't . . ." Lucas looked around the hallway, "here."

Joey laughed and followed the group to the same scene generator he and Poly shared. The white walls were still there and there was no sign of a grassy meadow with a blanket for two.

"Julie found this awesome program," Lucas said.

Joey uncomfortably looked at Poly. She was busy studying her fingernails.

"Okay, here we go." Julie pulled out her Panavice and pressed some buttons on it.

The room changed to a city with people walking around them and small tube-looking cars going down the road silently. The people were beautiful here and they moved around them, not giving the group of five any notice as they went about their day. He recognized the outfits. They were similar to the ones in the mall scene used during training.

"There it is," Lucas called and grabbed Julie's hand.

Poly gave Joey a sharp look and hurried across the street. She wore a similar dress as before, but with red and white color-changing flowers on it. Where was she keeping her knives in that dress?

A wooden sign displayed above the door read *Giuseppe's Toys*. He entered the store, amazed. It was much larger on the inside than he expected. Toys hummed around the store. Flying metal birds landed on a perch near the door and tweeted at him. He pet one on the back and it flew back to the second floor. The stuffed animals' eyes followed him as he rushed by.

Lucas grabbed a kid's bow and arrow and shot a foam dart at Poly who slapped it away. She grabbed a large foam sword from a bucket near the end of an aisle.

"Come on, gunslinger. Let's see what you can do against a sword," she said, waving the sword at Joey.

He grabbed a toy gun and shot rubber discs at her, but Poly swung her sword with grace as she dodged the discs, striking them away with her foam sword. He shot another and she moved toward him, slapping the projectile away with her sword. In one second, he found the end of her sword at his neck. Her narrow eyes and scowl gave Joey good reason to hold his hands up in surrender. Her expression wasn't all fun and games anymore. There was something else there.

She lowered the sword and he realized how deadly she'd gotten, or maybe she had always been that dangerous. Poly took a second sword from the foam weapon bucket and spun them both around.

Joey set down his toy gun for a foam sword. He stood sideways and tried to give his best fencing stance, the end of his sword pointing at Poly. "En garde."

"Oh really?" Poly raised one eyebrow and moved closer. In two quick motions, she pushed his sword clear and struck him in the chest.

He grabbed her sword and then hit her on the top of the head with his.

"No fair," she claimed.

"There's no rules in love and foam-war." They stared at each other. "Poly—"

"Look at this, guys," Julie interrupted as he started to speak.

Poly yanked her sword away from him and stuffed it in the barrel. She marched over to Julie and Lucas, each bent over a large glass aquarium.

Joey's stomach sank. He'd already hurt her feelings.

Joining the group, he thought they were looking at a train set with little houses. However, as he got closer, he saw tiny people doing laundry in a pail outside of their house. He leaned in with his face next to the glass. Some goats were in a pen nearby, and their neighbors were all working around their houses. Everything looked so real.

"Is this some kid simulation toy?" Hank asked.

"Oh no, this is real. Rather . . . we're in a simulation, but they aren't. I mean, they exist outside of here, I think. Here, watch." Julie reached over the display, picking up a goat. The tiny people nearby screamed and ran into their house. They poked their head out of their tiny house windows.

"Look at this goat. It's mechanical. MM put a ban on all robots, except for small toys and dolls. The tech that would go into creating something like this . . ." Julie's wide eyes stared at the goat for a bit, and then she placed it in Joey's hand.

He inspected the goat. A fascinating creation. The realistic small village had tiny people and animals moving around. How was it possible? He placed the goat back in the pen.

"Watch, there's a rain button here," Julie said and pushed the button marked rain.

The clouds moved in above the tiny town and it rained down on their roof and fields, collecting in small puddles. The tiny people scattered around, pulling their laundry into their dry houses. A small baby goat stumbled into a rising puddle. It struggled against the sticky mud but couldn't get out.

Poly rubbed against Joey as she jostled for a better view. The goat's head submerged under the puddle. He reached in, lightly picked up the goat, and set it in the dry pen next to the other goat. They greeted the baby goat with a few licks and the goats huddled together for heat.

"Joey, Hero of Goats," Lucas proclaimed.

The rain stopped and the people came out of their tiny houses and looked to the sky. They moved to their goat pens to check on their livestock, then to the gardens. But they kept looking up. Were they wondering if the large arm was going to come back and take one of them away?

Joey squinted and watched the goat family as they shifted from brown to white and then back again. In a second, the whole room shifted to its white base. Joey looked for Harris at the doorway but there was no one.

"What happened?" Hank asked.

"I don't know. The power is fluctuating—" Julie said as her fingers slid on her Panavice, before an intercom voice cut her off.

"Attention, attention. Hull breach. Everyone report to your designated zones, and await further instructions." The message kept repeating.

An explosion from above shook the room. Joey covered his head with his hands.

"What's going on?" Poly mouthed.

"MM. I think they've found us," he called out over the warning blaring.

CHAPTER 23

THE INTERCOM REPEATED ITS MESSAGE and Joey cringed. He didn't know their designated area. *Where should they go?* They moved toward the scene generator door—it flew open.

"We have got to go, now!" Harris yelled. He stood at the doorway of the room. "Go to your rooms and grab your weapons. Meet me at the elevator. *Run!*" Then he was gone.

They all sprinted back to their hallway. Joey bolted into his room, intent on getting one item. He opened the drawer next to his bed and pulled out Samantha's box. He ran to his door, adjusting his guns under his jacket, and opened it. Harris paced the hallway. Another explosion from above shook the floor.

Harris's eyes darted to Joey, glanced at the other doors, and resumed pacing. If Harris was nervous, then Joey felt a near panic building in him. He moved to open Lucas and Hank's door when they opened it themselves. Poly and Julie came out of their room a few seconds later.

"What's going on?" Poly asked.

"He's found us. We may only have minutes," Harris said. Another explosion rocked the structure.

Joey looked up and gripped his gun. Tendrils of dust fell from the ceiling. He didn't want to run. He wanted to kill. He wanted to end it now. "Let's stay and fight," he suggested.

"No, not here. He'll have the upper hand. He's prepared." Harris shook his head. "Listen, we have no time for debate. Almadon is nuking the mainframe as we speak. With any luck, they might not even know you were here. Your rooms will be ablaze in a matter of minutes as well." He jogged to the elevator, the doors opened and he stepped in. Joey stayed in the back and made sure all his friends got on.

The elevator plunged to the lower levels of the complex. The doors slid open and they ran down a long hallway, to a door at the end.

"The Alius stone is in the next room." Harris said, pointing at the big steel door.

"Where do we go?" Lucas asked.

"Back to your home," he replied.

"Preston?" Poly looked horror-struck.

"It's the best place to go right now."

"Is it clean?" Joey asked.

"Clean enough," Harris said.

The sound of clanking metal emanated from the elevator, as if someone dropped a can of soda on its metal top. He turned to the doors as an explosion blew the elevator doors off, sending smoke down the hallway. They were far enough away to be safe from it, but the concussion blew by them.

Something landed behind the smoke in the elevator with a thud. Joey struggled to see the movements masked by the fog. He pulled out one of his guns, and three silver assassins emerged into the hallway.

Harris shot them dead at the elevator doorway before Joey even got one shot off. He couldn't believe Harris could shoot from that distance. But his admiration had to wait, as three more fell into the elevator and ran at them. Harris shot two more and Joey took out the third.

Harris's Panavice chimed and he held it to his ear. "Okay, I'll get there as quick as I can." He lowered his hand. "Compry and Nathen are pinned down, I need to go and help them." Harris pointed at the Alius stone room. "Get in there and don't wait for me. I'll hold them off."

Joey grunted an argument, but Harris ran down the hallway toward the elevator. *Go on without him?* He stuffed his gun in his holster and followed his friends into the Alius stone room. It smelled clean and didn't have a hint of zombie goo anywhere in it.

Lucas and Julie rushed to the stone in the middle.

"You know what you're doing?" Hank asked.

"No, not really, I mean Almadon showed us a few times." Lucas kneeled next to the stone. "Julie?"

"You were better at it in the simulation."

Lucas shrugged and looked put out. "We were supposed to spend most of the day tomorrow learning this." He rubbed his hands together, and held them over the stone. He paused, hovering over the stone.

Maybe Joey shouldn't have been avoiding his friends the last few days. They were learning how to travel with the Alius stone and he didn't even know.

Gunfire erupted in the hall followed by a large explosion. Smoke poured into the stone room. An Arrack ran in with a dagger in hand. He shot it three times before it fell on the floor. Another Arrack emerged from the smoke; its large eyes regarded its dead friend, and lunged for Hank. Joey shot it in midair.

"We got to get out of here," he called to Lucas.

Lucas shook his head and looked to Julie.

Julie looked several times between her Panavice, Joey, and the stone. "You got this."

Lucas nodded his head. "No problem, I got this," he said, as if trying to convince himself.

Rapid gunfire echoed down the hall. Joey trained his gun on the open door.

"I hope this works," Lucas prayed aloud.

The dome went black.

CHAPTER 24

WATER SEEPED INTO JOEY'S SHOES. A familiar smell hit his nose and the blood left his face. No other place smelled like it.

Joey pointed his gun at the moans coming from behind him. In the darkness, he used his ears to guide his aim. Julie lit the room with her Panavice, at the same time, Lucas screamed. He thrashed in the water with a zombie's mouth attached to his leg. Pulling an arrow out, he stabbed it in the head until it fell from his leg.

No one could see Lucas's leg under the water, couldn't tell if it was bitten.

Glancing at the broken ceiling, Joey confirmed where they were . . . Ryjack. Under the casino.

The dark, domed room filled with the sounds of splashing water and moans of zombies. They weren't alone. A zombie sloshed toward Poly and Joey shot it in the head. The sound thundered through the small space. Poly spun with a knife in hand and threw one at the zombie approaching Joey. It fell next to him and splashed water on his pants. The thing was only a few feet from taking a bite out of his back.

"Get us out of here, Lucas!" Poly squealed.

Lucas dragged his leg and kneeled next to the stone. A zombie fell from the ceiling and crashed next to him in the water. He stumbled back as it emerged from the water, clawing after him. Joey shot it in the head and it echoed through the bowels of the casino.

"Now! There'll be more any second," Joey ordered.

Julie directed her light to the stone and Lucas. Lucas's red-covered leg came into view. He froze, transfixed at the sight of his leg. He knew—they *all* knew—what it meant. Placing his hands next to his wound, Lucas peeled back the damp clothes.

Another zombie fell from the opening above, sending foul water splashing on everyone. Hank smashed its head with a large piece of concrete.

Julie bounded to the stone. "Anywhere is better than here." She punched her fingers against the stone and it hummed.

The ceiling changed to a steel dome. However, the foul water and smell still filled the room.

Julie ran to Lucas. "You're bit." She helped Lucas to his feet.

"Where'd you take us?" Lucas clutched his leg and winced.

"I don't know."

He laughed—his face already pale. "Maybe somewhere awesome."

"Maybe," Julie sobbed.

Lucas fell to his knees and bent his head back.

Julie grabbed his arm and tried to get him up. "Help me. We need to get him out of here."

Hank rushed to help her carry him across the dome to the steel door, while Joey avoided the carcasses littering the floor. He kept his gun trained on each body as he passed it. He wouldn't let another of his friends get hurt.

Poly took her place next to him as they reached the door. He pulled the handle and climbed out of the room and onto a stone ledge in the middle of a hill. He helped Hank lay Lucas on the ledge. Joey swallowed and turned away from the blood trailing down his leg.

Of all the places, in all of the worlds, Lucas had to choose the one filled with zombies. He wanted to be mad, but settled for pacing. "Is he going to be okay?" It was a stupid question and Lucas answered with a moan.

"I don't know." Julie flailed her hands as she knelt next to Lucas's leg. "Hank, open that bag and get me the white box with the tree on it." Her face contorted with fear.

Hank flung the bag open and pulled the box out. She rummaged through the white box as they hovered over her.

Poly paced nearby, her face occasionally peeking from behind her hands. "You know what you're doing?"

"Almadon showed me some basic medical stuff." Julie held a glass bottle with red liquid in it. "Can you guys give me some room?"

Joey stepped back and scanned their surroundings, realizing they had no idea where they were. A zombie could be nearby, or who knows what else. He looked up to the cliff they were next to, waiting for a zombie to fall off the edge. Above them, he saw large pine trees. Below them, an ocean splashed its waves on a sandy beach.

"This may hurt." Julie had put on gloves and pulled up Lucas's pant leg. She dipped her finger in the red liquid and pulled out a glob of the goo. She grimaced and watched Lucas's face as she rubbed the medicine over his leg. It stopped bleeding immediately and Lucas's face changed from total agony to complete wonder.

Lucas half-smiled. "Wow, what's in that stuff?"

"It's a bit of everything."

Julie studied the wound with the blood cleared off. Two crescent-shaped bite marks marred his leg at the calf.

"I'll put some bandages on it."

Hank covered his mouth and turned away. Joey knew what the big man felt. He felt it as well. He saw it on everyone's face. The question hung in the air like a neon zeppelin over them. He looked Julie in the eyes; someone had to ask.

"How long do we have?"

She stared at Joey, her eyes full of tears. She didn't want to hear the question, as much as he didn't want to ask it. "I don't know."

"I'm fine." Lucas climbed to his feet as Julie gasped. "See? All good now." He walked in a tight circle, holding his arms out with a big smile.

"He needs a hospital," Poly pleaded. "We need to get him somewhere where he can get help." She pointed at the stone room.

"No can do. That's a one-way stone we came in on, a slave stone," Lucas said. "What? I listened to stuff Almadon said."

Joey sighed. Stuck in an unknown world got his heart beating. Were they still on Ryjack? Harris said the stone seemed to have a mind of its own when you tempted it. Could the stone be so vengeful, it would send them back there?

"Where's the nearest stone?" Joey asked, staring at the crashing waves below them.

Julie held the Panavice in her hand. "About fifty miles to the south, there is a master stone we can use."

"Can you walk on it?" Joey pointed at Lucas's leg.

Lucas raised an eyebrow. "You want to race?"

Joey smiled and shook his head. "You couldn't beat me with two good legs."

"I was talking to Hank. I could beat him with zombie bites on both legs."

"Not if I got my hands on you first," Hank added.

"Can we just race out of here and get to that master stone?" Poly stared at Lucas's leg.

A small dirt path hugged the cliff wall and led down to the beach.

"If we keep close to the water, it'll cover our tracks." Julie shrugged. "I don't know if they can follow us or not."

Joey glanced back up at the ledge. "Yeah, sure, why not?" He hoped Harris could follow them. It didn't feel right not having him around. They now had no safety net; bad decisions could not be made. Making the wrong choice would most likely get them killed.

Waves crashed nearby, sending a mist over them. He felt the salty water on the back of his hand. He'd never seen the ocean, and admired the massive body of water as he moved closer to the water line.

THEY'D MADE GOOD TIME JOGGING down the beach, trying to close the distance to the master stone. Joey's legs and chest burned as he slowed down and gazed at the sun nearing the ocean's edge.

"It's going to be dark soon. We should find a place to make camp," he said between breaths.

"Not on the beach, we'll be sitting ducks." Julie bent over, panting.

"I think I see a path up the cliff," Hank pointed out.

Joey led the way up a crooked path on the rocky cliff. The climb up the narrow path was slow, but when he reached the top, he looked back at the setting sun over the ocean, with its thin, golden clouds stretching over the horizon.

"We're on the west coast. I'd say northern California by the look of the trees," Julie said.

"You think we could be back on Earth?" Poly squeaked with hope.

"I doubt it, no trash on the shore line, no planes."

"As long as we're not on Ryjack," Lucas said.

Poly looked distant as she let the sun warm her face. "My mom took me to San Diego once for some convention. I stood on a beach and watched the sunset . . . just like this one. It's amazing."

Joey thought the sunset made the world familiar. Maybe, by some miracle, they were on Earth. Maybe it was a no-fly zone. He turned away from the view and faced the forest. Pine trees lined the bluff, with ferns and bushes filling in between.

"Let's get far enough in so we can't be seen," he said. "And don't make any noises."

"You think we might still be in Ryjack?" Julie asked.

"Don't say that," Poly begged.

"It's a possibility," Julie huffed. "Let's just find a place to camp for the night."

Joey didn't think it smelled like Ryjack, but things could be deceiving. A lurking zombie might be behind a pine tree in the distance. He led the walk into the forest with his gun out, straining to see deep into the darkening forest.

The rocky edge of the coastline gave way to a pine needle floor. Joey stepped into the dense forest, feeling the strange similarity of stepping into Watchers Woods. He wished he never stepped in there. If he'd just listened to his parents, maybe Simon would've never found them.

What was done was done. He gripped his gun and tried not to look back.

With the forest around them, he took in the sweet, moist smell. It was amazing compared to the recycled air of the bunker and the horrendous smell of the Ryjack zombies. He stepped over a rock covered in moss, enjoying the new surroundings. The bunker had dragged him down more than he realized. It felt great to be outside and away from the cold walls and artificial lighting.

After a few minutes of walking, he couldn't see the ocean, but the drone of crashing waves gave Joey enough reason to push farther into the forest. They walked until twilight set. He found a clearing with some grass and thin layers of pine needles spread around the forest floor.

"We can camp here tonight," Joey said. He cleared an area with his foot and then piled pine needles to create a makeshift bed. Poly watched him as he made his bed and matched his style, fashioning her bed next to his.

Darkness overcame the forest and the night sounds appeared. The crickets creaked and the owls hooted. Joey listened to the familiar noises, but refused to let the familiarities set in. His gut told him he was far away from home.

"This place sounds like home," Poly said, echoing his thoughts. "But it sure feels different."

"Yeah, it does." Julie eyed the surrounding area. "You guys think they're okay? You know, Almadon, Compry, and them?" Julie asked.

"They're pros. There's no way they didn't have a hundred ways to escape that situation." Lucas sat down, favoring his leg.

"How far away are we from the stone, Julie?" Joey asked.

"We have a long trek tomorrow and we should see it the day after next."

Another night in the forest didn't seem like a bad idea to him. He was starting to make out the stars in the darkening sky peeking through the tree canopy. A branch cracked from behind him and he jumped up, his gun in hand, only to see the branch had fallen from a nearby tree.

"We probably shouldn't make too much noise. We don't know what could be lurking out there," he said.

"I know, freaking zombies, grinning at us in the dark," Lucas agreed.

"Shut up, Lucas," Julie said as she nervously looked around. "Here let me change those bandages." She pulled out the medical box and worked on his leg. He seemed to relax as she spread more goo over the wound.

Poly scooted closer to Joey and grabbed his arm. She seemed scared as she looked around the forest.

She isn't scared of anything, usually. He slid his arm around her back and pulled her closer for a quick hug. She seemed to relax and lean against him for support.

A gust of cold air blew by them and stirred the forest canopy.

"We better keep watch," Lucas said looking at the swaying branches above.

"Yeah, I'm not sure if I'll be sleeping much anyways," Julie said.

To keep it fair, they decided which two would take first watch with a game of rock-paper-scissors. Joey was with Julie on the first shift.

As the others settled into sleep, he found a spot next to Julie and sat down. Studying her Panavice, she curved around it protectively. The screen produced little light. She must have had some kind of night setting on it.

"Hey, Julie," he whispered.

She looked at him with a blank expression and then glanced at Lucas. The darkness hid how bad he looked. "I'm freaking out."

"Lucas will be fine. We just need to get him out of here."

"I don't know. Look at him. He's pale and I know it's hurting him. He's just trying to look tough around you and Hank, but I know better. He's suffering."

Joey sighed. He and Julie never clicked like many of the others had. She was into her books and smartphone. Samantha was always closest to Julie. Samantha was their unifying bond.

"I keep thinking something awful is happening back home," Julie said. "It doesn't feel right without Samantha here."

"You miss her too?" he asked.

"Well duh, not having her around sucks." Julie paused and leaned closer to him. "I keep having nightmares about her."

He had nightmares involving Samantha too, but didn't want to scare Julie with them. "Samantha's with our parents. I'm sure she's fine. Probably worried about us."

"Yeah," Julie said, but with a distance in her voice.

He looked at her face. The corner of her eyes creased and her features sagged. He hated seeing any of his friends sad. He sighed, thinking of any way to brighten the situation—the way Poly would.

"What's up with that Panavice?"

Her eyes brightened at the question and she smiled. "You have no idea what these things are capable of. It's almost endless."

"Endless?"

"This makes any smartphone look like a jerk. I'll show you. What do you want it to do?"

He thought about this and it seemed a ridiculous question. Then he knew something that he would like. "Can it make us warm?"

She smiled and slid her finger around the screen and then pushed a button. The Panavice's screen began to glow red and then he felt heat radiating from it. He looked at her smiling, putting his cold hands closer to the red screen.

She whispered into the Panavice. The glow stopped, and cold night air took over.

"Can it make us Twinkies?" Joey asked.

She laughed and shook her head. He smiled back, but he had really hoped it could.

Julie stared at Poly's sleeping body and then turned to him.

"You know, at first, you freaked Samantha out with that attempted kiss," Julie said.

The darkness covered the redness on his face. Samantha had told Julie about the kiss. His curiosity beat out his embarrassment. "What did she say?"

"She just had never looked at you that way."

Did she know about their actual kiss on the porch?

"Don't look all down like that, because she does now."

"What do you mean?"

"I don't know. She just said you were hot and stuff," Julie said. "God, this is getting uncomfortable."

I'm hot? He couldn't stop smiling.

"You know," Julie whispered, nodding at Poly. "She doesn't know. About the earrings, or the kiss. I don't even know if she realizes you like Samantha."

Did Poly tell Julie about their time on the blanket? He gazed at Poly's sleeping body. Thoughts of fireflies and her warmth ran through his mind. "Poly's an amazing person. Truly."

"She is," Julie said. "Do not hurt her."

"I won't," Joey said. The thought of hurting Poly seemed impossible. He glanced at her again, curled up on her side. She was the kind of person you'd die to protect.

IN THE MORNING, THEY SHARED some meal bars from their bags.

Joey cleared his throat and spoke up. "We better get moving."

With bags packed and more goop applied to Lucas's leg, they jogged deeper into the forest, following deer trails—at least what he thought were deer trails. Joey hadn't seen one yet. He searched the surrounding forest, looking for a familiar part, something that told him they were not on Ryjack. The wind starting playing with his senses, the sways of branches and rustles of leaves whispered black-mouthed breaths.

As leader of the hike, Hank stopped abruptly. Oblivious to the group halting, Joey bumped into the back of Poly. Grabbing her waist, he pulled her upright and quietly apologized in her ear. She seemed to think it was funny and nudged him with a giggle.

"Look, there's a house over there," Hank whispered.

Joey and Poly froze in their playful back and forth and locked in on the distant small house. Through the trees, Joey made out the thatch roof and plastered walls. He was scanning the area around the house when he saw it. He stumbled backward and pointed at the silver creature hitting the dirt with a long pointed tool.

"There's an Arrack," he whispered, his shaking hand pointing at it. He looked at the gun in his other hand, not remembering pulling it out.

"Oh my god." Poly covered her mouth.

Joey glanced at her and then moved against a tree, pulling her behind him. "I think I can hit it from here." His shaky hand raised the gun and he rested it against the tree, pointing at the silver creature as it swung its tool into the dirt. The Arrack filled the space at the end of his sights. His finger flirted with the trigger. It was a long shot, but he thought he could make it.

A sound emerged from the house behind the Arrack. It turned to face the house when a small Arrack ran into its outstretched arms. Scooping up the small Arrack, it held the child in a long hug.

Joey's mouth hung open and he watched the two Arracks for a second longer before turning back to his friends.

"There are Arracks on this planet." He kept his gun trained on the pair.

"How can that be?" Hank asked and stepped closer, vying for better view of the pair.

"Is that a kid with its parent?" Poly whispered. "Joey, put the gun down. We aren't killing some family."

He complied and stuffed it back in the holster, while keeping an eye on the pair.

"Where did they come from?" Hank asked.

"Look at that house, it's proportioned for them, short doors and windows. Bits to bytes, this is there planet."

"That's crazy—" Hank began to say.

"They have to come from somewhere," Julie interrupted with a bit more volume and Poly shushed her.

Lucas paced with a limp. "Oh great, we get away from freaking zombies and now we are stuck on a planet of Arracks? Why can't we just, for once, land on some Hawaiian Tropic bikini competition island?"

Joey eyed Lucas's leg as he favored it heavily. "This doesn't change the fact we have to get to that master stone. Consider it lucky we found them before they found us." Although, that island Lucas mentioned did sound awesome.

"Joey's right." Julie glanced at the Arrack's house with disgust. "We should get to that stone as fast as we can and get off this planet."

Rubbing his chin, Joey watched the two Arracks walk hand in hand to their house. No daggers hung from their waists, nor did they have three yellow lines on their shoulders. *But* those zombies didn't want to kill us either, until they saw us. These Arracks might change into the crazed killers they'd witnessed in the forest.

"We need to avoid them for as long as we can," Joey said. "Which way, Julie?"

With a task given, she jumped at the chance to use her Panavice. "That way," she pointed past the house.

"We'll find a way around it. Hank, you want to keep leading the way?"

He nodded and headed to the right, deeper into the forest. Poly and Julie followed behind and Joey slowed down to walk next to Lucas.

"How's the limb?"

"Hurts, but I'll manage."

Joey nodded his head and glanced quickly at the bandages wrapped around his leg. Each look sent a jolt of goose bumps through his body. He studied Lucas's face for a second and then looked ahead.

LUCAS HAD BECOME EVERYONE'S SILENT obsession. Normally he would have reveled in the attention, but he was too sick to notice. After several hours, Lucas began favoring his leg heavily, and the red dots on the white bandages had grown to one large red blob. Working a path through the forest was taking a toll on each of them with scrapped arms and legs but most of all it was killing their speed.

Hank slowed to a stop and motioned them to come to him. They kept quiet and moved next to Hank and the dirt path to which he was pointing. Not a deer trail, but a ten-foot wide dirt road with ruts on each side. Joey pushed through the last bush and rubbed his legs. He pulled a few twigs and leaves off his shirt and waited for everyone to get on the road.

"We're never going to make it trudging through the forest like that." Joey lingered his gaze on Lucas. "Let's take the road until sunset. Then, we can make camp in the woods."

"It would save time," Poly agreed, glancing back at the thick forest behind them.

"We're exposed on the road." Julie leaned in close to Joey. "It could be risky."

Joey's wide eyes pointed at Lucas. "We don't have a choice."

Her lips thinned and she nodded.

"Poly, watch our backs, okay?"

She jostled a knife in her hand and nodded. The road stretched deep into the forest in both directions until curving and disappearing into the foliage.

They jogged their way down the road, stopping for water and a snack before starting again. He saw the low sun through the pine trees, there was maybe an hour before darkness. He looked at Lucas's leg for the thousandth time of the day, his bandage red with blood.

Darkness spread over the forest and the night air cooled the sweat on his body. Joey's lungs hurt and his legs ached. He slowed to a walk and Hank stopped, bending over and breathing hard. Joey stopped as well and tried to shake the numb feeling from his legs. Lucas kept his hands on his hips and stared at the dirt road. Hank looked almost as bad as Lucas. He didn't want to push them too far, but with each passing minute, Lucas looked worse. Maybe he could get them to slump along for a bit longer.

"Let's walk for a few more hours," Joey said, looking over his shoulder. They could travel on the road well into the night. The moon gave enough light to see their steps. Everyone agreed to the slow go.

Joey looked to the sky, staring at the stars as they trudged down the road. The big dipper looked just like the one on Earth, or like the one in the simulator with Poly, when the fireflies formed shapes.

Lucas coughed and bent over, grabbing at his leg. "I'm fine. Keep going."

They slowed to a crawl, but kept on for two more hours.

"Let's walk into the forest and make camp," Joey said finally, his stomach growling. He led the way through the forest, struggling to find a path in the dark. Twenty minutes in and he found a clearing large enough to fit them all, and it was behind a small hill of rocks, giving them cover.

Clearing a spot, he watched as Poly created one next to his. He smiled.

"Let's get those bandages changed." Julie sat and opened her bag. Taking the bandages off, the red, swollen leg was exposed. His face lit up in anticipation as she pulled the white jar from the bag. She smeared the cream onto the bite, and Lucas's face relaxed and he let out a long breath. She wrapped fresh bandages around the wound. With her back to Lucas, she showed Joey the near empty jar before stuffing it back into the bag.

A gust of cool air blew over them and sent chills over Joey. The fresh smell and peaceful nighttime noises of forest were in deep contrast the feeling in his gut. If they did get to the stone, he didn't know if Lucas could even be treated. Harris had never mentioned a cure.

Julie stood and scanned the surrounding forest. Joey did the same, but nothing moved in the dark.

His sweaty clothes felt cool with the night air blowing over them. Another chill swept through his body and up his neck. He looked at his friends to make sure nothing went into slow motion. *Where were you, slow-mo, when that zombie bit Lucas?* Joey sat on his pine needle bed, bringing his knees close to his chest.

Silence.

The weight of it all kept the words choked up in his throat. Lucas would usually be the one to break the strange silence. He took a deep breath and let out a slow release, hints of mist floated out from his breath. "Julie, think you can heat up rocks with the laser gun on that thing?" he asked.

Julie stared at him, eyebrows lowered. "Oh, yeah." She slid her fingers over the Panavice and pointed it at a pile of rocks next to them. A red beam shot out, striking the rocks. She spread the beam around the pile until they glowed red.

Joey scooted on the ground, getting close to the warmth. The rest joined in, forming a half-circle around the rocks.

"How's the stub, Lucas?" Hank asked.

Everyone turned to Lucas.

Lucas leaned forward and touched his leg. He swayed a little before his eyes rolled back. Head slumping down, his chin rested on his chest.

"Lucas?" Poly asked.

Joey felt a weight pushing against his chest and a headache building as his blood pressure rocketed. Julie crawled next to him. "He's cold." Whatever color Julie had left her face.

Lucas jumped to his feet and screamed with his hands extended.

Joey feel backward, grabbing for his gun when Lucas pointed and started laughing.

"*Not* funny, Lucas," Julie scolded, holding her chest.

"I'm not freaking dead yet," Lucas said. "But man, you should've seen your faces."

Joey felt as if his heart might explode. He picked his gun off the forest floor and stowed it. Poly kept a stern eye on Lucas as she held a knife in her hand.

Lucas sat back down, proud of his accomplishment. Though after a while, some of the pain showed in his face again, as a red dot formed on his bandage.

They rock-paper-scissored for the first shift—Joey and Poly came up first. Julie heated the rocks again and set up her bed next to Lucas.

After a day of running, the sounds Joey was waiting for came quickly from his friends. They were asleep, and for the first time since under the oak tree, he and Poly were alone. He held out his hands against the heat of the rocks and glanced at Poly. She scooted close against his side and held her hands out next to his.

"This would be pretty cool if we weren't in an Arrack world and if Lucas were better," she said.

"Yeah, and we didn't have some mad man after us."

"Okay, so maybe it's not that cool."

He saw her staring at him from his peripheral vision and kept his eyes forward.

"What do you think's going to happen to us?" Poly asked.

He looked at her face. It amazed him to see the same sweet

note in her eyes, even after what they had seen. He took his hands from the warmth and placed them on his lap. "I don't know. I have no clue what to do." How could he fill in for Harris? He hated every decision he made, thinking it would be their last.

She placed a hand on his knee. "You've been doing great," Poly said.

"Great?" he asked. "Look at Lucas."

"You can't control everything."

Joey stretched his legs forward, feeling the warmth on his feet. "I don't know what we're going to do if something happens to Lucas."

"I think we know what will have to be done," she stated matter-of-factly, looking at the rocks.

Joey swallowed and stared at the side of Poly's face. He did know, but he could never talk about it the way she did. She was right though. It wasn't as if he hadn't thought it a thousand times while looking at Lucas's leg.

"Think they have fireflies here?" she asked, looking in the sky.

He laughed. "I don't know." It was a better subject than the impending doom that was Lucas.

"Julie said this is just another version of Earth. She said if they had the internet, she could probably pin down the exact point in history when this world turned different than ours. The smallest things can change the future in drastic ways. Sometimes for the worse . . ." she said, looking at him, "and other times for the best."

He bumped her shoulder and they both shared a smile. "You know, you're starting to sound like her," Joey said with a smile.

"I'll take that as a compliment."

The full moon stretched over the tops of the pine trees and produced enough light to see all the features of her face. She had such a brightness about her, an infectious spirit. She was pretty, but it was more about her presence—her aura. Being around her, he couldn't help but smile.

"Think there are Earths with no moons?" he asked.

"I think all possibilities are played out, but without a moon, the Earth wouldn't be stable enough for higher evolution." She stared at him with a wicked smile. "Okay, Julie talked about this stuff every night in the bunker. I might have listened to some of it."

He laughed and looked to the moon.

"You should have seen her back there, on the computer system, figuring out how all their stuff works. I don't think she slept for more than a few hours in that place."

"Yeah, well she seems pretty fond of her new toy."

"You have no idea." Poly eyed his body. "Can I see your gun?"

Taken aback by the question, he looked at her. She thrust her hand out. He took one of his guns from its holster, making sure the safety was on, and placed it in her palm. She rubbed the steel barrel and wood grips, inspected the sights, and handed it back to him.

"Just curious," she said. "Guns are barbaric. At least that's what Mom would say."

"What are knives then?"

"I'm not agreeing with her. I just wanted see what one felt like," Poly said. "I've seen you do some amazing things."

With her one eyebrow lifted, he knew she wasn't referring just to his guns.

"Well, anyone can pull a trigger, but how many people can do what you do with those blades?"

Poly pulled a throwing knife from her side and spun it on her fingertip. "Not many."

THEY HEADED OUT IN THE morning at first light, reaching the road as the sun peeked through the trees, casting long shadows over them.

"Should reach it today," Julie exclaimed, looking at her Panavice.

Joey nodded and started the jog down the road. After an hour, he saw Lucas lagging behind. He slowed and alternated from walking and jogging.

"Can we take a water break?" Lucas asked. He gulped down water, letting it spill over his chest. He was getting worse and Joey wasn't sure what to do about it.

Joey drank some water, and looked at the road. It stretched the edges of his vision to see ahead of them—nothing. Turning around, he spotted something far behind them, a horse pulling a cart. The sun would be in the riders face . . . maybe they weren't seen.

"Everyone off the road."

CHAPTER 25

FROM THEIR VANTAGE POINT IN the forest, they could see the Arrack approaching. Lucas, sweating and pale, got his bow out. Poly had a knife in her hand. Joey pulled out his guns.

"It looks like a horse drawn cart," Joey said.

"It could be some harmless traveler," Julie said, not looking up from her Panavice.

"Maybe, but why take a chance?"

They watched as the horse pulled a small cart with an Arrack holding the reigns. The Arrack stared straight ahead and passed by. They lowered their weapons and relaxed.

Making their way back down to the road, they continued on their journey. He tried not to think about the Arrack, but he saw the rest of the group looking over their shoulders.

Halfway into the day, Joey saw a glimmer of something far ahead—something reflecting light. "How much farther is it,

Julie?"

"Two miles, I think," she said, looking at her Panavice.

"I think we should move into the forest," he said.

They headed into the forest and walked parallel to the road. Joey peered through the throng of trees and undergrowth, looking for something out of the ordinary. He stopped about a hundred feet from the end of the forest, green grass spread out for a bit before it ran into a building. The same single story building lined the dirt road for about a half mile. Smoke rose from a few other building's chimneys and several silver figures appeared in the small alleyways between them. It looked like a town out of a Dickens novel. Just replace Tiny Tim with a silver assassin.

"Let me guess, the stone's in that town?" Lucas coughed.

Julie studied her Panavice and nodded her head. "Yep, I think it's in that large orange building in the back of the town."

Joey spotted the building and shook his head. Of course it was. An easy task would have been asking too much. The space between the buildings gave him enough visibility to see the Arracks meandering through the town, kids running by, some of the larger ones carried sacks on their backs. The orange building had several Arracks with the yellow stripes leaning against its orange plaster.

A bird whistled from behind them, but it didn't sound like any bird he knew, too much breath behind it. It sounded human.

They heard the call and a split second later, the forest filled with Arracks surrounding them, pointing daggers at their necks.

Where had they come from?

Joey reached into his holster, but stopped as a dagger closed in on his throat. He scanned his friends and they were all in the same predicament. Three Arracks surrounded Poly and she gave them fiery looks.

Her gaze met his and when he shook his head, her hand moved away from her knives. How could he have missed a group of Arracks directly on top of them? They were out-manned and at a disadvantage. Joey's heart pounded in his chest, but he tried to keep his expression calm.

An Arrack stepped between two others holding knives on Poly and Julie. This Arrack had a large necklace and his yellow eyes stared into Joey's.

"Who are you?" Its voice hissed through pointy teeth.

The thing spoke English. Joey struggled with the shock and answered the question. "Joey Foust."

"You're not in MM uniforms."

Poly crossed her arms, but Joey answered first. "We're not with MM."

The creature's eyes narrowed. "I don't know of any travelers other than MM."

When this one said MM, his eyes narrowed and his lip quivered in disgust. Joey put his hands up and declared, "We just want to use your stone and be on our way."

Another Arrack spoke in a slurred, hissing tongue and the necklace Arrack nodded his head. "We'll take you to Sharati. She'll decide what to do with you."

The necklaced Arrack whistled that same birdcall and pointed to the town. The others thrust their daggers at them, ushering them forward.

Joey counted eleven of them. If he could slow down time,

he could get them out of the situation. He concentrated on the fear and anger building in him. He pushed for the chill, but it wouldn't materialize. He huffed out a breath in frustration. Poly brushed up against him as they walked out of the forest and into the grass field next to the town.

The Arracks herded them across the field and to the back of a large gray building. Hope departed as they reached the door at the back. An Arrack pushed it open and motioned for everyone to enter. Joey stepped in first and saw the four walls with no windows. A door stood on the opposite wall, wedged between thick plastered walls. Hank, Poly, Julie, and Lucas filed in with him and then the Arracks closed the door and left them alone in the small room.

"Great, now we're in jail." Lucas dragged his leg and plopped down on the wooden bench.

"They could have killed us out there," Julie said. "But they didn't."

"For now." Poly flipped a knife in her hand and stared at the door. "I could have taken out a few."

"You're right. I could have taken out three as well. Hank bonks a few with those monkey fists of his and Joey . . . Joey, why the hell are you not going all slow-mo on these things?" Lucas asked.

"I can't just summon it on demand. Don't think I didn't try."

"Oh no, I saw, I thought you were going to mess your pants out there."

"Shut up, Lucas," Julie said. Lucas huffed and stretched out his hurt leg in front of him. Julie tapped the screen on her Panavice. "They left us with our weapons and stuff. Something doesn't feel right."

"Yeah, it doesn't feel right. We're in a freaking Arrack prison. Jeesh, take me back to Ryjack. At least then, I'd be reunited with my peeps." Lucas rubbed the top of his leg.

Julie scowled at him, but didn't tell him to shut up this time. Her face crunched up as her gaze followed his hands massaging his leg.

The door on the inside made a clacking sound as a small window opened. A veiled person stood on the other side of the door, staring in.

"You're not MM." It wasn't a question.

The inside door opened and the Arrack removed her veil, letting it drape over her chest. Her shoulder had the three yellow lines. She stepped into the small cell and kept a hand on the dagger at her hip.

"The question is, who are you and why are you here?" Her voice hissed in its slow delivery. When her gaze paused on Lucas, her eyes narrowed and her fingers tapped on the dagger at her waist.

"We're trying to get away from Simon . . . from MM. We need to get to the stone and get back to where we belong," Joey explained.

"So you're travelers? Which of you can control it?"

Joey shrugged and looked at his friends. "I think we all can."

"Interesting." Her steps slid across the concrete floor, closer to him. "Do you come from the same planet as them? You smell different." She breathed in deep with her nose and her eyes went wide for a split second and then narrowed.

"Yeah, we're all from Earth."

Her face told him she'd never heard of it. "Your type has ruined our kind, so don't think I trust a word you say."

"We're not with MM. We hate them," Poly said.

"Are you Sharti?" Lucas asked and then struggled to keep a straight face.

"Sharati," she corrected. "Yes. Who are you all?"

"Lucas, Hank, Julie, Poly, and I'm Joey."

Sharati moved to the door like liquid in motion. "I used to be an M'arrack. Forced to work for them." Her face contorted with anger. "They used us like objects, sending us to endless worlds, looking for babies. We lost so many."

Joey controlled the emotions building in him and flattened the expression on his face. He didn't want her knowing they were the ones she had looked for. "I'm sorry for your loss, but we have a sick friend and we need to get back home to get him help."

"One of the dead bit you?" she asked.

Lucas nodded his head.

"You'll be dead soon, and after that, you'll be something much worse." She looked at the rest of us. "If you were true friends, you'd kill him before he dies."

Lucas's face went a shade paler and he exchanged worried looks with Joey. Joey shook his head. He would not kill Lucas—he couldn't pull that trigger.

"If we can just get to the stone, we'll be gone, out of your town, off of your world."

"You think you can just come in here and demand things?" Sharati's eyes twitched and her fingertips danced on the dagger at her side. "MM's bound us to a deal." She slapped the shoulder with the three yellow marks. "But that deal is ending soon, and when it does, I'll be searching for the one they call Marcus."

"I'm sorry. I didn't mean to offend you. MM has wronged us as well." He hesitated, not wanting to give any information about being hunted since the day they were born, or how half their parents had been killed.

Sharati's gaze scanned each of them. "I don't know if I believe you. I've been lied to by your kind." She backed up toward the door. He was losing her.

"I know, and while I won't pretend to understand what you have gone through, I want you to know, we're not like them." Joey pulled his gun out. Sharati's hand wrapped around the dagger at her hip and she went into a defensive stance. "This is a gun given to me by my father for my eighteenth birthday. Now it may not seem like a big deal, but this is the first real present he's ever given me. It means more to me than any other object I possess." He held the gun out. "It is loaded and deadly, and I want you to have it."

Sharati took a few hesitant steps and kept her eyes on Joey as her hand pulled the gun out of his.

"It is forbidden for us to have such weapons." She slid her fingers across the barrel of the gun. "I've cleaned many of these, but I've never owned one." Her questioning eyes fixated on Joey's. "Thank you."

"I—"

"No. No more of this talk. I'll give you my decision tomorrow morning." Sharati opened the door and left.

"We may not have—" Julie stopped when the hatch clicked as they locked the closed door.

One gun missing on his right side made him feel lopsided.

He adjusted the strap as he stared at the closed door. Had he done the right thing? Maybe keeping the gun and fighting his way out would have been the smarter thing.

Julie held her Panavice close to her face. "There's not a single MM tech around here. They're off the grid."

Poly stepped next to the door and put her knife next to the door's lock. "I think I can break us out."

"No," Joey said. "These aren't the same kind of Arracks we've dealt with in Preston and elsewhere. These are just a bunch of families, farmers, and stuff. We need to get their trust if we can get into that building."

Their eyes doubted his words, and Poly moved her knife against the door.

He continued. "Yes, we can get through that door and maybe we can get out of this building without any trouble. If we're lucky, we can get across town to the orange building, and find a way to get into it without any problems. And maybe we can handle the dozen guards I bet are in there. Yeah, maybe we can, but with each step toward that building, we are risking one of us being killed. Breaking that door down may lead one of us to our death."

Poly pulled her knife back from the door. "Then what? We stay in here, like caged animals?"

"Yes, and if they try anything tomorrow, that's when we make the move."

"Who says we have a tomorrow?" Lucas laughed and dangled his leg out in front of himself.

"Not funny," Julie said. "Let me get you some new bandages."

Hank plopped the bag next to Julie.

Poly sheathed her knife. "If anything bad happens, you kill

that Sharati chick first, she's dangerous."

THE WINDOWLESS ROOM MADE IT hard to tell what time it was, but the hatch around the door let in a few pinpoints of light and after a while, those lights disappeared. Julie kept them entertained with quiz games and such, all stored in her Panavice. The games were a great distraction from thinking of Sharati's plans.

Shortly after dark, the door slid open a foot and an Arrack pushed a tray of food into the room. Hank rushed to it and picked it up. Mostly bread and a chili of sorts spread around in small bowls. Joey took one taste of it, but the stringy, white meat made him stick to the bread.

They rock-paper-scissored once again for who got the first shift. Feeling beat, Joey felt good about losing. He wanted to sleep, even on the concrete floor. He felt weary in every way. The conversation died off and slumber set in.

The door flung open and hit the wall. Joey jolted from his sleep and jerked his gaze at the open door with Sharati standing in it. Her eyes were wide and filled with urgency as she rushed toward them. His gun dangled from her hip.

CHAPTER 26

"THEY ARE COMING FOR YOU," Sharati said.

"Oh my god," Julie said, clutching her Panavice near her face. "I'm getting a hit from another Panavice, maybe a mile out."

"You turned us over to them?" Joey jumped to his feet, anger filling his head.

"No, we agreed to grant you your request, but someone must have seen you and turned you in." Sharati held the door open and motioned for them to come out.

They left the small room and entered what looked like an office. An Arrack stood behind a desk with his arms crossed. They passed by his desk to another door. Sharati opened the door and the cool night air rushed in with hints of burning oil. A small army of Arracks stood at the ready, many holding small wooden torches.

The yellow flames danced across their silver skin. They fanned out from the open door, like a rainbow of assassins blocking any chance they had for escape. Joey grabbed for his gun; he'd kill them all if it would give his friends a chance to escape. He took a step toward the door and Sharati placed a hand on his chest.

"They are here to help us." Sharati hissed out her words. She whistled two quick notes.

In one motion, all the Arracks turned their backs on the door.

"I don't understand," Joey said. Having the Arracks on his side felt as if he'd missed something important.

"We know who you are. Every M'arrack worth her narash does. It took me a second, but I smelled it on you. You're one of those babies—all grown up."

Frozen in shock, Joey closed his mouth and stared at Sharati. "Shouldn't you hate us?"

"He needs you," she hissed. "We believe he may die if he doesn't get you. You are the best chance we have of getting out of our agreement with Marcus." Sharati stepped in the doorway and the Arracks spread out from her. She motioned for them to follow. "We need to move."

"Why not just kill us?" Julie said and then covered her mouth with her hand. Joey had asked the same question of Harris, but never told them about that conversation.

"What do you think we are, soulless monsters?" Sharati stepped outside.

Joey ushered Poly and Julie past the door. "Keep your bow out. If Simon's here, we need to be ready."

Lucas's pale face nodded in response. Even in the cool

night, sweat formed on his forehead. Joey rushed out of the building. The whole group of torch-wielding Arracks moved with them down the dirt road.

A horn blew.

Sharati's attention jerked in that direction. "He's here." She whistled.

The Arracks grunted and moved faster, keeping a tight circle around them. They moved at the eye of the storm, surrounded by a hurricane of silver bodies. He held out his gun, searching the darkness over the heads of the Arracks. Poly stuck to the edge of the eye, holding a throwing knife. Lucas moved along in a skip, trying to keep weight off his one leg.

"He's getting closer." Julie stared at her screen, jogging near the center.

The sound of gunfire echoed on the other side of town— several quick shots and then silence. He was close. Joey gripped his gun and stared ahead as more shots sounded. The shots didn't seem to bother the Arracks.

"Let's run," she ordered. Sharati whistled in two quick bursts.

The Arracks jumped into a run. They kept pace, but Lucas grunted. Hank sidled up next to him, grabbed his arm and helped him run with the group.

"We're heading toward him," Julie said.

He barely heard her over the clatter of feet and rustle of weapons, but knowing the direction they were taking, he searched for an escape path through the Arracks. They might have been ten deep around him and kept shoulder to shoulder.

More cracks of gunfire sounded, and closer.

An Arrack watched the group moving down the dirt road.

She scooped up the child at her side and ran into a house. The flickering lights inside the houses went out and the last few remaining Arracks on the street rushed into their homes as they passed.

Ahead, Joey spotted the orange building. He slowed a step when he looked past that and saw another mob of Arracks swirling around a tall man with a gun.

"Simon," Julie said.

A few Arracks shoved him forward and he stumbled before gathering back into a run.

Sharati blew out three whistles.

A few rows of Arracks peeled off from their group and ran ahead, holding out their daggers. He and his friends weren't going to make it to the orange building, unless that small group slowed Simon's group. Joey pointed his gun out, hoping to help in some way, but the risk was too great.

His watched as Simon fired onto the approaching force. The front few skid to a stop on the dirt, but it didn't stop their collision with Simon's group. Simon fired into the fray, striking as many of his own Arracks as the others.

But the small attack worked. Simon's group stopped to handle the assault. Joey whispered a silent thank you before running into the back of an Arrack. His group had stopped at the stairs leading into the orange building.

"Into the building." Sharati ran to the front door of the orange warehouse.

Two wide wooden doors were their only way in. A bullet slammed into the wood door over Sharati's head. She didn't flinch. Behind them, clashes of steel filled the dark, dirt street.

Sharati opened the doors and they fell into the building.

The rest of the Arracks stood at the door as Sharati closed it. The thump and latch echoed through the insides of the large, vacant building.

He searched for the stone protruding out of the ground.

"Where is it?" Julie asked.

"This way." Sharati jogged toward the back of the building and into the shadows.

Darkness concealed the size of the building but their heavy breaths and steps on the stone floor bounced off distant, unseen walls.

The doors behind them rattled as something slammed into it. Joey jumped at the sound. Julie used her Panavice to shine light back at the double door. It vibrated again, dust falling from the edges. Gunfire peppered around the handle, but the locks held. Joey wondered for how much longer.

"Here it is. Down here." Sharati stood near three doors and grabbed the handle of the far right door, swinging it open. Julie's Panavice lit the stone steps leading down.

"It's at the bottom." Sharati pointed.

Julie darted downstairs with Hank carrying Lucas behind her. Poly touched Joey's shoulder as she passed and headed down the steps.

"Thank you," Joey said to Sharati. He searched for better words, but everything seemed insignificant for what they were contributing.

"Here, take this back." She extended the gun to him. "It was an honor to hold onto it, if only for a bit."

He took it and nodded.

They continued to pound on the front door. He wasn't sure where the other two doors led, but he didn't want to see her get shot down by Simon. Enough lives had been lost on account of him and his friends already.

"Why don't you come with us?"

She looked confused and glanced at the door to the left. "This human shouldn't even be here. I don't have anything to run from."

"He'll kill you."

"We all die." Sharati took a step back and slammed the door.

Joey ran down the steps, breathing in the stale air as it poured out of the cave opening. He stepped into the dome as Julie focused her light on the stone in the center of the room. He breathed in a sigh of relief, actually seeing the stone. With one thing cleared from his mind, he marched back to the stairs and leaned at the wall next to the first step, peering past the edge.

The double-wide door that had been keeping Simon at bay finally succumbed and crashed down. He glanced back at his friends and they were all looking his way. Simon was coming.

Joey gripped his gun, feeling the smooth rosewood and eyeing the sights at the opening at the top of the stairs. He'd take out a few and buy some time for his friends.

"Lucas, can you get us out of here?" Joey whisper-yelled.

Lucas limped around the stone, wiping the sweat from his face. A yellow stain covered his bloody bandage. Joey gritted his teeth at the new color and told himself it was probably from the exertion or sweat of the run. He kept his attention on the top of the stairs.

"This is different. I'm not sure about this," Lucas said as he moved his hands around the stone.

Joey bit his lip and glanced from Lucas to the stairs. *Come on Lucas, we don't have time.*

The door above crashed open. Joey controlled his breathing and held his gun against the wall, steadying it. He lined up the sights to the top of the stairs. If Simon peeked his pinky out, he would lose it.

At the top of the stairs, a black jacket appeared. He pulled the trigger, striking the jacket. Puffs of cotton stuffing flew out and the stick holding the jacket moved out of sight. Joey sighed and adjusted his stance.

"Is that you down there, Joey? Or maybe you sent the girl to try to kill me. Or is it the big, dumb animal, Hank?" Simon laughed.

Joey didn't respond. He didn't have a shot, and even if he did, he didn't think it would get past Simon's personal shield. What he needed was time.

"I can hear your breathing, Joey. I bet you have your hand on that gun right now. Your dad give you those guns?"

"Why don't you come into the hallway and find out?" Joey taunted.

"There he is. Listen, there's something we need from you. We own it. We made it and I intend on getting it back," Simon threatened, voice screeching at the end. He seemed to collect himself and started again in a calmer voice. "I only want you, Joey. The others are just a bonus, but if you come up right now and surrender to me, I won't bother your friends or family ever again. They can all go back to their lives."

He searched the faces looking at him. The soft glow of the Panavice was enough to see they all wore the same expression. Hank shook his head as if to make sure Joey understood. He didn't want to hurt his friends and everywhere he took them put them at risk. The idea of ending it was intoxicating. Maybe he should go with Simon and end it for the rest of them. Poly's hand touched his wrist.

Simon's voice floated down the staircase again. "Last chance, if you portal off right now, I'll follow."

"Good luck with that, jerkwad," Poly spat.

Simon laughed.

Joey frantically glanced to each of his friends. All he needed was a nod, something to tell him to do it and he would walk up those stairs.

Poly whispered in his ear, "You better not let this guy get into your head for one second. You're not going anywhere." She gripped his wrist hard.

"I think I've got it . . . or something close," Lucas said.

"Poly dear, is that you?" Simon asked. "I have a present for you," Simon entered the hallway, fired a shot and stepped back. Stunned at the speed of it all, Joey moved back but felt Poly's grip loosen around his wrist.

Poly groaned as she clutched her arm, blood seeping through her fingers and running down her sleeve. Julie ran to Poly and grabbed her arm.

"That one is on you, Joey," Simon said.

Joey fired into the stairwell, emptying his cylinders. He reached into his jacket and pulled out the explosive Harris gave him, tossed it into the stairs, and pulled the steel door close. It would blow in ten seconds.

"We need to go now!" Joey screamed.

The soft hum emanated from the room and everything went black. He knew Lucas had found another location. The dirty, musty smell let him know they were in another cave. Julie lit up the room with her Panavice.

Joey rushed to Poly's side, being careful of her bleeding arm as he hugged her against his chest, kissing her head. "I'm so sorry."

Her tears soaked into his shirt.

"You didn't shoot me," Poly said.

"I shouldn't have let him get that shot off." Joey shook his head and swore under his breath. He would've taken the deal in a second, if he thought he could have prevented Poly from getting hurt.

"What's that box next to the door?" Hank asked.

A small metal box sat near the door with a row of numbers on the top, counting down. The first number stopped on zero and the box purred with power and vibrated on the floor. The noise grew louder with each passing second. Another number stopped on zero, only four numbers remained.

"Some kind of countdown," Julie said. "Simon must have thrown it in here at the last second."

"Where are we?" Hank asked.

Lucas threw his arms up. "I don't know. I thought we were going to the bunker."

"The doors are locked from the outside," Hank reported as he pushed on the steel door.

"We need to get out of here," Julie warned. Another number on the box went to zero and the humming grew louder.

"Can you get us to another stone, Lucas?" Joey asked.

"I was only taught a few locations and the last one was back on Harris's world, the bunker."

The sound from the box revved, squealing with a mechanical noise. The box vibrated against the stone floor, kicking up small puffs of dust around it. Another number zeroed out, only two more left.

Hank pounded his foot at the steel door. "It won't budge."

Joey pushed Poly back so he could see her face. "How are you doing, Poly?" Joey asked, letting go of her and inspecting her arm. It bled on both sides of her bicep; at least the bullet went through.

She lifted her arm, gawking at it with glazed eyes. "I don't know." She swayed and Joey held her up.

"She might be going into shock," Julie said, staring at the countdown box. "Get us out of here, Lucas!"

Lucas moved his hands around the stone. The soft hum filled the room and the room became bright with light.

CHAPTER 27

THE ROOM FILLED WITH THE smell of recycled air. Joey squinted against the onslaught of light filling the room. The noise of people talking and cars moving by drowned out the humming from the box. A glass dome, much larger than anything he had seen before, soared hundreds of feet over his head. Twisted and fantastic skyscrapers towered above the glass.

A woman arguing brought his attention to the line of people nearby. Two guards moved their hands in a defensive manner, as a woman in a purple dress with her hands on her hips yelled at them. She gazed up and made eye contact with Joey. He made out the words as she pointed at them.

"They're allowed in and I'm not?"

Joey held Poly closer, as the men turned to face them.

"Hey!" the guards yelled and jumped from their seats. They pulled out square guns, an electrical type of gun Joey had seen in training simulations, and ran toward them. Joey held his gun in his free hand. He didn't want to kill anyone, but another number zeroed on the steel box. Only one left. He figured he had twenty seconds before it counted down. He looked to Poly with her wounded arm and Lucas, who struggled to stand straight; they were all going to die if he didn't do something.

He controlled his rapid breathing and felt the chill at the back of his neck flow over his body. Things slowed down. The scrolling numbers slowed to a crawl. He watched as the eight turned to a seven. The guards froze in a run, pointing their guns at him, and his four friends were all staring at the box. He had seconds to make the right decision, to get them to safety. Looking around, he found the back door on the opposite side of the dome from the guards.

He picked up Poly, carried her to the back door, and pushed on it—locked. He placed her next to the door and ran back to grab Julie. Lucas wasn't as easy, and Hank took everything Joey had left.

Muscles burning, he fell to the ground and the sounds crashed back. His insides wanted to come out, but he willed them to stay put, with great effort. Sweat poured from his face and he struggled to get to his feet, wiping his mouth.

His friends, confused, looked around at their new location. The last circle disappeared, the box vibrated on the floor and the guards slid to a stop.

"Bomb!" one guard yelled, running in the other direction.

The box clattered against the floor. Julie pressed her hands over her ears and then it went silent and still.

The bomb exploded with a bright, white light. The sound hit them like a shockwave and blew them back against the glass.

Joey fell to the floor after hitting the glass wall. The guards and some others unlucky enough to be next in line were on the ground, one struggling to get to his feet. Joey's ears rang and he touched Poly's shoulder. She looked up at him, terrified. The rest of his friends were on his other side. They'd all made it. He let a brief moment of relief enter his heart before he heard the noise—glass cracking.

Spider cracks ran up the glass wall to the ceiling, making a crunching sound. He followed the fractures as they splintered off the main fissures into a million tiny ones. These ran all the way to the top of the glass dome, small pieces were falling like snowflakes.

"We need to get out—" Julie words stopped as the glass above shattered, raining chunks of glass. Joey moved over Poly, covering her. He felt a few shards slice his back open, and warm blood trickled down into his pants. Julie screamed as a piece of glass stuck out of the top of her shoulder. Lucas hobbled next to her and pulled it out. She winced and gripped the wound. Bits of glass continued to fall as the entire dome shattered.

Joey grabbed the door handle—still locked.

"Hank, we need this door opened." Urgency flooded his tone.

Hank stood in front of the door and kicked at the handle. It flung open and more shards dropped around him as Hank shot out of the dome. Lucas and Julie ran right behind him. The sounds of the city burst through the open door. The cacophony of cars, music, and hovering crafts filled Joey's ringing ears. He helped Poly through the door and out to the alley behind the dome.

In the distance, sirens from emergency vehicles closed in on them. He had no idea where to go, but opposite the direction of sirens made sense. He looked back into the chaos of the dome. Purses littered the floor, people yelled while shoving and pushing each other to the ground, guards attempted to usher everyone to safety. He sighed, hoping everyone would make it out alive. After all, they had brought the bomb to them—even if it wasn't their bomb.

"We're in Vanar. I recognize some of these buildings from scenes Almadon had me do." Julie gazed at the skyscrapers towering above. "We're in MM territory."

"Great, any more good news?" Lucas said.

"Come on. We better get away from here." Joey scanned the sky. Some of it did look familiar. *Holy hell.* Out of all the places they could have gone.

The backs of businesses passed by, as they ran down the alley. Most had small signs displaying their wares. A man with a cigarette in his mouth, dressed in clothes resembling a chef's uniform, appeared from the back door of one. He dumped out a bucket of dirty water as they came near. The smell of bleach filled the alleyway. When the chef made notice of them, he dropped the bucket and went back into his store.

Joey took inventory of his friends. Poly had turned almost as pale as Lucas had, and was clutching her bloody arm. Blood streaked down the front of Julie's shirt. No wonder the man ran back into his store, they were a walking horror movie. Joey frantically looked for something to help him—no 911, no hospital, no Harris. He didn't know a soul here, and his friends needed help.

"Keep pressure on it, Poly," Julie said.

She nodded and squeezed her arm, wincing as she tried to

keep pace. He tried not to stare at Poly's arm for too long, the site sent him into vertigo. He blinked hard and concentrated, trying to figure out a way around the impossible. First thing, he needed to get out of the alley and get to a place where he might be able to help his injured friends.

They passed a building with a door covered in old, cracked plastic with a faded *Do Not Enter* sign. Joey grabbed at the plastic and broke it. He kicked the rest of the plastic down and entered the building.

Dim light snuck in, enough to see the tables and chairs filling the room. Thin pipes hugged the walls on all sides, with hoses sticking out at regular intervals. Many had signs like *Rose*, *Cinnamon*, and *Chocolate* overhead. He pulled a chair from the table and spun it on its leg.

"Poly, take a seat and let's look at that," Julie said, clutching her shoulder. Joey followed her moves, staying a foot behind.

"You're bleeding too, Julie," Poly said, as if noticing for the first time.

"Let's get you buttoned up first," Julie said. "And back off, Joey, you're freaking me out."

Joey took a half step back, waiting for the second he could help.

Poly sat in the chair, holding her arm and breathing fast. The pain in her face hit him in the gut, hard.

"We need to cut the sleeve off," Julie said.

"Can I borrow a knife?" Joey asked the patient.

Poly smiled. "Make sure I get it back." She produced a knife from somewhere in her outfit and handed it to him.

He slid the blade under the cuff of her shirtsleeve. The shirt was thick, but the knife sliced through it with ease. He peeled the sleeve back, exposing the wound. She watched his face as he stared at it. *Keep strong for her.*

"Ah, it's not that bad," Joey said.

The bullet went in one side and left a hole, but where it exited, produced damage that made him struggle to stand.

"Liar," Poly said and smiled.

"I'm getting dizzy," Julie said, leaning forward.

Hank moved over to help her stay up and she wobbled in his arms. The sounds of vomit splashing the floor drew Joey's attention to Lucas. He hunched over on the floor near the back of the store, heaving. Lucas couldn't even look up to see Julie limp in Hank's arms. His pale face had turned a shade of gray and Joey gritted his teeth, fighting his attention between each of his friends. They were in serious trouble and he had no idea what to do. His friends were dying.

The weight of everything crashed against Joey. He moved his hand over his face, pushing against his eyeballs. He wanted to cry, he wanted to help, he wanted to make everything go away. Taking a deep breath, he met Hank's steely gaze. A nod from his friend forced him to face the situation.

Julie propped herself back up and wiped her hair back from her face. Joey didn't think she notice Lucas on the floor behind them yet and he didn't plan on pulling her attention away from Poly. If something happened to Lucas . . . he'd be the one to deal with it.

"You can do this." Joey refocused and hunched next to Julie.

"I can do this." Julie sounded as if she was convincing herself. She pulled out a small tub of the white paste she used on Lucas.

Scrapping the bottom, she dabbed a bit onto her own wound first, then went to Poly and pushed the cream into her wound. Poly winced, but Julie moved Poly's arm and pressed the remaining liquid on the other side. The pain in Poly's face diminished and Julie placed a pad on each side of the arm and wrapped tape around it.

"She might be losing too much blood." Julie swayed. "I'm not feeling too hot myself." She swayed again and Hank held her steady.

His friends stared at him in silence. Tears pooled in Julie's eyes. Poly slumped in her chair, and Lucas stood above his puke and leaned on the table.

"I'm not feeling too good, guys," Lucas groaned, wiping his mouth. "I think I should just get away from you all before something bad happens."

"Lucas, you're not going anywhere without us," Hank said.

Joey took a deep breath and knew this was the end. If he didn't give in now, his friends were going to die. He'd have to put out a hand for help and hope it didn't get bit.

"Julie, can you find a hospital on your Panavice?" Joey directed.

She jumped when he said her name, but was quick to pull out her Panavice and search. Her mouth opened and she held her Panavice up so he could see the screen.

The top of the screen read *Wanted: Terrorists*. Below were close-ups of their faces, and at the end, a reward of $100,000. There must have been cameras at the dome.

"Can you get past that wanted screen?" Joey asked.

"Yep." She zipped her finger around the screen and the soft glow of the Panavice lit up her pale face as she pushed through the pages of screens.

"There's a hospital, I think, half a mile from here." She pointed out the boarded up front door.

Joey turned back to Poly, her face turned up at the ceiling, eyes closed. His heart stopped as he grabbed her wrist to find her heartbeat.

"We need to take her, now." He grabbed her waist to pick her up, when Hank put a hand on his arm.

"Let me carry her. It'll be faster," Hank said.

Joey nodded and faced Julie and Lucas. "Can you guys walk?"

"Yeah," they said in unison, but Lucas held onto his stomach and gazed at the floor. He looked wet with sweat and his eyes seemed different, as if some of the light had left them.

Hank picked Poly up like a child. Her arms flopped around Hanks back, one red with blood. They left out the back door into the alley. Joey peered down the alley and heard boots stomping in their direction and the sounds of radios buzzing with talk. He didn't have time for a showdown with the authorities here. All he needed to do was get to the doors of the hospital; they'd have to take them. He shot a look at Julie, begging for the directions.

"It's this way," Julie said, looking at her Panavice.

Joey ran down the alley and turned a corner before he slammed on his brakes and scurried back behind the corner. There were two black cars with flashing lights parked in the alley. He held out his arm, stopping his friends. Looking around, he saw a door marked with a marionette. Lucas hung on Julie as they caught up.

"Through here," Joey said, opening the wood door.

Stuffed bears and boxes of action figures filled the stock room before he entered the back of a toy store. To his surprise, it was similar to the one in the scene generator back at the bunker. He walked past the play swords and toy farms, striding to the front door. He looked back at Hank holding Poly, her head flopping around as he trotted through the store. Julie, panic spread across her face, held Lucas up as he stumbled past a group of metal chirping birds.

The shopkeeper got off his chair from behind the counter, raising an arm, and opened his mouth. He locked eyes with Joey and collapsed back in his chair, mouth still open. The TV on the wall behind the shopkeeper showed their faces on a newsreel.

A group of black uniformed men ran by the storefront windows. Joey ducked behind a stack of board games, watching them run by the front door. They were closing in on them. He felt claustrophobia weighing down on him.

Is the room getting smaller?

Joey felt dizzy. He needed to get out of there. His friends needed help, or they weren't going to make it. He concentrated on slowing down time but the chills never came. He clinched his fist and made eye contact with Hank. "I don't know what to do."

"If Harris were here, he'd know what to do," Lucas said, coughing into his shirt. His face poured with sweat and his skin had a hint of gray pigment.

"You're with Harris, Harris Boone?" the storekeeper asked.

"We *were* with him," Joey said.

"Oh no. Listen . . . We might only have seconds before they're here," the shopkeeper rushed to say. "They're going to take you, but I'll do what I can to see that Harris knows what happened to you. If I'd known you weren't terrorists, I would've never called it in."

Joey turned to the window to see what he feared. Black-uniformed men filled every visible space of the front windows, staring into the store. He heard a rustle in the back and saw black helmets over the aisles of toys, making their way into the store.

Lucas stumbled away from Julie, grabbing a spinning display of action figures, pulling it to the ground as he fell on his face. The toys crashed down around him. Julie fell to her knees, screaming as she shook his limp, gray body on the floor.

Was Lucas dead?

"Lucas!" Julie stopped pushing him and her bloodshot eyes connected with Joey.

He took a step toward them, fighting the tears welling in his eyes. Seeing his friend motionless on the floor was more than he could bear. His heart hurt and all rational thought flew out the window. He didn't know what to do. He turned to Hank. Hank's closed eyes didn't see Joey's plea for help. Joey stepped closer to Hank and saw his mouth move then he heard "Dear Lord. . . ."

Poly's limp body dangled from Hank's arms, blood dripping off her fingertip. He touched her cold hand. *How much blood could she lose?* Her blood smeared on his hands. It was a fitting end; her blood was on his hands. All of their blood was. Every misstep he made, led them to this toy store. He turned to the wall of men at the storefront. He concentrated, trying to slow things down. His body shook from the effort.

He yelled with his shaking fists and felt tears run down his face. They had lost; everything was for nothing. Joey fell to his knees and tossed his guns to the floor. He raised his hands as a small ball skipped on the floor near him. He knew they'd all be dead in seconds. This was the end, death by a grenade. He gazed up at Poly's face. He wanted it to be the last thing he saw. Her hair dangled over her face, but he still made out the shape of her nose and those lips.

"I'm sorry," he whispered.

An electrical bolt shot from the ball in all directions, striking him in the abdomen. His body went limp, crashing to the floor. He kept his eyes open long enough to see black boots stomping around him.

CHAPTER 28

"DID YOU DISPOSE OF THE bombs?" Harris asked.

"Yeah," Compry answered.

The Arracks had left bombs throughout the bunker when they left, leaving Compry and Almadon to diffuse them. With any luck, they never knew the kids were here.

Harris stared at the screens in front of him. News lines from around the world scrolled through at a rapid rate. He frowned at the information. It had been days since the kids left for Earth.

Well, they *should've* been back on Earth, but something had gone wrong. The video showed Lucas typing in a different location. Now they could be a million different places. *Were they ready for this?* He felt a hand on his shoulder and looked at Compry's painted nails. Her comforting face did little to slow down his heart. *If Simon got to them first . . .* No, he wouldn't allow the thought. The kids were smart and wouldn't let it get to that.

"They're out there somewhere. We'll find them," Compry said. "Or they'll find us."

The cleared bunker provided him with a safe option for now. The upper floors were hit badly, but most of it was still in operating condition. Smoke hung in the air, and an occasional warning over the intercom about a fire were the main reminders of the attack.

Harris lingered on the screen, showing the bunker's Alius stone. He kept a hand over a button in preparation of an attack, or the appearance of the kids.

The steel door behind him creaked open. Due to the strain of the attack, the structure of the bunker had weakened in many places, leaving some of the doors harder to open and close.

"Any news?" Almadon asked.

He shook his head and watched the screens. *Come on, guys. Get to a stone and head back here.*

"The craft is ready for launch, Harris," Almadon said.

He knew the craft was ready, but without the right passengers, he didn't plan on using it. He could not abandon them to Simon. He wouldn't let Simon use these kids for his sick purposes. He gave Almadon a nod and she stood behind him and Compry, joining them at the screens.

They couldn't stay here long, not anymore. Simon would figure out the bombs had not gone off and would be back. He felt a touch on his shoulder again.

"I won't leave until we find them again," Compry said.

He knew she'd stay with him until the end. If Arracks swarmed the building and flooded each room, she'd be at his side. He placed his hand over hers.

The door opened fast and the sound of it hitting the wall was loud in the steel room. Harris spun out of his chair with gun in hand. At the end of his sights stood Nathen. He still had his arm bandaged from a bad wound he sustained defending the bunker.

"You need to turn on the world broadcast channel," Nathen stammered out.

Harris hit a button and the screen changed from the scrolling text to newscasters. He turned the volume up.

"Breaking news, a terrorist attack at Capital's museum leaves downtown in chaos. Those responsible are still at large."

The all-too familiar faces of the kids popped on the screen. Harris leaned closer. He saw Poly's bleeding arm. They all looked terrified, except Joey, who had a determined look on his face. He figured the newscaster had selected each of the pictures for maximum effect to make them look like criminals.

"There is a reward of a hundred thousand dollars for any information leading to the capture of these terrorists."

The screen changed to a live, hovering shot over the museum dome. The broken glass on the floor the museum shimmered in the lights.

"If we're seeing this, it may be possible Simon's seeing this as well," Compry said.

He needed to get to the kids before Simon did, or worse, MM's police.

"Here's some strange surveillance video, taken moments before the explosion," the reporter said.

The video showed the kids appearing at the Alius stone and Harris cringed at the sight of Poly grabbing her bleeding arm. Lucas didn't look right, either. A familiar small box sat at the edge of the circle—a bomb. Then, suddenly, each of the kids disappeared.

The reporter talked over the video. "Slowing the video down, we can see one of them moving at what appears to be near the speed of light as he moved his fellow terrorists out of the bomb's path." The camera changed back to the reporter.

"This is another obvious terrorist attack from Mutant Isle. We must put the right to exterminate all inhabitants of Mutant Isle on the ballot."

Harris had seen enough. Capture was imminent in a city they didn't know, without any friends. He'd have to get his team ready for an attack.

"Let's get on the craft and get to Capital," Harris said.

He watched as they all stood and walked toward the door without hesitation, all but Compry. She took a step toward him, her eyebrows crunched with her questioning face. He always liked that look. The others stopped at the door.

"You think this is smart, going to Capital?" Compry stopped a few feet in front of him.

Harris stood from his chair, the warm feeling of watching Compry walk toward him went cold as he thought about the results the last time they went to Capital.

"Is this any less urgent than last time? We may even get to them first." He knew the chances were slim, but Marcus did miss stuff on occasion.

"My sister died last time, and many others."

Harris rubbed his bare ring finger. They had both lost someone that day.

"Is it worth it?" She pinched her facial features again.

He took a while to respond, searching his mind for the answer. He would give his life to save others he cared for, but he didn't think he could give the life of others. He had given far too many and each memory weighed on him, as if their souls were attached to him; they were his responsibility. "It is, and if something goes wrong, we can always blow the kids up."

Compry raised an eyebrow at Harris's words.

"It better not come to that." Compry paused. "How are we going to get in?"

"We're going to have to land a district over, if we have any chance of making it in," Nathen said.

"Trade district will be the fastest. We can get the papers and tags we need," Almadon said.

Harris nodded. It would take a day or two to cross the many layers of security. With each layer, there stood a chance a guard would take a second look; with each glance, there was a chance he would have to kill someone.

CHAPTER 29

JOEY STARTLED AWAKE. HE OPENED his eyes and saw nothing but white. He realized it was a dream, yet his heart raced and sweat beaded on his face. He tried moving his head to see more of the white room, and couldn't. Maybe he was still dreaming.

Attempting to wipe the sweat from his eyes, his arm wouldn't move. He tried to look, but could only move his eyes. He saw his arms strapped to a chair. His feet, locked down as well. Joey couldn't see it, but he now realized there was a strap across his forehead, locking it to the back of the chair. Nothing blocked his voice and he wondered if he screamed aloud while dreaming because his throat felt raw.

He looked around the room the best he could. The walls were white, and a door sat directly across the room. Squeezing his eyes closed, he tried to remember how he got there. The cloudy thoughts raced through his mind: guns, zombies, deserts, and heat. It was fuzzy, but it seemed important. *There is something I need to remember. . . .*

He felt panic building—something was missing. Not being able to move his body started to make him crazy. He felt as if the room was closing in on him and he was helpless to protect him and his friends. *Friends!* He was here with his friends. He remembered Poly, Lucas, and the others—what they had all endured . . . and Samantha.

The door opened. A man in a white, long jacket with an oak tree on the chest, walked in, carrying a thin screen. He noticed Joey and smiled. "Oh good, you're awake," the doctor said.

"Where are my friends?" he asked, shaking his body in futility. "Tell me!"

"Well, you and your friends are being held here for the safety of the people."

He remembered a toy store. Fighting Poly with foam swords, as she easily beat him in their friendly battle.

"Where is Poly? Is she okay?" he demanded.

The doctor smiled. "Now which one is she? The one with a gunshot wound?" The man raised his eyebrows.

"Yes."

The doctor wrote on his screen. "She's fine, although some of my nurses cut themselves on the knife collection she had on her. So, her name is Poly?" he verified as he wrote on his screen.

Joey's eyes widened and he bit his lip. He didn't want to give the man any more information about his friends. Panic bubbled up and made him dizzy. He blinked, trying to stay alert. His heart raced and sweat dripped into his eyes, making them sting. He struggled against the tight straps, but they didn't move. *How did he get here?*

"You don't look too good," the doctor said.

He felt a hand touching his neck.

"Your heartbeat is at a dangerous level. I'm going to give you a sedative."

He barely felt the sting in his neck.

CHAPTER 30

JOEY FELT A NEEDLE GLIDE out of his neck and the room popped into vivid detail. He'd never been so awake. He felt the smooth metal chair with his fingertips. The ceiling lights flickered. The toy shop crashed into his thoughts. His friends were dying. He remembered his last thoughts before the explosion. Who were the three people in front of him? He listened to their conversation.

"Oh yes, he'll be alert for a while. Although, I'll have to monitor his heart rate to make sure he doesn't go into cardiac arrest," the doctor stated.

"Fine. Now leave us," some woman ordered. She wore a black jacket with a tight, dark gray button-up shirt underneath. A gun stuck out from her hip, next to a badge attached to her belt.

The doctor left the room and a heavyset man sat on the

doctor's chair as he cleaned his fingernails. Joey saw the shape of a gun through his black jacket. *Cops or detectives of some sort.*

"I'm Unitas and this is my partner, Larry." The woman pointed to the portly guy in the corner. "We need to talk to you about what happened at the museum." She smiled, but not the kind of smile Joey got from Poly. This smile made him squirm in his seat.

Museum? She must be talking about the Alius stone. He remembered slipping with Poly's name and steeled himself not to repeat his mistake. Joey pushed his lips together and said nothing.

She paced in front of him. "You know, I have been an officer of the law for a long time. Don't go thinking I started here. No, no . . . I had to work and *claw* my way into Capital."

She stopped and took on a big smile, full of pride and teeth. "You know how many terrorists have gotten through my walls, my check points, and facial recognition?" She raised an eyebrow, but Joey kept silent. "None. And now, I have a mere kid strapped into a chair in front of me, and I know just by looking in your eyes, you weren't the one to organize this. You weren't the one to fund this. So I have to ask, who did?"

Unitas moved closer and Joey tried to move back from her advance.

"Silence then, that's fine." She shrugged. "You know, your friends are talking right now. The first person to tell us about the whole operation will get a deal."

"Better take the deal, kid," Larry said through a yawn, leaning back in the chair.

Joey thought of Simon's deal and pushed the thought from

his mind. She said his friends were talking. They were alive. It was the only information he wanted.

Unitas frowned at Larry, and then returned her attention to Joey. He swallowed, feeling like a mouse stuck in a glue trap.

"You're the mutant with the speed, right? I watched video of you moving your friends away from the bomb. Some are even calling you a hero. But you know what I think?" She moved closer to his face. "You're cowards. You and the others from Mutant Isle, thinking the city is the cause of your problems." She huffed, rolling her eyes.

"I didn't come from Mutant Isle."

"He speaks. Oh joy," she said, clapping her hands in fake excitement. "So where would a strange group of people like you come from then?" She batted her eyes and held her hands under her chin, staring at him.

Harris mentioned the island once before, some sort of place for Marcus to send his failed experiments. *Was he a mutant?*

"Arrack," Joey said. It was the last place he came from. Did people know about other planets like Arrack?

Larry, sighing, pulled a Panavice from his jacket pocket and let out a long breath as he moved his fingers across his screen. "Nope, no such place."

"Don't lie to me," she said. "I don't like when people lie to me."

"That bomb wasn't even ours. We were trying to get away from it." Joey struggled with the straps.

They both laughed. Joey wasn't sure what was so funny.

"Oh man, you've got to be more original," Larry said. "I suppose that walking biological weapon with you wasn't yours either."

Joey's mouth opened to say Lucas's name, but he slammed it shut, pursing his lips. He made eye contact with Unitas and quickly looked away.

"Are you scared of little ol' me?" Unitas questioned, putting one finger in her mouth and prowling toward him.

Joey wanted to scream. If Poly were in the room, she could calm him down and get him through it. He closed his eyes and tried to picture her encouraging face, asking him if he was okay.

Unitas snapped her fingers. "Stay awake, eyes open. Who helped you set this up?"

Her face popped into focus very close to his, when he opened his eyes. She had a whimsical look plastered back on her face, as if she were having fun with him.

"I want to see my friends," Joey demanded, not answering her question.

"Oh yeah, for sure. Let me see," Unitas said. She moved close to Joey and raised her hand. "I have all five of them right here." She held her five fingers in front of his face, made a fist, and slammed it into his groin.

Joey jumped in the chair with pain. He tried to grab at it or squeeze his legs together but he couldn't. The pain went deep into his gut and he felt sick. Tears fell down his face, as the pain radiated up into his stomach. He wanted to scream, but held it back, causing spit to dribble out of his mouth.

"Uh-oh, we've got a crier," Larry said, looking at his Panavice.

"I've had enough with the formalities. If you don't answer these next questions, I'll have to get nasty," Unitas hissed. "Let's start simple. What's your name?"

"Joey Foust." He didn't want to set the woman off again.

Telling the truth felt simpler.

Unitas looked back at Larry as he typed in the information. Larry shook his head.

"No really," he pleaded. "That's my name."

Her face contorted with anger. She moved close to him with her fist clutched. He tightened his body and squeezed his eyes shut. She punched him in the stomach, and this time, he threw up on her sleeve. He coughed and wanted to wipe his mouth, but his hands wouldn't move. She took off her jacket with vomit on it and laid it on the floor.

"I said I don't like to be lied to, didn't I?" she hissed, the playful look disappearing from her face.

His stomach and crotch throbbed as he tried to see through the tears in his eyes. The sour taste of vomit filled his mouth. Unitas pulled a cloth from her jacket on the floor and wiped Joey's mouth clean.

"Can't stand a dirty mouth," she said.

"One last chance here, *Joey*, before we start to have some real fun."

She knelt down to her jacket on the floor and pulled out a black pouch from the inside pocket. She placed the pouch on Joey's lap and unrolled it. Stuck into the black pouches were long, metal objects. Some had pointed tips and hooks, while others looked like scalpels. Joey shook in the chair, trying to get away from them.

"I hope you're not a screamer like Poly," she said.

"No," Joey yelled.

Spit frothed at his mouth and his face heated with rage. He pulled on his arms, trying to find wiggle room, but there wasn't any. The straps dug into the soft skin of his wrists as he kept pulling.

"Well, maybe I do." Unitas winked. "I hope, for your sake, you start being honest with us. Give us the names of the people who helped you with this stunt and you can be the one who signs the deal." She laughed. "You may even live to tell your cellmates about it."

Joey's thoughts raced for an answer not involving Harris.

"The pain in your balls, kid, will be a distant, lovely memory if you get this one wrong," Larry said, thumbing through his Panavice. He had yet to look at Joey.

"We acted alone. There's no one else," Joey said, breathing hard, scanning Unitas's eyes for validation.

Unitas' grin widened, showing perfect teeth. "Wrong," she said gleefully. "You know, we can make this fun." She ran a finger up his chest, her nail landing gently under his chin. "No? Too bad, you're kind of cute." Touching each metal pick with a finger, she made her selection and pulled it from the black bag.

Joey internally reeled back, giving her a pleading look for mercy, but found nothing behind her eyes. She looked at him like an object to play with, a thing on a mantle, a tchotchke on her desk. The deep fear that comes with knowing you are going to die started to building inside him.

"This is level one of York's kit," she said. "Most detectives swear by their shots and computers to tell them what they need to know, but what fun is that?"

She smiled, almost giddy. Then she moved the sharp objects to a table and sat sideways on his lap, with the metal pick in her hand. He tried to move away as she paraded the metal object close to his eye. He couldn't escape the nightmare.

"No, please, you can't do this," Joey said.

She lowered the shiny metal pick, but his eyes followed its path as the sharp tip brushed against his shoulder. He tensed up; her arm hauled back quickly, and then plunged the metal into his shoulder muscle. A sharp, shooting pain went down his arm and to his spine. His hands gripped the armrests and he screamed, but kept his mouth closed. Then she twisted it and he howled in pain. The metal rod slid out of his shoulder and the pain diminished. Sweat ran into his eyes and he breathed deep, quick breaths.

"Who shot Poly?" she asked.

The room spun and he tried to focus long enough to answer. "Simon… Simon Vang."

Unitas backed away from him. For the first time, he saw a questioning look cross her face. Maybe she didn't have all the answers—didn't have this one figured out.

"Simon Vang—out of all the people in the world, why would you use his name?"

"He needs me to keep Marcus Malliden alive. He shot Poly just to show me he could." The truth. They must see he wasn't lying. His eyes begged them to believe. He couldn't take anymore.

Larry seemed interested. He leaned forward on his swivel chair, and for the first time, looked at Joey. "Son, you shouldn't be dropping names like Marcus. That's not going to help you here," he said.

"Simon's been hunting us, and if you hurt us, he won't be happy," Joey said. He watched as they looked at each other, then Larry shrugged.

"You little mutant puke, how dare you use his name, trying to save yourself." The giddy look left her face, replaced with rage. "Level three."

There was no fanfare with this selection as she picked the metal spike and stabbed it into his knee, just behind the kneecap. He screamed and felt her moving the metal around inside. He bellowed again, as she dug it in. Nothing in the world mattered but the pain. It burned out all traces of himself and left nothing but agony. The room spun and went black.

His cheek hurt, and then again, a sharp pain. He opened his eyes to Unitas slapping his face.

"Oh no, you don't get to pass out."

His vision cleared and his body felt numb. Thankfully, the spike was out of his knee. She grabbed his hair and plunged the needle back into his knee. He screamed again, a guttural scream. He wanted to die. Anything would be better than the pain.

Larry got up from his seat. Joey thought he might intervene, but he stood with an emotionless expression as he watched Unitas punish him. He had died. This wasn't some hospital. He was in hell. He got his friends killed and these people were here to punish him for eternity.

His throat wouldn't allow more screams. His breath fell out in silence like a dog with its voice box taken out. He deserved it, maybe more. She stopped moving the metal rod in his knee and stood up. The pain lessened enough for his body to weep. All his clothes were soaked in sweat and his muscles ached. The straps were the only thing keeping him from collapsing on the floor.

Unitas wiped her frothing mouth and pushed back her disheveled hair. Her wide eyes stared into his.

"There are plenty of other kids in this," Larry said. "Why don't we off this one and move to the next? I bet we can get that girl, Poly, to talk before lunch."

Unitas's face, red with rage, glared at Larry. "No," Unitas yelled. "This kid will not get the luxury of a quick end. He puked on my jacket!" She moved to take the black pad of metal objects and showed Joey one of the larger ones. A metal rod, like the others, but she pushed a button on the back and three hooks shot out.

"This isn't going to be pleasant." She moved the metal bar in front of his face. Joey's eyes fluttered, but he stopped trying to move away. He was ready. He wanted it to be over. She brought the metal close to his eye. He slammed his eyes shut and thought of Poly and him on the blanket, under the stars, fireflies dancing above.

The door slammed open. He opened his eyes, to find Simon standing in the doorway.

"Oh, sh—" Larry's words died on his tongue when he realized Joey had been telling the truth.

Joey tried to break free, but he could only watch. Simon, in one motion, pulled a square-looking gun from his side and shot Larry with an electrical charge. The big guy fell to the ground, convulsing. Unitas pulled her gun out, but Simon shot her with his electrical gun first. She fell to the floor in a heap.

"Looks like I got here just in time. That was a nasty trick, collapsing the stairwell. I had to use the locals to dig it out." Simon sounded disgusted. "But *finally* . . . we're reunited, after so many years."

Joey gave up trying to move. His body ached from the pain and strain of it all. His focus bounced from Unitas to Simon. When he was sure she wasn't going to move, he focused on the man standing in front of him. The person responsible for shooting Poly. He hated Simon. He hated him even more for stopping the torture. How dare he be the one to save him? How dare he make it possible for him to feel relief at his presence? But he did. He was glad Simon sent her to the floor.

Simon yanked out the metal spike in Joey's knee and tossed it to the floor. "Let me get you out of those straps." He spun the bolts and released the bindings.

First, his legs were free and then his arms and waist. After the head strap fell to the side, he was free. Never had he had such a feeling in his life—being free from that chair was like waking from a nightmare. He moved his arms and leg to make sure it was real. Simon stood in front of him, smiling. That face built up the rage he'd known for Simon.

Joey lunged for his throat, but his leg didn't work right and he fell to the floor at his feet. "I'm going to kill you," he grunted, slapping Simon's shoe.

Simon laughed. "You might be surprised at how many times I've heard that, but at my age, you've heard it all." He knelt, face directly in front of Joey. "I'm not the one you should be fighting. I offered you a deal that would've saved your friends and your families. Now, the deal's gone and I'll make you watch as Marcus devours each of your friends."

"Harris will come for us."

"That fool? He and his small group have been bothering us for decades. In fact, if they hadn't interfered with the last donor, you wouldn't even be here."

Joey attempted to swing at Simon, but he raised his hand to block the weak punch.

Grabbing a clump of Joey's hair, he pulled his head back, making him look at his face. "You've kept me stuck for the last eighteen years." Simon spit out the words with such hate, he felt the wet droplets cover his face. Then, he pushed his head down to the floor and Joey couldn't move to defend it.

Two Arracks entered the room.

"Let's sedate this one," Simon said. "There better not be another scratch on him."

The Arracks moved to Joey. He felt yet another needle glide into his neck.

CHAPTER 31

AN OVERSIZED, BIZARRE HAT WITH a yellow veil covered most of Harris's face. His black jacket, with enormous puffy shoulders, had a black cape cascading to the back of his knees. His tight, black, vinyl pants with a fringe of white lace extended to his shoes. The black, shiny shoes scrunched his toes together with a large square heel. He would have normally felt ludicrous wearing such attire, but he had his mind on other things. Besides, everyone in Capital seemed to wear the ridiculous.

Past the line waiting in front of Harris—all people with equally outlandish outfits—a large screen lit up with *Capital Entry*, and under that read, *Have your papers ready*. Compry was next in line for the entry into Capital.

Behind the entry, a tall, concrete wall ran to the left and right of the guards, with no openings, except for the one behind them. Car or plane travel into Capital was banned, unless you were with MM, or an official of the government. The common person waited in line.

Harris watched as guards asked Compry questions. He was too far away to make out what they said, but he saw the guard smiling and scanning her card. Compry sauntered past the guard post and behind the concrete wall. The guard waved for the next person to come forward. He exhaled, relaxing his hands. Almadon's hack into the guards' computer had worked.

They'd been through many checkpoints to get to this one—the last and most protected. Body scanners looked for changes in your heart rate and body temperature. A camera scanned eyes for suspicious behavior and facial recognition. This is where Almadon's hack came in handy.

"Line's moving," a man behind Harris said.

Harris looked at the small space in front of him. He might've corrected such a person on their rudeness, but he had to keep a low profile.

"Sorry." He stepped forward.

Almadon was next in line to the guard post. He heard a few words between her and the guard. Almadon played a haughty role and never dropped her eyes to the guards, answering their questions, as if they were wasting her time. He liked the way Almadon could take on a role with such ease.

Harris was next in line and Nathen was a few people behind him.

"Card," the guard said, holding out his hand.

Harris handed him the card, the guard scanned it, and a picture of Harris's fake identity showed on the guard's screen. The body scanner, a metal plate, moved closer to his head. Harris concentrated on the construction of a combustion engine while the scanners moved near him. Pistons, camshafts, valves, and headers bounced around in his mind.

"What do you need in Capital today, Mister Tre Hoffer?" the guard said, reading the screen.

"Here on business," Harris said.

"You planning on doing anything that could harm the people of Capital?" the guard asked, not looking up at Harris.

"The people of Capital? No."

The guard looked up at him. "Yes or no, please."

"No," Harris said.

The guard picked up his card, slid it down the side of his screen, and then handed it back to Harris.

"Go ahead."

He glanced up at the smooth, concrete wall towering above him, and strolled toward the small arched opening. Two guards stood on either side. He stuffed the card back into his tiny pants pockets and tried to walk normal in his shoes through the archway.

Past the first concrete archway, he entered the dead zone, a thirty-foot space between the two concrete walls. This was the last place they might be stopped. Capital stood on the other side. A chain-link hallway connected the two walls. He looked down the dead zone, seeing the wall curve, as it wrapped around the city.

Two guards stood at the second archway. He walked past them, as if he had gone through the hallway a hundred times. They never looked at him.

He was in Capital.

Pulling back his veil, Harris was glad his yellow-tinted vision was gone. He pulled out his Panavice and looked on the map for the meeting place, *Giuseppe's Toys*, two miles away.

Harris never heard of it, but Almadon said the owner, a friend, had direct contact with the kids a few days ago. He strutted through the throng of people crowding the streets. Twenty years had passed since he was in Capital. The streets and the people seemed unchanged. There were more hats on men than last time he was here, but the fashion changed frequently. Feeling the silky smooth pants he wore, he longed for his simple jeans and jacket. He sighed as he looked at the two miles he had left.

Despite the shoes, he made good time, striding through the streets in his man-heels. Harris made it to the last corner before the toy store. Across the street, he viewed *Giuseppe's Toys*, looking for a person out of place, or a hint of a stakeout. Satisfied it was clear, he scampered across the street to the toy store. The sign in the window said *Closed*.

The glass door creaked open and he saw an elderly man with glasses looking at him.

"You looking for a toy?" the old man asked.

"A Gem doll," Harris said the arranged password.

The door opened and the old man ushered him inside. Harris hadn't been in a toy store for so long, he was actually in wonder, looking around at the vintage and new toys scattered around.

He took off his shoes and hat and placed them on the counter. He moved his toes and feet, trying to bring the blood back into them. He hoped never to put them on again.

"Hello, shopkeeper." Harris extended a hand.

The man shook his hand and he felt the soft, wrinkly skin of an older hand. He held his hand for longer than standard, feeling the strange texture of old age.

"You're the first here, but I think you already know that," he said. "Oh great, here's Almadon!"

He watched as the old man opened the door and ushered her in. He thought they must know each other well, bypassing the password. The two embraced in a long hug.

"Harris, you see the others yet?" Almadon asked, breathing hard.

"Not yet, it's just us."

There was a knock and he saw Compry and Nathen at the glass. He was starting to think they should move to the back of the shop; a closed store shouldn't have so many customers visible from the windows.

Almadon waved them in. "So glad you made it."

Harris moved to the back of the store. The shopkeeper locked the front door and they huddled together behind stacks of board games.

"So what do we know at this point, Giuseppe?" Harris asked when the shopkeeper joined them.

"My name's not Giuseppe. I use that name because Lenny's Toys doesn't sound as good." Lenny paused, smiling at them. Harris motioned for him to continue. "Oh yes, well, I feel really bad about this, but I was the one who turned them in."

Harris sneered at Lenny.

"It wasn't that I was trying to hurt them. Once I found out they were with you, it was too late," Lenny said in a hurry.

"In the video it appeared as if Poly, Julie, and Lucas were badly injured. Did you get a good look at them?" Almadon asked.

Lenny took off his glasses and rubbed his eyes. "The big boy carried one girl like a ragdoll, blood dripping steadily from her arm. Another sick young man looked like the dead walking, until he finally just fell limp to the floor. The other girl with the bloody shoulder was as pale as a full moon. The boy with guns looked to be in a sheer panic."

"Who came here to take them?" Harris asked.

"Capital guards."

Harris let out a long breath of relief. Guards would take them to the hospital first.

"How long has it been since they were here?"

"Three days, but they took them just across the street to the hospital."

Three days. They could be anywhere by now. If the injuries were bad enough, they might still be in the hospital. "Almadon, can you get into the police database and see where they have them?"

She got out her Panavice and looked at him. "Yes, but it may set off alerts."

"I don't think we have time to jump through proxies and setup dummy servers. Once they're in MM's bunker, it'll be much more difficult to get to them." He didn't want to think about that, not yet.

Almadon placed her Panavice on top of a box of a flying-car labeled *Car of the Future*. A screen projected above the Panavice and she began typing on the digital keyboard.

Harris was good at the computer, but he always kept to practical stuff, like learning how to break into a lock, start a fire, or hack a security system. Almadon was a master. He watched her as she flipped through the screens, typing at a furious pace.

"Okay I'm in, but it won't take long for their anti-hacks to find me."

"Look for any medical releases in the last few days," Harris said.

"Way ahead of you. I found them. They're in the hospital still—in the guarded wing." Her face went pale.

"What is it?" Harris placed a hand on her arm to get her attention.

"Simon had them signed over to him and they're transporting them in thirty minutes." The screen went blank. "They just booted me off the server."

"Do you think they spotted you?" Compry asked.

"Yes, but it doesn't matter because it will take them hours to figure out what I was looking at. Lenny, they might be able to track it back to here."

Lenny adjusted his glasses. "Oh that doesn't matter much."

"It matters to me. Can't you find somewhere to stay for a while?" Almadon asked.

"Nope, never had much family. My wife died quite a few years ago in a car accident."

"I'm so sorry. I remember Margaret when I was a child. She would spend so much time helping me create the perfect doll."

Harris watched Lenny, wrinkles at all the corners of his face. How long could that face hold out against an MM interrogation?

"They will come for you, Lenny. When they do, they won't be asking friendly questions. Do you think you can withstand the interrogations?" Harris asked. He wanted to be blunt, having no time to waste.

"I stopped drinking Orange some time ago. Living after Margaret passed seemed wrong. Let them do their worst. I won't say a word."

Harris nodded. He admired Lenny for going out on his own terms. Nevertheless, if he talked about what happened here today, he would find him and make his short life shorter.

He glanced at the clock on his Panavice. "Lenny, did you get the packages?"

"Oh yes, they're right over here."

Two large, stuffed bears sat on the ground nearby. Lenny grabbed one by the top of its head and sliced the bear's stomach open with a box cutter. The stuffing poured out of its belly and onto the ground. Harris saw the silhouette of his gun holster and guns. Other toys held Compry's knives and Nathen's bow.

They all collected their weapons with cold determination set in their eyes.

"Do we have a plan?" Nathen asked.

"When don't I have a plan?" Harris said.

CHAPTER 32

JOEY'S NOSE BURNED AT THE ammonia smell and his eyes opened. Simon pulled a vial away from his face and Joey lunged at him, but straps over his wrists and ankles held him firmly in place. Simon turned without a word and walked away. The chair Joey was strapped in followed him down the hallway. From the white walls and the smell of ozone, he thought he was still in the hospital.

He turned his head, happy to have full use of it. His arms and legs felt better. The strength was back in them. How long was he out?

Over his shoulder, he saw a shiny, silver hand pushing his chair. He heard its raspy breath, feeling each exhalation on the back of his neck. His chair stopped at a door and another Arrack pushed Hank through the doorway. The joy of seeing Hank filled him. He struggled in an attempt to reach out. Hank struggled against his bindings until he made eye contact with Joey.

"They told me you were dead," Hank said with disbelief, eyes bloodshot.

"Still here. You okay?"

"I think so." Hank spotted Simon walking farther ahead. He strained against the straps and his chair creaked under the pressure, but the straps held. "Hey, Simon. When I get out of this chair, I'm going to crush your skull!"

Simon responded with his back to them. "Your mom thought she had a chance against us. How'd *that* turn out for her?"

Hank's face went red with fury and he yelled obscenities as he struggled against the straps.

They stopped at another door and Julie, Poly, and Lucas appeared next to them. It didn't seem real. They were all alive. Joey's mouth hung open.

They looked healthy. Lucas was still pale, but he seemed much more coherent. The color was back in Poly's face. Joey felt the corners of his mouth turn back in a smile. It was more than he could've wished for. He watched as her eyes widened and she eyed him up and down.

"You're alive?" Poly's voice wavered. "I heard you screaming." Her chin quivered and the tears welled in her eyes. "I thought you were gone." The Arrack pushed her chair next to his.

"Can't keep me down," Joey said. Unitas's wicked smile crept into his mind and he shivered involuntarily. "How's your arm?" He glanced up and saw Simon turning around to saunter over to Poly, a coy look in his eyes.

"So this is the one you like?" He asked Joey. Kneeling in

front of her, he brushed back her hair and touched her neck.

"Don't *touch* her."

"Like this?" Simon grabbed Poly's bandaged arm and squeezed hard. She yelped. "You think I woke you all up 'cause I like conversation?" He moved his face within a few inches of Poly's face. She shook and kicked. He let go of her arm, grabbed her face with both hands, and kissed her forehead. Lingering at her hair, Simon made eye contact with Joey and took a deep, exaggerated sniff.

"Get away from her." Joey's face was hot with anger. He pulled at the straps and shook his chair, trying to get at Simon. He could hear Hank wrestling with his own restraints.

Simon stood and laughed. "*This* is why I woke you up." He pointed at Joey. "You kids took eighteen years of my life and I plan on seeing you suffer as much as I can before I turn you over to him." He frothed at the mouth as he spoke. Then he blinked, and the anger flooded out of him. His expression changed to a pleasant smile.

"You're crazy, you sick f—"

"We have a schedule to keep," Simon interrupted, talking over Joey's rant. He turned and marched down the hall. The Arracks followed behind with their chairs.

Simon ruined the moment, but Joey quickly remembered his friends were alive. He hadn't killed them. Even Simon's presence couldn't stop the joy of seeing them. He looked over his shoulder.

"Julie, how are you doing?" Joey asked.

"Fine," Julie said. She didn't struggle, but he noticed her looking intently at everything around her. He heard Harris's voice telling him how slow he was at noticing what surrounded him. He glanced around him, looking for what he was missing.

"You can thank me for saving Lucas," Simon said, looking back over his shoulder. "Hope you all enjoy this reunion because after *he* gets his hands on you, there won't be any joy left." He laughed maniacally as they continued down the hallway.

Lucas struggled in his chair, giving up quickly. He still didn't look a hundred percent. Had Simon saved Lucas? Joey watched as Poly and the others seethed, looking at Simon's back. She moved her wrists, trying to pull them back through the straps. She made progress, but the straps were so tight it looked impossible to squeeze a hand through.

Simon stopped at the end of the hall, extended his right finger and pressed a button on the wall. The button lit with an arrow pointing down.

Maybe the elevator wouldn't be large enough to fit all of them. They'd have to split up to take the elevator. Hopefully, there'd be a chance he could get one of these silver guys close enough to grab its knife during the separation.

The elevator dinged. The doors slid open, revealing a man dressed in all black, with *R8* on his chest.

Simon's eyes narrowed.

"We've changed plans. You'll be taking them out through the basement," the man told Simon.

"Max, I don't care which way I take them as long as you stay out of my way."

Max locked eyes with Simon. Simon looked away first.

Max then turned his attention to Joey. His gaze made Joey shudder, as if he was looking at a science experiment. There was something familiar in those eyes to Joey.

"So this is them?" Max stood at the elevator door and used

his foot to stop the door from closing, without taking his eyes from Joey. "We'll be taking off from the roof. Don't mess this up, Simon."

Simon's face twitched. "Just get in your birds and be gone."

Max shook his head and walked back into the elevator. The doors slid closed.

Simon stomped to the next elevator and pressed the button. The second elevator over dinged. When the doors finally slid open, they revealed a space large enough to park a car.

Joey slumped in his chair as the Arrack pushed him and Poly all the way in, until their knees hit the far wall of the elevator. The rest moved in with noises of feet shuffling and metal chairs clanking as they rolled over the threshold.

A camera pointed down at them. What a sight they must have been. A bunch of people strapped to chairs with small, silver creatures pushing them. Would the footage be deleted? Would those detectives report what happened? Would Harris learn of their fate? He lowered his head, trying not to think about the future. Maybe if he had taken the deal with Simon back in the prison, his friends would be safe now. Joey felt a something graze the side of his hand.

He jerked away, until he saw Poly's fingers stretched out to his. He outstretched his pinky to touch her. When they made eye contact, she narrowed her eyes and nodded with a determination. Joey clenched his jaw and nodded back. He wouldn't let them take his friends. He'd find a way.

"So what, are you Max's bitch?" Lucas asked.

Simon walked to Lucas and raised his hand. He held it above him for a moment before pulling it back to his side and walking away.

The elevator moved down. It stopped at two different floors on the way down, with people trying to get on. He heard comments from behind him like "I'll get the next one," and after one stop, a woman screamed. The elevator dinged again and he felt his chair move backward. He reached for Poly's fingertips, grazing them with his. Uncertain future be damned. At that very moment, he felt elated. She was alive. He was touching her warm fingertips. The same fingertips that dripped with blood, from what seemed like only an hour ago. In that moment, he felt as if he had something to fight for again.

The bright sunlight filled the lobby through the large windows at the front of the hospital. On the road outside, four large, black vans were waiting at the curb. The lights dimmed and the view of the lobby disappeared as they entered a hallway off to the side. He didn't think Simon would take them through the front doors.

He tried to look around for some way that could help him out of the situation, but he found nothing.

At the end of the hallway, an elevator was marked with *Parking Garage*. Simon pressed the button, typed into his Panavice, and placed it in his pocket. Joey pulled at his wrist straps, wanting to slap the grin off Simon's face. Glaring at the smug bastard, Joey wanted to say something, but he felt useless. If he could only get one hand free, he might have a chance.

"Simon," Lucas said from the back of the line. "You're going to be dead soon."

Simon raised an eyebrow. "I have lived through more than any of you insignificants could imagine. If it's my time, it won't be at the hands of some kid like you."

"We'll see," Lucas seethed.

Words. It was all they had for an attack.

Simon frowned and pushed the elevator button again. It dinged and slid open. Simon paused, looking into the small elevator.

"These three first. Not this one. He stays with me." Simon grabbed Joey's wheelchair.

The Arracks rushed Poly and Lucas into the elevator. Hank's wheels squeaked as he rolled next to him, in queue for the first trip down. He saw the rage on Hank's face as he looked at Simon.

"Hank. . . ." Joey locked eyes with his friend. He wanted to tell him how much he meant, but the words sounded like a goodbye and he choked them back.

Hank's expression lightened and he nodded. He wasn't a big talker and Joey liked that. He expressed himself without words. A simple nod and Joey knew how he felt.

The elevator door closed with Hank, Poly, Lucas, and their Arracks inside. Joey felt this was his best chance of doing something. He pulled on the strap binding his wrist to the chair. He pulled past the pain and shook at the effort, but he couldn't get his wrist through.

After a minute, the elevator returned for Joey and Julie. Simon followed them onto the elevator and pressed the ground floor button. A few pops sounded from below. Simon froze with a frown, cocking his head toward the noise. Joey did the same, trying to discern if the noise came from the elevator or something else. He fantasized about it being gunfire—that someone had come to rescue them. Another sound, like a screech.

Was that a scream?

The elevator continued to move down, stirring the silence with a hum and metal clanks. Simon paced, staring at the door. He heard the sounds as well and probably thought the same as Joey—it was gunfire. Did they kill his friends? Did this Max guy have other ideas?

Joey jerked on his chair.

"Quiet," Simon gripped the wheelchair. He looked back at the Arrack and motioned for them to push their chairs closer to the door. Simon stepped around and stayed behind the chair with his gun drawn, pointing at the closed elevator doors.

Simon let out a whistle, but it sounded more like a hiss. The Arracks both responded by drawing their daggers and placing them directly on Joey and Julie's neck.

Joey reeled back and flashes of Unitas popped into his mind. The blade grazed his throat and he felt a warm trickle of blood run down his neck.

"Joey," Julie said.

He looked to her and she had wide eyes as if trying to tell him something without words. He knew what she wanted from him and it was the same thing he wanted. But what use would slowing down time if he couldn't get his hands free. He could spend an hour trying to get free and for nothing, he'd still be stuck and at the moment all he could think of was the blade touching his neck.

"They're cutting me," Joey said.

"If you kill him, I will end your line," Simon said to the Arrack.

The Arrack moved his blade back an inch, giving his neck a reprieve.

"Joey, when the door opens," Julie said.

A few more pops sounded and Joey was sure this time of gunfire and so was Simon. He slammed the stop button on the elevator and it jerked to a stop. He pulled out his Panavice and his finger shot over the screen. His face contorted with anger he finger punched the screen.

"She's blocking you, isn't she?" Julie said with a triumphant smile.

"Doesn't matter." Simon took a deep breath and pressed on the screen of his Panavice.

It hummed and the air around Simon shimmered. He pulled out a second gun and pointed at the door, hiding behind the two wheelchairs and their occupants.

"Whoever is on the other side of these doors will die."

"I can save you the wonder. That person blocking you out of your Panavice is Almadon and if she is down there, I can all but guarantee she brought her friends with her," Julie said.

"Shut up," Simon said and slapped the side of her head.

"Don't touch her!" Joey jumped up in his chair, staring at Julie. He shook up and down, trying to get free and the Arrack moved his knife further away to keep from mangling him but he didn't care. The rage built as he saw tears in Julie's eyes and her cheek redden.

The elevator stopped and the door dinged. He stopped his frantic hopping and stared at the line between the two doors, waiting for them to part. That was when Joey felt the tip of Simon's gun pressing against the back of his head.

CHAPTER 33

THE DOORS PARTED.

On the ground in front of the elevator sat a pile of Arracks mixed in with MM guards in black uniforms. Black and red blood smeared the floor and scents of gunfire filled the air. Beyond that were rows and rows of parked cars in the massive underground parking garage.

"Yoo-hoo. . . ." Simon called out. "I have your two pretties in here with guns pointed at the back of their heads. I suggest you put your guns on the floor and kick them toward the elevator or I will kill them."

The gun pressed against his head as if to prove the point, he had them. Joey stared into the blank parking garage, looking for signs of life from his friends. They were out there. They could be just on the other side of the wall, waiting for the moment to strike.

"I will give you three seconds before I shoot Julie, and don't think I won't. She isn't a critical person to him."

Joey looked at Julie.

She shook with fear and more tears fell down her face. "No, don't do this," she pleaded.

"One."

Julie jerked at the number and slammed her eyes shut. Joey needed to do something. He had to take control of the situation and slow things down. He didn't care if it took him a year to figure it out, there was no way he could watch his friend get shot and do nothing about it.

The Arrack kept his blade away from his neck and it gave him an idea.

"Two."

Julie whimpered and shook her head back and forth, saying no repeatedly.

This was it, the last second he would have any chance of stopping what was about to happen. He had no doubt Simon was about to do the unthinkable. Simon's finger tapped the trigger of the gun and Joey felt the familiar chill rush down his neck. The sounds of the room dulled and stillness crept into the air. The Arrack's blade stayed a few inches away from his neck, just far enough for his idea to work. He crunched down and bit the blade, being careful to only use his teeth. With a tug, he pulled the knife free of its hand.

Half way there. Don't drop it.

He crunched down to his awaiting hand and grasped the hilt of the dagger. Flipping the dagger around, he sliced through the fabric and breathed a sigh of relief at his freed hand. A few more seconds and he had the rest of his body free.

Julie's face froze with her eyes slammed shut and a tear hanging off the edge of her cheek. He shifted her head away from Simon's gun and cut the straps from her chair. He wasted a second looking at Simon and thinking of taking the dagger he had in his hand and stabbing it through him, but he didn't know how long the slow-mo would last, or if it would make it past his shield.

Stuffing the dagger in his back pocket, he picked up Julie in a fireman's carry and stepped out into the ramp. Just past the elevator, he saw them all waiting. The sight shocked him even though he expected to see them. He stumbled back, almost dropping Julie.

On each side of the door stood Harris, Almadon, Nathen and Hank on one side, and Compry, Poly, and Lucas on the other. Black blood covered Compry's hands, one holding a gun, and in the other, a short sword.

He placed Julie behind Poly and next to the elevator wall. The white exit sign pointed to a ramp leading into the daylight. Somehow, he needed to get all of them out of the garage. He'd moved them all in the museum . . . he could do this.

The sounds around him crashed into him and he fell to his knees.

"Three." A gunshot blasted from inside of the elevator.

Joey might have had a chance to imagine the shocked look on Simon's face but his stomach sent him into a deep nausea. He hunched to the ground and heaved. The garage spun and all his senses felt numb. The screams and gunshot barely registered to his weak ears.

"Joey," Poly said, shaking him. The sounds cleared and he felt her pulling him to his feet.

"You won't get out of here alive," Simon laughed from inside the elevator.

Harris spoke up. "We have the kids. We have you surrounded. You lost Simon. Just take a ride back up with the elevator and we'll be on our way."

Simon laughed and an Arrack came skidding out of the elevator as if it had been thrown. The thing scurried on its feet and lunged for Harris. "I've spent too long searching for them to let them slip from my fingers once more. I will not yield an inch."

Compry shot the Arrack dead, while Harris kept his focus on the elevator door. Gritting his teeth, he stuffed his gun into his holster. They had to get past the open elevator door to get to the ramp on Joey's side.

"He got a message through," Almadon reported, staring at her Panavice.

Joey staggered to the wall next to Poly. She held his hand but kept glancing back at the elevator.

"You okay?" she asked.

Joey nodded and did quick self-assessment. He felt better with each passing second.

Harris pulled a small canister out of his jacket and showed Compry, She nodded and pushed her back against the wall. Harris kneeled down and bowled the canister into the elevator. Joey braced for the explosion.

An Arrack jumped out but only made it to the door when the canister exploded. The shockwave blasted the Arrack back, sending it sliding along the concrete floor, into the parking garage. Its body stopped at the foot of the ramp.

Joey's ears rang and smoke poured from the elevator. The

first few breaths didn't come easy after the impact of the explosion. Harris didn't waste any time and rushed everyone across. Joey kept waiting for Simon to take a shot at the runners but nothing came out of the elevator but more smoke.

Could the blast have killed him? The thought sent chills down his spine and he hoped the man was dead on the smoke. He wanted it over. He wanted his friends to be free from the run and the pain and the near death. He wanted to step into the elevator and see the man's mutilated body.

Harris placed a hand on his chest.

"Can you run?" he said with a voice full of urgency that snapped Joey out of his fantasy.

"Yes."

Harris grabbed Compry's gun and thrust it into his hand. "Good." He glanced back at the elevator.

Nathen took lead and darted toward the ramp. Joey kept next to Poly and found his legs worked better than expected, even the hint of pain in his knee didn't slow him down. Glancing back, he saw Simon lumbering out from the thinning smoke cloud. With a shaky hand, Simon pointed his gun at them, but they were at the bottom of the ramp now and a good distance away. The flash from the muzzle shined for a split second before the crack sound of the shot. Compry, at the back to the pack, screamed and clutched her side.

Harris slid to a stop and returned fire. The shots hit Simon but bounced off his shield, sending only sparks around his face. He shifted his feet and hid behind a column.

"Compry," Harris called out, shaking his head.

"Run, you fool." Compry pushed Harris toward the ramp. Near her stomach, her shirt reddened with blood

"We've got a van incoming." Nathen yelled from the top of the ramp. "I got it."

"Faster, they'll try to pin us in here," Harris said.

Joey glanced back at Simon. He was making good ground, even though he staggered along. The shield must not have protected him completely. It was hard to tell, but he appeared to have blood dripping down his face.

The sound of the squealing van tires made its way down the ramp. Nathen stood with an arrow cocked, and then let it fly.

"Get to the side!" Nathen motioned everyone to hug the far wall.

They ran up the ramp, angling toward the wall just as the van screeched sideways and flipped on its side, skidding into the underground parking garage and halfway down the ramp. Moving forward, the group made their way into the light of day at the top of the ramp, as stayed back and Harris shot the driver through the windshield. He kept firing as he walked backward toward the group.

Joey raised his own gun at the vehicle and waited for something to appear. With the van lying on its side, one tire still spinning, the back door flung open, unleashing a small army of Arracks. Harris fired into the melee and ran sideways away from them.

Joey's heart raced at the sheer numbers stuffed into the Van. Too many. He raised his gun and fired into the lot. Some fell, but most made it closer and closer to them.

"Keep them in the ramp. If they get out, we'll lose this in a hurry," Harris instructed.

Joey fired to the front line but more seemed to be coming from the van as they kept moving sideways, away from the fray.

Too many, they were going to lose the ramp. Joey searched the nearby city, looking for an escape path.

"I don't have many bullets left." Joey kept his gun pointed at the ramp. He glanced back at Harris hunched over Compry. Almadon had a white box next to her and put something on her wound with one hand, holding her Panavice with the other. "We need to get out of here," Joey called to Harris.

"Just a second, if we move her, she dies." Almadon said. Joey hadn't noticed that Compry had collapsed on the ground with Almadon treating her wound.

Small glimmers of silver moved around in the darkness on the ramp. He fired a random shot into the ramp, hoping to keep them from running out. A man in black walked near the Van. He whistled and the Arracks moved close to him.

"Yoo-hoo," Simon called. He stuck his face into the light, squinting in their direction. "Where are you guys going? We own this city. There's nowhere to hide." He pointed to the sky. A black aircraft hovered far above.

There had to be a way out of there. Joey scanned the high-rise buildings flanking them in every direction. Any number of them would have to do. He took a few steps back when he heard the screeching of tires. He glanced back to witness a car veering off the main road and onto the hospital sidewalks. It bounced over two curbs and over a grassy area. Its tires screeched as it made a hard right, coming straight for them. The car's driver, an old man, nodded to Joey as he passed. In the back seat, he had two large containers. Joey turned, following the cars path toward Simon.

CHAPTER 34

THE CAR CAREENED WILDLY TOWARD Simon. At that speed, there would be no turning back. Simon stopped laughing and shot into the oncoming car. The windshield exploded and the old man slumped on the steering wheel. The front tires wobbled but kept course. Simon jumped back into the darkness a second before the car slammed into the back of the vans. The car exploded into a large fireball, sending a black cloud up the side of the building, over the parking garage.

"No," Almadon cried, running toward the parking garage, holding out a hand.

The flames engulfed the entire ramp with black smoke trailing high into the sky. The car melted in with the two vans, popping and cracking under the extreme heat. There was no way a person or Arrack could make it past the blaze. Whoever the old man was, he thanked him for his sacrifice.

Joey didn't move at first and something tugged hard at his arm. Glancing down, he saw Poly's hand pulling him away. He tore his eyes from the carnage and moved with her, and everyone else, to the edge of the parking lot.

Harris stood, shaking his head. He held out a hand and pulled Compry to her feet. She brushed the bits of asphalt off her clothes as she stared at the parking garage. Whatever Almadon did, it appeared to be working.

"We need to get away from here. That fire won't hold back Simon for long," Harris said as a black aircraft flew by, high overhead. Joey made out the MM logo on its wing.

Across the street, people stepped out of the stores and offices to witness the chaos at the hospital garage. They pointed at the strange group of people in the parking lot and the fire. A shift in the wind brought the rancid smell of burning rubber and they grabbed for their noses.

"Where do we go?" Joey looked into the surrounding area of tall buildings.

"There's a safe house not far," Harris said. "Hank, can you help Compry?"

"Just give me a shoulder to lean on, honey," Compry said.

Hank obliged and put his arm around her back. They all ran past the parked cars in the street. People stood next to their cars with Panavices in their hands, taking pictures or videos. Joey ran by a man with an orange suit saying this was going to get him in the top ten on Glow Net tonight. Joey tried to keep his head down and his face covered as he ran. He rounded the corner behind Poly, and looked to the sky—no sign of the aircraft.

Julie and Almadon huddled next to each other as they ran.

Joey caught parts of their conversation, mostly bits and pieces about breaking down Simon's shield. Almadon pointed to her Panavice, but as the conversation turned to technical jargon, Joey stopped trying to follow. He only hoped they were finding a way to get the bastards shield down so he could get one good shot on him.

Fewer cars filled the next street. Harris kept the pace at a run, ignoring any protests. They shuffled into a small alleyway between two buildings, wide enough for them all, single file. Joey jogged behind Lucas through the alley, pushing Lucas through to the next street over.

Harris made several more turns and the bright, clean buildings turned into run-down, rusty-orange buildings with broken windows. Harris stopped next to a pair of large steel doors, opened them and motioned them to enter. Joey glanced to the sky—no aircraft.

They all went into the building and Harris pulled the doors closed behind him. The steel doors clanged as he closed the latch. The building looked like an abandoned warehouse. Joey felt the dirt under his feet and smelled oil. Yellow light filtered through the grimy windows.

Julie poured over her Panavice, while Lucas and Poly breathed hard but stayed alert, looking around with weapons in hand. It appeared Harris brought toys for each for them.

Hank came through the door last, dragging Compry along.

"Let's get her on this table." Almadon motioned to Hank. He carried her to the steel table and laid her down gently.

"She's losing blood. I can do a few more things now, but it won't be a fix." Almadon reached into her bag and pulled out a small white kit. Harris paced near the table. Joey studied his worried face, trying to think of what to ask or what to say.

"Was that your plan?" Nathen said with his hand on his head, pacing.

Harris stopped walking and looked at Nathen. There was no emotion in the look, but Nathen looked away first. Compry moaned as Almadon touched her. Harris rushed to her side, his face contorted with anger and guilt.

"We should take her to Sanct. Her dad can take her in," Harris pleaded with Almadon.

"That's hours away, even by flight, but I think she can make it—if we hurry."

"I know of a place we can get a craft."

The second-story window smashed into the warehouse and Simon floated through the space, holding a gun. Joey stumbled back, grabbed his gun, and shot, but the bullets bounced off his personal shield. Simon fired a single shot and Almadon screamed, dropping her Panavice to the floor. Julie rushed to Almadon and grabbed her shoulders.

"You bastard!" Julie screamed as she held Almadon's motionless body. Joey stared at Almadon and rage filled him.

Poly threw knives at Simon, and they too flew off his shield. Hank moved forward, but Simon flicked his wrist to send an electrical bolt at him. It hit Hank in the chest, sending him flying ten feet back. He rolled on the ground, grabbing at his chest.

"Are we done with this?" Simon said before jumping off the rope at the last couple of feet.

"I'm going to—" Poly said.

"Kill me?" Simon interjected, throwing up his arms. "I know. You *all* want to kill me. But that's not going to happen, even with your shepherd here."

"You're not leaving this room alive," Lucas threatened.

"I'll skip the banter and get to the point. I need these kids, Harris. The bounty on you is so huge it's tempting, but I'll let you and your friends go if you walk away now."

"So they can live in suspended animation for centuries, feeding your demented boss?"

Simon laughed. "I don't care what he does, as long as I can stop looking for them."

Joey saw Julie using Almadon's Panavice, pretending to hunch over Almadon. What was she doing? He looked away, not wanting to draw any attention to her. He kept his gaze on Hank, who moved to a sitting position.

"If you want me, then take me and let them go," Joey said. He stepped forward, offering himself. Simon smiled and pulled out his second gun.

"Joey, you could've made R7. I would've taken on a kid like you, to see you become great, like myself," Simon said. "But no deal. You all have given me too much trouble. There's a craft above us and it has room for everyone. If you refuse, I'll see to it personally that each of your parents are dead. Your town and all the people in it, dead. If you come now, willing, I'll spare their lives."

Joey heard Hank stirring behind him and fidgeted with his feet on the dusty floor. He never thought of his actions hurting his parents, or Preston. He looked to Poly for a reaction. She looked at the ground, knife lowered. Joey knew he saw the answers to his question across all their faces.

A grim smile spread across Simon's face. Through the dirty windows above, a black aircraft hovered in the sky.

"Fine, but we want—" Joey stopped when he heard a loud crackling sound and the humming of electricity winded down to silence.

"What the hell?" Simon patted his body as if searching for something in his pockets.

"I took down his shield!" Julie screamed.

Harris was the first to shoot, but Simon was incredibly fast. He ran across the room, Harris trailing him with bullets. Simon grabbed Julie and with his sword on her neck, used her as a shield. They all had their weapons out, pointed at Simon. With his other hand, he pointed his gun at Harris.

"You're my new shield." Simon shook Julie around.

"Kill him! Don't worry about me!" she pleaded.

"Let her go," Joey said. He kept looking for a shot, but Simon moved behind Julie, making sure they didn't have an opening.

Sweat formed on Simon's forehead as he stepped backward toward the door. He kept glancing above to the aircraft. Shaking Julie again, he stuffed the knife against her neck. "If any of you move, I'll take her head off."

Julie, wide eyed, shook her head.

Joey tried to slow things down, but nothing happened. He concentrated on the sword Simon held but still—nothing. Simon was almost to the door. Joey continued to put all of his concentration on his anger and his fear.

Poly stood to his left, her knife gripped loosely in her hands. She looked calm and determined. Hank, his face contorted with anger, walked next to Joey and shook. Joey nodded to them as they pointed their weapons at Julie. They would only have one shot at this.

"What are you doing? I'll kill her!" Simon yelled.

Joey whispered a countdown as he aimed at the tiny spot on Simon's shoulder, a muscle that would force his hand to drop the sword. A little low and he'd hit Julie, high and he'd miss entirely, giving Simon a reason to hurt her.

He couldn't miss. "Three, two, one."

Squeezing the trigger, he felt the recoil as the bullet left the chamber. Simon's hand opened, dropping the sword. His expression changed from shock to confusion as he stared at the gaping wound in his shoulder.

Julie pushed Simon's arm off her and dropped to the ground as a knife flew by her hair and into Simon's other arm. Lucas's arrow whizzed by Julie and grazed Simon's neck. He reached for his neck, his fingers turning red. Stumbling back, he grabbed for his gun but his arm didn't work properly and the gun fumbled out of his hand.

Hank ran at Simon and hammer-fisted him in the head, grabbed his neck, and spun it with a cracking sound. Simon collapsed to the ground.

CHAPTER 35

JOEY PICTURED THIS MOMENT ALL through his training, but as Simon lay dead on the ground, bleeding from his mouth in a dusty old warehouse, the magic evaporated. He saw him for what he was, a pawn. He was doing a job for a man, collecting a prize for someone else.

Outside, a loud alarm sounded.

"It's the craft. They're coming," Harris said. "Quick, there's a tunnel in the back room."

"What about Almadon and Compry?" Julie whimpered.

"Hank, can you carry Almadon?" Harris asked.

Hank nodded and picked up Almadon's lifeless body.

Compry sat on the table. Her head swayed as she balanced herself.

"You think you can walk?" Harris asked her gently.

"If I can hold on to you," she said softly. "Did you guys kill

Simon?"

"Yes," Harris said.

"Good, the kids will be safer now," she mumbled as he helped her off the table.

"Come on." Harris rushed them to the entrance.

Joey couldn't stop staring at Simon's body. They'd actually killed him; each took a part in it. Lucas and Julie were in the same trance, staring as he bled onto the dusty floor. Through the windows, Joey saw black ropes dangling into the alley.

"We've got to go, guys," Joey called out, being the first to move.

Lucas was next, and the rest followed as they made their way to the back room. Harris dusted off part of the floor, revealing a steel door much like the one in Ferrell's convenience store.

"Lock it." Harris pointed at the door they had walked through.

Joey pushed a large steel bar over the door, just as the sound of glass breaking sounded in the next room. He flinched and some of his memories creeped into his mind. Zombies crashing the glass at the store, Unitas's face close to his. He shook his head in an attempt to shake the memories loose. The old man, the hero, who saved them all in his beat-up car full of explosives. That's whom he wanted to think of.

"Come help me lift this, Lucas," Harris said.

The steel door creaked and groaned as Lucas and Harris pulled on the door. A layer of dust slid off the door as they lifted it to a ninety-degree angle. Under the door, a wheel stuck out of the bottom side. The rusty underside looked ancient and dripped with moisture. Harris motioned for them to go in.

An explosion in the next room rattled the windows above.

"They breached the first door. Hurry up," Harris ordered.

The sound of feet shifting in dirt filled the room next to them. The pounding echoed on the steel door, but the latch held.

"They're going to blow up the second door," Julie warned.

Joey stared down the dark staircase under the hatch—the last place he wanted to go. He took out his gun and made the first step down the concrete stairs leading into darkness. The damp smell intensified as he made his way to the bottom step.

Stepping off the last step, his foot landed in a small puddle, splashing the water. He turned around to tell them to come down, but Lucas was directly behind him on the stairs. They all were. Hank carried Almadon on his shoulder. Compry touched her limp hand, crying as Hank moved down the stairs.

"Keep moving. I'll close the door," Harris said.

Another death. Seeing Compry mourn her friend weighed on Joey. He couldn't help but feel responsible. She would never have been there if not for them. How many more people would die for them before someone said enough? He pulled his attention away from Compry and stared at the blackness of the tunnel ahead. It seemed brighter than what was behind him.

Water splashed around Joey as he strode down the tunnel. He felt wetness intruding his shoe and hoped it was water. A glow from Julie's Panavice filled the tunnel and allowed him to spot a ladder with a faint, white number seventeen behind it.

The sound of an explosion echoed through the tunnel.

"They blew through the second door. We had better hope the hatch gives them more trouble. What is this, a storm drain?" Julie asked.

"Yeah, it's the old drainage system," Harris answered.

Compry held on to his shoulder and gazed at the floor. Joey saw tears flowing down her face. Harris placed a hand on her shoulder and they stared into each other's eyes. "We need to keep moving." Compry sniffed and nodded her head.

Joey turned and jogged at a slow pace down the pipe. The ladders passed at steady intervals. He wanted to get out of this tunnel and off this whole planet. He hadn't wanted to be home this bad in a long time.

Hank's heavy breathing filled the tunnel. After a few minutes, he no longer heard Hank's breathing and turned to see he had lost the group. He slowed down with Julie and Poly right behind him and waited until a light from Harris appeared. Hank adjusted Almadon on his shoulder. Blood covered his shirt and a grim look spread across his sweaty face.

Muffled sounds of banging steel followed with the sharp sound of bullets striking metal. Joey peered past Harris into the dark tunnel.

"It'll hold for a while," Harris said. "Not much farther. Ladder thirty-two is the one we want."

Joey watched the ladders as he ran by them in regular intervals. He slowed down at the next one, *31* displayed behind it. One more to go.

Joey stopped at the next ladder with a faded *32*. The rest stopped next to Joey, with Hank coming in last. Compry took her grip off Harris and leaned against the wall, breathing heavy and holding her bleeding stomach.

The ladder led up to a small, round tube jutting above the tunnel.

"Lucas, go up first and open the door. Don't leave the room up there," Harris said.

Lucas nodded, adjusted the bow on his back, grabbed the first rung of the steel ladder and climbed into the dark tunnel above. There was the sound of steel sliding on concrete and a faint light illuminated the hole above.

"All clear," Lucas called down.

Julie climbed out of the tunnel.

Harris met eyes with Hank and then looked up the ladder and the small shaft. "I don't want to do this, but we can't take Almadon with us. It would cause a scene and we would be given up instantly." He looked at the damp floor and rubbed his eyes.

"We can't leave her in this sewer," Hank said, adjusting her on his shoulder.

"She gave her life to save you guys. She wouldn't want it wasted on traditions," Harris said.

"We're not animals, Harris." Compry's tears flowed. "We can cremate her here," she said as she leaned against the wall, holding her stomach.

He nodded. "The rest of you go up. Hank, lay Almadon here."

Hank carefully laid Almadon on the concrete floor. Joey stared at her dead face. He didn't get to know her well, but after the time he spent with her, he knew she was someone special. Joey fought back tears, more from seeing how much Almadon's death was affecting Compry, Nathen, and Harris. They loved her and now she was gone. He clenched his teeth and felt a tear fall on his cheek.

Harris pulled a small bag from his pocket and sprinkled its contents around Almadon's body.

"Get up the ladder, guys," Harris whispered.

Joey followed Hank up the ladder. He heard Compry and

Harris whispering below, but couldn't make out the words. He climbed through the hole at the top and into the room above.

A dim bulb flickered, bouncing light over the carpeted walls and floor of the small room. The light stopped flickering and stabilized, giving him a view of Julie and Poly. They scowled at Lucas, while he faced a large window, looking into another room.

Nathen and Compry climbed through the hatch and slumped against the door. Nathen grabbed hold of Compry and held her as she sobbed.

He looked down the hole and watched Harris climb out of the hatch. Harris slid the steel lid to an inch of closing, held out a Zippo-style lighter, lit it, and dropped it into the tunnel. He closed the lid and placed his hands on the steel, staring at it for a moment. Bright light beamed out of the holes in the lid. Compry let out a cry.

"I'm sorry," Joey whispered, placing a hand on Harris's shoulder as he stood. Harris nodded and dusted off his jacket.

"Where's Almadon?" Julie asked.

Harris walked to Julie, put an arm around her, and whispered to her. He couldn't hear said the words, but he got the gist.

Harris let go of Julie as she covered her mouth as her eyes welled.

"Almadon would want us to move on. She would want us to make it," Harris stated to the group. "Save your mourning for when we have the time. Pretend she's alive for one more hour." He looked at the round, steel lid on the floor.

"He's right," Compry said, wiping tears from her face and pushing away from Nathen. "She'd kick our asses right now, knowing we're wasting time over her."

Lucas turned to face them and a smile disappeared from his face. "What's going on?" he said.

Joey looked to see what Lucas was smiling about and he stumbled backward against the wall. A woman in skimpy lingerie looked at them, smiling, turning her body from side to side and looking up and down. *What the heck is she doing?*

"Dude, it's a two-way mirror," Lucas said and rubbed his hands together.

The woman posed in the mirror and then turned to the dressing room door as another woman dressed in red panties and bra opened a door.

Joey stared at the exhibition at first, but averted his eyes as the two women held hands, laughing at their mirror. It didn't feel right. Some pervert probably set up a webcam down there and took advantage of unsuspecting women. Lucas didn't seem to have a problem with the voyeurism as he smiled and waved at them.

"You're sick, Lucas," Poly said.

"What? They can't see me." He shrugged.

Joey glanced at Poly. It felt awkward being in the room with her while women in revealing lingerie put on a fashion show.

"I don't know what's grosser, the fact that Lucas is getting off on this, or the fact these women are trying on lingerie at a store," Julie said, wiping her eyes.

"It's not really a store," Harris said. He looked miserable and maybe it was a reflection off the light, but Joey thought he saw tears in his eyes.

"What do you mean this isn't a store?" Lucas asked.

The two women giggled at each other and one slapped the

other's butt.

"They're putting on a show for whoever is in this room. Once you entered here, their light went on and they come out," Harris said.

"Wait, so this is some Peeping Tom show?" Lucas appeared enthusiastic about the idea.

"Whatever Peeping Tom is, but sure, it's just a show. One of many here. This is the red part of Capital. No one wants to be noticed here, we should be good to go. Besides, I know the Madame."

Harris opened the door out of the room and leaned into the doorway, looking both ways. He motioned for them. A long, dark hallway with doors on each side and windows near each door, stretched out in front. Joey stepped onto the soft-carpeted hallway, resisting the urge to grip his gun as a few people mingled nearby. They kept their eyes forward, looking into windows. He relaxed and stepped forward, allowing Poly and the others to come out.

Harris walked down the hallway and waved his hand for them to follow.

The first window showed the two dressing women in lingerie hugging each other and laughing, and then they started bouncing up and down, holding hands.

The next window had a woman in a soapy bathtub shaving her legs. The next window was the last one Joey would look at. A large woman wearing a diaper and bonnet, riding a tricycle in circles while sucking on a Popsicle. She winked at him as he walked by.

Lucas looked at the woman on her bike, shaking his head in awe. "That must be the best-built tricycle in the whole world."

Joey moved next to Poly and Julie and followed their lead of looking at the floor.

"I think I'd rather be strapped back in that chair than be here," Poly said.

He laughed, but thinking of that chair and not being able to move while Unitas tortured him, made his stomach queasy. Keeping a smile on his face, he kept the thoughts from overtaking him.

Poly kept her eyes on him and he matched her, watching her face as they walked down the hall. He saw the words mounting on her lips, but she pursed them and looked ahead. They would have to wait for another time to have a talk. He had so much he wanted to tell her, and seeing death made the matter even more urgent. He wondered what she was thinking.

"This place is foul," she leaned over and whispered.

"They do anything to you back at the hospital?" Joey whispered thinking of the threats laid out by Unitas.

"No, they kept me under for most of the time. I'm not even sure what day it is."

Joey got a glimpse of a set of twins, in what appeared to be a pie fight.

Poly shot a glance at him and looked to the floor. "I heard you screaming. They told us you were dead." Even in the dimly lit hall, he saw the tears welling in her eyes and her voice cracking.

"I'm here and we're going to make it, Poly."

"I know and the sooner we can get out of this place," she glanced at a muscular, oiled up man doing laundry and took a deep breath of disgust, "the better."

Harris stopped in front of a pair of doors and turned to face them. "Before we go up, we've got to cover up Hank and Compry." Harris took off his jacket, holsters and his guns and placed them on Compry. She pulled the jacket around her body to conceal the bloodstains on her shirt. Joey copied him and handed his jacket and guns to Hank. The jacket was small on Hank, but it was enough to cover the gore.

"We look rough, but this is a rough place. Keep your head down, don't look at anybody, and follow me," Harris instructed quietly.

"Where are we going?" Julie asked.

"To see the Madame."

"Who's that?"

"She's the one who's getting us out of here."

CHAPTER 36

SHE'D NEVER BEEN IN A more disgusting place . . . and she just came out of a sewer tunnel. Poly didn't even want her feet touching the soft carpet, and made a mental note to replace her shoes. Better yet, just burn them.

She kept close to Joey, watching his eyes to see if they would wander to the peep shows. He slipped a couple times, but mostly he kept them pointed at the floor. Oh, how he tried to be the good guy.

Thankfully, the soft carpet ended at the steel staircase. Steel felt more sanitary; she could only imagine what lurked in the confines of that carpeting. The clanking sound of their steps on the stairs filled the crowded space. A few flights of stairs and they came to a door marked *3b*.

Considering what had happened over the last few days, she wasn't a fan of opening doors when she didn't know what was behind them. She felt the seven-inch, weighted, throwing knife at her leg—one of the few blades left after the parking garage, a gift from Compry. Feeling the steel on her fingertips comforted her.

Compry fell to one knee. Poly gasped and moved to help her, but Harris clutched her arm and got her back on her feet. Seeing her in a weakened state shocked Poly. Compry was the blademaster, a person she could only hope to become. There was no way that gunshot was going to stop her.

"You doing okay?" Harris asked.

"Yeah, I'll be fine." Compry gave Harris a weak smile.

Maybe this Madame has knives. Poly tried to think positive. A sturdy kitchen knife would work in a pinch.

Harris opened the door and walked past it. Joey stepped a few feet past the door, frantically looking around. Poly waited a few seconds before pushing past Joey. She let her arm graze his body and looked ahead into the hallway, hoping it wasn't another peep show for creepers. Compry had trained her to see the whole room, and now she wished she could un-see the whole room.

This hallway, thankfully, was windowless and void of any creepers, but it did have the awful soft, squishy carpet, like the back room at the movie rental place in Preston. Harris stopped at an arched doorway adorned with draping tapestries.

"Let me do the talking," Harris whispered.

Poly peered past the fancy entrance and inside the room. An assortment of high-tech computer monitors and a mix of old trinkets, glass globes, and brass figures spread across the large room. Not a knife in sight. It was like the home of the nerdy-psychic-grandma she'd never had. She liked this Madame and hadn't even seen her yet.

At the end of the room stood an older woman dressed in a large, gaudy dress that looked as if it was from the 1500s. She had on a round velvet hat that seemed to throw off the whole look with its modern curves. She looked up from her table with a shocked look that quickly turned to a wide smile as she stood.

"Oh my, is that you?" she said and paraded around her desk. She moved and spoke with her hands flowing around as if she were composing an orchestra.

"Yes, Veronica, good to see you again," Harris greeted.

"It's been a long time," Veronica replied, as she hugged him. "And everyone here calls me Madame V." She smiled and bowed.

Harris bowed in return. "I'm sorry to put this burden on you, but we need a ship and a way out of Capital."

"Dispensing with pleasantries? You must be in real trouble. I see you brought a rag tag group along to put your burdens on. When will you ever learn, Harris?"

"Never. The ship, do you have one?"

She eyed Harris and cocked her head to the side as if trying to see him from a different angle. "I owe you one, Harris."

He nodded once.

"I don't like debts and will be happy to be rid of this one. I have a private escort ship for special clients on the roof. You are free to use it."

"Thank you, Veron—Madame V," Harris said and turned. Madame V grabbed his arm and pulled him back.

"Death surrounds you, Harris. These kids look fresh. You leave them with me and I can see to it they get out safely."

"No, just a ship out of here will do."

Poly saw the crease in Madame V's eyes when she offered the help. She didn't want to oblige, but Harris had something on her that made her accept his request. Poly narrowed her eyes as Madame V glanced at her. "Hi, I'm Poly." Poly found it helpful to make sure acquaintances saw you as a person; giving a face a name makes them less likely to stab you in the back.

"Enchanted." She made the slightest roll of her eyes. "Brucius, would you please take our special clients here to the escort ship?"

Poly hadn't noticed the man standing at the archway. She hated being snuck up on. The large man's no-nonsense face surveyed them. He grunted and left the room.

"Thank you," Harris said and bowed.

"Yes. Are your friends okay? I have a doctor on staff," Madame V offered.

"No, we must be going," Harris said, walking backward out of the room. "Thank you again."

Poly followed Harris as they caught up to Brucius standing at the stairway. He didn't say anything as they grouped up at the bottom of the stairs. After climbing a few floors, they were on the roof. A large, flat roof with a great view of the city and the setting sun.

She wondered how long they had been in that tunnel of debauchery. Her brow lowered as she tried to think of what day it was. She opened her mouth to ask when someone interrupted her.

"Fine evening we're having," the loud voice said.

Poly took her knife out in an instant and looked for the person. A man dressed in a black suit stepped out from behind a metal box attached to the roof. His shirt had a mark of R8 on his right chest and MM on the other.

"Max," she said. Remembering the man pushing Simon around next to the elevator. She closed her eyes and shook her head. Would they ever be rid of these bastards?

Harris, in one quick motion, grabbed Hank's jacket, pulled out Joey's gun and fired three quick shots. Max didn't jump out of the way, and as far as Poly could tell, he didn't flinch. The bullets bounced off him in small sparks. He had some kind of shield like Simon's.

Those dang cowards and their shields.

She looked to Julie to tell her, but she was already on her Panavice, sliding her fingers across the screen. She gripped her knife in her better throwing hand and waited for the word from Julie.

"I don't know. It's not like Simon's—it's so complex." Julie shook her head as her fingers skimmed around the screen.

"Ah yes, Simon," Max drawled. "It's a shame you killed him. Hello, Harris."

"You can go to hell, Max!" Harris hollered.

"It's been a long time, brother," Max said with a partial nod of his head.

Poly turned to Harris with her knife in hand. *This was his brother?* How could he keep something like that from them? Joey adored Harris, but she'd kept a skeptical eye on him from day one. Even Julie's attempts to find out about him led to dead ends. Julie said he was a ghost. Any record or mention of him online was always immediately deleted.

"Just let us go, Max, and there won't be any losses," Harris said.

"Oh no, I can't do that. *He* wants him . . . needs him." Max pointed to Joey. "And the others, too, for backups." He stepped closer. "Come on, Harris. You can't really think you can win here. We had trackers implanted on these kids at the hospital. You can't go anywhere without us finding them."

"I won't let you take them."

Damn right, you're not taking us. Poly nodded and glanced at Julie, waiting for that moment when she could send a knife in between the R and 8 on his chest.

Max pulled out his gun and shot twice. The shots were so close that they sounded as one. Poly didn't have the time to react before she watched Compry and Nathen collapse to the ground with a hole through each of their hearts.

She moved to attack Max with her knife, but Hank was ahead of her, running at Max. Three feet before reaching him, Hank hit something unseen and fell to the ground. Max looked annoyed. Hank shook on the ground, face straining under great pain.

"Please, Harris, can you control them before I start killing more?" Max said.

"Stay back, everyone," Harris seethed through gritted teeth.

Mouth agape, Poly stared unblinking at Compry's dead body. This man killed her in cold blood and she couldn't get within stabbing distance. Her blood boiled and she roared at Max, lunging at him with knife in hand.

Her arm stopped its forward motion and she looked at the fingers grasping her wrist. Joey's tight grip gave no room for her to pull away. He shook his head as she tried. *Damned Joey.* His soft blue eyes stared into her soul. Poly's eyes filled with tears and she collapsed into his arms, laying her face on his chest. She felt Joey's strong arms around her body. Why couldn't they just float away together, go somewhere away from all the pain, death, and danger?

Poly glanced at Compry on the ground, motionless.

No.

She pushed away from Joey and darted to Compry's body. Taking her jacket off, she draped it over her face. She couldn't hide from what happened. She wanted to face it head on. This woman had showed her so many things, and taught her in more ways than she could recall. She placed her hand on Compry's side and pulled out her knife. The shiny eight-inch blade with etched green dragons at the hilt. She never got the story behind the blade, but it meant the world to Compry. She slid the blade into her sheath at her waist.

"I'm sorry," she whispered into Compry's ear.

Poly stood and glared at Max.

"Julie, check to see what they've deployed around us," Harris said.

The soft glow of the screen on her face in the dimming daylight exaggerated her expression of concentration.

"Do you really think she can break into my team's network?" Max asked.

"There are four gunships surrounding us, and a small team of men are on their way up the stairs, and a dozen or so transport cars on the surrounding streets," Julie reported.

Max's smile left his face. Poly loved that Julie disrupted his confidence. He wasn't some infallible being.

"Now you know the situation. You realize there's no escape this time, no tunnels or Alius stones to use. Surrender and I'll keep their Earth safe. Fight us and I will turn their Earth into a Ryjack, starting with their families."

Poly gripped Compry's knife hard, her nails digging into her hands. She picked the spot on Max's neck. She would even use Compry's knife to do it.

Harris stepped closer to Max, his face contorted with frustration. "Just as you have implanted trackers on them, we have also implanted something." He looked to them, apologetic. "We knew there was a good chance you'd take them and we couldn't let it happen. So we implanted a small explosive in each of them."

Max smiled. "You're a devious one. I can tell from their faces, they weren't aware of this little gift. What else have you kept from them?"

"Listen. I could blow them all up right now and I don't think *he* would be happy when you returned with corpses."

Max paced back and forth, and even in the fading light, Poly saw his face red with anger. Was Harris bluffing? There was no way he put bombs in them. She tried to think of when they would've had time to implant something—the only time would have been when they first arrived in the bunker and into the medical wing.

She felt the blood in her face rising and touched the spot on her neck where they'd received their "vaccine." It did feel weird when the shot went in. How could he have placed bombs in them? Her nostrils flared and she turned to Harris.

"What are we to do then?" Max asked.

"You only really want one of them—Joey. You can have him in return for a transport ship for the rest of us and a guaranteed safe route to the Marshall Islands."

Max laughed, but Poly's heart sank deep in her chest. She

wouldn't let Harris bargain away Joey. She met eyes with Joey, seeing that he was okay with the trade. He was just noble enough to go through with the deal. He'd sacrifice himself for them. *The damned fool.* Facing him, she took in a deep breath, hoping he would say the words of rejection.

"Don't listen to this, Joey." She punched at his chest. She closed her eyes and felt a tear fall down her cheek. His finger caught the tear. She smelled the gunpowder on his hand and opened her eyes.

"Fine, we'll collect the rest in due time though. I'll personally see to it." Max took a step forward.

"No!" Poly screamed. Was she the only one to say something against it? "You can't give him Joey!" She rushed to Harris with her knife. Harris didn't move to defend himself. He looked defeated as she raised her knife, intending on bringing it across his neck. He stared forward, unblinking as she stopped the blade an inch from his neck. Holding it there, she shook with anger and disbelief. Joey tugged on her shoulder and she turned to face him, dropping the knife down to her side.

"The transports will be here in a minute for you, Joey," Max said. "Say your goodbyes, kid." He crossed his arms and watched on, as if amused by their suffering.

Joey looked at her with hurt eyes. She fought the tears.

"Poly, I have to do this. If going with them gives you another day, then it's worth it," Joey said.

"But . . . *no!*" Tears filled her eyes and she hugged him tightly. It felt right being with him and for a second, she got lost in him, forgetting the horrible situation around her. She held him with her eyes closed, head against his chest. He released her and held onto her shoulders, pushing her back and staring at her. She couldn't bring herself to look at his face.

He gently placed his hand under her chin and lifted her head. "If we only had more time," Joey whispered, brushing her hair back.

Tears fell down her cheeks and she didn't care if the others saw.

A ship floated over the roof and landed nearby. Dust flew up in a cloud on the roof and Joey, standing in front of her, disappeared for a second. She thought she felt a soft kiss on her cheek before he reappeared in the same spot in front of her. He had done his Speedy Gonejoey trick. The others hadn't seemed to notice.

Hank walked to Joey and hugged him, whispering something in his ear that she couldn't hear and Joey nodded.

Lucas dragged his feet to Joey. "This sucks." They shook hands and pulled it in for a hug. "I don't know what to say, man. Thanks."

Julie marched up and whispered in his ear as she hugged him. Poly caught the whisper in the air. "I can trace the tracker on you. We'll come back for you."

Joey nodded and Harris walked up. He didn't say anything as he simply placed a hand on his shoulder, met his eyes, and then walked away.

Poly stood there, not wanting to leave his side, not wanting to say good-bye. She always figured they would face whatever came at them, *together*. She could not deal with the world without him. He locked eyes with her.

She wanted to say something profound that would encapsulate all the feelings she had, but he broke the silence first.

"Promise me, you won't come after me."

Her heart sank for a second. His last words to her were about her giving up on him?

"I can't leave you with them." She glared at Max as the transport ship hovered above, sending gusts of wind toward them.

"Please, you have to. You can't live your life trying to save me, but you can remember me."

The fool boy. She wanted to punch the stupid out of him. It wasn't some simple switch she could turn off. She'd never give up on him and she knew he'd do the same for her.

"I'll find you again," was all she could get out. She wouldn't accept this as goodbye forever.

"Time's up." Max walked toward them.

Joey gave quick glances from Max to Poly.

"Promise me! I can't make it knowing you're not living your life out there. If you come after me, then we both are in a prison."

Poly felt another tear streak down her face. She wanted to explain so much to him, but Max approached and she lied to Joey. "I promise."

Getting on her tiptoes, she grabbed the back of his neck and kissed him on his lips. His hand came up to the side of her face, his thumb stroking her cheek. She felt the heat in her body build as he deepened the kiss.

"That's enough. Time to go," Max said, pulling Joey from her embrace.

She scowled at Max.

"Poly, I'm sorry," Joey said.

The aircraft blew the air around, making her hair stick to

her wet cheeks. She couldn't move. She couldn't step away from him.

A ramp lowered from the ship and a few soldiers in black ran off the ramp, stopping next to Max. Julie, Hank, and Lucas ran up the ramp into the ship. Harris stood at the bottom of the ramp, looking at her. She would deal with his betrayal later.

"Please, Poly, go!" Joey pleaded.

She took a deep breath, then turned and ran to the ramp. Her mind screamed at her with every step she took. If she'd hesitated even one second, she would have never made it. She ran past Harris and into the ship.

The ship had chairs on each side, like an airplane, but everything was military gray. All she wanted was a window. She jumped over a row of chairs and stared out the portal window.

She looked out just in time to see Max shoot an electrical bolt into Joey's neck. Poly slapped the window with her palm and moved her face close against the glass, screaming his name.

Joey collapsed and Max threw a blanket over him. The blanket wrapped around him, leaving nothing but his head sticking out the end, and lifted off the ground. Joey, wrapped in a blanket, floated next to Max.

She wanted to turn away from it, but she felt like she owed it to Joey to watch. Max leaned over him, probably gloating about his fantastic victory. Poly slapped the window with her hand. The pain felt good, and she hit it again. She had made Joey a promise, but not the promise he thought. She made a promise to herself. She'd never stop, until Marcus and Max were dead, and Joey was back in her arms.

THE CARNIVAL STYLE MUSIC WOKE him up. Gears squeaked and he swayed. Sitting up, Joey put his hand on the wooden bench beneath. The sun light shone through the metal mesh surrounding him. Large metal bars wrapped around his cage and held him high in the air. Looking around, he saw cages above and below him, and they swayed as the metal structure moved in a circle.

"Hello," he called out, searching the other cages for another person. His cage descended in its circular path and when it reached the bottom, it stopped.

The metal door clicked and he pushed it open. Joey surveyed the small boardwalk full of carnival games as it came into view. He looked back at his cage and the giant Ferris wheel moved in its circular path. A large cartoon head adorned the center of the Ferris wheel. It was of a smiling girl with pigtails and large eyes—Mindyland written underneath her face.

"Hello?" He called out again.

Electronic music played through speakers, but he was the only one there to hear it. He felt weak and rubbed his eyes. When he felt something hard and clunky, he stopped and looked at his wrist. Each had a metal bracelet on.

Blinking and rubbing the top of his head, he tried to remember how he got there. Max had been laughing when they put the bracelets on—they blocked him from speeding up. However, that wasn't why he was laughing.

Joey fell to his knees and put both hands over his face.

"No!" He screamed at the sky. Now he remembered it all.

"We shot them down," Max said and then laughed. *"Don't worry. I'm sure it was a quick death."* He laughed again.

Joey buried his face in his hands and wept for them. He was alone. He thought he remembered seeing Poly's face looking through the porthole right before he'd been shot with the bolt of electricity.

They couldn't be dead. But the vivid memory of Max making him watch the missile streak through the clouds and strike the aircraft hit him hard. After everything they'd been through . . . for them to die like that was incomprehensible.

He grimaced at the thought and gritted his teeth as tears flowed down his face. What did he have to live for now? How could he go on knowing what happened to his friends?

He glanced back at the rotating wheel behind him and contemplated going into one of the cages, closing the door and never leaving. The world must want him dead, but not before it could drain him of his will to live.

"Joey?"

Startled at the noise, he pulled his hands away from his face. That voice . . .

"Joey, is it you?" she asked, but didn't wait for his response. Running into his arms, she hugged him.

She felt real, but how—?

"Samantha?"

Thank you for reading the first installment in The Preston Six series. This is my debut novel and I appreciate the time you've given my characters' story. The next four books in this series will be released in quick succession, as the editing is already complete. And also be on the lookout for my other series coming soon, *Alchemist Academy*.

For the latest information about releases, or if you have questions for me, visit me at: www.authormattryan.com or https://www.facebook.com/authormattryan.

A new book series needs all the help it can get, and reviews matter. So, as a bonus to my loyal readers: leave a review of *Rise of the Six* on Amazon, send me a link or screenshot of your review, and I'll send you a free advanced ebook copy of *Call of the Six*. Authormattryan@gmail.com.

CHAPTER 1

POLY FELT A TEAR STREAK down her cheek, more gathered in her eyes, distorting her vision. She blinked and another one cascaded down as she glared through the airship's window. Joey was gone; the airship that took him, gone. She pressed her face against the glass and stared at the spot he filled just a few moments ago.

The vibrations of the airship's motor resonated through the window and against her cheek. The ship lifted, dust floated out like a cloud over the roof, covering the bodies of Compry and Nathen. That was their burial. It wasn't fair, but nothing seemed fair anymore.

She closed her eyes and seared in her mind the man's face who took Joey from her, the man who killed Nathen and Compry—Max Boone.

"I'll find you," Poly whispered. Her breath fogged the glass. The words were for Max and Joey.

"We have maybe ten minutes before they get the bomb out of Joey's neck," Harris yelled over the sounds of the aircraft.

Poly jerked away from the window at the mention of Joey's name and wiped the tears off her face. Harris looked frantic as he ran around the aircraft grabbing bags off the walls and throwing them in a pile.

Thunder boomed and a bright flash of lighting pulsed through the windows. Heavy rain pelted the aircraft and dulled the roar of the motors. Poly peered out the window, the roof was gone, nothing but streaks of rain and dark clouds rushing by.

"What do we need to do, Harris?" Hank asked.

"Get those suits on, the ones in the gray bags," Harris said as he rummaged through a steel box. He turned and none of them had moved. "Now!" He went back to the box and tossed out a couple more packs. "Where's the water packs?" Harris mumbled to himself.

Hank yanked open one of the gray bags and pulled out a black jumpsuit, he held it to his large body and tossed it to Lucas. He tore into another bag, but it contained an even smaller jumpsuit and he handed it to Julie.

Poly opened a bag and pulled out a small suit, sliding her feet into the built-in booties, and then pushing her hands through the sleeves and into gloves. The rubbery material felt smooth and had a new-purse smell. She slid the zipper up the front, all the way to her neck, and then realized what she was wearing. "Wait. We're getting off this plane?"

"Julie, how's it going?" Harris asked, ignoring her question.

"Only have Hanks left." Julie never looked up from her Panavice. Her fingers moved across the digital screen.

"Good, how much time do we have?"

"Six minutes."

"Poly, can you help Julie get her suit on?" Harris asked.

Six minutes until what?

Poly frowned at Harris for not answering her question, but he kept his back to her as he rummaged through another steel box. She stopped wasting her scowl and conceded to helping Julie. She knelt in front of her with the suit in hand. Julie's transfixed face glowed from the light of her Panavice. Sighing, Poly took Julie shoes, grabbed the suit and slid her legs into it. She'd never dressed a woman before but—

"Done!" Julie yelled and almost knocked her down. "Sorry, Poly."

"Nice job, Julie." Harris climbed a net on the sidewall to get into a high up compartment.

Poly helped Julie get into the rest of her suit.

"Thanks. We're going to get him back, Poly," Julie said with fire in her eyes.

Damn right we are.

Poly nodded her head in agreement. She touched her knife and wanted to add 'killing Max' in the mix, but kept the anger stowed. She glanced out the window with rain rushing past the glass.

Julie studied her suit, inspecting the zipper and the lining around her neck. She probably knew exactly what the suits were for.

"We don't have time for me to explain everything, but we need to put on the black backpacks and securely fasten the straps. *Now.*" Harris tossed more bags to the middle of the aircraft, and then grabbed one for himself and put it on, mumbling to himself about not finding water.

Poly picked up a black backpack and put it on. It had thick straps over her shoulders and waist, and they clicked together much like a seat belt. Her heart beat faster, as she put it together in her mind. The suits, the backpacks, the aircraft . . . *no.* She had to be wrong, they couldn't be jumping. She opened her mouth to ask the question again, but Harris turned to face them with a grim expression.

"Okay, now comes the hard part. They are going to shoot us down in a matter of—"

"Four minutes," Julie interrupted.

He nodded and continued, "We're going to jump from the craft at high speeds and you need to follow my instructions to survive. First thing, at the back of your neck you'll find a tag. Pull the tag up and this will activate your helmet."

Fear built in Poly. She blindly felt for the tag and pulled it up. A clear dome moved over her head and locked in around her neck. A puff of air hit her face.

"The suit will keep you warm and let you breathe, even underwater." The helmet dulled Harris's words.

"Underwater?" Lucas's muffled voice could be heard through his helmet.

"Yes, we're over the ocean right now."

Poly gripped the straps on her shoulder and pulled them tighter. Her shaky fingers felt for any holes around her dome. She'd never seen the ocean, except for TV, and now she faced jumping into it from a plane. Was the man insane?

"At this speed and altitude, we'll die on impact," Julie said, searching for a spot to place her Panavice. She unzipped her suit and stuffed it in.

"That's what the backpacks are for. We don't have time for explanations, you'll have to trust me and follow my directions," Harris said. "When the back ramp opens, we'll need to jump ten seconds apart to stay off their detectors. A parachute will deploy automatically and when you hit the ocean; your backpack will turn into your flotation craft."

They all talked at the same time, muddling their questions. Harris didn't respond and pressed a red button at the back of the hull. The back of the aircraft opened and the sound of the wind eliminated any chance of conversation. Harris walked to the edge of the large ramp. The wind tussled his hair and he motioned for them to come forward. The dark opening at the back of the aircraft lit up from a strike of lightning and the rain fell sideways as they flew through it.

Great, lightning. As if it wasn't dangerous enough.

They formed a line with Poly toward the back. Hank staggered to the edge of the ramp and Harris spoke to him, but Poly couldn't hear the words. Then, Hank jumped. She gasped and her heart raced. Was she really going to jump from the aircraft? Julie stepped forward to the edge of the ramp. She heard Harris yelling instructions to Julie and then he counted down from three. Julie jumped after he said one and Poly stepped forward.

The ramp vibrated under her feet and tilted toward the black clouds flying by. The wind swirled around her, making her take baby steps and spread out her arms to keep balance. She made the mistake of looking below the ramp, into the infinite darkness. She took a step backward and Harris put his hand on her back.

Harris yelled, "When you land, stay put and I'll find you.

But if I don't, set the prop at one-thirty-two. You will reach the island in a few days."

"Wait, what?"

"Three, two, one," Harris said and pushed her out.

Black clouds rushed by and she had a second to curse him before the wind hit and took any words she had left from her. Spinning, she moved her arms and legs out, trying to stabilize her chaotic descent. The wind slowed and she stopped tumbling. Rain smeared across her helmet in the free fall through the clouds. She flailed around, idiotically trying to grab the clouds to stop from falling. As she passed through the last cloud, she reached up, but it was long gone.

The dark ocean below rapidly moved toward her. She breathed in deep for the first time since the fall started, and with filled lungs, she screamed. Rational thoughts gone, nothing but fear and anger for Harris shoving her to her death.

Poly's backpack popped and she jolted forward from the sudden slow down. She turned her head and behind her a thin parachute stretched out from cords on her backpack. She wasn't going to die, but the feeling still filled every part of her body. Her shaky hands firmly grabbed the two cords rising above her. She let out a long breath, thanking the parachute above.

A missile screeched by, roaring through the dark clouds. A large section of clouds lit up in a flash. A few seconds later, the sound of an explosion hit her, crackling and resonating around her helmet.

"*No!*" She yelled into her helmet. She stared into the darkness, looking for a parachute from Lucas and Harris. They *had* to have gotten off the aircraft in time. She couldn't lose any more people around her, even Harris. She wanted to hurt him for bargaining Joey away, but she didn't want him dead. They had to be alive, she wouldn't accept anything else. The merciless storm laughed at her with thunder and rain, making it impossible to see into the distance.

She turned and looked over her shoulder, searching the sky for Hank, or Julie, *anyone*. The storm shot a lightning bolt through the clouds. She winced at the massive thunder that followed. Frantically searching around, only dark clouds and rain appeared. She was alone, falling to the ocean.

Large raindrops ran down the face of her helmet and she swayed back and forth in the embrace of the parachute. Below her feet, she saw the swirling black closing in. A hundred feet down, then fifty. At twenty feet, she saw the huge waves splashing, crashing into each other. Ten feet above the water, her slow descent ended.

The backpack made a pop sound as it detached her from the parachute. She yelped at the free fall and hit the water. Her whole body submerged into the ocean. She held her breath inside her helmet, as she swam back up to the surface. The buoyant backpack pulled her most of the way up. With her head above the surface she breathed in and felt her helmet puff air around her dry face. Large waves rolled by, splashing water over her head. She slapped her arms, trying to keep her head above water. After a few terrifying moments, she stopped panicking, realizing her helmet was providing protection from the water. Her backpack acted as a life preserver, but it began to shake and she turned, trying to look at it.

Another pop sounded and her backpack began to grow. Poly felt it move down her legs, as it lifted her feet out of the water—laying her back, strapped to the expanding backpack. It inflated around her and in a few seconds, she found herself in a small teepee-like hut, floating on the water. A wave pushed over the teepee and it rocked, but no water came in.

Poly lay on the floor with her back strapped to it, staring at the black fabric peak of the ceiling. Taking the straps off, she sat up just as a wave hit the craft, sending her tumbling into the inflated wall. She flattened her body out on the floor and stretched to touch all sides, stabilizing herself, as each wave wanted to catapult her around. It was like she was in a bouncy house with someone jumping next to her.

I'm alive. The thought pounded in her head. Her friends had to be alive as well. She had to find them.

Attempting to get up so she could look around, another wave crashed into the small craft, sending her to her butt. How could she find them when she couldn't even stand? She gripped the fabric on the wall and forced herself to her knees. Moving around the perimeter of the craft, she found a zipper and moved it up. A gust of wind and rain entered the opening. She raised a hand and squinted past the deluge long enough to see a wave crash into her. Water poured into the craft and she slammed the zipper back down. The calf-deep water sloshed around in the craft.

She took deep breaths, trying to stop imagining the craft sinking into the ocean with all the extra weight. Rapid puffs of air pelted her face, but it didn't feel like enough air. Poly felt like she couldn't breathe with the stupid helmet on. She reached for the back of her neck and pulled the tag. Her helmet retracted into her suit and the noises of the ocean rushed to her. Cold, salt water splashed her face.

What was she supposed to do? Her friends were in the same

ocean as she was, they could be a hundred feet away and she wouldn't know—ten feet, even. She could scream, but the ocean and thunder would drown her out. Poly had no clue what direction she was going, left to the mercy of wherever the ocean took her. She'd never felt so small, so insignificant.

Slumping down, she put her back against the craft as the cold water splashed against her and thought about everything Harris had said. *He'd find them.* But, did he make it off the craft?

She shook her head and refused to think about it. Harris said if she were alone, to set the prop . . . the craft must have had some sort of propulsion system. She waded through the water, feeling the edge of the craft, and then found a flap on the inflated edge.

Poly peeled the flap back with the scratching sound of Velcro detaching. She slid her fingers over the digital panel and it lit up. A flashing label read *Water Bilge* and she pushed it. A faint humming sounded and the water level lowered in the craft, until a small puddle in the middle remained. Okay, good. One problem solved.

Searching the screen's glowing labels, it wasn't much different than her tablet. Poly pressed the one labeled *Prop*, and the screen changed to an arrow. She slid her finger over the screen and moved the arrow. As the arrow moved, the number below spun around. She moved the arrow slowly, until the numbers one-thirty-two were displayed. The boat hummed much louder than the pump. She braced herself as the boat pushed forward. But what direction was it going? She took her finger off the screen and unzipped a couple of inches of the front of the boat.

Peeking through the small hole, she watched the dark blue waters splash the front of her boat, as it bounced over the choppy waters. In the horizon the clouds were breaking up, revealing the moon.

With the boat bouncing along the surface of the ocean, Poly slumped against the inflated insides of the craft. Sitting on the tubular edge, she put her face in her hands.

At least when she was falling to her death, there was a moment she didn't have to think about Joey. Images of him being zapped by Max filled her thoughts, followed with jumping from the plane and seeing it explode. Then came images of Nathen, Almadon, and Compry being murdered.

She slapped the side of the boat and stared at the zipper on the door. Where was she even going? Some island? She was in a foreign world, apart from her friends, and in a tiny boat, flopping around in the angry ocean. She wouldn't allow tears to fully form in her eyes. Taking a deep, cleansing breath, she lifted her head. There was more she could do, she needed to keep busy.

Going back to the screen, she examined the other buttons. Pressing the camouflage button, the boat turned a dark blue color. The one next to it read *Open*, and when she pushed it, the top of the teepee opened, forming a parapet wall. Poly crawled on her knees around the inside of the tiny boat, if you could call it that—more like an inner tube with a four foot wall around it—and scanned the expanse, looking for any of the others. Her friends were out there, somewhere.

After an hour, the storm clouds grew and she closed the top, sealing the rain out of the craft. Her whole body felt weak, drained. She slumped against the edge of the boat. It wasn't possible to find her friends and they weren't going to find her. There was nothing she could do, but wait for her boat to hit land, or for a wave to take her to the bottom of the sea. At that moment, she didn't know which she'd prefer.

Feeling weary, Poly laid down on the floor and felt the ocean push against the bottom as it moved along. A wave crashed against the craft, rolling her on her back, the rain outside peppered the fabric lining, making an orchestra of noises.

At some point it had to end, didn't it?

TWO DAYS PASSED.

The boat hummed along across the ocean. The boat seemed to have endless power. It was the only positive. She lay with her face bouncing off of floor, staring at the sliver of blue sky peeking its way through the zipper slit. The first day she spent in the bright sun, yelling, searching for her friends, seeing nothing but ocean.

At least it stopped raining. *Ha!* There are all kinds of positives, if you search long enough. Of course, the rain brought fresh water . . . too bad she hadn't collected any of it.

Her swollen tongue stuck to the dry sides of her mouth. She hadn't drank anything in two days. How long could a body go without water? Getting up on her knees, Poly pulled back the Velcro panel protecting the screen that ran the boat. The arrow still pointed in the same direction, but what did it even mean? She'd lost all sense of direction. She blindly hoped and feared the boat wasn't traveling in a large sweeping circle, perpetually sending her dying body on a round trip.

Her mind played through awful scenarios. She'd be found dead, dried up and shriveled, ten years from now. They'd run finger prints, DNA samples, and dental records, before she'd be declared a mystery person who didn't have a place on their planet. Her withered body would be dumped into a mass cremation. After spending many hours going through different scenarios, this one seemed the most likely.

She slapped the flap closed and jerked the zipper, blocking out the sun. Poly was sick of the sun.

Spending much of the last two nights trying to find a comfortable spot, she'd finally found it—a soft spot near the door. She lay there for the next few hours. It could have been longer, or it could have been ten minutes. Alone, with nothing but thoughts to occupy her, made time impossible to tell. She decided not to get up anymore; laying there until the mass cremators found her and disposed of her shell. The urge to open the craft and feel the salt water hit her face and the sun burn her skin, faded.

Her chapped lips ached, but she didn't think about that anymore. Poly wished she could say Joey and her friends consumed most of her thoughts, but she had to be honest with herself, it was water. She would push Joey to the ground to get to an ice-cold lemonade with extra sugar. She groaned thinking about it. No. Joey was in the hands of MM, probably being experimented on at that moment. She shouldn't have such selfish thoughts.

After Joey, her thoughts went to the plane exploding and if any of her friends were still alive. Were they waiting for her on this supposed island? Even if she lived to see it, she didn't know what she would do there.

Forests, grass fields, even school, seemed like a dream. Preston felt like a distant place, somewhere made up by

Hollywood. Her mom had to have been an actor, and her dad was still alive, just kept away from her. Why did they take her dad away? Everything Poly loved was gone and she was stuck on some stupid boat, alone. She pulled out a knife and stabbed the tarp above her head. She kept stabbing it, her dry lips splitting as she screamed, watching the slits of light shoot through each new hole.

Poly dropped the knife onto the floor, exhausted, letting her body fall down next to it. She couldn't hold back the tears, but there wasn't anything left to spill forth. She brought her knees close to her chest and hugged herself, her body wracked with tearless sobs.

She would die here. Her body would float on forever.